BLOOD RAGE

Brent Pilkey

for Army
friend, partner, brother

Blood will have blood
-William Shakespeare

Friday, 7 December
2157 hours

"Shots fired! Shots fired!"

The frantic shout crackled over the police car radio, and Jack dumped his half-eaten chicken dinner out the window. Revving the engine to life, he gripped the wheel and waited anxiously. *Where, where?* Running off blindly could send him farther away from the coppers who needed help.

"Sackville and Oak," the female officer yelled, her voice stressed but controlled. "We need a rush on an ambulance!"

"Shit, that's Jenny." Jack tromped on the gas and the Crown Vic fishtailed onto Shuter Street, slewing Aaron across the passenger seat. The psych nurse scrambled to buckle up while balancing his dinner on his lap.

Through his open window Jack could hear sirens wailing across the division, a pack of angry, vengeful wolves. He hit Parliament Street and hammered the brakes. Aaron, still frantically jabbing one-handed at the seat belt clasp, was thrown against the dash. His dinner, barbecue chicken and fries with gravy, spurted out lewdly from between his chest and the dash.

"Ah, fuck m—" he started, then slammed into the passenger door as Jack dived into the turn. He glared at Jack and opened his mouth, but his words were forced down his throat as Jack powered out of the turn, standing on the gas again, and Aaron was pushed back into the seat.

"Put on your seat belt," Jack told him as the cars parked on Parliament flashed by.

As they drew closer to Jenny's location, the scream of sirens grew louder, harsher in the cold air. In the violent sea of discord the dispatcher's voice was an island of calm professionalism. *"Unit at Sackville and Oak, update your situation. Ambulance is on the way. Can you advise of injuries?"*

Silence. Jack knew every officer within reach of a radio was waiting anxiously, straining to hear an answer. Who was shot? A criminal or a copper?

"Please God, not Jenny," Jack pleaded almost silently. "Not Jenny."

Traffic was mercifully light. The threat of rain must have kept everyone at home, or they were all elsewhere doing their Christmas shopping. A slow-moving pickup, more rust than steel, was trudging up Parliament, belching oily smoke with every pothole it hit. Jack laid on the horn as he dumped his valuable speed, cursing the unmarked scout car the Crisis Team was equipped with. A plain white car may have been less stressful to the mentally ill—at least that was the theory—but it sucked having no lights or siren.

Jack swerved into the southbound lanes then jerked back to avoid a van bearing down on them. Once the van with its blaring horn and irate driver was past, Jack slid the car across the centre line again and, whispering a prayer to the police gods, accelerated past the pickup. Aaron hissed, a nervous sucking of air, as Jack tore through the intersection at Dundas an instant after the amber light had flicked to red. Angry horns added their bleating to the cacophony of sirens, but Jack ignored them; shots fired and his partner wasn't answering the radio.

Please, God, not Jenny.

Then Jenny was on the air, sounding stressed and scared, but alive, thank God, alive. "5106, one adult male shot in the chest, semi-conscious, laboured breathing. Where—damn it, lie still, I'm trying to help you! Where the hell is my ambulance?"

"Ambulance has been rushed, less than a minute away. Can you give any more of an update? 'Is it just the one victim?" Dispatchers were trained and taught to be composed under pressure, to remain detached from the shit happening at the other end of the radio, but they were as humans as the officers and needed to know who it was bleeding out on the ground.

"Just the one victim," Jenny responded. "No suspects outstanding and all officers accounted for."

Jack gasped out a relieved sigh but didn't slow down. The tires squealed in protest as he cornered onto Oak Street, charging into Regent Park, the unofficial centre of the shit holes that together made up 51 Division. A sprawling government-housing project, Regent Park festered on the skin of downtown Toronto like an open, cancerous sore. The parasites of civilization lurked in the stairwells and shadows of squat, tired apartment buildings, preying and feeding upon the weak, the solitary, and the frightened.

Someone should burn it to the ground and be done with it.

Regent Park was dissected east to west by Dundas Street and the north was halved again by the Oak Street walkway. Oak was one of those interrupted streets, dead ending off of Parliament Street then continuing on east of the Park. Technically dead ending, that was. But then, technicalities didn't matter much when hauling ass in a police car.

Oak stopped abruptly in a miniscule cul-de-sac—Jack always thought it must look like an enormous thermometer from the air—but carried on arrow-straight through the complex as a concrete walkway wide enough to be a two-lane road. Jack hit the brief ramp at the end of Oak without slowing, and the car bounced painfully beneath them. Cop and nurse would have been slammed into the roof had they not been belted in.

Where are you, Jenny? Where are you?

The walkway stretched ahead of the police car, poorly lit by lights spaced too far apart and frequently dark, either burnt out or shot out. Jack reluctantly cut his speed and clicked on the high beams, wishing for a set of takedown lights and once more cursing the unmarked car.

The heavy clouds that had hung low over the city all day finally made good on their threat as an intermittent rain began to fall. Fat drops, more snow than water, splatted on the windshield.

"There!" Aaron called, pointing ahead and off to the right.

On a patch of winter-dead grass caught between the walkway and the brick wall of 248 Sackville, Jack could barely discern a small group of people motionless in the dark. He slid the car to a stop, bathing the scene in the headlights' stark glare.

"North end of 248 Sackville!" Jack snapped into the radio before jumping from the car.

Jenny knelt next to a large body collapsed on the ground. Beyond her, Connor Lee, the copper riding with Jenny this night, had a male against the wall at gunpoint. "Connor! You got him?"

"I'm good," the Pest called back, never taking his eyes from his prisoner. "Help Jenny."

Jack dropped to the ground opposite Jenny. She had her hands pressed down on the man's chest, blood painting her skin a bitter red in the uncaring cold light. She looked at Jack, half her face thrown into shadow by the headlights, her one visible eye wide and frantic.

"Jesus, Jack, where's the ambulance? He's dying. God damn it, he's dying."

"It's coming, Jenny, it's coming." Sirens sliced through the night, screaming against the rain.

The man bucked beneath Jenny's hands, almost flinging her away. He was a big man, but Jenny raised her weight above her arms and shoved him back down.

"Stay down, damn it. Stay down."

The man—no more than a boy really—moaned pitifully, the pain sounding lost in the dark. The rain washed his black skin, glistening in the light. His hands groped weakly, blindly. "Nana. I wan' my Nana."

"He's just a kid, Jack." Jenny was crying as she desperately fought to dam the blood behind her hands. "Jesus, he's just a kid."

Aaron shouldered Jack aside. "Get the fuck out of my way," he ordered as he ripped open the car's first-aid kit. "Go help the other one."

Jack stumbled to his feet. He was loath to leave Jenny,

but Aaron was right; as a nurse he was better suited to help the man and, by doing that, help Jenny.

Connor, better known as Pest thanks to Jack, had his Glock aimed unwavering at a second black male, this one leaning face first into the wall, his hands splayed high and wide above his head. Jack glanced at Connor as he unsnapped his handcuff pouch.

Connor nodded once sharply. "Listen up, asshole." Like Jenny's, his voice was tight, quivering, but still strong. "Look at me. Keep your fucking hands on the wall and look at me."

The man twisted his neck to peer at Connor over his left shoulder. Jack could just make out the male's left eye, wide and terrified. Jack doubted the man saw anything beyond the muzzle of Connor's Glock. When a gun was pointed at you, the smallest pea-shooter looked as big as a fucking canon.

"Another officer is going to handcuff you." The rain-slush was falling heavier but Connor was a statue. "If you so much as fucking twitch without being told to, I'll shoot you. Do you understand that?"

The man nodded, a jerky up-down.

"Do you believe I'll shoot you?"

"Yes, boss," the man whispered carefully, as if he feared speaking too loudly would cause him to twitch.

Jack slid in on the man's blind side and brought the man's arm down behind his back. He snapped a cuff in place then tapped the man's shoulder. "Other hand," he ordered, and the man obediently lowered his left arm, never taking his eyes off the gun aimed at his head. Jack clicked the steel around the man's wrist and, to Connor, said, "Cuffed."

Connor holstered then sagged, his hands on his knees, his head hanging limply. "Fuck me," he breathed.

Red lightning slashed the shadows as scout cars pulled up, spilling more officers into the scene. Jack waved over a pair and thrust Connor's prisoner at them. "Search him and dump him in your car," he instructed before turning to Connor. Laying a hand on his slumped shoulders and leaning close, Jack asked softly, "You good, man?"

At first, all Connor did was bob his head mutely. After a moment he stood up, rolling his shoulders. He wiped rain from his face, and Jack noted how pale he looked. Connor was half Korean, and his complexion usually made it look like he was perpetually working on a base tan. But right now it looked like the rain had washed away his colour.

Connor nodded again, more confidently this time. "Yeah, I'm good."

"Then get moving, Pest," Jack said, not unkindly. "You've got a prisoner to handle."

Connor hustled off and Jack paused to survey the scene. Since pulling up—maybe, what, a minute ago?—the area had flooded with cops and cruisers. A couple of uniforms, possibly Morris and Goldman but he couldn't tell because of the rain, were busy roping off the area with yellow police tape. The plastic tape hung limp, strung from trees, light poles and cars to seal off a perimeter well beyond the shooting site. When it came to crime scenes, going big was always better than being conservative. Jack only had to be chewed out once by a detective early in his career to learn that lesson.

He searched for Jenny but couldn't find her amid the lights pulsing scarlet flashes and shadows through the rain. An ambulance was on the walkway next to Jack's car, its rear doors thrown open. Aaron was in the ambulance, leaning over a loaded stretcher, his locked arms and upper body pistoning as he performed chest compressions.

That doesn't look good.

A paramedic slammed shut the doors, and Jack spotted Jenny leaning against the ambulance. She was slowly, methodically wiping her hands on a towel, oblivious to the cold rain and the controlled chaos swirling about her. To Jack, her posture, her whole manner, spoke of pain, distress. He knew where he was needed and headed to her.

"Warren!"

Sergeant Rose caught him by the elbow before he had taken more than a couple of steps. Rose was the road supervisor and, now that a set of stripes was on scene, Jack could relinquish his unofficial command of the growing headache. The sergeant was a big woman and at five-ten looked Jack in the eye. Right now the look she was giving him was not happy.

"You involved in this?" Rose had her hat pulled down low to keep the rain out of her eyes and it accentuated her pissed-off expression. Jack figured she must have been getting ready to pull the pin on the night when this shit erupted.

Jack shook his head. "No. First on scene, though. Helped Connor cuff his prisoner. Aaron helped with the guy shot."

"Who the fuck's Aar—" Rose hastily noted Jack's modified uniform: blue raid jacket, gun belt and jeans. "You're on that nut squad this week, aren't you? Christ! There's a civilian inside my scene?"

Jack gestured at the ambulance. "He went straight to the—the suspect." Jack had almost slipped and called the wounded man a victim. Force of habit; usually whoever was bleeding the most was considered the victim. Jack knew there'd soon be enough people involved who would be seriously calling the asshole the victim, but Jack wouldn't be one of them. He had no doubt his partner had every right to shoot, so that made the asshole anything but a victim. "Last I saw Aaron, he was doing CPR on the guy."

"Not good." Rose studied the scene. The tape was in place and officers had taken up positions along the perimeter, keeping the curious and the stupid back where they belonged. It was truly amazing how many people would walk under, around or into crime tape—not through, though; that tape stretched beyond belief and was almost impossible to rip apart—if there wasn't a copper there to yell at them, to which most idiots said, "But I'm going that way." As if their destination was far more important than whatever was inside the tape.

Despite the miserable weather, a substantial crowd was gathering. *Must be a night of Christmas reruns.*

"All right, Warren, you're with the victim." Sergeant Rose shook her head in disgust. "I mean the suspect. Go."

Jack hesitated, glancing at his partner. Jenny had wandered away from the ambulance and was standing alone. Rose followed Jack's gaze.

"Don't worry," Rose said, the gruffness momentarily gone from her voice. "I'll look after her. The best thing you can do now for her is to do your job."

Jack nodded and ran for the ambulance. "Where you headed?" he asked when the medic rolled down the window.

"St. Mike's, along Shuter," the medic responded, his impatience clear in the brief answer.

Jack got in his car. "CIT1, call," Jack radioed as he pulled shut the car door. "Ambulance is transporting the male to St. Michael's Hospital. 10-4?"

"10-4, St. Mike's. Do you want to set up an emergency run?"

"It'll have to be quick, dispatch; the ambulance is already leaving. They'll be travelling along Shuter." Units blocking traffic at intersections could shave some valuable time off the run to the hospital. St. Mike's wasn't far, just a few blocks really, but even a few seconds saved could pay off.

"I'll see if I can get some 52 units to handle the intersections in both divisions. All of our cars are tied up at the shooting."

"10-4, dispatch. I'm following the ambulance to the hospital and my escort is riding in back." Jack didn't mention that Aaron would probably be performing CPR for the whole trip; no need for that little tidbit to go over the air. Jack just hoped Aaron's efforts wouldn't be in vain.

Jesse Polan was horny.

Not that pleasant urge a quick fuck or blow job could satisfy. No, that was weeks past. Now it was a constant need, a crushing vise locked onto his balls that no amount of whacking off could relieve.

How fucked up was it, when he couldn't even get laid by some skanky crack whore? But ever since that shit with Kayne, nobody came near him. Not out of fear, no, nothing like that. They hated him. All of them. Buying crack was a bitch, but at least he'd found one guy who was willing to sell to him. At fucking three times the regular cost. Jesse could probably get laid if he was ready to fork out the cash, but paying extra for rock was one thing, no way was he going to give some whore more than she deserved.

"It's like I'm one of those piranha things, no one fucking wants to be near me," he grumbled bitterly.

And it wasn't like he could just make up a new name or something. After that beating back in the summer his right eye wouldn't open all the way and his nose was way off to the side. Everyone knew who he was and stayed clear of him.

"Probably wouldn't piss on me if I was on fucking fire. Fuck 'em. Fuck 'em all." He jammed his hands into his pockets as he limped along. The same ass-kicking that had left his face looking like a sack of rocks had also fucked up his knee. It always started hurting like a motherfucker when it was about to rain.

He glanced up at the night sky. Not a single star stared back. "Fucking perfect." Now he had to find somewhere to crash before it started pissing down, and a hostel was out of the question. Too many people scarred up by that fuck Kayne, or friends of them, stayed in the Seaton House or Sally Ann. Jesse had barely escaped being stabbed twice since making bail.

"Fucking cops took my gun." He spat contemptuously. "If I had my gun, no-fucking-body would fuck with me. Fucking cops." He sneezed, then moaned piteously. Sneezing fucking hurt. "Fucking bitch cop. Her and her fucking muscle-head partner. Just like that fucking Kayne. If I ever get me a gun…"

"Hey, honey, you looking to party?"

The voice, cracked with a need Jesse had suffered himself more than once, startled him out of his self-pitying thoughts. A sickly, stick-thin girl—if she was over seventeen, he'd bend over and suck his own dick—shivering in a worn, ragged hoody eyed him uneasily, desperation and wariness flickering across her gaunt face. She was jonsing bad. Jesse had never seen a fucking more beautiful sight in his life.

"You bet, baby." He hooked her arm. "Let's find some place private."

They were at the back of a school on Shuter—Jesse dimly recalled sitting in its classrooms a lifetime ago—and he frantically yanked the crack-hungry whore towards a shadowed corner; he had needs, too. His dick was a piece of steel and his balls ached so much he had to walk hunched over.

"Get your fucking pants off, bitch," he ordered as he fumbled with the buttons on his jeans.

"You gotta pay me first, mister," she whined.

Jesse stopped dead, his pants half undone, his mouth gaping. "What the fuck did you say?"

She cringed before him but held to her demand. "You gotta pay me first," she repeated. "You gotta pay me, mister."

"Fucking... *bitch!*" Jesse backhanded her across the face hard enough to send a jolt of pain up his arm. She hit the school wall and collapsed.

"You can forget getting paid, bitch," he snarled, looming over her. "When I'm done with you, you'll get on your fucking knees and thank me for not killing you."

She cowered away from him, whimpering, and her fear stiffened Jesse's dick until he thought it would rupture. With a sadistic smile twisting his ruined face, he reached for her.

Strong hands clamped onto Jesse's head, and he was violently swung around, then catapulted into the air. He struck the same brick wall he had knocked the whore against, but with far greater impact. He bounced off the wall then hit the ground face-first, the rough asphalt scraping gouges into his cheek.

Whoever had attacked him was about to be one sorry-assed motherfucker; Jesse had had enough of being pushed around and beaten on. He snuck his hand into his pocket, gripped his knife. Someone was about to get a bellyful of steel. He pushed himself to his knees, his left hand held out beseechingly, his right tucked alongside his thigh.

"Hey, man," he mumbled, trying to make out his attacker, but in the poorly lit schoolyard all he could see was a man-shaped figure.

The man stepped close, and Jesse swung the knife, meaning to bury its length in the fucker's gut, but the man jumped back and the knife missed him entirely. On his knees, Jesse's swing unbalanced him and he toppled forward. A heavy boot stomped down on his knife hand, and Jesse felt bones snap. He howled in pain, but the man slapped a leather-clad hand over his mouth.

In a calm voice, as if he did this shit every day, the man told the whore, "Find someplace else to be." She did, and Jesse was alone with his attacker.

In the distance, a single gunshot rang out, faint but sharp. The man, still crouched on Jesse's hand, paused, his head tilted quizzically, as if he was scenting the air. A handful of heartbeats after the gunshot, sirens erupted in the night.

The man shifted his weight as he leaned down, grinding the bones in Jesse's hand. "Bad news for you, ass-wipe.

Sounds like the cops are going to be busy for a while." He plucked the knife from Jesse's fingers, then hauled him upright and flung him against the wall one more time.

Jesse cradled his injured hand to his chest. The waves of pain throbbing out of it were making him light-headed. He felt like he was going to puke. This wasn't fair, it just wasn't fair.

"All I wanted was a blow job, man," he sobbed. "You broke my fucking hand."

The bone-breaking motherfucker stepped close, and his dark face held no sympathy or mercy. Jesse knew he was in trouble, just like the time that had started all that shit with Kayne. *Another fucking whore and nigger*. Although this time, he doubted he would be saved by some stranger. This time, the stranger was the one fucking him over.

"I hate cowards who hit women." The man's voice was low, hushed, but Jesse could hear the tension in it, the violence barely held in check. "Consider yourself lucky, ass-wipe. If you had time to do anything more to her, I'd kill you."

Jesse looked into hate-filled eyes. "Ah, c'mon, man. I just wanted—"

The punch caught Jesse on the ear, and his head exploded in sharp, unbelievable pain. His legs folded, but the man pinned him to the brick wall. Jesse was hit again, but he never knew how many times; his head was a massive explosion of agony, a pain that never lessened, only grew upon itself.

At last he was allowed to fall, and the slap of the pavement against his face was a tender kiss compared to what he had suffered. *Please stop*, he silently begged. He just wanted to lie where he was until the pain went away. But it was not to be. His upper body was hoisted off the ground. Distantly, he felt his feet and legs dragging on the broken asphalt.

"What...?" He tried to speak, but only drooled blood from his shattered mouth.

The world slipped in and out of a great darkness, and he desperately wanted to throw himself into that nothingness where the pain couldn't follow. There was no new hurt, no punishment the man could inflict that would surpass what Jesse had already suffered. Jesse kept telling himself that as his hand was positioned on the wood surrounding a sandbox, and he believed it right up until the stranger drove Jesse's own knife through his hand and deep into the wood.

The boy died. Twice. But each time the surgical team brought him back. Each time Jack closed his memo book without jotting down a time of death.

The doctor backed away from the operating table as he peeled his surgical mask free. The blue fabric fluttered almost gracefully to the floor to land on a piece of blood-soaked clothing—*Tyrone's shirt*, Jack thought. The cloth immediately began to darken, a tiny dot of red so deep it was nearly black, that quickly and smoothly grew to engulf the mask.

The air in the trauma room was subdued, the slow but steady beep of the heart-rate monitor interrupted by the quiet clatter of metal as the team cleaned up the surgical tools. The doctor studied the twice-lifeless body in front of him for a moment, his face worn and tired. It was a look Jack recognized easily; he saw it in the mirror every day.

The doctor stepped around the bloody clothing. "I didn't think we'd get him back that last time."

"But you did," Jack said. "Thank you."

"Whoever shot him," the doctor said, glancing back at the boy, "knew what he was doing. One round, dead centre of the chest. I'm amazed he's still alive. Do you have a name on him?"

"Tyrone Johnson, eighteen." One of the medics had tossed Jack the kid's wallet after fishing out his health card. Jack had gone through the slim wallet but found little to add to the ID. No driver's licence, no credit or bank cards. Just a list of three names and phone numbers written in a child's large, unsteady hand—friends, family?—and a photo of a smiling, heavyset black woman with a small boy on her lap, his "say cheese!" grin stretching from ear to ear. Tyrone in his younger, more innocent days, perhaps.

What were you doing, bud? Jack asked the unconscious Tyrone Johnson. *What did you do to make Jenny shoot you?*

"Was it gang related?" the doctor wanted to know.

"I don't know," Jack replied honestly.

"Whatever the reason, he's too bloody young to be getting shot." The doctor rubbed a hand across his eyes. "Is there any family waiting?"

"Shouldn't be. We'll send officers around to notify next of kin once we get an address on him."

The doctor nodded. "Better you than me. I hate doing that shit. Could be worse though. He isn't dead, yet." He shouldered open the door and as it swung shut behind him, Aaron slipped into the operating room.

Aaron watched the slumped shoulders of the doctor walking away. "Dead?" he asked, glancing over at the operating table.

"Not yet."

Aaron nodded as if he expected nothing more. "Jack, you better come out to the waiting room."

Aaron Wallace, the psychiatric nurse St. Mike's provided for the Crisis Intervention Team, was stocky and a couple of inches shorter than Jack. A decent, solid guy to work with. A lot of cops mistrusted the nurses on the CIT, thinking they were cop-hating tree huggers. Jack hadn't met any of the other nurses but had no problem working with Aaron. He was damned good at his job—he could calm down a psychotic drug user or talk a jumper off a bridge with nothing more than the promise of a cigarette—and was almost cynical enough to be a cop.

Aaron had ridden the stretcher right into the trauma room, straddling Tyrone as he continued with the CPR. As soon as he had climbed down from the stretcher, he had ducked out of the room to wash up. Gloves or not, you didn't take chances with someone else's blood. Jack suspected Aaron had also taken the opportunity to catch a breather; doing chest compressions was damn tiring.

Sure enough, the bright operating lights exposed a faint sheen of sweat still clinging to Aaron's shaved scalp. And judging from the way he was smoothing his goatee— black with the first traces of grey—and glancing back in the direction of the waiting room, there was something else causing him anxiety.

"What is it?" Jack asked. "I should stay with him—" he jerked a thumb over his shoulder "—until he gets settled in a room."

Aaron slid his hand over his goatee once more. "All I'm saying is you should take a look and maybe call someone."

"How long until he's ready to go?" Jack threw out to the three nurses still in the room.

A young Philippino-looking nurse flashed Jack an enticing smile. "Won't be for a while yet. You've got time."

"Thank you."

"Any time," she told him, still smiling. As she turned away, she bent over, giving Jack a very good and very deliberate view of her shapely ass. If anyone thought hospital scrubs weren't sexy, they needed to see what Jack was seeing. The invitation was clear, but the last thing Jack needed was another woman in his life right now.

I'm having trouble enough with one.

Outside the trauma room, Jack could hear a woman's raised voice coming from the direction of the waiting room, sounding stressed and scared. Never a good combination. The short hallway led to another set of double doors, and Aaron toed one open. The woman's voice was louder now, painfully loud, and Jack peered over Aaron's head.

The doctor who had saved Tyrone's life was standing near the triage station just outside the waiting room, his back to Jack and Aaron, and judging from the droop of his upper body, he didn't want to be there. Facing him was the yelling woman, and although she was older and heavier now, Jack recognized her from the picture in Tyrone's wallet. She had aged considerably since the photo was taken, a lot undoubtedly in the last few hours.

"Where's my Tyrone?" she demanded of the doctor, her voice barely controlled. "Where's my baby?"

The doctor gestured off to the side, obviously wanting to take the conversation somewhere private; telling a mother her son was barely clinging to life was not something to be discussed in public, but Mom wasn't budging.

"Where's my baby?" she nearly screeched.

Surrounding and supporting Mom—studying her more intently, Jack reassessed her as Grandmom—was a group of five people, possibly family: two women of an age with Grandmom and three young men, very irate.

One of the men, his face a furious mask beneath his baby dreadlocks, placed his hands protectively on Grandmom's shoulders and confronted the doctor. "The police shot him and brought him here. Don't be lying to us. Just because we're black don't mean we're stupid. You tell us where Tyrone is."

Two security guards had joined the scene and were standing a respectful distance from the group. Jack hoped they had the sense to stay out of it unless absolutely necessary.

Grandmom's yelling had subsided. Her head lolled back against the man's chest, and Jack could hear her muttering, "My baby, my baby."

The doctor leaned forward and once more held his arm out to the side, futilely it seemed as Grandmom ignored him and began yelling at the top of her lungs. "Tyrone! Where are you, baby? I'm here, Tyrone. Where are you, Tyrone?"

The people in the waiting room who had been watching the commotion with bored curiosity now looked decidedly uncomfortable. The security guards moved closer.

Jack didn't hear what the doctor said; he didn't need to. Grandmom's face, twisted with fear and anxiety, froze as the doctor leaned in to her. For a moment, a lifetime, her face was stock-still, a mask representing every parent's greatest nightmare, and then it collapsed beneath a wave of anguish. She let loose a wordless wail of agony and crumpled to the floor. Bending down, the doctor placed a hand on her shoulder, but the man at her back knocked the hand away.

"Don't you be touching her," he warned. Where Tyrone's grandmother was the image of sorrow and suffering, the man was rage incarnate. Tyrone obviously was important to him, and very clearly the man wanted to vent his anger on someone. The security guards moved forward, but the doctor waved them away. The young man turned on the guards.

"That's right, motherfuckers. You stay the fuck away from us." He contemptuously showed them his back as he knelt to huddle with the people around Tyrone's grandmother.

Jack tapped Aaron on the shoulder, and they backed away from the door. Aaron cast one final glance past the doors. "I thought you guys always did the notifications."

"Someone beat us to it." Jack flipped open his phone and dialed the station. He needed to let the higher-ups know that the bad situation had just turned ugly.

Saturday, 8 December
0417 hours

Fuck me, what a day.

Jack didn't want to know what time it was but checked anyway. The numbers on his watch glowed a cold green. 4:17.

Too late to still be night, and too early to be morning.

This used to be a favourite time of night shift for Jack, a time not shared by many. The streets were quiet, the odd taxi cruising about, early workers heading out for the day, delivery trucks loading up. It was a secret time, the time when tomorrow became today, when the city was still mostly asleep but starting to stir and stretch. A favourite time, once. Now the hours before dawn were a no man's land, a hellish mix of bone-deep weariness if he was working and the frustrating inability to sleep if he was at home.

What do you expect? With all the shit going on in your

life, you're lucky you haven't ended up in a padded room someplace.

The night was chilly but nowhere near as cold as it should be for the time of year. Despite Christmas being just a couple of weeks away, the weather felt more like mid-autumn. Granted, it was always a toss-up whether Christmas in Toronto would be green or white, but so far this year there was yet to be a heavy frost, even in the city's surrounding 'burbs.

We'll probably get dumped on in January.

Jack tucked his head down into his old leather jacket, enjoying the comforting, familiar feel. Karen had hated the jacket, said it was a worn-out, embarrassing eyesore and refused to be seen in public with him if he wore it.

Don't have to worry about that anymore, do I? he thought bitterly. As far as a consolation prize went, though, it sucked.

The parking lot was quiet, almost tranquil. Leaning against his car, sipping a Coke, Jack kept his eyes turned away from the lot's lights. A sour, nauseating ache behind his right eye, growing over the past hour, turned the weak fluorescent light into jagged spears of pain. Knowing he wouldn't be able to make it home, not with the speed at which the migraine was building, he popped open a pill bottle and tapped two capsules into his hand. He downed the medication with a swig of Coke.

The station's back door swung open, spilling pale fluorescent light across the asphalt. Jenny stepped out, shoulders hunched, her shadow briefly thrown out ahead of her until the door slipped close.

Hurriedly stuffing the pill bottle into a pocket, Jack pushed off from his car as she drew near. "Hey," he said softly.

She started; it looked as if she had jerked up from deep thoughts. "Oh, Jack. I didn't see you there."

"Sorry. I didn't mean to startle you."

"It's not your fault," she said with a tired smile. "It's been a long night."

"Yeah," he agreed. "It has. How are you doing?"

"Okay, I guess. Considering."

But Jenny didn't look okay, not at all. She was a tall woman, like Sergeant Rose, but height was where the similarity ended. Rose was a thick, stocky woman while Jenny had a lean, athletic body that Jack had dreamed—and daydreamed—of on a few occasions. Her hair fell in gentle waves to her waist and was a black so deep it reminded Jack of the comic books he had collected in his teens. If the superhero's costume was black, the artist would highlight it with dark blue so the character wasn't a simple silhouette. Jenny's hair was that solid a black.

But body and hair aside, to Jack, his partner's most captivating feature was her eyes. Crystal blue, the colour of deep ice on a lake, her eyes spoke of hidden secrets while seeing to the depths of Jack's soul. But now those eyes were listless, exhausted. In them he saw a swirl of emotions that few could understand.

It was a look Jack had seen in his own eyes, and he hated it that she now knew how it felt.

"You don't look so good, partner." *That's comforting, moron. What's next? Pat her on the back and say, "There, there"?*

"I'll live," Jenny said, and Jack felt her pain in his guts. "What are you still doing here?"

"Waiting for you," he explained.

Jenny smiled again, this time closer to her normal

self but still a lifetime away. "That's sweet but you didn't have to."

"I wanted to. By the time I got back from the hospital, they had you locked away with the Association rep and the lawyer. I wanted to see you, to see how you were…" He hesitated, then told her, "I know how you feel right now and if I could, I'd take it from you so you wouldn't have to carry it."

"Thank you, Jack," she whispered and stepped into his arms. Jack pulled her to him, holding her tight, wishing he could shield her from the days to come as easily. They held each other, not speaking, not needing to, until Jenny eased away. Reluctantly, Jack thought. Hoped.

She nodded at the Coke can sitting on Jack's car. "Regular Coke? Do you have a headache?"

Jack shrugged her concern away. "A bit of one. I was hoping the sugar and caffeine would keep it in check until I got to bed."

"Jack, you shouldn't have waited," she scolded. "Not if you're getting a migraine."

"It's nothing, really." No need to tell her, to worry her, that he had just popped his second hit of Fiorinal, a powerful muscle relaxant, in six hours. "Listen, Jenny," he said, steering her away from his problem; she had enough of her own. "If you want, you can crash at my place tonight. You know I have plenty of room. Or, if you want, I can swing by and grab Justice then head over to your place." The Service taught that after a "critical incident" the involved officer shouldn't be left alone—although Jack knew from firsthand experience that they tended to dump the officer in a room to sit alone until the lawyer arrived—and if possible should spend time with someone who had gone through something similar. And when it came to shooting people, no one at 51 Division was more experienced than Jack.

"Thank you, Jack. I would but Brian's coming to pick me up." She huddled inside her black leather coat as an errant breeze spun cold air about them. Jack thought she used the opportunity to avoid meeting his eyes. Was she relieved Brian had given her a reason to turn him down, or saddened?

Jenny had been seeing Brian Tripp for close to six months now, which was a record, she said. Jenny didn't have good luck when it came to men. The civilians she dated couldn't handle her strong personality or the fact that they weren't the one in the relationship who carried a gun and occasionally kicked ass for a living.

The cops who asked her out never looked beyond the body and her undeserved party-girl reputation. So when she didn't jump into bed with them partway through the first date, they dumped her, and usually capped off the fiasco by bragging to their buddies about how they'd gotten into her pants. According to the high-school-like gossip floating around the station, Jenny had done pretty much every copper, male and female, in 51.

Unfortunately for Jack, his wife had added him to the list.

Brian was a doctor at St. Mike's—Jack had half expected to see him in the ER tonight—and so seemed invulnerable to the civilian-female cop curse. So if his partner was happy, then Jack was happy for her.

I am. Really.

"Has Brian gotten used to the kids?"

Jenny laughed. A weak, almost not there laugh, but a laugh just the same. "You know the kids. Hammer thinks she's a lap-dog and Mugsy goes around snarling at everyone. Brian keeps threatening to take him to the hospital for plastic surgery."

Hammer was Jenny's ninety-pound Rottweiler and Mugsy was a chubby twenty-pound pug who thought he was a ninety-pound Rottweiler. He had a harelip that exposed one fang in a perpetual sneer. As tough as he thought he was, Mugsy was a wimp when it came to strangers and other dogs, and his favourite place of refuge was peeking out from between his big sister's legs.

"So he's becoming a dog person?"

"Not quite," Jenny admitted ruefully. "He still has a problem with all the hair, and Hammer likes to stare at him while he sleeps."

"But did she wipe herself on him when she met him?"

"God, no!" Jenny laughed, really laughed this time. "I think that would have ended the first date right there."

Jenny lived in a basement apartment just outside the division and sometimes had to drop in at home during the shift to let the dogs out. The first time Jack had accompanied her while working the dogs had dutifully relieved themselves in the yard then run spastically back into the house. They had met Jack before but never in their home so they were acting like kids, goofing around in front of company. Once they had calmed down—Mugsy watching Jack intently with his Elvis-sneer lip—Jack was able to squat down without fear of being knocked over. Hammer had promptly sat on his thigh for a good butt scratching, and when it was done she left a tiny wet spot on Jack's uniform pants. Jenny had been mortified but Jack had laughed it off, taking it as a compliment that her dog was comfortable enough with him to wipe herself on his leg.

"What's so amusing?" Brian asked, appearing out of the parking lot's shadows.

"Nothing you'd find funny." Jenny hugged her man and the good doctor held her close, one hand smoothing her hair. Jack averted his eyes, assuring himself he wasn't jealous, just giving his eyes a break from the lights.

"When did you get here?" Jenny asked, moving to stand with her arm around her boyfriend's waist.

"I've been here a while but I didn't want to interrupt. You two looked like you were having a partner moment."

Dr. Brian Tripp was tall, six-two easily, with the trim build of a swimmer. Add blond hair and a square jaw, and he looked more like a soap opera doctor than the real thing. He also had this annoying habit of looking stylish, even when he was wearing an old sweatshirt and jeans. Thicker and heavier with muscle, clad in his eyesore jacket, Jack felt like…well, like a street cop next to a doctor.

It didn't help that Brian reminded Jack of his father-in-law.

"Jack was just checking on me, that's all," Jenny was quick to assure Brian.

"And I guess I should let you two get home. Call you tomorrow, Jenny?" For cops, tomorrow was always after sleeping, regardless of the time.

"I'd like that." She brushed his cheek with her lips. "Thanks for making me laugh. I needed that." She paused, studying his squinted eyes. "Are you okay to drive?"

Jack forced a smile as he fought to keep the pain from his face. "I'm good. Besides, concentrating on driving helps me ignore the headache."

Jack watched them walk to Brian's car and lifted his hand in response to Jenny's goodbye wave. They drove off and Jack was left alone in the parking lot, trapped in the no man's land before dawn.'

Blood Rage

Jack turned on to his street just as the dashboard clock tripped over to five. Most of the houses were still dark but more than a few already showed signs of life, people hoping to get a jump on the commute into the city. The drive wasn't bad for Jack; because of the shift work, he only had to deal with rush-hour traffic after day shift, but on those days, the time he spent in the car could easily double if not triple. He did not envy his neighbours who had to endure that twice a day, every day.

Some houses still had their Christmas lights shining, the owners having either forgotten to turn them off or purposely left them on all night. Jack wouldn't doubt the intentional all-night displays; the neighbourhood, his street in particular, was into the holiday pageantry big time. Every house on the curving street had something aglow, whether it was a simple string of white lights, a lawn-to-roof extravaganza or inflatable snowmen and reindeer tramping across the front yard.

Jack's house was the dark exception, an ink stain on a multicoloured quilt. No lights sparkled, nothing pranced across his lawn, not even a wreath brightened the door. As he pulled into the driveway, the idea that he should put up some decorations crossed his mind, not for the first time, not even for the tenth, but he knew he wouldn't follow up on it. Jack planned on skipping Christmas this year.

The holidays had never been important to Jack, at least not since his childhood. He was an only child and his parents had long since divorced. He rarely spoke with his father and had no idea where his mother had moved to once his father had found himself a younger wife. But after meeting Karen, the whole Merry Christmas, Happy Holidays feeling had been reborn in him.

Christmas morning was always spent with her family, Evelyn and Dr. George Hawthorn and George Jr., the doctor to be. Those mornings were like a Christmas painting, stylishly perfect and posed, and Karen's parents were lavish with the gifts. Back in those days they had simply disliked Jack, presuming their daughter's relationship with a cop would be nothing but a fleeting infatuation or a brief rebellion. Whichever, it would be short-lived. Jack figured the expensive gifts were initially meant as subtle bribes, complemented with not so subtle hints, to encourage him to leave. Later, when it was apparent his presence was becoming permanent, the presents were to remind him of his place: a lowly civil servant who would never be good enough, or make enough money, for their daughter.

Christmas dinners involved the entire Hawthorn clan, with aunts, uncles and cousins descending on the house for another perfect holiday affair. Evelyn never cooked the meal herself but was quite comfortable taking credit for it. After all, she planned the feast and oversaw the people who cooked it. How much they paid to have a meal prepared and served on Christmas Jack didn't know and didn't want to know.

He tolerated and endured the stuffiness and pretense of a Hawthorn Christmas because of Karen and the love they shared. But Christmas Eve, that belonged to them. Jack remembered the first eve they had celebrated in their new house. The living room had been bereft of furniture—her parents had 'gifted' them with those god-awful wing chairs the next morning—and they had lounged on a comforter in front of the fire. The gift they gave themselves was the new Honda CR-V, but Karen had one more for him and had slipped off her robe to reveal the lingerie that she had purchased. They ended up sharing that gift as well.

Jack shook his head, chasing away the painful memories. It was cruel how recalling happy times could hurt so much.

He walked up to the house. He didn't consider it a home anymore. It had been a home when he and Karen had lived and loved in it. Now it was just an edifice, a construct of wood and brick, where he happened to sleep and exist when he wasn't working.

Justice greeted him at the door, the German shepherd rubbing up against Jack's thigh like the world's biggest house cat. Jack ran his hand along the thick fur, and Justice thumped his tail enthusiastically.

"Bet you need to go out."

Justice dashed down the hall, stopping on the kitchen tile to look back at Jack as if to say, *You coming, or what?*

"Yeah, I'm coming." Jack detoured by the fridge to snag a bottle of cider before sliding open the door for his furry friend. Justice darted onto the deck then cleared the steps as he leaped into the darkness. "Guess he had to go."

Jack followed, moving much slower than his dog. He settled on the stairs leading down to the lawn and cracked open his drink.

Mixing alcohol with migraine medication probably isn't a good idea, he told himself but countered the argument with, *I really don't give a fuck.* To prove he really didn't give a fuck, he took a long pull of the sharp, cold cider.

He smiled a sad, lonely smile, thankful for the mild winter, but even if the deck had been coated in ice and snow, he'd still be sitting here. The no-longer-a-home house was just an item, a thing, a curio from the past he had shared with Karen. It had been purchased with their money, the mortgage payments had come out of the joint account. The house and all it stood for was theirs, but the deck, that belonged to Jack. He had designed it, built it, then extended the lower level to encompass a hot tub. There was more than a bit of his blood stained and smoothed into the wood.

A job's never done until the gods get their sacrifice. Who had told him that? An uncle, a contractor hired by his father? Certainly not his father; manual labour was beneath Jack's sire. Jack rubbed the wood lovingly. Mitchell Warren would never understand the satisfaction of building something himself. Not that Jack gave a fuck what his father thought, not about the deck, not about his job, not about his life.

Justice trotted out of the dark and curled up beside Jack. "Doubt he would have approved of you either."

But his father had approved of Jack's wife, had actually expressed amazement that the daughter of Dr. George Hawthorn—both fathers moved in the same no-policemen-allowed wealthy circles—had married someone of Jack's standing. No doubt dear old Dad had heard of the impending divorce.

"Well, here's to you, Dad." Jack hoisted his bottle. "If I ever run into you, you can tell me you told me so."

Justice whined softly, shifting to rest his head on Jack's thigh. Jack stroked the thick black and tan fur to calm his friend. "Yeah, that's what I think, too."

The cider was gone; his migraine was down to a sickening ache. "Time to go to bed and stare at the ceiling," he told Justice. The shepherd flipped to his feet and followed Jack into the house.

"Oh, fuck me."

The day was overcast, mild for December but still damp and chilly. After five hours of broken sleep, Jack had given up on the hope of a full night's rest and dragged his ass out of bed. Ignoring the fuzziness in his head—a consequence of the meds or the cider or both, he really didn't care—he had made a tea to go, hooked up Justice and headed out.

Now he stood on the sidewalk, oblivious to the rain wetting his head and leather jacket. Justice was at his side, tongue lolling in a happy, doggy grin. They were heading home from the hydro field after twenty minutes of playing fetch. Jack used a tennis racket to spare his arm, belting the balls as far as he could in a vain attempt to tire out the dog. To date, Justice had never given up before Jack.

The game had been called on account of the rain. He'd had no intention of stopping for a paper until the headline—in big, bold, damning letters—caught his eye.

"Oh, fuck me," he repeated, fishing out the necessary coins. Ripping a paper free, he scanned the article, his stomach turning to ice. He crushed the paper in a fist and urged Justice to a run. He needed to get home and call his partner. Now.

Ted Huntington finished reading the article then folded up his copy of the *Citizen* and dropped it on his desk. If he wasn't saving it for the crossword, the newspaper would have ended up in the garbage. Folding his hands behind his head, he leaned back in his chair and stared at the ceiling. The story Millie had written was more prose than reporting but that seemed to be what the bosses wanted these days.

Ted was a career newsman. He often joked that when he died, they wouldn't need to embalm him; there'd be too much ink in his blood. In his forty-plus-year career he had seen much and told it all in black and white, sticking to the facts. Even now, as a columnist, his opinions and views were always anchored in the facts, in the truth as he saw it.

"Not this...this crap." He swept the paper into his wastebasket. He'd do the crossword online. The clack of heels and Millie's annoying voice—to Ted, her voice was too nasal, like she was talking down at everyone through her nose—let him know she'd soon be passing his cubicle on her way to her desk.

"That was quite the article you wrote about the shooting," Ted said to her in lieu of hello when she came into sight.

Millie Templeton had been on the *Citizen*'s staff only for about six months, a hotshot small-time reporter from some small rag up Sudbury way. She'd broken a police scandal in her hometown—*probably caught a cop snoozing in his car*—and ridden the story to Toronto and onto the *Citizen*'s payroll.

And then the shooting had fallen right into her lap. It was an opportunity even veteran reporters would kill for. Ted held no jealousy towards her for landing the story; she'd been in the right place at the right time. What he had a problem with was what she had done with it.

It was pretty obvious Millie didn't want to talk to Ted, not this morning after such a late night, but she perched herself on his desk—there was just enough room among the clutter for one hip—not bothering to tug her skirt down.

Ted smiled to himself. If she thought she could derail him by flashing some leg—rather appealing leg, he was willing to admit—she had a lot to learn about veteran newsmen. He was also willing to concede that female reporters had a God-given advantage when it came to coaxing co-operation out of men. It wasn't a woman's fault that some men would let themselves be distracted by a length of leg or persuaded by a show of cleavage. And God had certainly blessed Millie with advantages. Dark hair that fell in luxurious waves past her shoulders, long, shapely legs, and ample cleavage, as the slight strain on her blouse buttons attested to.

"Quite an article good or bad?" she asked, toeing the paper in his garbage can.

"Bit of both, actually." He nodded at the headline. "Your idea?"

"It was," she replied proudly. "I wasn't sure the boss would go for it but there it is: Cops shoot unarmed 'child.' You don't approve?"

"It's sensationalism. I'd expect it from a tabloid, not a newspaper."

"If you don't like it," she said, with a defiant toss of her hair, the burgundy streaks in the brown catching the overhead fluorescents, "take it up with the boss. Oh, right, I forgot. You're the one with a soft spot for the cops."

"And you're the one with the hard-on for them," Ted shot back. The police beat had been his turf for decades. "Yeah, I cut the cops some slack; they do a shitty job nobody else wants to, but I'll be the first to go after them if they fuck up. Or if they try to hide a fuck-up."

"So why the attitude? If shooting an unarmed retard isn't a fuck-up, I don't know what is."

"Retard? Really, Millie?"

Millie rolled her eyes. "Save the political correctness for interviews and writing, Ted."

"Did the officers know he was mentally handicapped?" Ted challenged, and when she opened her mouth to answer he rolled over her. "Did they know he wasn't armed? Was there any way they could have known either prior to the shooting?"

"They should have." Millie flipped her hair again. "And none of that changes the fact they—"

"Gunned down an unarmed innocent," Ted finished for her. "I know. You made that perfectly clear in your article. Repeatedly. All you left out was 'in cold blood.'"

"I thought it was too clichéd."

Ted shook his head. "You're a reporter. Reporters report. They stick to facts. Leave the opinion to the columnists."

"So that's what this is all about," she accused. "You feel I'm trespassing on your precious domain. What's the matter, Ted? Feeling threatened?"

"Hardly," he scoffed.

Millie stood up, glaring defiantly. "I was in the right place at the right time to hear the call come over my police radio. I got the pictures, I got the quotes. The story is mine and it's pissing you off. Now, if you'll excuse me," she said with a slight mocking bow and stormed off.

Ted watched her stomp off like some spoiled brat having a tantrum. He grieved for the future of news reporting. "Incompetent bitch."

"Sanctimonious asshole."

Ted Huntington may have been some hotshot reporter back in his day—in the dusty, best-forgotten age of typewriters—but now he was nothing more than a self-important, duller than dog shit columnist.

Sitting at her desk—her orderly desk, a professional's desk—she pulled a copy of the day's paper to her and felt her irritation melt away as she proudly studied the photo, her photo, under her headline. The picture was dark—a flash could only do so much at night—and just a touch out of focus, but that only added to its harsh effect. She'd caught the female officer, the shooter, crouched over the victim. Was she giving first aid? Was she watching her prey bleed out? The interpretation was for the reader to make.

A second photo, also hers, accompanied the article on page three, positioned so it slapped the readers right in the mug when they opened the paper. It showed another male up against a wall, his almost comically wide eyes peering fearfully over his shoulder at the cop training a gun on him. The caption read, *A second suspect is arrested at gunpoint despite not possessing any weapons.*

Ted could go fuck himself and his criticism. Millie had spoken with enough people at the scene to confirm the retard's—*fuck you again, Ted*—mental capacity. And she'd lucked out to overhear a big, dyke-ish sergeant tell another cop no gun had been found. The dyke was quoted as a source close to the investigation.

Just as other news crews were arriving, Millie had bailed on the scene; she'd milked it for all she could. She busted her ass over to the hospital and had lucked out for the third time that night, running into the retard's grandmother right after she'd been told it didn't look good for her precious little baby.

Millie checked her watch. Plenty of time before her appointment. If Ted had problems with today's write-up, wait until she'd had her exclusive interview with the grieving—*no, grief-stricken sounds better*—grandmother.

Smiling in anticipation, she turned on her computer.

"Could they have made it any more biased?" Jenny shoved the paper off the table, drawing curious and annoyed stares from the other coffee-house patrons. She ignored them.

Jack retrieved the paper, placing it face down between them, but that accusing headline hung in the air like an executioner's axe. *Cops shoot unarmed 'child.'* Had the author of that sensation-grabbing banner been in the room, Jack would have gladly throttled him. No, make that her, he corrected.

"How were we supposed to know he had the mental age of a six-year-old?" Jenny's voice was a ragged whisper but still it carried, and Jack was regretting the decision to meet his partner outside of her home; not all of the customers were pointedly ignoring them. But Jenny had insisted; she needed to get out.

"God, Jack, I didn't want to shoot him." Jenny's eyes, sunken from a sleepless night, welled with tears. "I didn't want to. I swear it, but I had to. I had to. I thought he had a gun."

Jack grieved for his partner, his friend, grieved for the pain she was feeling. "Jenny, please, keep your voice down." He took her hands, could feel them trembling in his grip like two small, frightened animals. Jenny was shuddering as she fought to keep her anguish inside.

Jack bundled her in her coat, the same mid-thigh leather jacket she had on at the station last night, and guided her out the door. He left their drinks on the table; he doubted what her frayed nerves needed right now was caffeine. Jenny allowed herself to be led outside; she buttoned up her coat against the chill in the air. The temperature may have been well above seasonable but a nip in the air said winter was out there, waiting.

Jenny sniffed. "Guess that was pretty stupid, huh?"

Jack put a comforting arm around her. "Don't worry, I've done worse."

Jenny lived in an old residential section just east of the Don Valley, the green swathe that divided the city like a giant, serpentine wedge. If it hadn't been drizzling over the last two days or if the ground had been frozen, they could have walked in the valley, but today it was a quagmire of thick, icy mud. Instead, they wandered the sidewalks of her neighbourhood, beneath the winter-bare arms of aged trees.

Jenny was quiet, alone with her thoughts, and Jack didn't push the conversation. He knew his partner would talk when she was ready to. The dreary rain had withered away, but grey clouds still filled the sky, drab and cheerless.

Kind of like my life right now, he thought then immediately chided himself for being selfish. *Jenny needs me and I'm thinking about myself. I can be such an asshole.*

"I'm glad you're here, Jack." She slipped an arm through his and huddled against him. Her voice was steadier and her tears, for the time being, were gone.

"Hey, where else would I be?"

"At home, sleeping. You couldn't have gotten more than six hours of sleep."

Less than five, really. "The furry alarm clock went off and there's no ignoring him."

She nodded in understanding. After all, she had two of those alarm clocks herself. "How's your head?"

Jack shrugged. "Okay for now. The drugs took care of it."

She nodded again. "That's good. You looked like shit last night."

"Why, thank you. Love you, too."

She nudged him in the ribs. "You know what I mean. You seem to have a migraine more often than not, nowadays."

"Sometimes it feels that way," he sighed. "It used to be that lack of food was my only trigger, but now it seems everything gives me a migraine. Lack of sleep, stress—" he waved a hand at the clouds "—the weather. Life in general."

"What's happening with Karen?"

Jack glanced at his partner. Easy to do when they were the same height. Jenny was watching him with those crystal-blue eyes he loved so much. He knew what she was doing, had done it enough over the last year or so himself. By asking after Jack's troubles, she could avoid thinking about her own. It was a simple tactic, effective, but worked only for as long as the other person's tribulations.

Lucky for you, I've got plenty.

He shrugged again. "Not much. I told you she moved out back in July."

"Yeah, right after we arrested what's-her-name."

"Taylor Furlington." How could he forget? A few months after saving her when she had cut off her own breasts and tried cauterizing the wounds with a blow torch, Furlington had nearly beaten Jack to death with her bare hands. An embarrassment he couldn't forget. He touched his nose, fingering the slight crook. It hadn't healed well.

"Has she come back?"

"I fucking hope not. I'm still recovering from the last beating."

"Stupid." The last they had heard of Taylor Furlington, she'd been declared criminally insane and shipped off to a padded cell somewhere. "I meant Karen."

"Oh." *That beating's still in progress.* "Only to pack. And only when I'm not home."

Jenny hugged his arm. "I'm sorry, Jack."

"Me, too, but really, it's my fault."

Jenny pulled back, shocked. "How can you say that? *She* left *you*."

"Yeah, I know," Jack admitted. He gave her a tug and she reluctantly fell into step with him. "But come on, life with me wasn't exactly easy. Sy, Charles, Kayne, Furlington." So much blood on his hands, a litany of guilt. "That's a lot to ask anyone to put up with."

Jenny didn't reply, and Jack snuck a look at her. Her mouth was set in a terse line, a look he was well familiar with; she had directed it his way more than once.

"You know what I think about that," she said at length and seemed satisfied to leave it at that. They'd covered this ground before, Jenny arguing against his feelings of guilt and responsibility over a dead partner and a soon-to-be-dead marriage.

But Jenny hadn't been there, hadn't knelt in Sy's blood as he died, hadn't seen Karen taken hostage, threatened with rape and murder. Jenny hadn't shared a bed with him on the nights, so many nights, when he had screamed himself awake, lived with him during the investigations as he faced possible criminal charges. What marriage wouldn't have crumbled under such enormous pressure? Especially when he had turned a deaf ear to Karen's pleas to save himself, to quit the job.

"She could have met you half way, Jack," Jenny declared as if interpreting his thoughts. "But she didn't. Not an inch. Not to mention trying to get pregnant behind your back, her and her mother planning on using the baby to control you. Accusing you of adultery." She all but hissed the last.

"Kind of wish that part was true," he said, repaying the nudge. "If I'm going to be accused of it…"

That earned him a brief smile. "I can't believe she thinks you cheated on her. With me."

"It's understandable how you'd be willing to," he said dryly. "Who could resist? With this scar and the broken nose, I'm irresistible."

"Well, they do add a touch of danger to your usually cheerful scowl." She stopped and faced him, her tone growing serious. "I'm sorry Karen saw these in the wrong way."

Her fingers gently traced the scar running through his right eyebrow, squinting up his eye.

Jack snorted. "There's a right way to see them?" He knew what they meant. The scar, the broken nose and rib, the bullet wound, they all represented his failures, times when people had suffered because of him.

"They show you care. You wouldn't have them if you didn't care, if you weren't willing to do what had to be done." Her hand fell away, slowly, and she added sadly, "But you don't see it that way, do you?"

It seemed that Jack couldn't find the words to answer Jenny's question so she asked, "Have you met with a lawyer yet?"

Jack shook his head, starting to stroll again. "Only hers, and I wouldn't call him a lawyer. He's more like a hired assassin."

"Can Karen afford someone that good?"

"Nope," Jack replied with a mock cheerfulness. "But her parents can. I don't know if it's both of them or just her mother, but someone's out to get me. This guy they've hired, he normally handles the divorce cases that deal with millions, maybe billions, so to him I'm nothing but a bug to be stepped on."

"That's not fair."

"Life's not fair, but apparently—or so I'm being told—Karen and her lawyer aren't out to fuck me over. All they want is half the house, the Honda, a chunk out of my pension and any furniture Karen feels attached to."

"Which is?" Jenny asked apprehensively.

"Everything but the bed," Jack told her with a stiff smile. "In the meantime, I'm carrying the mortgage and car loan and have been told I should consider myself lucky."

Jenny tightened her grip on his arm. "I'm sorry, Jack. You don't deserve that."

"What can you do? Shit happens and payday's Tuesday. That's all you need to know." They walked in silence for several steps. "Do you know what hurt the most, though? While we were meeting in this guy's office—which probably cost more than my fucking house—I had a migraine, a bad one. I mean, seven out of ten on the pain scale and I had to leave. If I stayed any longer, I would've been leaving in an ambulance. And do you know what Karen said to me?"

Jenny shook her head.

"She looked at me," Jack began, his voice hitching with emotion, "and she told me that my migraines were awfully convenient."

"That bitch."

"Yeah, it hurt hearing she thought I used the migraines to my advantage."

"If she had seen—" Jenny started to protest.

"She has," Jack assured her. "She's seen me curled up on the floor waiting for the medication to kick in, but I guess she's just… misremembering." On the outside, Jack tried to pass off his wife's comment as a little barb meant to sting his feelings, but inside, down deep where he kept his emotions penned up, it hurt more than he thought possible. Compared to those few icy words from Karen, being shot was nothing.

Overhead, the grey clouds drifted sluggishly across the sky while the partners wandered the sidewalks aimlessly. Jenny had lapsed into a stillness, her reserve of deflecting questions seemingly drained.

"Did Brian get you home okay last night?" An innocent enough question, capable of steering the conversation to harsher grounds if Jenny wished to go there.

"Yeah, he did." She paused, long enough for Jack to think she didn't want to talk about the shooting, but in the end, she did. "He couldn't stay long, he was needed at the hospital." She sighed, heavy with regret. "I should have taken you up on your offer. Not because he couldn't stay, not that. He's a doctor and he's had people die on him before but…"

"But he's never shot anyone." Jack said it as gently as possible, but there was just no blunting its edges.

Jenny nodded, wiping her nose with her jacket sleeve. "I shouldn't be talking to you about this. The lawyer told me not to discuss it with any cops."

Jack concurred. "And you shouldn't talk about it to Jack, your partner. Good thing he's not here right now and you're with Jack, your friend."

She slid her hand down to his and gave it an appreciative squeeze. "I'm glad he's here, too." They walked hand in hand, a hush following them. Jack knew Jenny would talk when she could. It wouldn't help to force her; she'd had enough of that last night.

"Have you heard anything?" she hesitantly asked. "Has he…?"

"No," Jack assured her. "I called the station but there's been no change. He's still critical."

"We thought he had a gun," she whispered, almost to herself. "How were we supposed to know he was mentally challenged?"

"You couldn't."

She snickered harshly. "Not according to the newspaper. The way they wrote it, we should have known everything about him as soon as we ran into him. Did you read it?"

"I did," Jack said solemnly. "And I suggest you skip the news for the next little while. It'll only upset you more."

He had indeed read the article and it had royally pissed him off. He could only imagine what it had done to Jenny. The headline—"Cops shoot unarmed 'child'"—was horrible but he figured "Police shoot suspected gunman" wouldn't sell as many papers. The reporter had gone on to paint an inflammatory, gruesome picture. Tyrone Johnson was an innocent, loving man-child whose greatest joy was pleasing his struggling, poverty-stricken grandmother. The reporter had highlighted that not only was this man-child not carrying a gun or a weapon of any sort, he had not been involved in any suspicious activity at all.

Makes it sound like we go around shooting people for the hell of it.

But it got worse. The reporter had to point out that Tyrone, a young *black* man, had been *mercilessly gunned down*—the reporter's phrase—by a *white* officer.

Like that makes a damned bit of difference.

Jack, like most cops, saw skin colour simply as another physical descriptor. Gender, age, height, build, hair colour, skin colour. All the same. Not surprisingly, the reporter failed to mention that one of the officers was female and the other Korean.

"How do you handle it?"

"A day at a time," Jack told her. "Sometimes, an hour at a time. Did you think you had to shoot?"

Jenny hesitated. "I did, but now—"

"None of that shit." Jack cut her off, slicing his hand through the air. "Don't let what you hear now cloud your memory. No 'what ifs.' You're a good cop and a good person. I know you wouldn't have shot unless you felt you had no choice."

"Thanks, Jack. How'd you get so smart?" she joked.

"With situations like this?" he laughed. "Practice. Lots of practice."

"Well, at least they have a nice day for their protest," Jack observed as he joined Detective Mason at the window.

The head of the division's Major Crime unit nodded glumly as he stared down at the line of protesters marching up and down the sidewalk out front of the station. "Yeah, I wish it would fucking hail."

"C'mon, Rick. Where's your community spirit?"

Mason was a big, beefy man with a buzz cut and a grey goatee long enough to braid. He possessed a frowning glare that was known to cause rookies, and some not so rookie cops, to require a change of underwear. He focused that oh-so-pleasant demeanor on Jack.

"How come you're so fucking cheerful?"

"Drugs," Jack said simply.

Mason grimaced in understanding. Jack's migraines were gaining legendary status at the station. "Do you have enough to share?"

Jack waved a hand at the protesters. "They're bothering you that much?"

About two dozen people were down below, most of them carrying homemade signs. From his position on the second-floor office, Jack could read "Justice for none", "police = murderers" and "Who speaks for Tyrone?" A host of media trucks clogged Regent Street and St. Bartholomew

Street, the little side street that ran straight from the station into South Regent Park. Reporters and cameramen buzzed around the protesters like bees searching for a ripe flower.

"Nah. The Superintendent told me to hold off on some search warrants slated for Regent Park. Figures there's too much tension right now to go kicking in doors."

"The search warrants too important to wait?"

"Only if you consider the division's last couple of homicides important," Mason griped.

Jack gave the detective a knowing grin. "Shouldn't Homicide be handling the warrants, then?"

Mason shrugged. "Only if they are directly involved with the investigation. The warrants are for drugs and weapons, but if we find something related to the murder… Well, shit happens."

The division had been immersed in a gang war for the past two months as the Park Boyz duked it out with Downtown Hoods for supremacy in Regent Park. At stake, the lucrative drug trade in and around the Park. The conflict had been punctuated by three stabbings, two drive-by shootings and a host of radio calls—fight and sound of gunshot—that could not be definitively credited to the gangs, but no one was doubting who was responsible.

None of the self-styled gangstas had been able to kill any of their adversaries yet, but the last drive-by—only a week ago—had come close to claiming a civilian life. Patricia McQueen, a young mother on her way home from Christmas shopping, had the miserable misfortune to walk past Dorian Scott, a 'lieutenant' in the Hoods. A stolen Honda Civic loaded with hyped-up Park Boyz had slowly cruised by, and the assholes in the car had opened fire, aiming at Scott, but obviously not caring who they hit.

Their intended victim escaped the hail of gunfire, but Patricia wasn't nearly as lucky. She was hit by four bullets. Two caught her in the leg, shattering her femur, while another gouged a deep gash across her abdomen. The fourth one tore through her left cheek and out the right, blasting apart several teeth. Had she been facing the shooters, the slug would have taken off the back of her skull.

She was lucky to be alive. A bona fide Christmas miracle.

After the shooting—and a hell of a lot of noise from the community and the media—someone at headquarters had finally decided to give a damn, and 51 was loaned some extra manpower, with the two gangs firmly in police sights. But stopping gangs from fighting, especially over territory and drugs, was like getting dogs on either side of a fence to stop barking at each other. As long as they could see each other, no one was about to get them to shut up.

The drive-bys and the open violence had quickly dried up, but in place of open warfare, the Boyz and Hoods had progressed to assassinations. Within three days of the bungled drive-by shooting, each gang had lost a member—both pretty high up in the pecking order—in very precise, almost professional manners. As Jack understood it, one had his throat slit and the other's forehead had grown a hatchet. Seemed like gangstas could learn, after all.

Jack grinned at the gruff detective. Whatever happened in 51, on his streets, Mason took personally, and Jack could see him going after the killers without waiting for Homicide.

"One of these days, Rick," Jack cautioned, "you're going to step on the wrong person's toes."

Mason snorted. "Like I care. Besides," he justified, "Homicide's busy with other cases, and a couple of gangbangers getting offed won't be high on their to-do list." He abandoned the window in favour of his desk. The chair creaked alarmingly as he settled his bulk on it.

Jack chuckled. "Tank stealing your chair again?"

Mason grimaced. "I wish. They're just all falling apart. Just like everything else around here." The MCU office was similar to every other office in the police station: too old and too small. Banged-up metal desks and beaten-up filing cabinets fought for space in the shadowy office. Mason usually kept the blinds drawn, casting the room in a perpetual twilight. He said he didn't want anyone with a grudge taking potshots at him through the windows.

Changing the topic, Mason asked, "How's Jenny doing?"

It was Jack's turn to grimace. "As good as can be expected, I guess. I talked with her this morning. She's stressed, and all this media attention—" he gestured blindly at the window "—isn't making it any easier."

"Has she been told when her SIU interview is?"

"Not yet." Jack's lips puckered as if he had bitten into a rotten lemon. He and the Special Investigations Unit—every copper's favourite civilian agency responsible for investigating police incidents where someone other than the cop suffered serious injury or death—had a lengthy history. They'd gone after him twice. Once for shooting Anthony Charles, the second time earlier this year for dropping Randall Kayne off a bridge. In both cases they were unable to come up with enough evidence to lay charges against Jack, and he imagined that there was now a most-wanted poster in the SIU office with his picture on it.

"She isn't rethinking the shoot, is she?"

"Trying not to, but it's difficult not to second-guess yourself. She thought the kid had a gun. Connor had a second guy under arrest. Anything come of him?"

Mason snorted. "Freddy Franklin. That little shit was going around telling people he had a gun." Mason leaned back in his chair, revealing what was written on his T-shirt: *Do I look like a freaking people person?* "He didn't have one," he said, forestalling Jack's hopeful question. "All we could get on him was a simple possession of cocaine. He'll walk later today most likely."

"Well, that's something, at least. It could explain why Jenny thought the Tyrone kid might have had a gun. I'll see you later, Rick." Jack stood up to go.'

"Have you seen this yet?" Mason asked, sliding a sheet of paper across his desk. "You might want to take a look before you go on the road."

Jack scanned the officer safety bulletin. "You're just full of cheery news, aren't you?"

Mason smiled. "Always."

Alone in the office, Mason sagged in his chair, cradling his throbbing head in both hands. *Shit, if it isn't my gut killing me, it's my head. I should have pressed Jack for some drugs.*

Berating himself for being a wimp, he straightened up and turned his attention to work. His desk was littered with folders. Despite having a computer on his desk, Mason preferred reading reports on paper. Feeling the weight of the report in his hands, having the ability to jot notes and ideas down as they came to him, felt like police work.

So I'm a dinosaur. Fucking computer's probably giving me cancer, anyway.

He flipped open a folder—the Scott murder; someone had cleaned up on the drive-by—and slowly and meticulously went through the stack of paper for the third time, hoping to catch some little detail he missed the previous reads. The cause of death may have been a slit throat, but Scott had suffered plenty before dying; the autopsy revealed he had been thoroughly beaten with a blunt object. According to the coroner, the baseball bat left at the scene was most likely the weapon.

Yeah, like the bat being splintered and covered in his blood wasn't a clue. Guy thinks he's Quincy.

Two days after Scott met his messy and well-deserved end, Clayton Felcamp, a rather nasty and sadistic bastard in the Boyz, was found in an underground garage with a hatchet buried between his eyes. Like Scott, Felcamp had not died easy or quickly. The small axe had been used extensively on his lower body before becoming lodged in his grey matter.

Homicide considered the Felcamp murder as retaliation for Scott's, and was looking at both deaths as two pieces in the gang war. Even though the murders showed a severe increase in the conflict's violence, the community and police were somewhat content—as long as the gangs kept the executions private and off the streets. Let the gangs kill each other.

But Mason wasn't convinced. The two gang members 'hadn't been just executed, they had been tortured.

"Or punished," Mason speculated to the empty office. Like someone was making an example of them. But he didn't want to consider that possibility; if it was true, there would be a shitload more trouble than a mere turf war.

His stomach gurgled painfully, followed by a nasty belch that burned its way up from his guts. *Probably got an ulcer, the way my luck is going.* He opened his desk drawer, grabbed a bottle of antacids and crunched a few to quell the riot in his belly. *Too much stress. Maybe I should take a vacation.*

With no family to share Christmas—no kids, his wife long since dead, his sister married and living somewhere in Europe—he could easily bugger off for an extended period of relaxation. Problem was he just wasn't the relaxing type.

Mason's cell phone rang, and his heart did a little stutter-step. The detective carried two cells with him, a personal phone, and a blank one that couldn't be traced back to him. The blank was the one presently ringing. Only a handful of people knew the number: Tank, Kris and Taftmore, his trusted team of officers, a Crown attorney and one judge. You could never predict when a surreptitious call for legal advice or a backdated warrant would come up.

There was nothing going on right now that would necessitate a call from any of his officers, and the judge and lawyer, even though they had the number, never called; Mason called them.

The phone continued to ring, its electronic chirruping demanding it be answered.

Only one other person knew the number, knew the phone even existed. It couldn't be him. Couldn't be.

Chirrup, chirrup.

Mason hadn't heard from him in six months, but the detective knew it was him calling. Half a year of silence, despite Mason's best efforts to track him down, and now he calls.

Chirrup, chirrup.

Don't answer it, he warned himself. *Throw the fucking thing in the garbage. Hell, flush it down the toilet.*

Answering the call would mean trouble, but he had no idea what ignoring it would result in. He pulled the phone free of his belt just as it fell silent. Mason stared at the hateful device, wishing he could simply toss it and everything it represented away. His hand strayed over the trash bucket, paused, then he tucked the phone back onto his belt.

Palming sudden sweat from his forehead, Mason blew out a deep breath. Maybe it was time to take a vacation, after all.

Millie Templeton, the *Citizen*'s newest rising star reporter, freed herself dejectedly from the huddle of cameramen and TV news personalities. She clicked off her recorder and shoved it into her pocket, for all the good it would do her. The protest's spokesperson, an older gentleman who reminded Millie of Morgan Freeman, had talked at length about the injustice that the black community endured at the hands of 51 Division officers, about their ' outrage over this latest shooting, and their demand to see the officer responsible brought up on charges.

Blah, blah, blah, Millie thought. *How am I supposed to write something interesting out of that mediocre bullshit?*

"'The protesters vow to remain until their demands are met,'" she phrased for herself. "Like that will accomplish anything."

"Bitch, you don't think we can fight back?"

The harsh, hate-filled words came from beside Millie, and she jumped. The young man beside her was staring aggressively at her, his eyes narrowed slits of hostility. There was something in his glare she found familiar, but she couldn't place him. If the spokesman was Morgan Freeman, then this one was a young Denzel Washington from *Training Day*. Younger, with short dreadlocks. And a whole lot angrier.

"You think we should just smile and say 'Yes, boss' when they be killing us?" He spat contemptuously. "You ain't nothing but a white bitch who never had to fight for a thing in her life."

Now, this is more like it. "What I meant," she explained, giving the young man a sympathetic smile, "was that this—" she swept a hand at the protesters across the street "—if they're lucky, will be a thirty-second spot on tonight's news before a commercial break. Everyone watching it will have forgotten it by the time the weather is on."

The young man—it was hard to judge his age; there was so much intensity to him—looked at Millie speculatively. "What would you do, then?"

Millie shook her head. "I honestly don't know. But waving signs and marching up and down the sidewalk won't accomplish anything. I know that, and I'm willing to bet you know that as well." She fished a business card out of her purse. "I'm a reporter for the *Citizen* newspaper. If there's anything I can do to help, let me know."

He took the card, but eyed it disdainfully. "What could you do for us?"

"The police are a big corporation, and like any business, they have a powerful PR section. Having your own voice in the media certainly wouldn't hurt." She checked the time as the man tucked her card away in a pocket. "I have to get moving. I have an appointment to talk with Tyrone's grandmother this afternoon."

That surprised the man. "Auntie Dee said you could talk to her?"

"That's where I know you from! You were at the hospital with her." Her brow scrunched up. "She said your name. It's Leon, right?"

"Lyron." He gave up the name reluctantly. "If Auntie Dee says you can talk to her, then you must be okay."

Millie noted Lyron's Caribbean accent faded in and out like a weak radio station on a stormy day. "Auntie Dee? Are you related to her or Tyrone?" *The grieving grandmother and enraged…cousin?* New York Times, *here I come.*

Lyron shook his head. "Everyone calls her Auntie Dee. And everyone looked after Tyrone. Until these fuckers…" He fell silent, but the anger still played about his face. "When you go to see Auntie Dee, look in the stairs."

"The stairs? What am I supposed to see?"

Lyron's grin was predatory. "Some of us be using different signs."

"Here, take a look at this." Jack handed the officer safety bulletin to Aaron and started the car as the psych nurse read it over.

"Well, that's a kick in the balls." Aaron passed the flyer back.

Jack crumpled it up and dropped the paper ball to the floor. "More like a declaration of war."

The bulletin Mason had shown Jack was being posted all over the station and stacked by the front desk. It warned officers of graffiti appearing throughout Regent Park since the shooting, accompanied by a photo. The picture was in black and white but its message was clear nonetheless. Spray-painted on the cinder-block wall of a stairwell was the number 51, crossed out in a circle, with 187 scrawled across the top.

"One eighty-seven?" Aaron asked. "They know this is Canada, right?"

"I guess it would confuse too many fuckheads if they used the section number for homicide from our Criminal Code."

"Is it legit or just someone talking big?"

"I was thinking the same thing. I asked Rick Mason about it—he's the detective in charge of Major Crime—and his guys have heard from different informants that people are talking about killing a cop to even the scales for last night's shooting."

Aaron twisted in his seat, showing his back to Jack. "Is 'crisis team' in big enough letters? I don't want to be mistaken for one of you guys."

"You're fucked, bud," Jack pronounced with an evil grin. "You work with the police, you ride in a police car. Guilt by association."

"I went through all the trouble to become a nurse," Aaron pouted, "and now I'll get shot 'cause someone thinks I'm one of you."

"You could always walk around backwards," Jack suggested.

"And risk my life on the public school system? I think not." Aaron sulked for a moment then asked, "I guess we won't be doing any calls by ourselves tonight, huh?"

"Not in the Park."

With only one cop on board, the CIT car was considered a solo unit and wasn't supposed to respond to calls alone. Ideally, the uniforms were supposed to show up first, determine if the crisis team was required, then call for them. In a division as small and as busy as 51, Jack and Aaron were frequently on scene first, saving the need for a uniformed car to attend.

The Crisis Intervention Team was a year old, having started up in November of 2000, and was well received by both the coppers and the EDPs. Cops generally didn't like dealing with the nut jobs—emotionally disturbed people, in political correctness—because they could be extremely time-consuming. An apprehension under the Mental Health Act meant a trip to the hospital where the cops could end up sitting with their prisoner for hours waiting for a psychiatric assessment. And all too frequently, the EDP who had been standing on the wrong side of a balcony railing or screaming about the voices telling him to slash his wrists would walk out of the hospital before the cops were done with the paperwork. All because the EDP had calmed down and knew what answers the doctor wanted to hear.

The CIT was to change all that. The team's nurse, an employee of St. Mike's, was to speed up the process at the hospital, mostly by legitimizing the apprehension in the doctor's eyes. Aaron could also refer people to community services if an apprehension wasn't warranted, an option the police didn't have. When it came to the mentally ill, the police had two choices—apprehend or not—and most of the time erred on the cover-your-ass side. No copper wanted someone taking a header off a balcony after deeming the person sane enough to be left alone. Safer to let the doctors make that call.

Aaron had urged Jack to volunteer to fill in for the regular police officer, who was on annual leave, and Jack was glad he had. While he missed working with Jenny—he was kicking himself for not being at her side last night—the CIT was an enjoyable change from the cars although it wasn't that much of a change in pace. Jack had always known there were a lot of EDP calls in the division, but he had never realized just how many until he was responding to all of them. Or how pitifully little he knew about mental health.

Jack had quickly discovered that what he had been taught in the police college wasn't even the tip of the iceberg. More like the pile of penguin shit on the tip. Before working with Aaron, Jack had never really known what schizophrenia was, and had never even heard of borderline personality disorder, but Aaron was a good teacher and realized Jack's glaring ignorance wasn't his own fault.

"You hungry?"

"I can always eat," Aaron said, patting the paunch under the vest. "What do you have in mind?"

"I was thinking Peking Express."

"That the one with that chicken and broccoli thingie?"

"Yeah." Jack had 'discovered' the little take-out Chinese restaurant at Parliament and Shuter after driving by it hundreds of times. Run by a brother-sister team, it had the best General George chicken Jack had ever tasted and it had taken only one serving to hook Aaron.

"Is CIT on the air? CIT?"

"Did you hear a call?" Jack reached for the mike. "Must have come over when we were in the hospital." Aaron, as a St. Michael's employee, started and ended his shifts at the hospital, not the police station. "Go ahead for CIT."

"It's 5106. We're heading to a call at 251 Sackville. You available?"

"10-4. Dispatch, can you throw us on 6's call?"

"So much for the chicken thingie," Aaron sighed.

"Quit being a little bitch," Jack said jokingly. "We'll grab lunch right after this call."

"Fine." Aaron sighed dramatically and pulled up the call—the other nurse on the team refused to use or even touch any police equipment—and read it out. "Mother's calling. Her son is schizophrenic and off his meds, getting violent. There goes lunch."

"That's up to you," Jack informed Aaron. "Maybe he's just an asshole."

Aaron grinned. "One not-insane assessment coming up."

When the crisis team had been revealed to the public, St. Mike's had touted it as a vital, long-needed link between the police and the mental-health community. Too often, the hospital cried, the mentally ill were being thrown into the criminal justice system because the police were lacking in knowledge and understanding of their condition. With a mental-health nurse on board, able to assess the situation first hand, these unfortunate souls would be routed away from the cells and into the hospital.

That was the idea, anyway.

Jack placed EDP's in one of two categories: those who truly needed help and the assholes who hid behind their mental illness. The first group was rarely involved in a criminal activity, the second, almost always. Those were the ones who got in people's faces, stole, assaulted, caused shit great and small, and when the police showed up, started crying about the voices in their head, or their depression, or their…well, the list went on. They may well indeed be sick, but they had learned that a few key phrases could steer the police car from the station to the ER. And since they were almost never admitted—they knew the right words for the doctors as well—they were back on the street in a few hours.

But Aaron was changing all that.

He despised the frequent flyers as much as the coppers did. He had no problem sitting down with people who were genuinely in distress to make sure they got the help they needed, whether at the hospital, outsourced to the community, or just listening to them vent. But he had no patience, no tolerance whatsoever, for those using their illness to circumvent the law. On average, it took Aaron five, maybe ten minutes tops, to determine if someone was sick or should have his ass dumped in a cold cell for the night. Word of the team had spread quickly through the division, and many EDP's welcomed the familiar sight of the casual uniform while others had learned to dread it.

All in all, Aaron was cynical and hard-assed enough to fit right in at 51.

251 Sackville was the twin apartment building opposite 248, the scene of Jenny's shooting. The parking lot between the six-storey buildings wasn't much more than an exaggerated driveway with little room to maneuver, but 5106 was parked right in the middle, even though there were empty spaces on the sides. Jack pulled in behind the marked car, forgoing the vacant spots as well; some idiots thought it was hilarious to block in police cars.

Jack stepped out of the car, adjusting his blue raid jacket. The idea of having the CIT cop dressed more casually, away from the intimidating uniform, so as to help relieve the anxiety of the EDP's—or clients, as the hospital liked to refer to them—was fine by Jack; he'd wear jeans over polyester pants any day. Unfortunately, he had to borrow a jacket from the cop he was replacing as no one had thought to buy extras for the subs, and the jacket was a little too snug for Jack's liking. He knew he was lucky the weather was so mild; there was no way he'd get a sweater under the nylon jacket.

As he tugged the jacket into place, he scanned the area around him. Cops who went directly to the call without seeing what, or who, was near them could easily end up dead cops. To the north, a mother with a toddler in hand made her way along the Oak Street walkway, while out front of 248 a small group of hostile faces glared Jack's way. Jack studied the group, made up of different ages and sexes, trying to determine if they were going to be a problem. The group turned their backs on him.

Nice to see you, too.

"You see the memorial?" Aaron asked, pointing to the north end of 248.

Sure enough, on the strip of winter-brown grass butting up against the walkway where only hours before police and civilian investigators had attempted to dissect Jenny's shooting—the rain had necessitated a hurried examination of the scene—stood a flowered wreath and small white cross. Beneath the cross lay more flowers, and as Jack watched, the mother he had seen on the walkway led her child to the cross and reverently added a bouquet to the growing pile.

The mother, bundled in a parka, said something to her child as she gestured at Jack and the police cars. Jack may not have been able to see the mother's face, hidden within her hood, but the toddler's face, framed by a heavy toque, was visible. And so was the intense hatred. An all-consuming hatred that only an innocent and naïve soul could produce.

Still squatting next to her child, the mother brazenly gave Jack the finger, and the child instantly copied the motion although his—Jack assumed it was a boy due to the blue snowsuit—was lost in his mitten.

"Nice, huh?" Aaron joined Jack by the driver's door.

Jack wondered what the mother would do if he suddenly started walking towards her then decided he really didn't give a shit. "Job security," he said simply.

"How so?"

"With that kind of parenting—" mother and child were leaving, the boy stomping on a strip of police tape sagging from a light pole "—do you really think he's going to grow up to be a law-abiding citizen?"

"Guess not." Aaron shook his head. "Nothing like setting your kid up to fail."

With a final tug on his jacket, Jack said, "Let's get this done then grab some lunch."

Like its twin across the parking lot, 251 was shaped like a giant dog bone with the building's ends jutting out to form a wide courtyard on the east and west sides. Not satisfied with a single entrance, the building sported two lobbies, each tucked into the courtyard's corners. The two officers from 5106 were standing on the low cement steps at the north door. A distraught woman, the worry clear on her dark skin, stood with the cops.

The problem with working the CIT and starting early in the afternoon—the team worked a steady one-to-eleven shift—meant Jack spent the first half of his shift with the platoon on days and not the officers he was used to working with. The early half of B platoon wouldn't parade for duty until four. Jack recognized the two young coppers, but if they had ever introduced themselves, he had forgotten their names. He was bad with names.

One of the officers, a redhead with a heavy case of freckles, stepped away from his escort and the woman to meet Jack and Aaron in the courtyard. "Hey, Jack. Glad you could make it." Jack may not have known the copper's name, but everyone seemed to know the name of the guy who was potentially going to take an EDP call off of their hands.

"What have we got?" Jack asked, wondering where the woman's son was.

"Maybe nothing," the redheaded copper said, flipping open his memo book. "The complainant, Maria Smith there, says her son, Justin, is schizophrenic and stopped taking his medication."

"How long ago?" Aaron wanted to know. Before working with Aaron, Jack wouldn't have cared when the kid went off his meds, but now he knew it was an important piece of information; going cold turkey from psychiatric medication could mess up a person worse than the illness.

Redhead shrugged. "She doesn't know. A week ago, a month ago. She really doesn't know. What she does know is that he's back on the crack."

"A schizophrenic off his meds and on crack. Oh, joy." Lunch was looking further away by the minute. "Where is he now?"

Redhead bobbed his shoulders again. "Dunno. He took off before we got here." Smiling, he tucked his memo book away. "So, I guess we can leave the report with you guys, right?"

"No," Jack snapped, his anger stirring. *Fucking rookie trying to sluff his call off on us.* Jack may have been shitty with names, but faces he remembered, and this little punk hadn't been around the station long enough to be anything but a rookie.

Redhead's smile collapsed. "But it's an EDP call," he protested. Weakly.

"No," Jack corrected, feeling a stab of sadistic pleasure at the rookie's discomfort. "It's a missing person if she wants to go that route, and that makes it yours."

"Oh, I just thought..." Redhead glanced at his escort, who was still standing with the complainant, too far away to help.

As quickly as Jack's anger spiked, it crumpled as the rookie floundered. "Sorry, but I was on the shooting last night," Jack explained, "and didn't get much sleep. I'm just a little on edge." *And I feel like I just kicked a puppy.*

"And hungry," Aaron added with a smirk. "You don't want to be around him when he's hungry."

"Oh, no problem. I just thought because the son is... Never mind." Redhead looked beseechingly at Aaron. "Could you talk to the mother? She was asking questions we can't answer."

Aaron nodded. "Lead on."

"Maria, this is our Crisis Intervention Team," Redhead said by way of introduction. "They can answer your questions about your son's condition."

The woman was wringing her hands nervously as she glanced from Jack to Aaron.

"I'm a nurse from St. Michael's Hospital," Aaron clarified; he was used to being mistaken for a cop. "I understand your son has been diagnosed with schizophrenia. Is that correct?"

Jack stepped back and let Aaron do his thing. Redhead and his escort, an even younger-looking blonde PW, hung back as well, and Jack kept an eye on them to make sure they didn't try to slip off to their car. He doubted they would—seniority still counted for something—but he could never be sure with the newer recruits. Redhead was still shooting Jack nervous looks as if he was some feral dog that might attack. The blonde ignored Jack, writing in her book, the end of her ponytail brushing the side of her neck.

Fucking dumb. Some asshole is going to use that as a handhold and fill her face in. Jack shook his head disgustedly. *Bloody sergeant shouldn't have let her out on the road like that.*

Jack was only at the halfway point of his eighth year, but even in his modest time on the job he had seen a change in the officers being hired. Jack's training officer had taught him that seniority was as important, if not more so, than rank, and if a twenty-year vet called you rookie when you were five years in, then too bad, you were a rookie.

And you did the job. You looked after yourself first, then whoever you were riding with—a partner if you were lucky enough to have paired up with someone—then the rest of the shift. And you did the job.

But more and more of the recruits, not all—not yet, anyway—saw the job differently. It wasn't a calling, it was a career, a good paycheque with room for advancement. To these new-age officers, only rank mattered. Forget time on, dismiss experience. They'd go out of their way for a sergeant with six years on but totally blow off a member of the division's quarter-century club.

And with this new attitude came a lack of passion for the job, an unwillingness to put your ass on the line for what was right. As far as Jack could tell, the spine was slowly melting out of the Toronto police.

Fuck, I'm in a foul mood today.

"There he is now," Maria said, her words jolting Jack out of his reverie. "Oh, no. That isn't good."

"What isn't?" Jack asked over his shoulder as he watched a young man—*Redhead said his name was Justin?*—cutting across the parking lot. He moved in a quick, jerking stride, like a marionette controlled by a demented puppeteer. Despite the cool weather, Justin was wearing a baggy tank top over equally baggy jeans, and as he came closer Jack could see sweat glistening on his black skin. He had a backpack clutched in one hand, and that turned out to be the problem.

"That's not his bag," his mother said, distressed.

"Aaron, do we have enough for an apprehension?" Justin was getting closer but wasn't slowing down, no matter that a small group of uniforms was waiting for him with his mother. Jack wanted to know what he was going to do before Justin reached them.

"More than enough," Aaron answered quickly.

"Good." Jack shot a look at Redhead and his escort. "We're going MHA right now. We can figure it out later if he stole the backpack or not." Jack didn't wait to see if they agreed with him; it hadn't been a question.

Justin came striding through the courtyard, his eyes fixed firmly on nothing, his limbs swinging spasmodically. He made to brush past the officers—Jack wasn't sure if he even saw them—but Jack snagged him by the arm.

"Justin, you're under ar—"

Justin swung the backpack, slamming it into the side of Jack's head. The bag must have had something heavy in it; it thumped painfully against Jack's head but not hard enough to knock him down.

Jack dropped and drove his shoulder into Justin's slim belly. They landed hard on the concrete stairs, Jack's two hundred pounds driving the air out of Justin in a loud *whoosh*. Jack was getting ready to flip Justin onto his stomach for handcuffing when some idiot fired off some pepper spray. The orange gush caught Justin full in the face, and at the first touch of the searing spray he wrenched violently beneath Jack, trying to escape.

If he manages to suck in a breath right now, he'll get a lungful of that shit. Jack almost felt sorry for Justin; he hated pepper spray.

Jack didn't want to risk turning his head toward the orange stream to see who was doing the spraying, and the cop continued to hose him down. Jack turned to tell the copper to stop, and one of Justin's flailing arms connected with the spray can. And knocked it directly into Jack's eyes.

Jack hated pepper spray, really fucking hated it. Because it worked so fucking well on him.

The heavy, oily mist swept across his face and he was instantly blinded as a thousand pinpoints of blazing pain stabbed into his eyes. Jack jerked backwards, trying to keep his hands from his face—rubbing only ground the shit deeper into the skin—but his legs were tangled with Justin's and he fell, his left hip smacking hard on a cement step.

Jack yanked his legs free and rolled off the steps, landing on his hands and knees. His eyes and skin were burning, a nuclear sunburn, and his nose was spewing snot. The asshole copper had missed his mouth, but there was enough of the shit in the air—what happened to the two quarter-second bursts they were taught to use?—that Jack had breathed in a sickening amount. He started coughing, deep hacking barks that did nothing to clear his chest.

I'm going to kill whoever fucking did that. Fucking kill.

Jack could hear a scuffle close by. Something whacked into his foot. He tried to still his coughing, to listen to the fight. Aaron was capable on his own, but handcuffing someone, especially someone who didn't want to be cuffed, was never as easy as it appeared on TV, and neither Redhead nor the PW was exactly formidable-looking in the black uniform.

"Justin, don't fight them! Please, baby, don't fight!" That was the mother screaming, and from the sound of it she was still at the top of the stairs, keeping out of the fight. For now. Jack hoped she didn't suddenly decide to jump to her son's rescue.

But, as it turned out, the mother was the least of Jack's worries.

"Let him go!"

"Get the fuck off him!"

"You ain't gonna kill another of us!"

The angry—fuck angry, furious—voices were almost on top of them. Jack forced his burning eyes open and could barely make out a heavily blurred group of people rushing across the courtyard.

The group from across the street. They must have been watching us. Not that it mattered. One irate mob was as bad as another.

"Let him go!" they were yelling, and it quickly fell into a chant. "Let him go, let him go, let him go." The strength of the chant was building rapidly, and Jack was worried—fuck worried, scared—what would happen when the chanters drew others to the scene, or worked themselves into a frenzy. Three cops, one all but blind, and an unarmed nurse. They were in shit and sinking fast.

Jack fought through the pain and kept his eyes open. He found Justin at the base of the stairs with two dark blobs on top of him, smudged arms thrashing as they struggled to control him. A third blob—Jack couldn't tell if it was Redhead or the blonde, and he fucking prayed it wasn't Aaron—was facing the indistinct mass, and from its many throats rose the chant.

"Let him go. Let him go. Let him *go!*"

Jack didn't need to see to know they were about to be overrun; his ears told him enough. And if that happened, then the best they could hope for would be to get out of this mess alive.

Jack crawled over to the thrashing blob that turned out to be Aaron and Redhead. Justin was face down and groaning pitifully. His moans ebbed and swelled like a medieval war horn, urging the crowd on. Aaron had one of Justin's arms pinned; Redhead had hold of the other arm but was nowhere near to controlling the boy. Justin was swinging the cop back and forth like Justice shaking one of his chew toys.

Jack grabbed Justin's arm and planted a knee on the back of the boy's elbow. "Justin, calm down!" he roared, loud enough to be heard over Justin's moans, loud enough to briefly drown out the chant. "We need to get you to the hospital!"

Jack groped, found Redhead's jacket and pulled him close. "Get the fuck up and help her," he hissed, jerking his head towards the PW facing the mob. "Calm that fucking crowd down or keep them the fuck back. Do it!" He shoved Redhead away, praying it was enough. Praying, but doubting.

"How many people?" Jack's back was to the crowd, and he could feel the hostility crashing into him like waves.

"About twenty, but more keep coming." Aaron lowered his voice. "They're really pissed."

Jack nodded, wiped away a trail of snot. "Fuck, my eyes are burning. What's idiot doing?"

"They're trying to calm things down," Aaron answered, seemingly designating both uniformed coppers as idiots. "But it ain't going to last."

The chant was growing in volume, ominous and threatening, throbbing all around Jack and Aaron like the clichéd drums in an old jungle movie. And like those old black-and-white thrillers, the shit would hit the fan once the drums stopped.

Jack wrenched Justin's arm behind his back—there was no time for niceties. The arm pinned, Jack grabbed his cuffs and held them out to Aaron. Jack didn't doubt he could cuff Justin blind, but it would be faster if Aaron did it. Seconds later, Jack heard the wonderful *snick* as the cuffs clicked shut. "Cuffed," Aaron announced quietly.

Jack reached for his radio but Aaron stopped him. "I called for backup as soon as I saw the crowd coming."

Distantly, Jack could hear sirens, but from the sound they were still a distance away, perhaps as much as a minute's worth of traveling. And a minute could be a lifetime when facing an ugly crowd.

"You got him?" Justin had given up the fight, his only movements quivers that ran through his upper body as he softly wept.

Aaron nodded. "What are you going to do?"

"Buy us some time. Hopefully." Jack wiped his nose once more and flung the steaming snot on the ground. Pushing himself to his feet was hell. All he wanted to do was curl up on the cement next to Justin and tear the skin from his face, his eyes from his skull. What he would give for a snowbank right now. His face was on *fucking* fire.

"That...is...enough!" he yelled in his best cut-the-shit police voice. And miraculously, for a brief second or two, the mob fell silent. Even Redhead and Blondie paused to stare at him. Whether it was his yell that quieted the crowd, or the sight of a cop covered in orange pepper spray, snot, and tears, he didn't know and cared even less.

"We're taking him to the hospital," he said, projecting so that everyone could hear him. "We need to help him, and right now this isn't helping."

"He didn't do nuthin'," a voice called from the side of the crowd. "You started beatin' on him for nuthin'." The crowd murmured its agreement.

"You ain't gonna kill another of us!" This from another voice—*fuck, I can't see shit!*—somewhere in the back.

"We're not going to kill anyone," Jack declared, beseeching with empty palms.

"Bullshit!" someone yelled. "You're the Reaper. You've killed three black people already."

Jack groaned. That fucking nickname. 51's criminal community had gifted him with it after Jack had tossed Randall Kayne from the Rosedale Valley pedestrian bridge. The Reaper, because everyone who went up against him ended up dead. And, for the record, only one of the two had been black. Where the guy got three, Jack had no clue.

"He shot Tyrone! I seen him."

"I never—" Jack began but the mob drowned him out.

"They be sayin' some white chick shot him but I seen him, too! The Reaper shot Tyrone!"

The sirens were closer now, only seconds away, but the crowd was oblivious to them, lost within its madness. Gone was the chant, replaced by angry growls and calls for justice, demand for the Reaper's blood.

Jack should have been scared. A lynch mob was calling for his head. He should have been terrified.

I don't need this fucking shit.

Jack's anger, molten and raging, rose up, fuelled by the shit that was consuming his life. Karen's betrayal, her accusations, her parents and their bloodsucking lawyer. All the sleepless nights, the never-ending migraines. The anger at Karen for leaving him, the hate at himself for driving her away. It burned up from his stomach and erupted.

"You want the Reaper?" Jack snarled. He ripped out his collapsible baton and snapped it open. "I'll fucking give you the Reaper."

Jack still couldn't see anything beyond fuzzy, indistinct shapes, but that didn't matter. He didn't need to see the faces he wanted to smash. The rage, held tight for so many months, was free, and it wanted to hurt someone. Anyone.

A startled hush fell on the crowd, and into the sudden silence screamed three police cars. Two screeched to a halt in the parking lot while the third jumped the curb, scattering the crowd as it fishtailed to a stop in the muddied courtyard.

It was over in a few frenzied moments. Some of the crowd, possibly fearing retaliation, fled. Others backed off but stayed in the area, keeping sullen, suspicious eyes on the police.

Jack sagged against a wall, his anger gone, dispersed with the crowd. Someone, Aaron maybe, pressed a bottle of water into his hand. Jack murmured his thanks and upended the bottle over his eyes, but it was like trying to extinguish a bonfire by pissing on it. Too quickly, the bottle was empty and Jack's skin was still aflame.

"Better?" Aaron asked.

"Slightly." Bent over, Jack coughed and spat. "Is everything under control?"

Aaron paused, probably checking the scene. "Yeah."

"Good." Jack held out the car keys. "Get me to the station. There's a hose in the sally port."

Aaron hesitantly took the keys. "Um, don't you need to be a cop or have a special licence to drive a police car?"

"You've just been deputized. Let's go."

Millie was ecstatic. If there was a patron saint of reporters, he or she was certainly smiling on Mrs. Templeton's little girl this week. First she scooped the shooting, and with photos no one else had, then she scored an interview with the grandmother. And now, after that tearful, juicy meeting, she lands right in the middle of a near riot. Well, not right in the middle. The periphery was better for pictures and safer for the non-combative types.

I must have horseshoes up my ass.

She fired off her camera as quickly as it could focus. She got shots of the crowd, shots of the cops, lots of shots of the victim pinned painfully against the concrete. The crowd was chanting, yelling at the cops to let go whoever it was they had in handcuffs. Millie shivered in delight. The air was practically vibrating with the intensity of the situation.

If she was really lucky, there'd be another shooting. Her career would be made.

C'mon, somebody pull your gun. C'mon, you fucking pussies.

Millie hurriedly checked her camera's picture count; she didn't want to run out of memory. Lots of room.

The crowd's chant had fallen off, the chanters seemed to be targeting one particular officer, a big bastard with orange pepper spray smeared across his face. Millie smirked. Probably sprayed himself. The cop, dressed in a quasi-official uniform, looked like he was trying to calm things down. Millie didn't bother photographing that, but she had to give the cop points for tenacity; his eyes and face had to be on fire. She'd got a taste of that shit back home once, and it was an experience she never wanted to repeat.

She was beginning to wonder if anyone on either side of the confrontation would have the balls to push it to the next level—sirens were screaming closer so there wasn't much time left—when a sudden change came over the cop. He whipped out his club and yelled at the crowd, "You want the Reaper? I'll fucking give you the Reaper."

As volatile as the crowd was, it was nothing compared to the absolute fury emanating from the cop. Millie took an involuntary step back, so fierce was the cop's visage, but she didn't forget to raise her camera. Even as she backed away, she was snapping pictures as fast as she could.

Millie jumped out of the way as a police car slid to a stop in the courtyard. More cops poured into the area, and as quickly as it had begun—faster even—the almost riot was over. She hung around a bit longer to make sure it was truly done, then ducked out of sight before some nosy cop wanted to see what was on her camera.

Away from the scene, Millie took out her notebook and jotted down, "blue jacket, jeans, special unit? The reaper?"

She added her impressions of the confrontation to use later when she wrote it all up. There was nothing better than first-hand accountings to make a kick-ass article. Except for kick-ass pics. She flipped through the photos until she reached the pepper-sprayed cop then zoomed in on his face.

"Yes," she hissed triumphantly. She'd caught him with a snarl of inhuman rage contorting his face. "To serve and protect, my ass." Too bad he had that gunk all over his face, but it could probably be Photoshopped out of the picture. Thank God for digital cameras.

The day had been so unbelievably lucrative. The demonstration, Auntie Dee's open and candid talk—the old woman had really poured her heart out—and the mini-riot. Even the unexpected meeting with Lyron felt positive to her. True, he could turn out to be a dead end, but she didn't think so. After all, he had tipped her to the graffiti in the stairwell. Hopefully, no one else had shots yet of the 187'd 51. Yup, there definitely might be more to Lyron than an angry pretty face.

She stowed her camera away in her purse. As she crossed the parking lot of 248 Sackville—the cop cars were clearing out—she realized that Tyrone had been killed just outside his home. She scribbled "Mercilessly gunned down steps from where his grandmother lay sleeping" in her notebook then hustled for her car. She had some writing to do.

"How are your eyes?"

"The eyes are fine." Jack took a sip of tea, Earl Grey, heavily laced with honey. "My face feels like I've got one fucking nasty sunburn though."

The breeze coming off the lake felt good on Jack's skin, cooling, moist. He had the car door propped open with his foot on the armrest, enjoying his tea and the quiet. It had been quite the hectic start to the day. Justin had been carted off to the hospital for decontamination then promptly driven to 51 where he was now sitting in a cell, waiting for court tomorrow morning. Turned out the backpack he had hit Jack with wasn't his, just like his mother had said, but belonged to a twelve-year-old boy on his way home from school who had the misfortune of running into a cracked-up Justin. For reasons only he could understand, Justin had taken the bag and dealt the kid a few solid blows to the face in the process.

So instead of a warm, comfy hospital bed, Justin was sitting his ass on a cold steel cot facing robbery and assault to resist arrest charges. The detective who had processed Justin's arrest had been less than eager to lay charges against someone with a mental-health history as extensive as Justin's until Aaron had assured him the robbery was motivated more by the need to feed a crack habit than to placate whatever voices Justin claimed to be hearing.

"Justin's mom says he's an okay kid when he's on his meds. Maybe this'll convince him to stay on them."

Jack snorted. "'Your faith in humanity is greater than mine."

"So you got hit in the head then sprayed in the face. Poor baby." Aaron finished the last of his hot chocolate—with whipped cream and chocolate sprinkles, of course—

belched, and dropped the cup on the floor. He was becoming a regular copper. "At least what's-his-face bought us lunch." Aaron laughed. "You should have seen him when he asked if you were mad at him for spraying you. I thought he was going to dump a load in his pants."

Jack harumpped. After bringing Justin back from the hospital and talking to Aaron, Redhead had made a dash for Peking Express and offered an olive branch in the form of General George chicken. Now fed, and in Jack's case rinsed off, they were sitting at Cherry Beach, secluded from the rest of the world; every winter, the eastern parking lot was closed off, but barriers meant little to someone willing to do a bit of off-roading.

"How's your partner?"

"Okay, I guess. I saw her this morning before work." Jack swirled his cup, stirring up the honey that had settled to the bottom. "The media is hyping the whole unarmed, mentally challenged angle, and it's killing her. She says they thought he had a gun."

Jack had no problem discussing the shooting with Aaron; in his year in the division, the nurse had proven himself to the coppers, and they had unofficially adopted him as one of their own. As a civilian riding in a police car and a psychiatric worker, Aaron had a unique perspective on the job, and some cops had even gone to him, unofficially again, for some…well, not counseling. More like discussions. Cops were the ones who did the helping, they didn't need it.

"How about you?"

Jack cast Aaron a suspicious look. "What about me?"

Aaron shrugged, a little too casually for Jack's taste. "Nothing. You've been through a couple of incidents yourself. Just wanted to make sure Jenny's shooting wasn't stirring anything up."

Jack laughed. "You're a shitty liar. You worried I'm going to snap and lose it?"

"No, not really," Aaron mumbled. "But when you were facing that crowd, you looked like you wanted them to rush you."

"Relax. I'm not about to go postal." Jack drained the last of his tea and shut the car door. "Not yet, anyway," he said with a malicious grin as he started the car.

Jack carefully navigated the Crown Vic around the crater-like potholes scattered across the dirt parking lot. He gave driving his full attention, hoping Aaron wouldn't pursue the conversation. Aaron was a good guy, but how could Jack tell someone how he had felt confronting the mob? How could he explain the mindless rage that had exploded in him, the murderous fury that had wanted to attack the crowd, swing his stick and feel flesh and bone break beneath it?

This anger wasn't new; it had been growing in Jack for some time now. Exactly how long, he couldn't say. Karen would say, if he was stupid enough to ask, that it had started the first day he stepped foot in 51 Division. Regardless of when it began, it was with Jack always now. Even when relaxed, he could feel it coiled within him, waiting.

And what scared him, what he was reluctant to admit even to himself, was that the rage felt…good. In its grip, he was alive, fully alive. Not that miserable quagmire of beaten-down emotions wandering aimlessly through an empty house. Empty house? Try empty life. So, yes, the rage felt good, like a pure, cleansing fire sweeping through his body, his mind.

Is it the rage that feels good, or something else? a doubtful voice from the back of his head asked.

Fuck off, Jack told himself. *It makes me feel good, and right now I can use all the good feeling I can get. It's not like I'm out of control,* he assured himself.

Oh, really? the voice asked. *Would a sane man attack a group of angry people by himself?*

Jack refused to answer; he hadn't attacked the crowd. *And besides, it gave the cars time to get to us.*

It was a weak excuse but fortunately the dispatcher saved him from arguing with himself. *"CIT, call radio."*

"Go ahead."

"Could you attend with 5103 on their call? A female's calling, saying she's pregnant but doesn't know how it happened. Possibly EDP."

Ya think? "10-4, dispatch. Throw us on the call."

Aaron pulled up the call on the car's computer, an old hand at the mobile work station. Unlike the second nurse on the team who refused to use the radio or learn how to work the MWS. Jack was thankful he didn't have to work with her.

Aaron scanned the call. "Thought so." He scooped up the mike. "CIT to dispatcher. You can cancel the scout car. We've dealt with Hermenia before."

"We have?" Jack asked as the dispatcher cleared 5103.

"Well, not *us*, but we, the team." He chortled. "You'll get a kick out of her."

"If you say so."

Homewood Avenue was a little street running north off Carlton Street, opposite Allan Gardens. The top end of the street, at night, was part of the track walked by the division's transvestite hookers. The bottom end, across from the park, sported a couple of highrises and a group home for people with mental-health issues.

There was an ambulance already parked at the curb, and the paramedics were wheeling out the stretcher. An Amazon of a blonde—she had to have four inches at least on Jack—perked up when she saw Aaron.

"I was hoping you guys were coming." She swung the medical bag onto the stretcher like it was a lunch box. An empty lunch box. "Breaking in a new cop, Aaron?" she asked, eying Jack keenly. "What happened to the old one? Got tired of your ugly mug?"

"He's on holidays, that's all," Aaron said defensively. "This shouldn't take long," he speculated. "This isn't the first time Hermenia's called."

"What's her deal?" the Amazon asked as she hauled the stretcher after Aaron. Her partner, an average-size guy made small by the Amazon's stature, brought up the rear with other equipment slung over his shoulders.

"Around once a month, she figures she's pregnant and about to go into labour. After tonight, she should be good 'till the new year."

The house boasted a large front deck, and Hermenia met them outside, perched apprehensively on one of the benches built into the railing. She was wearing an oversized parka and even without the puffy coat, she was a big lady, her protruding belly parting the coat as she stood up.

She isn't pregnant? Jack looked questioningly at Aaron, who shook his head and puffed his cheeks out.

"Hi, Hermenia, how are you?"

"Not good, not good." Placing her hands on her substantial belly, she offered it up to Aaron for examination. "I think I'm going to have a baby."

Aaron sat her back down on the bench and settled beside her. "Now, Hermenia, how could you be pregnant?

I was here last month and you weren't pregnant then, and as much as I think women would like it, you can't get pregnant and go into labour in just one month."

Hermenia looked at him, squinting her eyes. "You were here before?"

So much for reason, Jack thought, but Aaron wasn't deterred. "How about if I could prove to you you're not pregnant?"

Hermenia's face lit up, astonished. "You could do that?"

"Sure could."

"Oh, thank you!" She reached for Aaron with lips puckered.

Aaron slid away, somehow making the movement seem not disrespectful or rude. "Now, Hermenia, no smooching on the first date," he chided.

"Oh, right." She folded her hands primly in her lap, flashing Aaron a coy smile.

The Amazon leaned down to whisper to Jack. "I think someone's crushing on your nurse."

Jack nodded. "Better him than me."

Their whispering obviously needed work as Aaron shot a scowl their way. Gesturing at the medics for Hermenia's benefit, he carried on. "The ambulance here has a machine that measures heartbeats. We'll hook you up to it—don't worry, it just clips on your finger—and it'll tell us how many heartbeats there are. If you're pregnant, it'll read two, yours and the baby's, but if you're not, then it'll only show one. Right?"

Hermenia hesitated, processing what Aaron had told her, then nodded sharply. "Right!"

"But we don't have—" the male medic began but stopped abruptly as the Amazon shushed him with an elbow to the ribs.

"Yes, we do," she insisted, glaring at him meaningfully.

"But…oh, right. We do," he agreed, finally cluing in.

Moments later, Hermenia was watching the heart-rate monitor intently, and let out a relieved sigh as a single electronic beep flashed across the screen.

"That should hold her for awhile," Aaron figured once Hermenia had been sent off to bed, happy and not pregnant.

"That was a neat trick," the Amazon declared, slamming shut the ambulance doors. "Good thing numbnuts here—" she hooked a thumb at her partner "—didn't blow it." Chagrinned, her partner shrugged then slunk around to the driver's side.

"That's a different kind of delusion, isn't it? Thinking you're pregnant?" Jack started up the car as the ambulance pulled away, lights flashing back on. The cops weren't the only ones the division kept jumping.

"Not that uncommon," Aaron explained as he snapped on his seat belt. Being tossed around in the car the previous night had made a lasting impression. "From what I've been able to gather, she was sexually abused by her father. When she was thirteen, he and a bunch of his drinking buddies gang-raped her. She ended up pregnant but the baby was stillborn, and she's never gotten over it."

"Fuck me," Jack swore. "But how come she keeps thinking she's pregnant?"

Aaron shrugged. "Guilt, I guess. Part of her wants to have a baby, but she's terrified it'll end up dead again. She's in therapy now, but it'll take a long time to get her over it. If ever."

"What a life." *Makes my problems seem pretty small.*

"Don't know about you, but I'd gladly castrate her asshole father with a shotgun."

"Amen to that," Jack said, dropping the car into gear.

The air inside the Regent Park Community Centre was a storm of strained emotions, a swirling, volatile vortex of fear, confusion, hatred. But mostly outrage. And that anger had a target.

"The police don't care!" someone shouted from the depths of the throng amassed in the meeting room. "They're always shooting black folks."

"And getting away with it!" another added. Grumbles of agreement rolled through the crowd, angry fists spiking overhead.

At the room's front, one of the impromptu panel beseeched the assemblage. "Everyone, please calm down! This is not helping us."

Voices began to call for quiet, and slowly, reluctantly, an uneasy silence took hold. The meeting, originally planned to be a gathering of the stronger voices in the park, had uncontrollably mushroomed until the room was packed from wall to wall. Only a small slice of open floor before the panel's tables remained clear of bodies.

The watcher leaned comfortably against a wall, up by the stretch of no man's land. The mass of people did not bother him, only strengthened his anonymity. Within this heated crowd, he was merely another forgettable face among hundreds.

The periphery was a good vantage spot. The front was never good. Front and centre focused attention on you and blinded you to what was behind. He preferred to work, to attack, from the rear, but to observe, he was happy where he was.

The crowd was quiet, or as quiet as it could be expected to be considering the high emotions. The speaker lowered his arms. "Thank you. I apologize for the lack of seating but we really weren't anticipating this many."

"When the police are shooting innocent children? What did you expect?"

A sharp, edgy laugh rippled through the room, and the unofficial moderator, a slim black man with a fringe of grey around his head, smiled appreciatively. The watcher recognized him as the spokesman from the morning's demonstration. "That's exactly what we're here to discuss. Not the details of how it happened, but what we're going to do in response."

"Kill a cop!" someone yelled. The watcher attempted to locate the yeller, but the crowd was too dense.

"No, no," the speaker said, once again raising his hands, imploring calm. "Violence will only beget more violence. How do you imagine the police would respond? Some of you may be too young to remember when a 51 Division officer was stabbed on his way to work. That was about ten or twelve years ago, and I can still recall how the police invaded this community and held it hostage until the attacker was found. Or just two summers ago?" the speaker continued, pre-empting any arguments. "Surely, you all remember how the police terrorized us as they searched for the murderer of a police officer. How many of our young men were senselessly and brutally beaten if they were seen wearing leather gloves? And you want to bring that down on us again?"

The crowd rumbled, some in agreement, others still in protest.

"What would you have us do, Frances? We can't let them get away with this." This from a stern-faced woman sitting next to the speaker.

Frances reached down and gave her hand a reassuring squeeze. "I'm not saying we should, or will." He faced the assembly again, his voice sure and firm. "We work within the law to ensure the officers involved in Tyrone's tragedy are held accountable for it. I have already spoken with Tyrone's grandmother—most of you know her as Auntie Dee—about hiring our own lawyer. There are several firms willing—"

"That's bullshit and you know it!" A young black man forced his way free of the crowd and stood defiantly in the thin strip of barren floor. He wore a close-fitting red tank top over a lean, muscular body. Baby dreadlocks framed a face of sharp, enraged features. The watcher eyed this man with interest, recognizing him from the demonstration out front of the police station. Not involved in the protest, but viewing it—contemptuously, judging from the expression the watcher remembered—from the sidelines, like the watcher had done.

Why had the watcher bothered with the demonstration? Risked getting that close to the station? Habit, mostly. He had learned in war never to ignore the unusual or unexpected. Either could become an advantage, or kill you.

"Ain't no lawyers gonna help us, so we gotta do it ourselves," the young man stated. "We—" he swept a hand behind himself, indicating a small group of men of similar age who stood with him "—been letting the pigs know they ain't getting away with this."

"If you're the ones responsible for the graffiti, I beg you stop," Frances pleaded. "Tensions are strained enough as it is."

No, they ain't, old man. Not even close, the watcher thought, as an idea suddenly took shape. Not much of an idea, not yet. More like a suggestion, but he figured this angry youngster, bent on vengeance, could easily play a part.

"Bullshit!" the gang's spokesman repeated. "You talk to your lawyers, you old fool, and we'll do what needs doing."

The small gang—there were eight of them, and the watcher was already thinking of them as his—gave Frances and the rest of the panel their backs, cutting through the gathering as easily as an axe through winter-dry wood. One of the group stopped at the rear of the room, brandishing cans of spray paint. The people bunched at the back pushed away from him as he brazenly painted a black "51" across the wall, then, switching cans, he scrawled a red "187" over it.

He stalked away as the paint dripped down the cinder blocks, the red and black running together in ugly patterns.

Lyron Dove fumed outside of the community centre, the cold night air doing nothing to cool his temper. He shrugged into his leather jacket and furiously jammed his fists into the pockets. Those fools in there wanted to talk and march around, waving signs in the air. Couldn't they see the truth? If they didn't push back now, the police would never learn to respect them, would never learn there were consequences for every action.

He blew out a frustrated breath and watched as the chilled air from his lungs quickly dissipated on the winter air. If only troubles could be swept away as easily. But life was strife, and the conflicts fought and overcome defined a person, a community, a people. And his people had faced hatred since the time darker skin had been equated with inequality. The Jews could whine about persecution, but as they cried they controlled the world's purse strings. Suffering with money was no suffering at all.

That was something his father never understood. Or refused to understand.

Carter Dove, Lyron's estranged father, was born in Jamaica and had fled his birth land, running to Canada for what he called "a better life." What his father had meant by better life was a *whiter* life, but that was a truth Lyron hadn't learn until university. The senior Dove had raised his only child in a predominantly white, middle-class neighbourhood, and the young Lyron had grown up listening to his father preach the holy trinity of education, hard work and perseverance. Lyron's father had surpassed his father financially and it was expected, practically demanded, of Lyron to accomplish the same.

Lyron had graduated high school with grades strong enough to earn him entrance to the University of Toronto, much to his father's ultimate, brag-to-his-friends, delight. But it was in university where Lyron's life changed. His childhood and teen years had been spent with friends of similar persuasion and economic background, despite their ethnic or cultural heritage. Lyron's father had done everything in his power to ensure his son grew up white, well distanced and ignorant of his roots.

In the fall of his first year at U of T, Lyron met by chance a member of the Caribbean Student Alliance. Nothing really more than a social group, the CSA had introduced Lyron to a part of himself he never knew existed, and he embraced his newfound self with a fervor nearing obsession. His studies and grades suffered as he immersed himself in his ancestors' world. Much to his father's ultimate, don't-tell-his-friends, shame.

Through the CSA, Lyron met other friends, members of organizations focused on racial and economic discrimination, groups that were dedicated to their cause, radical in their beliefs and actions. Soon, Lyron was an eminent presence at rallies and demonstrations, a crusading force in the perpetual fight for social justice and equality. His grades, which had dropped, eventually disappeared altogether.

A confrontation with his father was inevitable and unavoidable. Carter accused his son of throwing away his education and his life, spitting in his father's face by casting away everything his father had fought for.

"Throwing it away? You were the one who turned his back on who he was," Lyron countered, unassailable in his belief. "You never let me know about our past, our heritage."

"I gave you my father's name!" Carter argued. "Isn't that enough?"

"But you kept me ignorant of everything else. You robbed me of my identity."

The argument had degenerated into threats and ultimatums and ended when Lyron stormed out of the mortgage-heavy, conservatively decorated house, vowing never to return.

The second, and more pivotal, watershed moment in his life came on June fifteenth, 2000, when he proudly stood shoulder to shoulder with hundreds of other protesters laying siege to Queen's Park, the seat of political power in the province. That was a glorious day when their leaders announced the time for talk was over and the time to fight for what was right and just was at hand.

On that day, under the bright summer sun, Lyron cared little for the cause and yearned only to strike back at the symbols of oppression. They clashed again and again with the police and the daunting police horses. Lyron's moment of triumph came when the cobblestone he pried from the ground felled a cop.

With the pitching of one stone, his thirst to fight those he saw as his enemy—the racist police, the corrupt government, the greedy money brokers, all that contributed to and profited from the oppression of the African-American communities—was insatiable. Many of the organizations he once was affiliated with disowned him, fearing, they said, the attention and retaliation his actions would incur. He cursed them for cowards and sought out those who shared his views and desires.

Since then, Lyron had drifted through a shadowy unseen world, an underbelly of the city, striking where he could, alone or with others. Robbery, arson, vandalism were his weapons, anonymity his armour. But now the time for working in secrecy was past. With a single gunshot, the blood-thirsty police had declared war, and Lyron was ready to lead the counterattack.

"But those fools and their lawyers won't listen," he bitched as he cupped his hands around a match, touched it to his cigarette.

"Some of them listened, I saw it in their faces."

Lyron turned. The street—which looked directly at the front doors of the damned police station—was bathed in the sterile light of streetlamps, but the man who spoke to him was deep within the darkness behind a tree. Lyron dragged deeply on his cigarette, saying nothing. He had learned long ago that sometimes silence was the best answer.

Despite the shadow, Lyron got the impression the man smiled. "The question isn't what those sheep are willing to do, but what are *you* willing to do?"

Lyron drew on his butt again. "Buddy, you don't want to know what I'm willing to do."

The watcher stepped from the shadows, and he was indeed smiling. "Oh, but I do."

"And just who the fuck are you?"

"If the cops found out you knew my name… Well, we've seen they'll kill over a lot less than a name." The watcher smiled. "Call me…Ghost. I'm just a ghost in the machine."

"Another threatening suicide?" Jack shook his head. "I never realized there were so many. How many have we done since yesterday?"

Aaron did a quick mental count. "This'll be five, I think. But remember, one of them wasn't an actual suicide attempt, just a cutter. It was…?" He looked expectantly at Jack.

"Borderline personality disorder," Jack said after a moment's thought. Aaron liked to quiz him on his fledgling mental-health knowledge. "She was using physical pain to relieve emotional pain, right?"

Aaron nodded. "Very good. Your sensei is proud of you."

Jack snorted at the sensei remark but let it go without further comment. He had always known there were a lot of suicide calls in the division—threats, attempts and the occasional successful—but never really appreciated how many until he was responding to them all. If nothing else, the crisis team was earning its paycheque on the suicide calls alone, sparing coppers lengthy waits at the ER. Of the five suicide calls they had yesterday and today, Aaron had deemed only two serious enough to warrant a trip to the hospital. One had gone to the station after Aaron had deduced his suicidal ideation—*how's that, sensei?*—was just a ruse to avoid responsibility for criminal acts. The last two he had referred to community resources.

All in all, probably saved the division about a day and a half in man-hours.

The call for the cutter, just a few hours before Jenny's fateful run-in with Tyrone Johnson, had left an impression on Jack. The poor girl, nineteen, alone and wrestling with a host of demons from an abusive childhood, had been sitting in Allan Gardens methodically slicing herself with an old razor blade, blood dripping steadily from the fresh cuts to her forearm. Her face had been blank as the dull steel had dug at the flesh on the back of her forearm; the inside of the arm, from wrist to elbow, was a mass of twisted scar tissue from years of self-mutilation.

Jack had not slept well that night, the call bringing up violent memories of Taylor Furlington and how she had hacked her own breasts off. The nightmare had ended as Taylor hurled Jack from a balcony. Even less sleep than normal that night.

"Do you remember that call up in 53?" Jack asked, dispelling unpleasant thoughts. "The depressed guy who burned his sandwich? Whatever happened to him?"

"He jumped," Aaron stated, making a diving motion with his hands. "About a week later."

"That's too bad," Jack said, surprised to find he actually meant it. The poor sap had been so depressed that when he had burned his grilled cheese sandwich it had been the final straw. And what had Jack done? Stomped all over the guy's feelings. "I owed him an apology."

Aaron shrugged. "You win some, you lose some. The night he jumped, he never called."

"Just like Brett," Jack realized.

"Who?"

"Oh, sorry. Just thinking out loud." Jack sighed. "He was a copper I worked with up in 53. One night after work, he took his gun home with him and blew his brains out. No one even knew he was depressed. I didn't know and I worked with him. I thought he was just having trouble sleeping because of his divorce."

Aaron nodded. "High-functioning depression. Some people, even though they're clinically depressed, can hold down a job, keep going to the gym, make it look like everything's fine. Doesn't mean they're any less depressed than the ones who can't get out of bed."

"I should have clued in, but I never did."

"Don't beat yourself up about it," Aaron cautioned. "The high-functioning ones can hide it pretty easily. Not sleeping well, stress, headaches, just about anything can be used to explain depressed moods."

Jack reluctantly agreed. "I guess."

"It's easy," Aaron maintained. "When someone asks how you're doing, what answer do we usually give? 'Okay,' or 'not too bad,' and my favourite, 'life's a bitch,'" he said, answering his own question. "People don't really want an honest answer when they ask that. It's just another way of saying 'hi.' Could you imagine how someone would react if you said 'Actually, I'm thinking about jumping off the balcony when I get home tonight'? They don't want that kind of honesty, so it's easy to brush off their concern by saying you're tired, or fighting off a bug."

"You keep saying 'you,'" Jack observed with a wry grin.

"I hope you're not making those comments about me."

Aaron studied Jack with a clinical eye. "Are you thinking about jumping off the balcony tonight?"

"I don't live in an apartment," Jack said dryly.

"Well, that's good, then."

Blood Rage

Sunday, 9 December
1030 hours

Jenny sank her fingernails into Brian's chest as she rode the violence of her orgasm, shuddering as the intensity whipped through her. As the last of the spasms quivered out of her, she rolled off him to lie on her back, gasping quietly as she listened to the thunder of her heart slow and settle.

"Good thing you don't have much in the way of nails, love," Brian decided as he checked himself for blood. "Any deeper and I'd need stitches."

"What?" she asked, his words barely penetrating the blissful fugue that had clouded her thoughts for a few precious minutes.

He propped himself on an elbow to display the red crescents she had dug into his skin. "Not that I'd mind bleeding for you, but explaining the injuries to my co-workers at the hospital would be a bit embarrassing."

Jenny flapped a hand in the sweaty air. "More like a chance to brag, you mean." As her body and mind settled back into a more normal rhythm, the melancholy that had haunted her since Friday night slipped back over her. The brief respite she had found in Brian's bed was gone.

"I wish I could help you. I don't like seeing you hurting." Obviously, her sudden mood change had not been unnoticed.

"Don't worry about it. You do enough for me already." She forced a smile and traced her fingers through the sweaty hairs on his chest. Brian was tall, which was nice for a change—it was frustrating not being able to wear heels with men her height or shorter—with a lean, athletic build. The late morning sun coming in through the condo window haloed him in his own blond hair.

He's prettier than me, she thought, but kept it to herself; her doctor did not like to be called pretty.

Six months with the same man. A personal record for her. Brian was confident enough not to be intimidated by her job or her tendency to "cop-up a situation," as he liked to describe it. Intelligent, fun, good-looking, and damn good in bed—all those biology classes came in handy, she could attest to it—he was almost the ideal man. So why didn't it feel ideal?

They connected in so many ways, but…didn't. Jenny had shown up for their first date with her left eye and cheek a mess of swollen, bruised flesh, gifts from a drug dealer and that man-chick, Furlington. Brian had been sympathetic and an attentive listener when she described the two fights, one brief and amusing, the other epic and near fatal. At that point, most men would say something relationship-ending like, "I wouldn't let my wife do that work," or "That's too dangerous a job for a pretty woman."

Brian had said neither. He never doubted her abilities as a cop or judged her choice of careers. He even liked Jack, the few times they had met, and did not feel threatened by her partner. The violence she saw—and sometimes participated in—on the job never fazed him. After all, what physician in a downtown ER hadn't seen his ample share of brutality and human suffering? But the violence he saw and repaired was somehow second-hand to him. He didn't experience it the way Jenny did as a uniformed cop.

What am I bitching about? I should be ecstatic he hasn't let all the shit touch him, that he can keep himself separate from it.

But she wasn't, and couldn't figure out why. She'd tried explaining it to Jack once, and he had instantly understood. To him it was as clear as delivery pizza versus eat-in. "Delivery is good, but pizza's better when it comes to the table straight from the oven."

And he was right. It wasn't a big difference, but it was a difference. Just like how Brian always called her "love." She'd heard it from him hundreds of times, but never, "I love you."

Not that she wanted to hear it. She liked Brian, cared for him and lusted after him, sometimes like a teenage schoolgirl, but no love. Could she love? She loved her dogs, and she definitely loved Jack. But that was different. He was her partner, her work husband, as some PW's said. Was being a cop slowly robbing her of her ability to love?

More like encasing it in the shit we see each day. Is policing the job for me?

"Thinking profound and deep thoughts?"

Again, Brian's words brought her out of a brooding daze. "Sorry, my thoughts were wandering."

Brian gave her a supportive smile. "Don't worry about it, love. I'm sure you did what you believed you had to do."

Jenny stiffened. "What do you mean, what I believed?"

He brushed hair off her brow and she forced herself not to pull away from his touch. "You told me you thought he had a gun."

It was her turn to rise up on an elbow so she was facing him. "Believed or thought?"

His smile slipped a little. "Thought, believed. Same thing."

"No, they aren't." Dine-in or delivery.

"Hey, if I said the wrong thing, I'm sorry. I didn't mean anything by it."

She sighed, her head drooping. "I know you didn't and I'm sorry. I'm just stressed out right now."

"You shouldn't be," he told her, reaching out with what was supposed to be a comforting hand on her arm.

"But I am," she said through a grim smile. "You're not the one facing possible attempted-murder charges."

"You didn't do anything wrong, love."

"You don't get it. A lot of people are saying I did," she corrected him. "And I'm pretty damn sure that's what the SIU thinks."

"You—"

"But I have to go," she cut him off. "I need to take the kids out for their walk, and you need to get some sleep before you go back to work." She leaned in to give him a quick kiss. "Thank you for breakfast and the romp. Believe it or not, I actually managed not to think about it for a while." No need to say what *it* was.

Brian watched her as she pulled on the clothes she had recklessly scattered across the floor in her haste to fuck away the ever present guilt and stress. As she was buttoning up her shirt, he wrapped his arms around her from behind. Nuzzling her ear, he encouraged her: "Let it go, love. You have nothing to worry about."

You just don't get it, do you? Jack understands. She let herself be held and pretended it was a different set of arms.

"Dispatch, can you mark CIT out at 291 George Street?"

"10-4, CIT. 291 George."

"You don't have to come in," Jack told Aaron. "I'm just dropping off a Christmas present." Jack went around to the trunk and retrieved a large bundle wrapped in a plastic bag.

Shrugging, Aaron pointed out, "Nothing else to do."

The rooming house had seen better days, but probably not since the sixties. Its bricks and wood were eroded and worn by decades of weather and neglect. A pall of misery shrouded the old building.

"You have a friend who lives here?"

"Not everyone who lives in 51 is a shithead," Jack said, and it sounded to Aaron as if he was reminding himself as much as telling Aaron. Curious, the nurse followed Jack up onto the porch.

The front door was unlocked. Incapable of being locked, Aaron saw. It must have been kicked in, or forced open somehow; the wood frame was shattered, but long ago, the splintered damage dull with time. At the end of the ground floor hall, Jack rapped politely on the only door decorated with a wreath.

"I don't think I've ever seen you knock quietly," Aaron observed.

Jack gave him a look. "I can be civil. If it's required."

The door opened, revealing an elderly—very elderly—black man. "Officer Jack! This is an un'spected surprise." Unlike most people, this gentleman seemed genuinely pleased to have the police at his door. Jack smiled and Aaron realized it may have been the only time he'd seen such an expression on the tough cop's face.

"Hello, Phil. This is Aaron, he's a nurse from St. Mike's Hospital. Sorry he's not as good-looking as my usual partner."

"Nice to meet yuh." Phil extended an arthritis-gnarled hand which Aaron shook with great care. Phil eyed Jack suspiciously. "A nurse? I ain't dyin', am I?"

Jack laughed. "No, you're not. This is a social visit. Can we come in?"

Phil swung the door wide and beckoned them in. His home was a large single apartment sectioned into living room, bed room and kitchen by the furniture. The building itself may have looked ready for a condemned sign, but Phil's residence was clean and comfortable with an abundance of flower pictures and paintings to compensate for the boarded-up side window. Aaron doubted any real plants could survive in the apartment. It may have been immaculately clean, but years—decades?—of cigarette smoke had sunk into the walls and ceiling like water into a dry sponge.

"Where's my buddy?"

"Oh, you know Bear, Officer Jack. He's hidin' somewhere 'round here."

Jack reached into the bag he had brought with him. "This is from Jenny and myself, Phil. Merry Christmas." He presented the old man with a gift basket chocked full of bottles of beer. "Hope it fits."

"Ah'm sure it will," Phil proclaimed with an elated grin. "You two didn't have to get me a present."

"Yeah, we did. We couldn't afford to buy you an around-the-world trip so we opted for the beers of the world."

Phil set the basket on the card table that doubled as his dinner table and peered closely at the bottles' labels. "Well, ah'll be buggered! Them's the pricey ones." He straightened up—a slow process for his frail body—and wiped a tear from his cheek. "You shouldn't have, Officer Jack, but ah'm sure glad you did. You give that lady o' yours a hug 'n' kiss for me. Well, ah'll be buggered," he repeated. "This's been the best damn day ah've had in a long time."

"Why's that?" Aaron asked, feeling there was more to the aged man's happiness than some premium beer.

"Well, ah'll show you." He shuffled over to a rack of coats by the door and came back displaying a Blue Jays jacket, flourishing its crisp blue and white colours proudly. "Muh great-gran'daughter came by t'day t' give me this and t' invite me t' Christmas dinner. Ah ain't seen her in over ten years."

"Ten years? How come?" Jack asked as he knelt down. Aaron wondered what Jack was doing then spotted a small dog creeping out from behind the sofa. The little guy's doggy years must have rivalled Phil's; he appeared as stiff with age as his owner, but the stub of his tail perked up when he caught Jack's scent.

"There's the little bugger," Phil said, the tremendous affection he had for the dog unmistakably clear in his voice. "You be a good dog 'n say hello t' Officer Jack."

But Bear didn't need any encouragement. He trotted to Jack as quickly as he could—cats and mice had no reason to fear him—and actually managed to get his front paws up onto Jack's thigh before collapsing to the floor for a belly rub. Aaron watched, bemused, as the Reaper, one of the most, if not *the* most, feared cops in 51, rubbed the belly of a pudgy old dog.

While Jack sent Bear into doggy ecstasy, Phil gave a quick accounting of his family history. "Muh son and his wife were killed in a car accident long time ago. Their child'un don't want nothin' t' do with an old man livin' in a roomin' house. Last time ah saw muh great-gran'daughter, she was only twelve years old. Now, she's all grown up 'n wants to get t' know her great-gran'daddy." Phil dropped Jack and Aaron a wink. "She hinted she might be makin' me a double great-gran'daddy soon."

"Congratulations, Phil." Jack stood up and dug into his gift bag once more. "Do you remember when you told me about the little prick who was abusing his German shepherd?"

Phil nodded sagely. "Ah do. Man who's mean to animals don't deserve to be on God's good earth."

Jack pulled out a framed photograph. "I thought you might like a picture of my dog, Justice."

Phil tucked his jacket under his arm to take the picture. Under the glass, a happy shepherd grinned joyously around a tennis ball clamped in his jaws.

"You're ridin' with a good man, sir," Phil told Aaron. "He rescued this dog from a cowardly boy who was hittin' him day and night."

"I've heard the story," Aaron admitted. "Haven't had the pleasure of meeting Justice yet."

"A good man," Phil stated again, tapping Jack's chest with the picture. "You 'n' your lady." The old man's wizened face creased up even deeper. "Ah hear what they bin writin' 'bout your lady in them papers, Officer Jack, 'n ah don't believe a word of it. Not a word! If she did what they say she did, then she had t' do it. Ain't no one's fault but the fool who got hisself shot. If you need me t' tell anyone that, you come 'n' get me."

Jack smiled, a little sad. "Thank you, Phil, but let's hope it doesn't get to the point where she needs character witnesses."

After final wishes for a Merry Christmas, Jack and Aaron headed back to work. Aaron studied Jack and was not surprised to see by the time they had reached the police car that Jack Warren, bringer of gifts and giver of belly rubs, was gone. In his place was the Reaper, his face set in a grim scowl, his eyes hard and unforgiving. Aaron knew Jack hated the nickname but he wore it well.

Aaron was at the beginning of his second year on the Crisis Team, and in that time he had worked and socialized with a good chunk of the coppers at 51, had even dated a few. He had known long before joining the team that police officers—like anyone who worked in a front-line emergency job—have two personalities, one the public sees and one that is revealed in their private lives. For some the difference was slight, the shift from civilian to cop minuscule, seamless. For the unfortunate ones, there was no separation, the cop having overwhelmed and consumed any non-police traits. For these few—mostly male and from a different era—the job was everything, and they rarely lived long into retirement.

And then there was Jack, an even rarer circumstance. Aaron had done calls with Jack prior to their time together on the team and had chatted with him over drinks at several after-shift functions. Today was the first time he had observed the complete non-cop Jack, and detecting the enormity of the gulf between Jack and the Reaper was unsettling. He knew of Jack's impending divorce and the events leading up to it, was aware of the extreme situations he had survived at work, and the amount of stress bearing down on him. Add to all that his partner's shooting, and it was a wonder the man could function at all.

Beneath the Reaper's harsh, stony exterior, Aaron had sensed a deep sadness in the man he considered a friend. At first, he had assumed it was solely the Reaper's property, but now, having seen the civilian side, Aaron knew both sides of Jack laid claim to it. That joylessness had been in Jack's eyes as he listened to Phil talk about the reunion with his lost family.

Everyone had secrets, pieces of themselves hidden away behind walls—Aaron knew that better than most—but the Reaper's defences were insurmountable, and Aaron worried what his friend was refusing to admit, even to himself.

"Ident 5 to radio."

"*Ident 5?*" The dispatcher sounded surprised having an Indent unit pop up on the air; there weren't any crime scenes in the division for a change.

"Can I see a car in Allan Gardens? I've got a male here who needs to sleep off a nasty drunk, and I don't have a caged vehicle."

Jack laughed. "I bet Manny's the only Ident guy in the city who makes drunk arrests." To the dispatcher he said, "CIT will head up and see that unit in Allan Gardens."

"Thanks, Jack," Manny said, recognizing his old partner's voice. "I'm out front of the greenhouse."

"This the guy you used to work with?" Aaron asked as Jack pulled a U-turn on Sherbourne.

Jack nodded. "Yeah. He's in the forensic unit now, but still cruising his old stomping grounds apparently."

Allan Gardens was a city-block size park on the western edge of the division, an oasis of nature amid the concrete, famous for its flower beds and greenhouse. And a preferred drinking site for the local hounds, outside in the summer and inside the humid hothouse once the colder weather hit. For Jack and a few other coppers, keeping the grounds safe and derelict-free for the area's residents was an ongoing battle. The crackheads had gotten the message relatively quickly, but the rubbing alcohol and mouthwash drinking crowd was like a bad rash that just kept coming back.

The Forensic Identification Services van was easy to spot in the winter-bare grounds. Manny, dressed in khakis and a black golf shirt, was leaning against the van's grill, an amused smirk on his face. Using the concrete wall of a barren flower bed to stay upright, Manny's candidate for cell thirteen, the drunk cell, was searching the pockets of his ratty parka with the deliberate slothfulness only the royally smashed can achieve.

"What's he looking for?" Jack asked as he got out of the car.

"His bottle," Manny explained joyfully. "I dumped it before I called you guys and he's been looking for it ever since. He must have searched the same pockets a dozen times." Manny grabbed Jack's offered hand and quickly pulled him into a hug, slapping him vigorously on the back. "Good to see you, dude."

"Manny, you've met Aaron, haven't you?" Nurse and cop exchanged nods, Manny's with the obligatory, "How's it going, dude?" The first time he had seen Aaron at a call, Jack had briefly mistaken him for Manny, a slightly shorter version, but with the same clean scalp and non-regulation goatee.

"I hear you guys might be in uniform soon."

"Yeah," Manny grumbled. "With all the shit that's going on, the politicians are screaming for more cops on the street."

"They're going to put the Ident guys back on the platoons?" Aaron asked.

"Nope, just back in uniform," Manny clarified, his amused grin back in place. "That way, the chief can say there's another fifty cops in uniform. Not his fault if everyone thinks that means they're in the cars answering radio calls. It's a numbers game, dude, and it sucks."

Snapping on a pair of latex gloves, Jack squatted near the drunk, but not too close; vomit could travel an astounding distance. "Hey, do you know who this is?"

"'Course I do," Manny scoffed. "Everyone knows Lloyd."

"Yeah," Jack agreed. "But do you know *who* he is? This is the man who puked all over your buddy's legs."

"Dude!" Manny exclaimed. "Oh, man, Lloyd, I'm sorry. You told me someone barfed on him, but I didn't know it was Lloyd. If I'd known that I'd've given him a lift to the Seaton House."

Earlier in the year, Staff Sergeant Greene had transferred Manny, kicking and screaming, to Ident. The arrogant prick had thought that banishing the hyperactive human puppy to the meticulous, snail-paced work of FIS would be the ultimate punishment, the *coup de grâce* in his hate-on for Manny. The last *fuck you* went to Manny, though. He fell in love with the work and had his temporary transfer made permanent.

"He's better off in the cells. Come on, Lloyd. Up you get." Jack grabbed an arm and hauled Manny's newest hero to his unsteady feet. Lloyd mumbled something that might have been *Go fuck yourself*, but he was short a few nouns and syllables. "Let's see if you can puke on Greene again."

"You're not going to park in front of the doors?" Aaron asked as Jack drove by the building's entrance.

"Driveway's too narrow. Don't want to block it," Jack explained as he wheeled into a little parking alcove at the north end of the apartment building.

"My, aren't you in the Christmas spirit."

"Yeah, right. Me and Kris Kringle, we're buds." Jack tapped the At Scene button to let the dispatcher know they had arrived at the call. Aaron climbed out of the car and tossed his dinner debris into a Dumpster that was hogging most of the parking niche. "Now look who's being all nice and neat."

Aaron dusted off his hands. "Just trying to be professional. I figure a woman who's starving herself to death wouldn't appreciate me finishing my lunch in front of her."

201 Sherbourne was a high-rise just south of Dundas, across the street from the rooming house where Jack had dealt with another memorable EDP call. In that case, a man with cockroaches in his toes. From a man with bugs dining on him to a woman who was attempting suicide by not eat-

ing. Same shit, different day. Today's shit was a fifty-something year old woman too weak from lack of food to get out of bed. Her daughter had found her when she came by for a visit.

Waiting for the elevator, Aaron surveyed the lobby. "I don't think I've been in this building before. Doesn't look too bad."

"Yeah, kind of middle of the road for 51. Not too many calls here," Jack said in a lifeless voice.

"C'mon, man. Cheer up. Things can't be that bad, can they?"

"Sorry. I was just thinking of Phil getting back together with his family this Christmas."

"And that's reason to sound like a zombie?"

Jack uttered a tiny chuckle. "No, I'm happy for him. I guess I'm just a little envious, is all. Christmas this year is a bit of a bust."

Aaron nodded in understanding; he knew all about Jack's domestic troubles. "Is your shift working?"

"Nope. Got Christmas off this year." Jack sighed. "Jenny's invited me to her family dinner, but I think I'll see if anyone working Christmas wants to swap. Better than sitting at home alone."

Jack was spared from hearing what a mental-health worker thought of his plan when the paramedics joined them by the elevator. Jack was disappointed it wasn't the Amazon and her partner. The elevator finally *dinged* its arrival at the lobby. They got off at the twenty-first floor and their complainant, a young Vietnamese woman, was waiting for them by the apartment door. Her story was short and painful. Her father had passed away unexpectedly a few months ago from a massive heart attack. Not only was the coronary lethal, it was greedy, appearing intent on taking the wife as well, only not as quickly. Since the funeral, she had remained inside the apartment she had shared with her husband and was slowly starving herself to death.

She lives on the twenty-first floor, Jack mused as Aaron questioned the daughter. *I can think of a faster way to commit suicide than starvation.*

"How effective can this be?" Jack asked Aaron as they followed the woman into the apartment. "I mean, it's not like she's on a deserted island."

Aaron shrugged. "I guess we'll see."

And see they did. Whatever Jack had been expecting—an anorexic middle-aged woman, Maris from *Fraser*—it was nowhere near the grotesque sight they found curled up on the bed. Mai, the mother, was naked so there was nothing to blunt the horror of the inhuman creature she had become.

Back in high school, as a bit of a World War Two geek, Jack had seen many disturbing pictures of concentration camp victims, but no amount of photos could prepare him for Mai. She was a living skeleton with waxy skin pulled taut over the bones. Her limbs were drawn into a fetal position, bowing her back so that every vertebrae from her straw-like neck to the jutting pelvic bones, which threatened to tear through the flesh, was sickly visible. Her face was the worst, a bony caricature of the person she once was, the face of a mummified corpse somehow still alive.

She saw the uniformed men enter the room behind her daughter and began a mewling sound as one arm—Jack's stomach rolled as he watched the bones move beneath the emaciated flesh—weakly twitched in the air.

My God, I think she's trying to scream at us.

A psychiatric evaluation wasn't necessary. Jack helped lift her onto the stretcher and had to fight down a shudder at the feel of her, at the utter absence of weight. The daughter stayed beside the stretcher, trying to calm her mother as the cadaverous woman fought uselessly against the straps holding her down.

"How could she get so bad?" Jack asked as he and Aaron watched the stretcher and its corpse-like passenger being loaded into the ambulance. "Didn't anyone see what was happening?"

"The daughter's been out of the country since the funeral—back home in Vietnam cleaning up the father's business—and just came to visit her mom today."

"There's no other family?"

"Oh, there is, but I guess there must be some money with the parents, and the rest of the kids were waiting for her to die so they could divvy it up. Ain't humans wonderful?"

"I'm getting to the point where I think the whole world would be better of without the human race. Maybe that's why I like post-apocalyptic books like *The Stand* so much." Jack finally allowed himself the gratification of that shudder, as if ridding himself of clinging foulness. "I don't know about you, but I could use a tea before our next call."

"Sounds good to me. I don't need to go to the hospital; they'll be busy with medical issues on her long before anything psychia—"

"What the fuck is this?" Jack fumed, cutting off Aaron.

The Dumpster that had been off to the side of the tiny parking lot when they arrived was now sitting directly behind the scout car, effectively pinning the car against the fence.

"We can just push it out of the way with the car, right?"

Jack didn't answer; a chorus of poorly suppressed laughter had his attention. He slowly turned his head and found a group of five teenage boys watching them with great relish. The question of how the Dumpster had moved was no longer an issue. The mirth choked away as Jack stared them down, the angry scar by his eye aggressively evident. Somewhat satisfied, Jack headed for the car, pulling the key free. *Fuck this.* He shoved the key back behind his gun belt and put his shoulder to the Dumpster.

"Um, Jack, it's pretty full and I bet it took all of them to move it."

I fucking hope so.

A new refrain of laughter, louder and more insolent this time, rang out as Jack heaved against the weight. Jack pushed, wanting to shove, to throw, this overgrown garbage can across the parking lot, to shove their fucking joke back down their fucking throats, and his body responded. He felt the strength in his legs, his back, and it was awesome. His life may have been going to shit, his thoughts getting uglier every day, but physically he had never been better, stronger.

At the first squeal from the metal wheels, the laughter stuttered uncertainly. When the Dumpster began rolling, agonizingly slow at first, then faster as Jack's legs pumped, the laughter died altogether.

Fuck you! Jack screamed silently as he thrust the Dumpster away. It struck the wrought-iron fence with a thunderous and satisfying crash. Jack took a deep, settling breath before walking back to the car, pointedly ignoring the little shits.

"That was, um, rather impressive," Aaron commented from the passenger seat.

"They pissed me off," Jack simply said.

"Um, remind me never to do that."

Jack stopped by the group of shits and lowered his window. They stared at him in a mixture of fear and awe. He glared at them.

"If you ever do that again, at least make it a challenge."

The van was filled with the acrid reek of gasoline. Bottles clinked softly as someone shifted, stretching out cramped legs.

"Careful, fool," Lyron hissed.

"Sorry," the man muttered in the darkness. "When's them gonna come?"

"Soon," Lyron reassured him.

"How do you know?" the third man in the back of the old cargo van asked. He was sitting next to a window, and Lyron could see his frosted breath outlined on the glass by the light of the street lamp. The light was not strong enough to reveal faces, muted as it was by the tinted windows.

"Cops are like trained dogs; they come..."

"...they come when you call them," Ghost had guaranteed. He had smiled when he said it, a feral grin. Lyron found himself smiling in return.

"As soon as you and your team—" Lyron liked the sound of that "—are in the van, I'll call 911. Nothing too big; we don't want a shitload of cop cars. Just one, two at the most."

"Why are we only doing the cars? Why not the cops?" Lyron had a hard-on just thinking about it.

But Ghost shook his head firmly. "Too much, too soon. Our people aren't ready for that yet." He patted Lyron on the shoulder as if he knew how eager the young man was. "Wait. There'll be blood, I promise you."

Lyron nodded, willing to bide his time. He trusted Ghost even though they had met just last night outside the community centre. A brief conversation had shown their goals were the same, the methods they were willing to employ, violently similar.

"It'll be fucking cold sitting in that van. Why don't you just tell the cops there's a guy with a gun. A *black* guy. That always brings them running."

Again, Ghost shook his head. "I told you, we don't want too many cops," he said sharply. "Never give your enemy the upper hand if you can prevent it," he explained to soften the sting of his words. "I'll call and say I heard a woman crying in an apartment, maybe a guy yelling. That'll bring them quick enough but not a lot of them. You won't have to wait long. Take some blankets or towels to sit on."

"How do you know what they'll do?"

Ghost eyed him, his face hard, unforgiving. "When you fight an enemy as long as I have, you learn their ways."

That Ghost had been wrestling with the police for years—decades maybe!—Lyron had no doubt. His new friend and mentor was not a big man, a couple of inches shorter than Lyron's own five-foot-ten, but his lean, muscular body radiated deadly violence. That Ghost had killed, Lyron believed with certainty. How many had died at his hands, Lyron could only guess; Ghost had never said.

And it was because of his past actions that Ghost could not take a visible, commanding position in the coming fight. His face was too well known to the enemy, and careers, he confessed, could be made on his arrest.

Why couldn't he have been my father? Lyron asked himself as he sat shivering in the van. As cold as he was, it would have been unbearable if Ghost hadn't suggested blankets to insulate against the van's frigid metal floor.

"Is that them?"

The question brought Lyron back to the task at hand. He peered out the van's rear window, squinting uselessly against the dark tinting. They were parked out front of 274 Sackville, just across the Oak Walkway from where poor Tyrone had been gunned down.

Tonight, we begin payback, brother.

Just as Ghost had predicted, a single police car pulled into the lot between 248 and 251 Sackville. And, again as Ghost had said, the pigs didn't bother to park properly, stopping their car in the middle of the lot, not caring if they pinned any cars in. Lyron smiled appreciatively. No other cars would be damaged.

Unless the gas tank blows. A minor concern; there were always casualties in war, and these were just cars.

Two pigs got out of the car, one of them a giant. He towered over the other one—a woman?—as they strolled into the building.

That's it, you fucking assholes, take your time. It's probably just some nigger girl getting beaten up. Why hurry?

Lyron's fists clenched on his two bottles as he gave the pigs another minute to get deeper into the building. "Don't wait too long," Ghost had cautioned him. "But don't rush either. We want them to be a couple of floors up before you move." Ghost's fake call would have the pigs heading to the top floor. Lyron's count hit sixty and he reached for the door handle.

"Your mask, bro."

Too eager, he had forgotten to pull down his balaclava. Cursing softly, he tugged the ski mask over his face, settling the eye and mouth holes comfortably. He didn't want to fuck up by tripping on something he couldn't see. Retrieving his bottles, he nodded at his team and jumped out of the van.

Ghost had told them to walk, not scurry, to the police car. "Walking like a criminal makes people think you're criminals."

But despite Ghost's advice and Lyron's own intentions, by the time he was halfway to the police car, he was hurrying in a hunched crouch, as if he expected gunfire at any moment. There were a few people about but no one close, and they took no notice of Lyron's team, scampering quickly themselves to get out of the cold.

Squatting next to a pickup listing on two flat tires, Lyron produced a lighter and touched its flame to the gas-soaked rag hanging from the neck of his glass bottle. Bright blue and orange flames blossomed, leaping up the length of the cloth. He offered his fire to his team, a solemn moment, but one of them still giggled as they used his flame to light their Molotov cocktails.

Lyron lit his second firebomb—two each; Ghost wanted the car doused from bumper to bumper—and stepped out from behind the pickup. Thrusting a blazing bottle into the air, he screamed, "For Tyrone!' and let fly.

The bottle hit the police car above the left headlight. The bottle shattered, spewing flaming gasoline over the hood to lick at the windshield. In rapid succession, four more firebombs struck the car, adding their fiery retribution to the inferno. Lyron aimed his second throw carefully and when the bottle punched through the side window, the interior of the car belched flames.

"Let's go, bro." A team member tugged at Lyron's arm; he was immobile, mesmerized by the fire. It was the most beautiful sight he had ever seen.

And that's when someone started shooting at them.

The man who called himself Ghost watched from the corner of 251 Sackville. He watched as the scout car pulled into the lot, as the cops headed to the fictitious domestic. He watched as Lyron and his companions approached the car, snickering as they scurried like mice wary of a hunting owl. They disappeared behind a pickup and seconds later the shadows on the truck's far side rippled and danced as the cocktails were lit.

One of them advanced on the car. Ghost figured it was Lyron and knew it was when he heard the boy shout, "For Tyrone!" Ghost didn't see the bottle hit—he was diagonally opposite the point of impact—but he heard it and saw the flames jump across the car's hood.

The car was soon engulfed in flames. Lyron didn't have to get his second bottle inside the car, but it was a nice touch. Ghost nodded in approval as he pulled out his gun. At this distance and blind to anything beyond the fire, Ghost had no hope of hitting any of the three firebombers. It was just as well; as he had told Lyron, it was not yet time for blood.

Aiming high—but not too high; he didn't want it to be evident he had missed intentionally—he fired off two shots. The roar of the Glock was incredibly loud over the background roar of the flames. In the silent wake of the gunshots, Ghost yelled, "Police, don't move!" then fired off another three rounds.

Assuming Lyron and the others were already hauling ass—he really couldn't see shit past the fire—Ghost slipped his gun into a pocket and simply melted into the night.

Monday, 10 December
0950 hours

"I'm surprised to see you here." Jack went to drink his tea then hastily added, "I'm glad to see you, but just surprised, is all."

Jenny smiled at her partner's discomfort. "Truth is, I was going crazy sitting at home. Even the kids were starting to get on my nerves."

Jack cocked an eyebrow at her. "And court is more relaxing?"

Jenny sipped her coffee—extra large, extra strong, extra long night—then sighed, her shoulders slumping slightly. *Damn it, I'm tired*. "Well, better than sitting alone."

Jack nodded in understanding, but watched her carefully over the rim of his Tim Hortons cup. The jumbo size for him as well. *Guess he isn't sleeping either. If we were together, we could at least make use of the time.* She chased those thoughts away. Even though Jack was technically no longer married, the last thing either of them needed was a relationship born out of convenience and stress.

They were standing in the main hall of College Park Courts, a road-wide corridor servicing the ten courtrooms. At a few minutes before ten, the hallway was packed with accuseds, victims, witnesses, lawyers and cops. Everything needed for the legal system to grind slowly forward.

Each type of person was easy to identify. The victims and witnesses usually had slightly stressed, perplexed expressions as the life blood of the courtrooms swirled around them. Unless they were repeat victims. Then they just looked bored.

Those facing charges also typically appeared tiresome while awaiting their turn in the limp-wristed, revolving-door process. Unless they were repeat accuseds on some serious charges. To the rest, this was just an annoyance.

The lawyers, the defence ones at least, were most often the best dressed in the show. They strutted around in their expensive suits—who says crime doesn't pay?—reassuring their clients, haranguing the Crown attorneys and pestering the cops. Or trying to befriend them if that suited their needs better. Jenny had learned very quickly never to trust a smiling lawyer.

The poor Crown attorneys were the ones staggering through the hall, more often than not hauling an overwhelming pile of case briefs. The composed, well-prepared Crowns of TV cop shows were nowhere in sight. Unfortunately, because the courts were so backlogged, the chances were good that the majority of those cases had landed in the Crown's lap just this morning.

That left the cops. The young ones, not too far from their days with a coach officer, were nervous and excited about going to trial, getting up on the stand and delivering some justice. They'd learn. At this level, cases rarely ended up in a trial. This was where the plea bargains were hammered out. Oh sure, defence lawyers would spout and assert they were ready to go to trial, until, that was, they found out the Crown had all his witnesses and officers present, and then it was time for *Let's Make a Deal*.

The rest of the law-enforcement grunts stood in small groups—coppers didn't sit much with so many assholes in the vicinity—drinking coffee, swapping stories and harassing the detective in charge of their case with the question that had been around since some idiot had thought up courtrooms: Can I go now?

Cops were always impatient to punch their court card and get gone. Court on a day off sucked, unless you lucked into a quickie and were out in an hour or less. Otherwise, you could end up hanging around all day and driving home in rush hour. And who wanted to do that when you were supposed to be enjoying a day off?

Jenny's non-police friends all thought court on night shift was the worst but it actually wasn't, unless it was afternoon traffic court. That was like a normal nine-to-fiver getting up at two in the morning for some extra work. No, court on nights was okay. Work finished at seven so staying up the extra few hours wasn't much of a problem. And regardless of when court finished, you could always count on grabbing some sleep before work.

Evening shift, that was the true bitch. Finish work at three a.m., head home and be in bed by four, up again by eight to fight traffic into the city. If court went anywhere past noon, forget about going home to catch some sleep. Yup, court on an evening shift was bad. Repeat appearances on evenings was killer.

"Lucky for you, you're on the CIT this week," Jenny told Jack.

"How so?"

"You're off at eleven, not three," she pointed out. "You can get some sleep before court."

"Oh, yeah. Lucky me," he said sarcastically. "More time to stare at the ceiling."

"Is it that bad?"

"No, no," he quickly retracted. "Some nights I just have a hard time staying asleep and it gets frustrating, you know?"

Jenny could relate. She'd managed maybe six hours total of shut-eye over the past three nights, and when she did sleep, it was only to relive that moment over and over, never changing. In her dreams Tyrone Johnson—God, it was worse, so much more painful, now that he was no longer nameless—reached into his pocket no matter how loudly she yelled at him not to. Reached in, grabbed something, a flash of metal. Her gunshot always woke her up.

"How about you?" Jack asked. "Did you sleep okay last night?"

"Good enough." She felt guilty about lying, but Jack had too much of his own stress. Time to change the subject. "Who's the new OIC for our case?" The previous officer-in-charge had been Detective Clarence, now a uniformed staff sergeant somewhere out in the west end.

Jack shrugged as he drank. "Don't know. Guess we'll find out soon enough."

The overhead speakers began crackling announcements, summoning people into their respective courtrooms, and the crush in the hall began to ease. Out of the thinning crowd came a Crown attorney, his black suit looking like it had doubled as last night's pajamas. Behind him squeaked one of those suitcases on wheels, its sides bulging with papers.

He stopped in front of Jack and Jenny. "Are you…" He had a stack of Crown briefs under his arm and he tried to shift them so he could read a note paper-clipped to the one closest to his chest.

"Warren and Alton?" Jenny finished for him, wondering why he just didn't let go of the suitcase.

"Yes, thank you." The Crown was a tiny Philippino man, not much over the five-foot mark, with round wire-framed glasses. "Have you seen…" He twisted to consult his note again. "Detective Daryl?"

The partners shrugged in unison. "If we have, we don't know it."

Jenny swatted Jack. "What my partner meant to say is that the detective is new to our division and we haven't met him yet."

"I see. Well, I'm sure he'll be here." The Crown finally released the suitcase to offer his hand. "I'm Raymond Navarro, the Crown for your case."

"Are we going to trial today?" Jenny asked, worried. "I don't know if anyone told you but I was involved in a…"

"Yes," Navarro said, rescuing her. "The detective mentioned it when we spoke on the phone this morning. Don't worry, it won't have any bearing on the trial," he assured her, having anticipated the question. "If defence is stupid enough to bring it up I'll turn it on him by saying it shows how dedicated you are to the victims and this matter by coming to court despite being involved in a stressful… What do you call those things?"

"Critical incident."

"Yes, thank you." Navarro beamed at Jenny. "I take it you're off sick right now?"

Jenny shook her head. "Injured on duty. Is Myers here?"

"He's in custody. Has been since his arrest."

Dean Myers was a low-life piece of shit Jenny had arrested for beating his girlfriend and child. Twice. In two days. But each assault had been a different girlfriend and a different child. Jack had been with her for the second arrest.

"Have you seen…"

This time Jenny saved Navarro. "Heidi Dubaine. She's over there."

Across the hall, huddled on the bench, pointedly ignoring the officers, sat a thin young woman, her strawberry blonde hair pulled back in a ponytail. She wore a long-sleeved black denim shirt. The colour made her appear even paler than she was, and Jenny figured the long sleeves were out of habit, not necessity, as Myers had been doing dead time since his arrest.

"Have you spoken with her?" Navarro wanted to know.

"No," Jenny replied while keeping an eye on their victim. "We tried when she first got here but she didn't want to talk with us."

"Yes, I see. Excuse me." The little Crown wheeled his suitcase over to Heidi, no doubt to introduce himself.

Jenny turned back to Jack. "You don't think she's going to be hostile, do you?"

"Wouldn't fucking doubt it," a gruff voice said from behind Jenny. And above.

A freak of a human had stepped up to them, and how such a large man could move quietly was beyond Jenny. He had to be six-five, easy, and big. Big like a professional linebacker. His salt-and-pepper hair was shaved on the sides and that, along with the loosened tie and unbuttoned collar still straining at the neck, gave the impression his head was about to explode. The rest of him just gave an impression of utter *hugeness.*

"I'm Dave Daryl." He stuck out a paw. His other hand was holding a half-eaten fritter on top of an extra-large coffee that looked like a medium at best with his colossal fingers wrapped around it. "You Warren and Alton? Good. I'm astounded she's here." He tilted a cinderblock of a head towards Heidi. "Have you talked to her?"

Jenny shook her head. "We tried, but she walked away from us."

The detective nodded, not surprised. "Had a bitch of a time serving the subpoena on her, and when I finally nailed her down, she said she wouldn't show up anyway. I had to threaten her with a material-witness warrant. I figured she'd up and disappear like the other one."

"You mean Myers's other girlfriend? The one he assaulted the day before Heidi?"

"The one and the same. I'm sure she'll show up once the charges are withdrawn. But we've got her here—" the cinderblock jabbed at Heidi again "—and she can cry all she wants about her boyfriend being a misunderstood saint. She can explain to the judge why we have her on video saying the little prick beat her and the baby."

On the night of Myers's arrest, Heidi had given a videotaped statement, disclosing a history of abuse that dated back well before she was even pregnant with Myers's son. But would it be enough? Jenny had her doubts. Like so many victims of domestic violence, Heidi didn't want to proceed with the charges. Jenny was surprised she had consented to the taped interview, let alone proceeding with charges.

How many times had Jenny been called to a domestic where the woman—be it wife, girlfriend, baby mother, whatever—had clearly been assaulted yet when the police started to haul away her man, had suddenly recanted her story? So many women called the police just wanting the abusive prick taken away for the night in order to sober up, cool down or "as a warning." Time and time again, Jenny had dealt with women who, once they realized prick head was going away for a lot more than one night, refuse to give a statement. Or, when the trial came up, accuse the police of pushing the statement in one direction or outright fabricating the whole thing. Harder to blame it on the cops with a videotaped statement, though.

Jenny didn't understand why women stayed in abusive relationships. Oh, sure, she knew some women were willing to trade the odd beating for financial stability, or that some women, the really fucked-up ones, equated abuse with love. But she just didn't *get* it.

If a guy hit me, he'd need a surgeon to remove his balls from his ass.

The Crown attorney was back from his conversation with Heidi, not looking pleased. He squinted up at Daryl. "Shall we?"

The big detective shoved the last of the donut in his mouth, gulped his coffee and belched ogre-ishly. "Let's do it." He passed his empty cup to Jack and followed Navarro.

"Well, he's certainly something, isn't he?" Jenny commented as the doors leading into the courtroom swung shut.

"He definitely has a certain…" Her partner floundered for an appropriate word as he looked for a garbage can.

Jenny didn't need a word. "Yeah, you can say that again."

"Officer Warren, are you a violent man?"

Jack wasn't expecting that question and hesitated briefly before saying, "No."

"You're not?" The young defence lawyer looked appropriately shocked. "May I suggest that, while you do not consider yourself to have a propensity for excessive physical violence, you in fact do."

Are you trying to show off by using big words or are you simply trying to piss me off? is what Jack wanted to say, but instead he said nothing.

"Well, officer?"

"I'm sorry. I was waiting for you to ask a question." That got Jack a few chuckles from the courtroom. Jack, like most cops, had an innate dislike for defence lawyers, and this one had been getting on his nerves from the moment he started his cross-examination.

Unperturbed, Myers's lawyer flashed Jack a little grin that said, *So, you want to play, do you?*

Before the attorney could rephrase his question, Navarro stood up, objecting quietly. "Your Honour, if Mr. Silvermann is going to bring up the two incidents involving Officer Warren where the suspects were killed, I can save him and the court some time by reminding my learned friend that both those cases were thoroughly investigated by the Special Investigation Unit and the officer was absolved of any wrongdoing. They have absolutely no bearing on this matter."

Silvermann smiled confidently. "I can assure the court and my learned friend—" *aren't we all so friendly?* "—that

I had no intention of re-opening cases that do not pertain to this trial."

"Then what do you hope to accomplish, Mr. Silvermann?" The judge was an older black man with a distinguished fringe of hair and a tone that implied he would tolerate no grandstanding, especially by a lawyer young enough to have been out of law school less than a few years.

"My questions concern the character and credibility of the witness, Your Honour."

"Very well, you may continue but the court would appreciate a bit more directness, this time."

The mild rebuke must have touched on a nerve. Silvermann's "Thank you, Your Honour," sounded a trifle strained.

From comments made by the Crown and judge since he had taken the stand, and the fact that Heidi had indeed been declared a hostile witness, Jack figured the young attorney had rifled a few judicial feathers during Heidi's cross. Didn't he know it wasn't smart to upset the judge? That was like a cop pissing off the dispatcher. Never give the person responsible for handing out the radio calls reason to dislike you.

While Silvermann was receiving his wrist-slap, Jack casually scanned the body of the courtroom. Jenny wasn't there, of course. Witnesses weren't allowed to sit in court and listen to testimony they may be corroborating or refuting later on. The benches—resembling pews in a church and just as uncomfortable—were about half full, people waiting for their cases to be heard, cops hoping to get a word with the Crown at the next break, lawyers—

Jack froze.

What the fuck is he doing here? He was sitting in the back row, partially hidden by the people in front of him, looking relaxed and at ease in his designer suit. *Is he here to see me?*

"—Reaper?"

"Sorry?" Jack tore his eyes away from the unexpected and disturbing—very disturbing—sight in the body of the court. Defence had just asked him a question. "Could you repeat the question?"

Silvermann smiled indulgently. "My apologies for disrupting your daydream, officer. I asked how a non-violent man such as yourself earns the nickname the Reaper?"

That fucking thing. "My understanding is that some individuals in the division gave me that nickname."

"Individuals?" Silvermann rested his chin in his hand, cupping the supporting elbow with his free hand. He probably thought the pose made him appear intellectual or serious. Jack thought he looked like an idiot trying to look smart.

"It's not uncommon for criminals to give police officers nicknames," Jack explained. "I've heard of Van Damme and Robocop to name a couple. Reaper isn't something I'd choose for myself."

"It isn't? That's interesting, but we'll come back to that in a moment. Do you know why you're referred to as the Reaper? As in the Grim Reaper?"

Sighing loudly, Navarro pushed himself to his feet once more. "Your Honour—" he began but the judge cut him off.

"No need, Mr. Navarro." The judge pinned Silvermann with steely eyes, and the young lawyer's pose wilted beneath the glare. "Mr. Silvermann, this line of questioning had better make some sense soon. You're trying my patience."

Silvermann nodded. "Of course, Your Honour. It will. Officer," he said, turning back to Jack, the flush from the reprimand still fresh in his cheeks. He paused to compose himself and re-establish the rhythm of his query.

Jack decided to keep him off balance just a little longer. "My understanding is that they call me the Reaper because whenever someone goes up against me, they end up dead."

Silvermann may have been young but he handled Jack's quick answer smoothly. "And you say it's a nickname you don't approve of?"

"No, of course not."

"And you'd never refer to yourself by it?"

"No." Jack hoped the judge would put an end to the questions; they were getting boring.

Silvermann may have been thinking along the same lines as he shot a nervous glance at the judge. "Then can you explain how two days ago, while confronting a group of onlookers, you called yourself the Reaper not once, but twice?"

Jack was puzzled, not sure what Silvermann was talking about, but then remembered the crowd at 251 Sackville. *How the fuck did he hear about that? And what has it got to do with this case?*

As if he heard Jack's unspoken question, Silvermann flourished a copy of the *Citizen*. "I'm guessing you haven't read yesterday's paper. There is a small but well written article about you on page five. And Your Honour," he quickly added, "it goes to character and credibility."

The judge nodded but made a twirling gesture with his finger. *Hurry it up.*

Silvermann laid the paper in front of Jack, folded open to the article, on the railing of the witness box. "You're quoted as saying, 'If you want the Reaper, I'll give you the Reaper.'" Silvermann took the paper back to study the article. "There seems to have been some expletives censored."

Fuck. "We were responding to—"

"I'm not interested in why you were there," Silvermann interjected. "I find it interesting that you referred to yourself by a nickname that you just told the court you did not approve of."

Jack took a deep breath and told himself to relax. "I was faced with a very agitated and possibly violent crowd. I was concerned the crowd might rush us in order to free a prisoner. I was trying to defuse the situation."

Silvermann looked shocked. "You attempted to de-escalate the situation by threatening violence? That is quite a novel approach, I must say, officer."

And this has to do with your piece of shit client beating his girlfriend and baby, how?

Navarro must have been thinking the same thing, but before the small Crown could get to his feet to object, Silvermann changed attack. "You're aware, aren't you, officer, that Mr. Myers has filed a complaint against you? Predominantly citing excessive force."

So that's what he's been aiming at. "I'm aware of the complaint."

At the Crown's table, Navarro sat down without speaking. Silvermann was back on safe ground, it seemed.

Silvermann brandished a sheet of paper. "This is a copy of the complaint filed by Mr. Myers." He presented it to Jack. "Officer, would you tell the court if this is the complaint of which you are aware?"

Jack took the paper and studied it, not wanting to agree to anything new that might have been slipped in. "It appears to be."

Silvermann was back to his intellectual pose. "Would you read the itemized points for the court?"

Jack was tired. Tired from not sleeping, tired of Silvermann's smug attitude and tired of him wasting Jack's time. What Myers's sissy complaint and the Reaper nickname had to do with Myers beating on his girlfriend and baby, Jack had no idea. But he did know Silvermann was pissing him off.

Jack locked eyes with the lawyer and didn't let go until Silvermann looked away. Only then did he lower his gaze to the complaint.

"The officer threw the complainant to the floor," Jack read. "The officer assaulted the complainant—" *yeah, after he tried to knee me in the balls* "—the officer threatened to throw the complainant down the stairs—" *I wasn't going to throw him, just let go* "—the officer put the handcuffs on too tight—" *you've got to be kidding me* "—and the officer did not read the complainant his rights to counsel." As Jack had driven Myers to the station, the little wuss had yelled, "I can't hear you! I can't hear you!" like some tantrum-throwing brat as Jenny tried to give him his rights.

"Officer, I would suggest you are overly prone to violence, and when you saw Mr. Myers, you saw a smaller, weaker man than yourself, and you took the opportunity to indulge in some unnecessary and completely unprovoked brutality. And may I suggest, you and Officer Alton forced Ms. Dubaine into giving a statement incriminating Mr. Myers to justify your actions."

Oh, bloody hell.

And so it went.

Jack ran his hands through his hair, clearly frustrated. "What a bloody twit."

"Who?" Jenny asked. "The defence lawyer?"

Nodding, Jack blew out a breath. "He just spent the last hour going over Myers's complaint against me. Every time I didn't give him the answer he wanted, he asked the question again, just reworded."

"You were sighing so loud, you sounded like a whale coming up for air," Daryl said, joining them outside of the courtroom. It was one o'clock and most of the courts had already broken for lunch. The hall was all but deserted except for the trickle of people coming out of the courtroom behind Jack.

"You okay, Jack?"

"Hm?" Jack glanced quickly at Jenny. "Sure. Why do you ask?"

Jenny pointed. "You're staring at the courtroom doors like you're expecting an attack or something."

Jack faced Jenny, and she could tell it took him an effort to keep his eyes on her, which was a first. Who was he looking for?

Navarro came out of the courtroom—Jenny wasn't sure but she thought Jack twitched as the door swung open— and came over to congratulate Jack. "Good testimony. The more time his lawyer spends on the complaint, the less he focuses on the charges. At this rate, he'll convict Myers all by himself." The little Crown attorney smiled appreciatively. "We've been put over till January. Detective, you'll notify everyone?"

"Sure." Daryl pulled out a pen to scribble the new trial date on his copy of the Crown brief and wandered off after Navarro.

"Do you have time for lunch before work?" Jenny wasn't all that hungry—her appetite, like sleep, hadn't rebounded from the shooting yet—but an empty apartment was even less appealing.

"You bet," Jack said, checking his watch. "I told Aaron I had court so he's not expecting—"

A man came up behind Jack and clapped him on the shoulder. "That was some solid testimony, Jack. I'm impressed."

The man was dressed in a dark suit that quietly but assertively stated the wearer had money. Jenny put him in his mid-fifties—she guessed his hair was prematurely white; she had the impression he was the sort of man who wouldn't hide behind hair dye—and there was something about his tanned features she found familiar, but she couldn't place him.

Jack, however, had no such trouble.

"What are you doing here?" he asked coolly as he shrugged off the hand. Whoever he was, Jack's reaction spoke volumes and none of it was good.

The man, seemingly unperturbed by his reception, smiled good-naturedly. "Silvermann here—" he gestured at the defence lawyer who was keeping a respectful distance "—is one of our new hires. I came down to watch him in action, see how he handles himself. Imagine my surprise when I heard you called to the stand."

"This case seems a little ordinary for your firm," Jack said. "Is Myers a secret millionaire?"

Jenny clearly heard the sarcasm in her partner's words but if the man—a defence lawyer from the sounds of it—did, he took no notice. He just chuckled at Jack's feeble joke.

"No, Myers isn't a millionaire. I doubt he's even a hundred-aire. But the firm does its share of Legal Aid work."

"And it's a good way to try out the rookies," Jack snorted, casting a derisive glance at Silvermann. "On cases that don't matter. To you, at least."

The lawyer didn't answer and the two men matched gazes. Despite the lawyer's smile, there was no love, no liking, between them.

After a few seconds, the lawyer broke away, turning to Jenny. "You must be Jennifer, Jack's partner," he said, offering a hand. "You'll have to forgive Jack. He was always an awkward child in social situations, and it appears adulthood has done little to smooth his manners. I'm Mitchell Warren, Jack's father."

Father. Jack's hostility suddenly made sense. The father who had all but disowned his son when Jack refused to follow in his father's legal footsteps. Jenny's guard was instantly up. She had never met the man, had no personal opinion of him, but Jack was her friend, her partner, and his enemies were her enemies.

"We haven't met before, have we?" she asked, full well knowing she had never laid eyes on him before today.

"I would have remembered if we did," Warren said, smiling a winning smile. "Just because Jack and I don't talk all that much, I still keep tabs on him."

"He knows Karen's dad," Jack clarified for her. "And I'm sure you're up to date on what's happening between Karen and I," he said to his father, sounding like an accusing lawyer himself.

"George has kept me apprised," Warren admitted. "I was sad to hear the two of you were divorcing."

"Really? You were shocked she agreed to marry me in the first place."

"Can you blame me?" Warren's eyebrows rose in surprise, and Jenny had the notion he practiced that and other expressions for court. "The daughter of Dr. George Hawthorn marrying a police constable?"

"I guess if I had been an associate or partner in some law firm, it wouldn't have been such a shock. Tell me, did Hawthorn have to ask you for the name of Karen's divorce lawyer or did you hand it over the minute he told you the good news?" Jack's voice was low, angry. Jenny had heard that tone before and it never bode well for whoever it was directed at.

"You had the perfect marriage, the perfect wife—"

"The perfect in-laws?" Jack taunted.

"Yes, the perfect in-laws." Warren's words were taking on their own rasping ire. Whatever stood between father and son, Jenny felt it was a hell of a lot more than a failed marriage. "With George and Evelyn behind you, your future was unlimited. But you threw it away, just like your education. And for what? To be a *cop*?" Warren's disdain was abundantly clear. He shifted his eyes to Jenny then back to his son. "Was it worth it?"

Warren's meaning was unmistakable—he was well apprised, indeed—and Jack's reaction was immediate. He stepped close to his father, almost going nose to nose with him. "Don't believe everything you hear," he snarled. "It could prove hazardous to your health."

Warren had a couple of fingers in height on his son, but Jack was by far the bigger of the two. "I see George's assessment of you is true," he said, stepping back and straightening a tie that didn't need straightening. "You have become quite the savage." He turned and walked away.

"Why did you come here?" Jack asked after his father's retreating back. "It wasn't to check up on your lackey; you stopped doing that while I was still in university."

Warren stopped and slowly turned to face his son. "Of course I knew you were on this trial. You think I'd come to court without reading the case? I had other reasons for coming here." He studied Jack and Jenny for a moment, then turned away. "Watch the news tonight, son," he called over his shoulder. "You might learn something."

Jack's father disappeared down the hall, Silvermann scurrying obediently behind.

"What did that mean?" Jenny asked.

Jack shook his head. "Whatever it means, it can't be good. Hang on." He stepped over to a bench and snatched up a discarded newspaper. After reading for a moment, he slapped the paper against his thigh. "Fuck me."

"What?" Jenny asked and Jack handed her the paper. As she read, she understood her partner's frustration.

Not twenty-four hours after Tyrone Johnson was shot and killed by police just steps from his apartment, officers from 51 Division were involved in another violent clash with residents of Regent Park.

The police Crisis Intervention Team had just arrested Justin Smith, a young black man, under the Mental Health Act, and when concerned citizens gathered to insure Smith was not subjected to any excessive force, Officer Jack Warren confronted them with his night stick in hand. Warren was heard to say, "If you want the Reaper, I'll give you the Reaper." It is unknown why Warren would refer to himself as the Reaper.

Additional officers arrived to support Warren and the vigilant residents were brusquely dispersed. Smith was taken to the hospital, but eventually charged with robbery.

One resident who witnessed Smith being thrown to the ground said the force used by the police was unnecessary. "I know Justin," the resident said. "He isn't violent at all." The resident spoke only on condition of remaining anonymous for fear of retaliation. "The police harass us all the time. Living here is bad enough without the police gunning for you."

Officer Warren was assigned to the Crisis Intervention Team, or CIT, a unit that has an officer partnered with a crisis nurse from St. Michael's Hospital. The purpose of the specialized unit is to improve the interaction between police and the mentally ill. Toronto Police have been criticized lately over their poor track record involving members of the mental health community.

Officer Warren rose to infamy in September 2000, when he shot and killed a young black man who had broken into his house. More recently, he was involved in the arrest of a suspect where the suspect fell to his death from a secluded bridge over the Rosedale Valley Road. Warren's regular partner is Officer Jennifer Alton who is currently being investigated for the shooting death of Tyrone Johnson, a young black man from Regent Park.

The photo accompanying the article showed Jack brandishing his baton, anger clear and unmistakable on his face. The caption read, *Officer Warren confronts citizens over arrest.*

"Strange how the pepper spray on my face isn't in the picture," Jack commented dryly.

Jenny could only agree with his earlier assessment. "Fuck me."

"She paints quite the picture, doesn't she?"

"Did you see the other article? It's by the same reporter." Jenny quickly skimmed the story and snorted. "Not much to it. She interviewed the grandmother and you can guess the rest. Tyrone was a 'gentle soul, loving and never caused any trouble.' Get this: he was 'gunned down steps away from where his grandmother lay sleeping.'" Jenny tossed the paper away in disgust. "She all but put a halo on the kid's head. I'm surprised she didn't say I was trying to murder him." Her voice broke on "murder" and she turned away, hiding her tears.

Jack's strong hands gripped her shoulders. "Don't give it any credibility," he whispered in her ear. "It's just sensationalism to sell papers. She's milking the story for all it's worth. It wouldn't be as interesting if she took our side, would it? When the SIU clears you, she won't even bother writing about it."

"But will they, Jack?" Jenny sniffed back tears. "Will they clear me? He didn't have a gun."

Jack gave her the tiniest of shakes. "Don't think that way. You thought he had a gun and he gave you no choice but to shoot. It wasn't your fault. Now let's get out of here. It's too depressing. You still good for lunch?"

Jenny nodded and forced a smile. "As long as I can get a drink with it."

"I'll second that, partner. Let's go."

"She's in her room on the second floor." The group home staff member looked equal parts tired, annoyed and fed up.

"Long day?" Aaron asked.

The man nodded wearily. "This is supposed to be my day off, but everyone's calling in sick." He rubbed his hands over the dark skin of his face, then across his tight hair. The hands ended up clasping the nape of his neck as he blew out a deep breath. It had the appearance of a well entrenched gesture.

Jack sympathized. He had no doubt working in a group home for teens with a mix of mental health problems, personality issues and good old-fashioned drug addiction could wear down anyone's patience. With the migraine that was building behind his eye, Jack figured he'd last about ten minutes working in here.

"I'm glad you guys could make it, though," Greg, the worker, told them. "These kids don't respond well to uniforms."

Probably because when they see a cop, it means they're getting arrested. Aloud, Jack asked, "The call said she was threatening to kill herself. She say how?"

The group home was in the stylish neighbourhood of northern 52 Division, tucked away amongst the old and expensive houses on St. George Street. Officially, CIT served only 51 and 53, as they shared the same radio band, but the 52 dispatcher had asked for a favour as she had no cars to attend the threaten-suicide call. The dispatcher had promised to send the first available car to back them up, but Jack wasn't about to hold his breath waiting; 52 coppers had a notorious reputation for avoiding radio calls. After all, you wouldn't want to take a call that could possibly, just maybe, end up in overtime and get in the way of a paid duty, now, would you? The downtown, central division—bordered to the east and west by 51 and 14, the armpits of the city—was renowned for its abundance of off-duty money-making opportunities.

Greg shook his head. "Nah. When I told her she wasn't getting her weekend pass to see her boyfriend, she ran upstairs screaming she was going to kill herself."

"Sounds more like a temper tantrum," Aaron suggested.

"Couldn't agree more, but..." Greg smiled apologetically. "When one of the kids says suicide, our hands are tied. We have to call."

"Understood," Aaron assured him. "There's someone up there with her?"

"Sally," Greg confirmed. "She's keeping an eye on her from the doorway in case she has anything in her room."

"Why don't you just pull her out of the room?" Jack asked, rubbing the heel of his hand into his right eye. The bastard was coming on fast.

Greg and Aaron shared a knowing look. "You'll have to forgive my partner. There aren't many teen group homes in 51. He comes from a more hands-on style of policing where you're not prohibited from touching people."

Jack looked unbelievingly at the poor worker. "You're not allowed to touch them?"

"Not without their permission," Greg sadly verified. "Unless we have to protect someone, that is." He led them deeper into the house. "Samantha—don't call her Sam, she'll go ape shit on you—has one suicide attempt in our records. Same shit, she wasn't given a pass so she took off. Cops found her in the subway, laying on the tracks."

"Laying on the tracks? Wouldn't it be more effective to wait for the train to be coming before jumping in front of it?" Jack asked.

"Exactly," Aaron said.

"Ah, got it."

There were four of the home's clients clustered at the bottom of the stairs. Greg shooed them off, but the one on the landing, standing defiantly in their way, didn't move.

"Zack, you have to let us pass," Greg said with a sigh.

"No way, man," Zack declared boldly. "You leave Samantha alone. Ain't no pigs gonna grab her."

Jack stepped past Greg and stopped two steps down from Zack, their eyes level. Samantha's self-appointed guardian was not a tall guy and he was even thinner than he was tall. The most intimidating thing about him was the amount of metal piercings decorating his face. Jack figured the studs and rings accounted for a good ten percent of the kid's weight.

"Zack, move," Jack instructed, not unpolitely. All he wanted to do was get this Samantha to the hospital or have Aaron declare her not dangerous to herself or whatever, then pop some of his meds. He could feel his right eye squinting up against the stairwell's dingy light.

"No fucking way, man—"

Jack took hold of Zack's arm and none too gently deposited him several steps down the stairs. "Stay put," he told him.

The look on Zack's face was one of utter incredulousness. Someone had touched him! Without his permission. "You can't do that," he protested, making to climb back up the stairs.

This time it was Aaron who laid a restraining hand on the teen. "He can, he just did, and he'll do a lot worse if you piss him off. Take my advice: stay here and live to fight another day."

Jack and Aaron made it to the second floor bedroom without further incident, and Sally, Greg's co-worker—*only two in a place this big?*—gladly stepped aside for them.

Samantha was a heavy girl with black hair and a pale complexion too white to be natural. On the plus side, she had only a fraction of the metal in her face that Zack had.

"You can't come in my room!" she screamed, huddled atop her bed.

"Really?" Jack said. "Ask Zack."

"I'm surprised you had us take her to the hospital," Jack admitted. "I would have bet you were going to write off her suicide threat as bullshit."

Aaron shrugged, sipping his coffee; they'd stopped at the Tim Hortons in St. Mike's after seeing Samantha safely deposited in a secure room. "It *was* bullshit, but now instead of relaxing in her room, she's stuck for a few hours at the hospital. And I thought Greg could use the break."

"Greg?"

"The guy at the group home," Aaron said, nonchalantly.

Jack gave the nurse a curious glance. "Guess you're just a big softy under your vest."

Aaron cleared his throat. "Aren't you cold? I know it's warm, but no jacket?"

The day was indeed warm. To say it was unseasonably so just didn't cut it. Instead of mid-December, the afternoon felt like a spring day, a cool spring day, but nothing close to winter. They were cruising up Yonge Street, the spine of the city as it cut Toronto in half east and west, and the sidewalks were busy with people enjoying the mild weather. The Eaton Centre, a huge, multi-storey mall occupying a good chunk of the downtown real estate, slowly slipped by.

"The vest keeps me warm," Jack said, rubbing the Kevlar under the shirt. After leaving Samantha in the hands of security, Jack had dumped the CIT jacket in the trunk in favour of the team's dark blue T-shirt. "Besides, the jacket's too small. If we get stuck outside, I can always throw it back on."

He also had the burgeoning migraine to keep him warm. Whether it was an increase in blood pressure or whatever, a migraine always made him feel like he had a low-grade fever. He'd managed to pop some of his Fiorinal back at the hospital so hopefully the headache would be subsiding soon. But only half a dose—although half a dose was still more than double what he'd been taking less than a year ago—as he was driving and the medication was a pretty potent muscle relaxant.

"Fuck!" Jack hammered the brakes, throwing himself and Aaron against the seat belts, as horns blared angrily around them. The Crown Vic lurched to a stop, just missing the legs of the male who had bolted across the street. The man, short and skinny with a mop of flaming red hair, hit the east sidewalk and hauled ass southbound.

Jack craned his head over his shoulder to watch the man run down Yonge Street. "That guy looked like he was running *away* from something." He turned, looking out the driver's side, and sure enough, here came two security guards sprinting across the road, cutting through the traffic stopped in the suspect's wake.

That the redhead was a suspect, Jack had no doubt; no one innocent ran that hard from security. What precisely he was wanted for—shoplifting was Jack's guess—could be determined later.

There was no room to turn the car around; the traffic was just too heavy. In a marked car, possibly. But without lights and a siren to carve a hole in the cars? Forget it.

Jack bailed and took off after the guards.

Redhead had a good lead on the guards, but to their credit, neither of them showed signs of throwing in the towel.

He must have pissed them off good.

Redhead, baggy white T-shirt and blue jeans flapping as he ran, turned the corner onto Queen Street, heading east in the general direction of St. Michael's.

That's good. Jack grimaced, the blood throbbing painfully in his head. *If he makes me run that far, he'll need the hospital.*

Jack pounded after the guards, anchor man in the pursuit. While Jack's head screamed with bright new pain, his legs felt good, strong. Like he could run down a car.

God, I love feeling like this.

He reached Queen in time to see Redhead once again throw himself heedlessly across the street. Luckily for him, this stretch of the road was between red lights and the traffic was sparse.

The guards were still hard on Redhead's heels but Jack knew that the longer the chase lasted, the greater the advantage tipped to the one not wearing Kevlar, boots and a belt loaded down with weighty law-enforcement tools. Crossing Queen, Jack was reaching for his mitre when Redhead button-hooked onto the street, cutting back the way he had come. He suddenly stopped, spinning to face his pursuers. Straddling the road's yellow centre line, he raised his fists. A ballsy move coming from a guy who might have weighed a buck forty. Maybe he'd had enough of running. Maybe he figured the guards were too tired to fight. Whatever. Jack wasn't about to stop and ask him.

Jack was coming at Redhead from the side and instead of easing up, he threw himself into a final sprint. Redhead must have spotted him at the last instant; he turned just as Jack lowered his shoulder and drove it into the smaller man's ribs. Redhead was blasted from his feet and hit the asphalt with a satisfying *thud!* Jack quickly flipped the unresisting man onto his stomach and snapped on the cuffs.

"Whoa, nice tackle," the female guard stated.

"Football?" her partner asked.

Jack grinned up at them from where he was crouched beside Redhead. "Rugby."

The guard nodded knowingly. "Sweet. Thanks for the assist. Oh, you may wanna smile while you're at it."

"What?" Jack looked up. There, not two lanes of traffic away, was a bus, stopped at the curb quite possibly because of the foot pursuit. And it wasn't any ordinary bus shuttling commuters home from work. It was a double-decked tour bus, and Jack found himself the attention of a dozen or more cameras.

Oh, fuck me.

Jack was leaning against the CIT car, rolling his right shoulder, trying to decide if the soreness in it was serious. The ache was not that severe, but the nauseous pain behind his eye certainly was. The migraine hadn't appreciated the jarring tackle. Or maybe it had.

Guess it depends on whose point of view you take.

Aaron plopped his butt next to Jack's. "How's the shoulder?"

"Sore."

"The head?"

"Even more so. Thanks for bringing the car around."

Aaron waved it away. "No problem. It's not like making a U-turn on Yonge Street is difficult during rush hour."

Jack scowled at him.

"You may want to get that looked at," Aaron suggested.

"Nah. The shoulder's fine, just a little banged up. I'll work it out tomorrow in the gym."

"Not that, you moron. That." Aaron pointed at Jack's forearm.

Jack checked the arm and whistled appreciatively. The skin, elbow to wrist, was scraped raw, a souvenir from the tackle.

My head must really be hurting for me not to have felt that.

"Doesn't look like it needs stitches anywhere," Aaron announced, peering at the road rash. "But we'll get it cleaned up at the hospital. Looks like Horner is ready to go."

An ambulance had been called for Redhead; his scalp needed some stitching, and he wasn't quite as steady on his feet as he had been during the chase. The security guards were jumping in the back of the ambulance with him for the short ride to St. Mike's Emergency.

"Horner?" Jack asked. "Joey Horner?"

"I think so. Why? You know him?"

Jack laughed, then groaned as his head complained. "I thought he looked familiar. Yeah, I know him, sort of. He's the guy I got my dog from."

"Poetic," Aaron declared. "Give me a minute, will you? Looks like one of the medics wants to talk to me."

Jack nodded, and the nurse wandered away to the ambulance. Jack lowered his head, shielding his eyes from the excruciating sunlight. *Man, I feel like shit.*

A pair of dress shoes and dark slacks stepped into Jack's field of vision. "Excuse me?" a heavily accented voice said.

Here we go. The first complaint of police brutality. I'm surprised it's taken this long. Jack raised his head, squinting fiercely against the bright light. *I've gotta get my sunglasses.*

A middle-aged Asian man with a camera slung around his neck and a huge grin on his mug was facing Jack. "Good…knocking down." He shot Jack a thumb-s up.

Jack smiled. "Thank you."

The man gestured at the tour bus, then raised his camera questioningly. Jack nodded and suddenly found himself facing the bus, a friendly arm flung across his shoulders. Flashes went off inside the bus and the tourist, with some decidedly unusual holiday photos, trotted happily back to his group.

Aaron was still chatting with the medic so Jack sagged back against the car hood, once more lowering his throbbing head.

"Well, that was certainly exciting."

Jack groaned inwardly. Couldn't he catch a minute of quiet?

This time the feet on the edge of his eyesight were female, clad in snug knee-high leather boots. The woman was Asian as well, but Jack was willing to bet she wasn't from the tour bus. Her black leather jacket was belted tight over a lithe but shapely figure, and her long black hair draped over one shoulder. Like Redhead, she looked familiar, but Jack's head was hurting too much for him to root through memories.

"You don't remember me, do you?" she asked with a quizzical smile.

"Sorry. I know we've met, but—" he tapped the side of his head "—thinking's a bit difficult right now. I may have given my head a bit of a rap a few minutes ago." Not exactly the truth, but it easier than explaining a migraine.

"I know. I watched the chase. It was very exciting."

Jack shrugged his indifference. "Not that exciting. You can get better on any TV cop show."

"But not as real," she reasoned. She held out a slim, well manicured hand. "I'm Lillian. We met at—"

"Hawthorn's party last winter," he finished for her, her face finally clicking. "And your husband. Scott?"

"Yes, Scott. I guess you didn't rap your head as hard as you initially thought." She paused, letting her alluring smile fade into seriousness. "I was sorry to hear about you and Karen."

Jack shrugged again. "Thank you, but I guess it was destined to happen. Karen never was happy with me being a cop."

"I would be," Lillian said, shifting closer. "I understand the worry, the concern for your safety, but I'd be proud if my husband was a police officer."

"Is Scott thinking of a career change?" Jack had a dim recollection of Lillian's husband and what came to mind did not scream "cop."

Apparently, Lillian thought the same. "Scott? Oh, no, not him." Her laugh was light and musical, but with an underlying throatiness to it Jack felt in his belly and lower. An image of Lillian in a red dress, the dress she had worn to Hawthorn's party, a dress that clung seductively, intimately, to her body came to Jack and he was in no hurry to be rid of it.

"Scott isn't the police type. He has an amazing intellect and is a gifted teacher, but he's not good at confrontation." She waved a hand at the ambulance. "I certainly couldn't see him chasing down a criminal and subduing him in such dramatic fashion."

Dramatic fashion? Jack felt like he should be shuffling

his feet and saying, "Aw, shucks, ma'am. T'weren't nuthin.'" Instead, he said, "Nothing special. Just a shoplifter who didn't want to be arrested."

"You're hurt," Lillian gasped.

Jack turned the forearm to reveal the injury. "Just a bit of road rash. I'll get it cleaned up at the hospital."

Lillian stepped closer to inspect the wound. Her fingers travelled above the scraped and bloody skin, as if she wanted to touch but didn't quite dare. In her rapt gaze, Jack saw… excitement? The tip of her tongue snuck out to wet her lips. Her fingers finally settled on his skin next to the injured area, and it was Jack's turn to wet his lips. Her touch was delicate yet heated, stirring the feelings her laugh had awoken.

Maintaining the contact, she slid next to him so that her thigh pushed against his. "I know you and Karen have been apart for some time now."

Jack nodded, at first not trusting his voice. After a moment to steady himself, he managed, "Since the summer."

"Since the summer," Lillian echoed, trailing her fingers up to his shoulder. "So long for a man to be alone. Especially a man of such…forceful instincts." With her free hand, she passed Jack a business card. "This is my private number," she whispered, leaning in although there was no one close by to overhear. Her warm breath caressed his cheek. "If you want to talk or…" She paused suggestively. "…or *need* anything else, call me. I'm always available."

Her touch, the closeness of her body, the undeniable sexual heat radiating from her had Jack's blood aflame, but he managed to ask, "Um, what about Scott?"

"Scott and I have an arrangement," she purred into his ear, and it was all Jack could do not to pull her to him.

"An arrangement?" he asked, his voice hoarse with…

not desire. What she had aroused in him was far more primal, more animalistic, than desire.

"An arrangement," she confirmed as she straightened up. "Call me, Jack. I think you want to, and I *know* I want you to."

She walked away, her hips swaying erotically to the rhythm her stiletto heels were tapping out on the sidewalk. She looked over her shoulder to see if Jack was watching. He was, intently. She smiled.

"Who was that?" Aaron asked, joining Jack at the car.

"Trouble," Jack admitted, but tucked her card in his pocket all the same.

"I don't get it." Aaron was frustrated. Frustrated and pissed off. "We bring her to the hospital, and while she's waiting to be assessed by the doctor, security let her out for a smoke. Idiots!"

Samantha, their I-wanna-see-my-boyfriend-or-I'm-gonna-kill-myself apprehension from the group home, had just eloped from St. Mike's. Luckily, Aaron had finished cleaning up Jack's arm after determining no stitches were required, and they'd been able to jump back in the car only minutes after Samantha had buggered off. She couldn't have gotten far. Unless she'd hopped a streetcar, flagged a taxi or made her way to the subway. And even if she was still on foot, this was downtown Toronto. Pick a direction, any direction.

They were making their way slowly—rush-hour traffic was in full, aggravating bloom—toward Yonge Street and the Eaton Centre, figuring a teenage girl would naturally head for the mall, while Jack was updating the dispatcher on Samantha's description. "...heavy set, wearing a pink T-shirt and ripped-up blue jeans."

"10-4, CIT. Units be on the lookout for..."

As the dispatcher rebroadcast Samantha's description, Jack scanned the sidewalks, looking for a pink T-shirt. Despite the above-seasonal temperature, most people were still wearing jackets, so a T-shirt, a bright pink one at that, should be easy to spot.

"There!" Aaron crowed triumphantly. "No, wait, that's not her. What about—damn, not her." The nurse was getting first-hand experience of a weird policing phenomenon. "I bet I didn't see a single person wearing pink today, and now it's all I see."

Jack grinned. "Frustrating, isn't it? It's one of the first laws of policing. That, and shit happens, payday's Tuesday."

"I thought the first law was a cop should never be hungry or cold."

"Or wet. And that's not a law, it's a rule."

They crept up Yonge Street through a seemingly endless parade of pink. Pink jackets, pink hats, pink pants, pink toques, pink hair, but no Samantha in a pink shirt. Jack was about to declare it a lost cause—she was 52's call in the first place—when Aaron announced, "There she is."

Sure enough, standing in Dundas Square was their Samantha. The square was an open, public space with fountains of water shooting up from the concrete in warmer weather, and a staging area for outdoor concerts and events. Right now, there was no music and no spurts of water, but the chairs and tables scattered across the area were full with people enjoying the last of the day's sunlight. Samantha was near the centre, staring up at an electronic billboard, seemingly spellbound by the flashing lights.

They approached her from different angles, Aaron taking the lead. "Samantha? We need you to come back to the hospital."

Her head snaked slowly from side to side as she eyed each of them in turn. Jack was uncomfortably reminded of Linda Blair in *The Exorcist.*

If her head spins backwards, I'm outta here.

Jack watched as awareness gradually seeped into her eyes. She may not have been gone from the hospital for long, but long enough to score something off the street. She faced Aaron. "The hospital?" she asked, sounding as if it was a new and alien concept.

"Yes," Aaron said slowly. "The hospital. We'll take you back."

Stoned or not, Samantha must have known she didn't want to go back to St. Mike's, so she bolted. Right into Jack. Normally, a sixteen-year-old girl running into him wouldn't have been a problem, but Samantha hit him harder than he thought possible, and the two of them went down. Jack twisted as they fell, and she ended up face down beneath him. He caught himself with his hands, not wanting to drop all of his weight on her.

It would turn out to be a mistake.

"Samantha, just calm down," Jack said loudly, partially for her, hoping she would calm down, and partly for the gawkers. The last thing he needed was to be accused of assaulting a teenage girl. "You have to go back to the hospital." He gripped her left wrist. Teenager or not, she was getting cuffed.

"No!" She tore her arm free and threw herself sideways, almost flipping Jack off her back.

"Aaron, need some help here," Jack called as he reached for a thrashing arm.

Aaron dropped down on Samantha's other side, grabbing her arm and pushing down on her shoulder.

"Good, keep her pinned while I—"

Samantha heaved herself to her knees, carrying Aaron with her as if he was nothing more than a knapsack filled with a few books. Cop and nurse shared a startled look across her shoulders then forced her—not without some considerable effort—back to the cement. This time, they both leaned their weight on her.

"Samantha, just stay still!"

But Samantha wasn't listening. Once more she pushed herself up from the ground, this time with the weight of two men on her, one wearing another twenty pounds of vest and belt. She slowly straightened her arms as if doing a simple pushup in gym class.

Jack thought of Zack, her boyfriend back at the group home, and what would happen to the hundred and twenty pounds of him if he ever pissed her off. Jack actually chuckled, and Aaron turned disbelieving eyes at him.

"What the fuck's so funny?"

"Tell you later," Jack grunted. "Hang on. Sorry about this, Samantha." Keeping his shoulders bearing down on hers, he wrapped both hands around her wrist and yanked back on the arm. She slammed down to the cement and Jack quickly twisted her arm behind her back. With Aaron's help, he snapped the cuffs on. With the final click of the steel, the fight was over, and Samantha lay unresisting beneath them.

Jack looked at Aaron and shook his head in wonder. "Whatever she's on, I want some for tomorrow's workout."

"I don't believe it. I don't fucking believe it."

Jack had stopped dead as he and Aaron passed the waiting room in St. Mike's ER. He was transfixed by what he saw on the television.

Aaron looked from the TV to Jack and back again. "What? It's the grandmother from the shooting. She's been on the news constantly. Come on, I need to sit down for a while. My head still hurts, asshole."

Jack tore his eyes from the television long enough to give Aaron an unsympathetic look and a sarcastic, "Please."

Samantha had been relatively quiet for the short trip back to the hospital, only muttering to herself and the occasional frustrated scream as she realized the handcuffs hadn't magically disappeared since the last time she tried to move her arms. Things had changed once they got her into the square little room security had ready for her.

There was just enough space in the room for the stretcher bed and maybe a couple of other people. A cop, a nurse and two security guards—not the morons who had let her walk out, thankfully—was well beyond the maximum capacity limit.

Samantha was a good little stoned-out girl as they got her up onto the stretcher. She didn't twitch a muscle as Aaron and a guard held her legs. It wasn't until the restraints came into sight that she decided to freak out one last time.

Without any warning, she began to kick and thrash, using her drug-induced strength to toss Aaron and the guard off her legs.

"Hold her!" Jack ordered the remaining guard, who quickly used his considerable weight to pin her shoulders to the bed. *Thank God her hands are still cuffed.*

Jack threw himself across her legs just as Aaron rushed back in, and suddenly Aaron was sitting on the floor looking like a cartoon character who had just been smacked in the head with an oversized mallet. All he needed was the tweeting birds circling his head. But Jack didn't have time to wonder what had knocked Aaron on his ass; Samantha was still bucking beneath him, and every time a knee came up, it threatened to toss Jack into a wall.

"Come on, Barry, get the straps on her legs." That from the guard holding her upper body.

Barry, the guard who had been kicked away, joined Jack, and together they got the left ankle secured with the heavy leather strap. By the time they were working on the right leg Aaron was back on his feet—none too steady—and the remaining limbs were promptly fastened in place.

They shut the door on Samantha, but it wasn't thick enough to muffle her outraged screams. The patients in this section of the emergency were keeping wary eyes on the door, as if they expected the shrieking lunatic to burst free any moment. The staff, however, were going about their work, business as usual. Yes, there was a drug-crazed adolescent who had tossed full-grown men around like they were stuffed animals just a few feet away, but ho-hum, another day in the ER.

"I can't believe you headbutted me," Aaron was now

saying as he rubbed his forehead. Apparently, Jack had given Aaron a bit of the old Glasgow kiss when he threw himself across Samantha's legs.

Jack shushed Aaron's complaints. "I want to hear this." He turned up the TV's volume.

The scene was from a news conference held earlier in the day. Devisha Lawrence, the grandmother of Tyrone Johnson, was sobbing quietly as a distinguished white-haired man stood confidently and protectively beside her. Jack's father.

"My firm has taken on the responsibility of ensuring Devisha Lawrence and her family find justice in the unnecessary shooting of her grandson, Tyrone. As the police are refusing to comment on the shooting, we will be in constant contact with the province's Special Investigation Unit, and we will insist all involved officers provide statements regarding that night's questionable events. Furthermore, I—"

Jack snapped off the volume. *That fucking prick. So that's why he was at court this morning. Was probably hoping to see Jenny on the stand, get a feel for her. And now this, acting like he's helping out from the goodness of his heart and not the free publicity.*

"You okay?"

"Fucking unbelievable. Of course the police aren't saying anything; we never do while an investigation is ongoing," Jack explained for Aaron"s benefit and anyone in the waiting room paying attention. "And saying Jenny and Connor will be forced to give statements, like the Charter of Rights applies to everyone but cops."

"You know that guy?" Aaron asked, obviously sensing Jack's personal rancor. "Who is he?"

"An asshole." Jack took a deep breath and blew it out. "Leave it at that."

"Okay. Now let's get going before I fall down," Aaron moaned, back on his preferred topic. "I've already taken a couple of extra-strength Tylenols, but they aren't helping much."

"Don't be such a baby," Jack scolded, forcing himself to let go of the anger his father's sideshow had riled up. "It couldn't have been that hard; I didn't even feel it."

"That's because you have a titanium forehead," Aaron bitched.

"Get real," Jack scoffed, then added smugly, "and it's not titanium, it's adamantium."

"Ada-what?"

"Read a comic book," Jack muttered.

Jack pulled onto his street a little before nine. He and Aaron had called it an early night due to headaches. Aaron had plodded into the hospital moaning he might get X-rays before heading home—Jack still couldn't remember head butting him—and Jack's migraine, which had been throbbing all day and had gotten an extra boost from tackling Horner, had been running rampant, making it all but impossible for him to open his right eye.

Another hit of Fiorinal—a full dose this time—and the brain-numbing drive home had actually combined to smooth out the migraine some. It was down to a muted roaring instead of a perpetual sonic boom, and he thought he might be able to take Justice for a walk before crawling into bed. In spite of everything, the day had turned out not to be a complete write-off.

Until he pulled into his driveway.

His soon to be ex-father-in-law's Lexus—he'd gotten rid of the BMW; after all, it had been a year old—was sitting pretentiously on the side of the driveway where Karen used to park the Honda. Jack was surprised Hawthorn hadn't parked right in the middle, taking all of the interlocking brick for himself.

Guess he didn't want to get his car too close to the oil spot. Wouldn't want people to think the leak was his.

Jack opened the front door and Justice was there to greet him. The German shepherd whined anxiously as Jack scratched his ears. But Jack's eyes were on Karen, his former wife, lover and best friend. He had caught her halfway down the stairs, frozen like a thief who had suddenly found herself exposed in the light.

Her shocked expression at seeing him—was it Jack's imagination, or did she look guilty as well?—was brief as she quickly recovered. "What are you doing here?" she demanded.

"I still live here," he explained, hanging up his coat.

Her lips—lips that he had kissed and had kissed him thousands of times—hardened into a tight line. "You know what I mean," she snapped. "You're supposed to be working."

She was angry, he could hear it in her voice. The plan had obviously been for her to be in and gone while he was at work, and his unexpected arrival had upset the schedule. He knew he could explain the different hours on the CIT or his migraine, but if she was going to play the bitch, then fuck her.

"Got a date tonight, Jack?" she asked, her tongue dripping venom. "Left work early so you could fuck your whore partner? I guess she has plenty of time to fuck married men now, doesn't she?"

Jack's anger flared, and before he could control himself, he had taken two steps towards the stairs. If Karen had been closer to him, he didn't know if he could have stopped himself from hitting her. As it was, the spark of fear he saw in her eyes was payment enough.

Through gritted teeth, Jack told her, "I never slept with her. I never cheated on you with anyone."

"That's bullshit, and we both know it, Jack." Now that Jack was staying at the bottom of the stairs, her fear was gone. The bitchy haughtiness was back.

An acid of suppressed anger, guilt and loathing ate at Jack's stomach. He hardened his face, pulling on his cop mask so she wouldn't see how much he hurt.

It was his turn to ask, "What are you doing here?"

"This is still Karen's house, Jack. She has every right to be here." George Hawthorn, Karen's dad, joined her on the stairs.

Jack kept his groan silent. *Haven't I had enough grief from one father today?*

"It may be half her *house*, but it's my *home*," Jack rasped. "What are you doing here? Seeing what else you can take from me? You've already taken most of the furniture. What else is there?"

"She has every right to be here," Hawthorn repeated, slipping past his daughter to come down the stairs first. Karen followed him, her face righteous and privileged but her steps cautious. Hawthorn stopped on the last step, just out of Jack's reach. "Until the separation agreement is signed, or the house is sold, Karen retains possession of one-half of it and the contents."

Jack snorted. "She's already taken more than half the

furniture," he pointed out. "Without discussing it with me, I might add. She's the one that moved out, not me. I should change the fucking locks and see how you like to be fucked around."

"Do as you please, Jack. We'll have Karen's lawyer discuss it with you. Now, if you'll excuse us."

Jack didn't move, blocking their path to the front door. He locked gazes with Hawthorn, and it wasn't until that moment that he realized how much Karen's dad resembled his own. Colour his hair entirely white—not just those egotistical white patches at the temples—and they could be brothers. And why not? They were already related by their disdain of Jack.

Only when Hawthorn's eyes dropped, nervously, did Jack step aside, hating himself for the petty satisfaction. He leaned against the doorway to the living room, his back to Karen and her father.

"You're nothing but an asshole, Jack," Karen said once she was safely out the door. "A bully and an asshole. I wish I'd never met you."

Her words cut Jack like no lawyer's papers ever could. "Just leave, Karen," Jack said, his head hung low. "If you wanted to hurt me, you did. Now just leave."

Karen didn't bothered closing the door, and Jack listened to the departing footsteps, the car doors and the car's engine as his life drove away.

Jack listlessly closed the door and stared at himself in the front hall mirror. Gone was the cop mask, stripped away by Karen's final words. Guilt at causing Karen pain, for wasting years of her life, warred in his face with anger and hate. Anger at Karen for wanting to hurt him. Hate at himself for being the man he was.

"Fuck!" Jack screamed. His fist lashed out, shattering the mirror and the face in it.

Jack leaned on the small bureau beneath the mirror, unmindful of the slivers of glass digging into his knuckles. His rage was sated for the moment, but not gone, and for that he was thankful; he'd take this low, furious simmer over the self-loathing any time.

A quiet whimper from Justice snapped Jack out of his fugue. The dog was pacing by the stairs, clearly unsure if he should approach his master.

Jack held out a warning hand. "Stay there, Justice. I don't want you to cut your paws."

Jack removed a broom from the front hall closet and quickly swept up the broken glass. He left the mirror frame where it was. Its few remaining pieces of jagged glass, jutting from the frame like a witch's rotted teeth, would be a good reminder for him to keep his temper well in hand.

Jack settled his ass on the stairs and wrapped his arms around Justice. "Sorry about that, boy. She just pissed me off something fierce." And the anger was still with him, a slow burn down deep in his belly.

"I could have cheated on her, you know," Jack confided to Justice. "Cops always have the opportunity, but I never did, not once. And now…" He shook his head. "Well, if I'm going to be convicted of the crime, I might as well enjoy it." He took Lillian's card from his back pocket and punched the number into his cell.

She answered on the second ring. "It's me, Jack." He listened for a moment then smiled. It wasn't a pleasant smile. "Yeah, I do. And wear the boots."

Evelyn, tucked away in the car's inner shadows, had watched as Jack went into the house, grinned as the self-important, too good to be her son-in-law policeman stalked past without seeing her. The look on his face had said he expected to find trouble inside, and Karen's expression when she came out indicated that the trouble had been found. Her daughter climbed into the back seat while George started up the car. No one spoke until the ink spot that was Jack's house on the gaily lighted street was safely banished from sight.

"I thought you said he wouldn't be home until much later," Evelyn chided Karen, who was brooding in the back seat. Outside the meticulously heated interior, the cold night passed by with the purr of the powerful motor.

"He must have left early," Karen sulked. "Probably going to fuck his slut of a partner."

"I understand you're upset, dear, but there's no call for such language. You needn't debase yourself by sinking to his level." Beneath the reprimand, Evelyn was relieved. Whenever Karen met with her future ex-husband, Evelyn feared her daughter's resolve would crumble and she'd throw herself back into the savage's arms.

"Sorry, Mom," Karen apologized. "It's just that he really hurt me, and every time I see him, the pain comes back. I can't believe he cheated on me," she cried softly. "Especially with that whore."

Evelyn let the vulgarity slide this time, content to hear Karen utter it with conviction, with the stubborn resolve she had inherited from both parents. "Some men just need their whores. Isn't that so, George?"

"Excuse me?" George said, sounding startled.

"I said some men, like Jack, feel compelled to visit prostitutes. You've seen it before in the university."

"Yes, yes I have. Men like that cannot be trusted, honey," he said over his shoulder to Karen.

Smiling, Evelyn proposed, "Why don't we stop somewhere? I would enjoy a hot cup of Earl Grey."

Not an hour after flipping his cell phone closed, the doorbell rang, and Jack opened the door with feelings of misgiving, but he was still too mad to listen to them.

Lillian stood on the front step, and although her body was hidden in a long red coat, Jack could see the stiletto boots she had been wearing this afternoon.

She smiled at him, her hunger naked and shameless, and purred, "So, do you want to talk?"

"No," Jack said hoarsely.

"Good. Neither do I."

She swayed into the front hall, saying nothing when she saw the shattered mirror. Jack could feel the sexual heat radiating from her. He closed the door on the night and any second thoughts.

She let the coat fall to the floor and stood before Jack, brazen in her desire, confident in his. Her body was lithe, smooth and strong. A body made for fucking. She wore nothing but the boots and a lacy black bra and panties. She slid towards Jack, the movement too fluid to be a step, until her groin pressed against his. The heels brought her within a couple of inches of Jack's height.

She trailed a hand up Jack's torso, pausing to press her palm on his chest muscles. She ground her pelvis against him, finding his hardness. "So," she sighed into his ear, her touch and breath shivering Jack's flesh. "Are you going to fuck me here in the front hall?"

The front hall. Where Karen had vented her hateful words, hurt him more than anyone else ever could.

Jack grabbed Lillian by the arms, lifting her roughly onto the bureau. She wrapped her legs around him as Jack sank his fingers into her thick, black hair. His mouth found hers and the kiss was savage, loveless.

She moaned into his mouth, then tugged at his shirt. Jack ripped the clinging obstruction over his head. Lillian ran her hands greedily over his shoulders, arms, kneading and caressing the muscles.

Jack was burning with desire, lusting for this woman who wasn't his wife, who was the wife of another man. Jack reached behind Lillian and tore the bra apart. He flung it away, baring her breasts, and she gasped in approval.

"Fuck me, Jack. Fuck me now."

Jack freed himself of his pants and pulled Lillian's panties aside. He positioned himself, but she stopped him with a hand on his stomach. Jack's anger wanted to swat it away, to take what he wanted.

"Are you clean?" Lillian panted.

"I never cheated," Jack growled.

"Then fuck me," she breathed and Jack entered her in a single thrust. Her legs held him tight as he drove himself deep inside her. She scored sharp lines of pain across his back as her fingernails tore at his skin. The pain only fueled Jack's anger, and he slammed his hips against her ravenously.

Lillian grunted in wanton pleasure. "Yes, Jack. Scott can never fuck me like this." She brought his hand to her mouth, the hand that had smashed the mirror, bore cuts from the glass, and licked at the split flesh. Her teeth nipped at his skin, tearing open the small wounds.

Jack snatched his hand away. Lillian smiled mischievously at him, her lips stained with his blood.

"Harder," she demanded. "Hurt me."

Jack pulled out of her and dragged her off the bureau. She looked questioningly at him until he spun her around. Grinning, almost snarling, she gripped the bureau and pushed her hips back at him. Jack yanked her panties down and grabbed her slender hips. Losing all thought and control, he thrust inside her, relishing in her whimpers and cries of pained pleasure.

She screamed as she came, and Jack was only seconds behind her.

**Tuesday, 11 December
0852 hours**

Rivulets of sweat streamed along Jenny's body, her face. She swept a towel across her brow knowing it was a temporary solution at best. She dropped the towel over the stair climber's handle and upped the pace of the revolving steps another level.

Beneath the sweat, her face was a mask of exhaustion. Bloodshot eyes peered out from within dark sunken pits. But despite how tired she was, it was never enough, and nightmares haunted what little sleep she was lucky to steal away from a guilty conscience.

Out of desperation she was at the gym, driving herself to a point where she hoped her body would have no choice but to collapse unconscious. She'd started with an hour-long Body Pump class, but no matter how much weight she used, regardless how hard the instructor, Mary, drove them, it was not enough. So she was forty-six minutes on the stair climber, pushing herself harder than she knew was reasonable.

I have to sleep. I'll go crazy if I don't.

She kept her eyes fixed on the overhead TV, the mute screen on CP24, Toronto's twenty-four-hour news channel. She knew Jack was right when he told her to avoid the news, to turn a blind eye, a deaf ear to the opinions and arguments of others. Others who hadn't been there, who had no idea what had happened or why. Keep tight to what she knew. Excellent advice, but impotent. Every day since the shooting she had read the papers, watched the news. She kept her car radio tuned to an all-news station. She couldn't help herself. It was like her tongue returning time and again to a gap left by a missing tooth, to probe at the tender flesh no matter how much it hurt.

Her interview with the SIU was next week and despite her Association-appointed lawyer telling her not to worry, the stress was a constant knot behind her eyes, a perpetual boil of acid in her stomach. Someone watching her, analyzing her actions, might presume her angst was fuelled by concern for her own welfare, her impending, unknown fate. If only she could be so selfish and callus. She shot a poor, unarmed man. No, a boy. A boy who had not understood what was going on, who had no doubt been acting out of fear and confusion. And now, because of her, he lay in a hospital bed, fighting for his life.

My God, what if he dies?

She was alone, plagued by remorse. Brian was great, but with his stupidly long shifts—without overtime, which was as common for doctors as it was with cops—the time he could spend with her was miserably brief. Hammer and Mugsy were her best support group right now, and the dogs may not have understood the excessive time she had with them or the frequent, unexplained hugs, but they weren't complaining. Except when her restless sleep kept them awake.

But as wonderful as the dogs were, they couldn't talk to her, couldn't give her the advice and understanding she sorely needed and craved. Jack could. If only he wasn't working. She knew she could call him and he would take time off for her, but she refused to act that selfishly. He had far too much stress in his life for her to dump hers on top of everything else.

She tapped the speed control on the display counsel until she was practically running up the stairs. She fell not a minute later. A horrified gasp stumbled her, and her toe caught on the lip of a stair. The escalator-style steps pitched her feet out behind her. She grabbed at the handles but her sweaty hands slipped and she tumbled to the floor. The treads continued to whirl triumphantly, doing a few victory laps before the machine automatically shut down.

She hurriedly scrambled to her feet, ignoring the pain in her ankle, the blood dribbling down her skinned shin, dreadfully hoping no one had witnessed her spill. A personal trainer broke away from his client to check on her, but Jenny brushed his concerns away. She was desperate to get off the gym floor, to make it to the change room before she vomited.

The trainer watched her flee, a puzzled expression on his face. Behind him on the muted TV, the news anchor carried on silently relating the day's news. Below his network-perfect visage, the breaking news banner continued to scroll the latest developments: Tyrone Johnson, 18, dies four days after being shot by police.

"How long we gotta wait? It fucking stinks in here."

"Patience, man. It'll happen soon." Lyron sounded calm, but he too was feeling the waiting, ants crawling up and down his spine, ants with hundreds of ice-cold feet. He fought the urge to glance at his watch. *A leader leads by example*, Ghost had told him. *Fear, uncertainty, are contagious.* To still his hands Lyron gripped the .22 rifle Ghost had provided for the operation.

Kyle was right, though. It stank in the car. Lyron cracked the window to let some clean air in. His crew—seven this time; there'd been no shortage of volunteers after the success of the car bombing—sat in two stolen cars tucked away in a parking lot just south of the cop shop.

"You think they'll shoot at us?"

"What you think? They shot at me when I torched a fucking car." Kyle could run like the fucking wind and could chuck a football farther than anyone Lyron had ever met, but fuck was he ever stupid. Some said that flat spot on his forehead was where his momma had dropped him when he was a baby.

"I don't get it, bro." Devon spoke up from the driver's seat. He had been with Lyron for the car bombing and had been the first to sign up for tonight's exploit. "Ty's dead and we ain't doing a cop? Ain't right, bro."

"We stick to the plan," Lyron commanded.

Kyle's hadn't been the only voice calling for blood after word of Tyrone's death had spread through the Park. Lyron had been just as eager. "Blood for blood," he'd argued with Ghost. "One of us dies, one of them dies."

"Not yet," his mentor assured him. "This is a war, and a war isn't won in a single battle. We hit the station, their symbol of authority, together, so they know they're facing all of us, not just someone in the dark with a gun. We let them know they aren't safe anywhere. We want them scared before we take what's due."

"Then we go for blood?" Lyron had bared his teeth in a wolfish grin.

Ghost had gripped Lyron's shoulder in brotherhood. "Then we go for blood. And they'll never see us coming."

"Man, I gotta shit—"

Lyron's hand shot up, silencing Kyle's bitching. In the distance, sirens howled in the night. Ghost was right, the cops were so simple to manipulate. Say the right words and you could have them running in circles chasing their own fucking tails.

Lyron's phone rang. He snapped it open, listened. "We're on it," he told the caller and killed the connection. "Time to play," he announced. He signaled to the car beside him, to the second half of his attack crew. Eight balaclavas slipped over heads, and the cars moved out.

"Go ahead with the hotshot," the dispatcher broadcast. *"5111's area, eleven Polson Street, the Docks nightclub. Man with a gun. 5106, 5110, this is for you."*

"We going?" Aaron asked as Jack wheeled south on Cherry.

"We'll head down to the area," Jack said quietly. His head

was throbbing despite the drugs he'd popped. "Sergeants frown on it when we take unarmed civilians to gun calls."

"I'm cool with it. If the shit hits the fan, all I have to do is run faster than you, and no offence, but you look like you couldn't run ten steps without puking. You sure you should be working?" It wasn't the first time the nurse had posed that question this night.

"Yeah, I'm fine," Jack assured him as he drove with his left hand shielding his eyes from the streetlights. "Nothing at home for me, anyway."

"Update for units responding to the gun call. Male, black, wearing... what?" The dispatcher paused as the call-taker repeated the description. *"Okay, male, black, wearing a black leather jacket with Mickey Mouse on the back. Male threatened the complainant with a handgun, last seen in the parking lot across from the nightclub."*

Jack stopped at Lakeshore as two scout cars blew through the red light, sirens echoing weirdly under the concrete of the raised Gardiner Expressway.

"5106, to radio." In the background of the cop's transmission—Paul Townsend, by the sound of it—Jack could hear a future echo of the two cars that had just passed him. "There's a large crowd of people down here. Can you spare any more cars?"

Jack didn't wait for the dispatcher to answer. Checking for traffic, he darted through the red light. Once across Lakeshore, he gunned the car down Cherry Street.

The south end of the division was a flat mosaic of vacant lots, industrial buildings both working and abandoned, and parkland. The Docks nightclub had opened before Jack's time in the division. Sitting on Toronto harbour at the end of Polson Street, it was an ideal location for a club as it boasted one of the best views of the city's nighttime skyline, and was removed from the city proper, so the only noise complaints came from the residents across the water on Toronto Island.

The only downside to the Docks was its inaccessibility by transit. Which meant just about everyone drove down, filling the inadequate parking lot quickly. As a result, cars lined both sides of Polson and Cherry. A traffic nightmare when the club closed its doors.

If the gunman was on foot, he was probably heading for a car.

As the nightclub's radiant glow became visible in the night sky, Paul was back on the radio. "Suspect spotted! Polson and Cherry." Behind Paul's words, Jack heard his partner yelling, "Police! Don't move!"

"Aw, shit," Jack muttered.

"What?" Aaron asked, sounding a touch on edge.

"You don't yell that unless your gun's out."

"Oh."

"When we get there, take the car and get the fuck out of the area. I'll call when it's over."

"Sure thing." Aaron didn't argue; being unarmed when a gunfight could erupt was not a way to stay healthy.

Cherry Street was a wide four lanes heading straight down to the beach, but it was blocked at Polson by two cruisers, their lights flashing in the well-lit intersection. One more scout car—Paul's most likely—was further down Polson, keeping cars penned in, but little could be done about the foot traffic. Bystanders spilled onto the road, fascinated by the live-action police show in front of them. The rubberneckers formed a huge circle, heavier on the sidewalk and near the police cars, but as more spectators arrived, the circle's far rim was filling in.

Jack bailed from the car and didn't wait to see if Aaron drove off. He joined the four cops behind their cars. They had cover, but Paul and his partner Sue Dennis—Mutt and Jeff, the shift had taken to calling them; the scarlet-haired PW dwarfed by Paul's bulk—were out in the open, and everyone's attention was focused on the suspected gunman. Straddling the road's centre line, he glared at the cops, arms crossed defiantly over his chest. Whether his leather jacket had a Mickey Mouse on the back, Jack couldn't tell, but when the coppers you work with all have their guns aimed at the same guy, you go with the flow.

The crowd was whistling and cheering appreciatively. Somewhere in the back, a chant of "Shoot, shoot, shoot" had started. Over this raucous din, police were yelling at the suspect, but the orders weren't meshing. Jack could distinctively hear Paul yelling, "Don't move!" but also heard others commanding the man to lie down, put his hands up, and get on the fucking ground.

Jack knelt beside Sammy Morris, the second of the platoon's two redheads. Morris glanced at Jack, then back at the gunman. He had his Glock resting on the engine hood, slowly tracking as the man began to pace back and forth.

"Fucking idiots think it's some kind of movie," he said to Jack without taking his eyes off his target. "That'll change if the bullets start flying."

"Never underestimate the stupidity of the general public."

"Ain't that the fucking truth."

As the crowd grew, so did their suspect's agitation. "I didn't do anything!" he shouted. That came through loud and clear, and so did his intention of not co-operating.

Fuck. Is this how it happened with Jenny? Some asshole not listening?

"I didn't fucking do anything!" the man yelled again, flinging hands out, and Jack's finger twitched. Not enough to squeeze the trigger—even if he was stupid enough to have it on the trigger when he wasn't about to shoot—but a twitch nonetheless. Jack wondered how many other fingers had jerked, and if the suspect had any idea how close he had come to dying just then.

The crowd was thickening up, filling in behind the suspect. If bullets started flying, someone—only one if they were lucky—was going to get hit.

"Leave me the fuck alone!" The man jammed his hands into the pockets of his jacket, and Jack was sure the same thought was going through all the coppers' minds. *If his hand comes out fast…*

The mob of spectators was still yelling and chanting; the cops were still bellowing orders. It was all one major fucked up mess.

Paul Townsend was a towering powerhouse of a man with a voice to match, and he used it now. "Everybody shut the fuck up!" His roar cut through the cacophony, stunning the crowd to silence and effectively shutting up all the other cops. Into this hushed breach, Paul stepped.

"You, in the Mickey Mouse jacket. Yes, you. Don't fucking move until I tell you to." Whether it was the single, clear voice, or the don't-fuck-with-me tone of that voice, the suspect froze. Completely. Jack noted the shrugged shoulders, the slight flare to the elbows, and realized the man had stopped in the process of pulling his hands free. Jack kept his eyes on those hands.

"I don't care what you think, right now," Paul yelled at the suspect. "We're looking for a guy with a gun and you match the description perfectly, right down to your jacket.

So, until I search you and know you don't have a gun, me and the other cops are going to assume you do have a gun, and if you don't do exactly what I say, I'll fucking shoot you. Do you understand?"

"But I—" The man tried to protest, but Paul was having none of it.

"If you move without me telling you to, I…will…shoot…you. Do you understand?"

It was so quiet as everyone waited to see what the suspected gunman would do that Jack could hear the music from the Docks drifting up the street. Up on Lakeshore a horn sounded. Somewhere in the crowd someone coughed. The throng was waiting, waiting, wanting…what? Blood?

"I understand." The man's response was meek, but it carried in the still, mute air, and the crowd sighed a disappointed groan.

From there on it was textbook. With short, precise orders, Paul had the suspect kneeling and cuffed in no time.

"Well, what's the verdict?" Jack asked after Paul shut the back door on their suspect.

"Nothing," the big cop said disgustedly. "No gun, no problems at the club tonight. So he says."

"Fake call?"

"Maybe," Paul admitted, rolling his shoulders to ease some tension. "I don't get it, Jack. Half a dozen cops pointing guns at him and he doesn't do what we tell him to. Just because he knows he hasn't done anything, he expects us to know that? He thinks we're aiming at him for no fucking reason?"

"Yeah, I know. It's frustrating. Never—"

A frantic, urgent call screamed out of the radios.

"We need backup at the station! We're under attack!"

Detective Rick Mason had the cramped and cluttered Major Crime office to himself. He had four files open on his desk: the Johnson shooting, threatening graffiti, a torched police car and two homicides. All connected, he was sure, but how?

True, the investigations into the homicides and the shooting—he'd be damned if he called a police shooting a murder, regardless of what that bitch in the newspaper said—belonged to other units and the SIU, but that didn't mean Mason couldn't keep tabs on them. They'd all taken place in his division, after all, and what happened in 51 was his business. Tank had once likened the Major Crime boss to a spider sitting in the crux of its web, attuned to any vibrations on the strands.

Mason's stomach gurgled painfully, eliciting a gassy belch. *A bloated spider, more like it.* Grimacing, he tugged open a desk drawer and popped some antacids. *Going through these things like candy.* With one hand unconsciously rubbing his belly—a belly that had gotten considerable larger over the last few years, he was loath to admit—Mason returned to studying the cases.

Okay, Jenny shoots the Johnson kid. Probably thought he had got a gun. Then we get all that graffiti shit. Understandable. People are pissed. The kid was unarmed and slow. Then someone torches a cop car. Again, I can see why. But who shot at them?

Paul and Sue, the two cops unfortunate to respond to the bogus domestic call and lose a car, denied firing any shots, and a check of both guns had confirmed that. But separate witnesses had sworn they heard someone yell the police challenge. And the casings found at the scene could have come from a police Glock. Had some idiot cop overreacted, realized his fuck up and was keeping his mouth shut? Possible. And of course, no usable prints had been found on the shell casings.

"Fuck," he swore softly. Leaning back in his chair, he laced his fingers behind his head and stared at the ceiling. Mason was a man old before his time. His goatee, only partly grey last year, was now fully grey with streaks of white. Heavy lines creased his face while his eyes, so deep and black-rimmed, seemed to gaze out from a cavernous skull.

He belched again, a slow-climbing churn of gas that seared its way up from his stomach. *Too much stress. I need a vacation*, he thought as he thumped his chair back down. But a retreat from the job would have to wait with the growing tension between the cops and the black community in Regent Park. And that bitch at the *Citizen* with her inflammatory articles certainly wasn't helping the situation.

Mason's gaze drifted wishfully to the *Cobra* movie poster. A really bad movie—horrible, in fact—crammed to overflowing with every tough guy, badass cop cliché there was. But it spoke to the detective of a simpler time in policing, when problems could be solved by kicking the appropriate asses and bashing a few select heads. Not today, not anymore. Now, the goal of the Police *Service*—fuck, how he hated that—was to reach out to, get in touch with, the community. Be their friend, social worker, babysitter. Toothless, spineless.

Just like the fucking court system. Trials weren't about guilt or innocence anymore. Lawyers argued technicalities, squeezed the biggest assholes through the smallest loopholes and the fucking judges just sat there, agreeing with it.

My client couldn't have robbed that old lady of her snakeskin purse, Your Honour, he's afraid of snakes. The three witnesses identifying him must all be mistaken.

My client wasn't selling the crack, all four bags of it was for personal use. The scales, debt list and cash found on him? He works in a deli.

My client can't be found guilty of raping that boy, Your Honour, the recording of it on his computer was seized without a warrant.

My client wasn't impaired, Your Honour. He was in diabetic shock when he ran that woman over.

"Here's to the old days, Sly." Mason toasted the match-chewing Sylvester Stallone with his Coke.

Who had put the poster up? Was it Taft?

That reminded Mason: John Taftmore's transfer request to Hold Up had come through; he'd be leaving the division in a couple of months, creating a vacancy in the Major Crime office.

I'll have to talk to Jack. See if he's still interested in the spot. A few months ago, Mason wouldn't have even questioned Jack's answer, but now… A woman as beautiful and sexy as Jenny could do strange things to a man's thought process. A fact Mason knew very well.

My client wasn't impaired, Your Honour. He was in diabetic shock when he ran that woman over.

But who knew what the outcome of Jenny's shooting would be. If the SIU laid charges, she could be suspended until the matter came to trial, which could take years. Civilians investigating cops. Another indication of how fucked up the legal system was. And that Templeton bitch had all but convicted and crucified Jenny in her articles.

On impulse, Mason snatched up the phone as he flipped through his Rolodex. There might be one thing he could fix. He punched in the number.

"*Citizen.* Ted Huntington."

"Ted, it's Mason over in 51."

"Rick, you old bastard. Haven't you retired yet?"

"Me? Weren't you writing for that rag when they were using hieroglyphics?"

"You should talk. You were probably around to see the new invention of the police call boxes," the gruff reporter fired back. "Now, what has my favourite detective calling me? Somehow, I don't see this as a social call."

"Wish it could be, Ted," Mason sighed. "What can you tell me about Millie Templeton?"

"Becoming a bit of a pain, is she?"

"Not my personal backside, but what she's writing ain't helping things over here. We're sitting on a powder keg, and she's tossing matches."

"If it's any consolation, I'm not a fan of her articles either." It was Ted's turn to sigh. "It's nothing but tabloid journalism, but it's what the boss wants. Sensationalism sells."

"Where'd she come from? She's new, ain't she? How'd she score this story?"

"Luck, my friend, luck. Right place at the right time. You know how it is."

"Yeah," Mason grumbled. Like most cops, he didn't like to admit how much of successful police work was sheer, dumb luck. Walk around a corner at the right time, you interrupt the drug deal. Ten seconds either way, you miss it.

Mason's most memorable piece of luck had happened way back when he was still in uniform. He and his partner were searching for an asshole wanted on a warrant and decided to check his old girlfriend's house to see if he was holed up there. On the way, a pigeon had decided to take a crap on Mason's shirt. Instead of going for the arrest stinking of bird shit, they'd returned to the station so he could change. As a result, they'd gotten to the house fifteen minutes later than they had planned and met the asshole on the sidewalk. After they pinched him, the man had admitted to coming to his ex's place with the intention of killing her for snitching on him.

If not for the fly-by pooping, they would have missed him, and the ex-girlfriend would have ended up very much dead.

Luck, indeed.

"And you're right, she is new," Ted carried on. "Been at the *Citizen* for about six months. Came down from Thunder Bay or somewhere way up north. Achieved a bit of fame—or notoriety, depending on how you look at it—on a local paper. From what I gather, she was dating one of the cops from the area, and one night he was stupid enough to tell her how he had bolstered a case against some lowlife dealing at the high school by—supplementing, shall we say?—the evidence."

"And I bet it ended up in the paper with her name on it."

"You would bet correctly," Ted confirmed. "The low-life walked free, the cop started looking for a new job, and she cashed in her little slice of success at the *Citizen*."

"All right, so she'll crucify her friends to get ahead. Charming. Anything else I should know about her?"

"That's about it. Anything new on the firebombing?"

"Not much. Waiting on some fingerprints we found in the van they were hiding in. That's about it."

"Well, if you can, let me know. I'd love to one-up our little princess."

Mason laughed. "You can count on it."

"Give me a call sometime when it's not work. We'll get together and smoke some stogies."

"Just so long as they're not those *genuine* Cubans you bought off that guy on the beach."

Huntington groaned. "I only got suckered the once. And they weren't that bad."

"Not if you liked smoking rolled-up wallpa—"

That's when all hell broke loose outside.

Glass exploded and the outside world flared up in a *whooshing* roar. Mason dropped the phone and sprinted to the windows. He kept the blinds perpetually shut, not wanting to give any would-be snipers or photographers access to his office and officers, and standing off to the side, he cracked the slats to peer out.

Two cars had skidded to a stop out front of the station, and masked men stood on the far side of the cars, flaming bottles in hand. As Mason watched, four bottles arced toward the station. One hit just below where he stood, and flames shot up, lunging hungrily for the window. Mason threw himself back as the sudden heat from the flames cracked the cold glass.

Mason heard officers shouting, swearing, a mix of surprised anger and fear. The Molotov cocktails continued to explode—*how many do those bastards have?*—and suddenly the second floor was filled with a copper's terrified screams. In seconds, the screams turned to agony, and Mason knew that someone was burning.

Gunfire erupted outside and for an instant the detective thought cops were firing on the arsonists, but the shots were too high-pitched and rapid for Glocks. At least one person was giving the bottle throwers covering fire. The windows in his office blew apart, the blinds twitching and flailing as bullets punched through them. Mason ran in a crouch to his desk as the bullets tore into the ceiling, rain-ing fragments of insulation and plaster on his head. He grabbed his gun from his desk drawer and threw himself against the wall next to the window.

He peeked through the ruined blind, eager to give the bastards a taste of their own medicine, but as quickly as the assault on the station had begun, it ended. Eight figures, not much more than black shapes in the streetlights, were sprinting down St. Bartholomew to disappear into the Park.

The attack on 51 station was over.

The air smelled wet, yet burned, with a faint whiff of gasoline still present. Firefighters splashed through puddles as they rolled up their hoses, and coppers stood on the perimeter, anxiously scanning the streets and shadows, hands resting on gun butts. Tension strained the night, as if reality had been chained to a medieval rack and stretched to the snapping point.

Jack joined Mason on the sidewalk, out of the firefighters' way. The detective gave the impression of being at ease, but Jack noticed his hand never strayed far from the Glock tucked into his waistband.

"Do they know what they've done?" Mason asked, gesturing to the station.

"They've declared war." Jack, like the rest of the officers, was outraged by the blatant attack and more than ready for some payback.

"We're going to fall on the Park like a sledgehammer on an anthill." Mason's voice was hushed, more suited for a church than a crime scene. "It'll make what we did when we were hunting for Anthony Charles look like a minor scuffle."

Jack studied the station, an old rundown structure he had come to respect and in some ways love. She was too small and outdated for the purpose, but she was a tough old bitch and got the job done. She represented the officers she housed: too few for the job, working with archaic equipment and weary from the constant toil. With her exterior blackened and scorched by God knew how many Molotov cocktails, the old lady appeared to be sagging, but Jack knew she, like the shell-shocked cops who had been here for the attack, would shrug this off and rise to the fight.

The firebombs had done little, if any, damage to the brick walls. The front doors and windows on both floors were shattered and shot out from a hail of bullets, but unbelievably, only one bottle had gotten through to the interior. Only one, but the harm done was immense.

"Any word on Keith?"

Mason shook his head. "Nothing new. That new detective, Daryl, put the flames out quickly, but the paramedics had Keith's face wrapped up when they wheeled him out of here. They were saying he might lose an eye."

The one firebomb that had breached the walls had exploded as it crashed through the CIB window, and the young officer, Keith—Jack didn't know his last name—had been doused with flaming gasoline. Detective Daryl, the giant Jack and Jenny had met in court, had smothered the flames with his suit jacket, but the extent of the injuries was still unknown.

"It could have been a lot worse," Mason reasoned. "If the shooter hadn't lain down covering fire for the bombers, if he'd waited for coppers to come to the windows or outside…"

Jack nodded. Yes, it could have been a lot worse. A young officer who had been at the wrong window at the wrong time could have been the least of the injured. And Jack knew that the chances of someone else—copper or civilian—being hurt or killed before this was over were awfully damn high. All because some assholes thought this was the right thing to do. As if it could bring back Tyrone Johnson.

"Blood is going to be spilt over this," Mason prophesized, as if reading Jack's thoughts.

"But not tonight," Jack prayed. "Let's hope there's nothing else tonight."

But sometimes, prayers go unanswered.

Freddy "Thriller" Franklin was having a shitty day. In fact, it was downright fucking horrible. Just like every day since that fucked-up night when Tyrone was shot. God, he still got the shakes thinking about it. He had nightmares about it, hadn't been able to sleep more than two hours in a row, and every time he relived it in his dreams, he was the one getting shot.

His girlfriend—ex-girlfriend now, the skanky bitch—said he was having nightmares on account of his guilty conscience. What did that crack whore know?

"It wasn't my fault Ty got shot," he declared. "Not my fault at all."

Thriller hastily looked about himself, making sure no one had heard him talking to himself. Since the shooting, he wasn't exactly the most welcomed person in Regent Park. Seemed everyone was blaming the cops and him for Ty being dead. How could it be his fault?

"I didn't shoot him. Fuck, I didn't even have a gun with me."

He'd picked one fucked-up night to come back to the Park. Word was someone had blown up the cop shop. Thriller didn't know if it was true or not, but there sure seemed to be a shitload of cop cars prowling around, and every cop looked royally pissed. If he hadn't been in such a fix, he would have stayed home.

The door to 260 Sumach Street was unlocked as usual and he ducked into the stairwell. Once inside, he jammed his hands into his coat pockets and hunched his shoulders to tuck as much of his face behind his scarf as possible. Not everyone in the Park knew his name, but everyone knew who he was once they spotted the pale patches on his skin.

The vitiligo had plagued him since his early teens. At first, it had been nothing more than a few pale patches on the dark skin of his hands. And then his face. And the patches grew, spreading across his palms to wrap up the sides of his fingers and onto the back of his hands. His face wasn't spared either.

The skin condition had earned Freddy the nickname Thriller. Whether it was because Michael Jackson had the same disease, or kids at school said Freddy looked like one of the zombies from the video, he didn't know. Or care.

By the time high school—or at least the first half that he had stayed for—was a distance memory, the vitiligo had taken most of his hands and consumed a good third of his face. The taunting and bullying of high school had followed him into his adult years. How many beatings had he suffered because someone thought he looked gross, weird or simply different? He had taken to telling people the disease was contagious. That had spared him a few thumpings, but isolated him, like he was some leper from the Bible. And if someone was really intent on whupping his ass, they wore gloves or used weapons.

He was doubly damned. First the vitiligo and now carrying the blame for Ty's death. If his regular crack dealer hadn't lived in the Park, Freddy would have stayed well fucking clear of it. But at least his dealer was still willing to sell to him; Thriller was a steady, reliable customer. And today, he was loaded with cash. The plan was to buy enough rock to keep him going for a week, longer if he didn't binge, and lay low until all this shit went away. He'd had his fill of people questioning him, yelling at him and yelling questions at him.

The cops had drilled him all night about the shooting. They wanted to know all about the gun, what Ty had been doing before he was shot. All of that shit. They'd only been able to get Freddy with a bullshit possession charge; the piece of rock they'd found on him was just a crumb, so small even he didn't know he had it on him. But because of that sliver of crack, plus a couple of fail-to-appears on his record, the cops got to hold him till court in the morning. They'd gone at him all night long, not letting him sleep, until he'd been crying like a fucking baby.

And it hadn't stopped once he got to court. Freddy had been dumped in a private little cell, and a couple of mean-looking bastards from that Special Investigating Bureau thing—they were the guys who went after the cops when the cops fucked somebody up or killed them—went after him just like the cops had. Except these guys wanted to know what the cops had been doing before Ty was shot.

And the gun. Everybody wanted to know about the gun.

"Hey, Thriller."

Jarred out of his self-pitying thoughts, Freddy stopped on the landing. A man he didn't know stood a few steps above him, his face hidden in the shadow of his ball cap. He was smiling down at Freddy but his right hand was held casually behind his back, out of sight. Out of sight wasn't good, and Freddy prayed he'd still have his money after the beating.

"I've been looking for you, Thriller," the man commented with no malice in his words.

"You have?" Freddy asked, tentatively hoping this wasn't going to end up with him bleeding.

"You bet," the man said, smiling more than ever. He brought his hand into view and Freddy knew this was going to be more than a beating.

"Turn around, Thriller," the man told him as he raised the gun. "It'll be easier that way."

Freddy "Thriller" Franklin did as he was told, and had just enough time to wonder if dying was going to hurt.

Ghost tucked his Glock into his jacket pocket as he trotted down the steps, careful to avoid any of the blood splatter. It wouldn't do to leave a shoe print that didn't match up with the intended story. He paused to give Thriller, lying face down on the landing, one last glance. It was amazing how much of his brains had ended up stuck on the cinder brick wall.

Don't feel bad, Thriller. Your life may have meant nothing, but your death will play a crucial part in my plans.

Ghost hurried down to the ground floor, not really worried about being seen; Park residents knew better than to stick their heads out of their apartments when guns were in play. And if he was observed leaving the crime scene? Just another male black in a baseball cap and baggy jacket. One of hundreds.

He nudged open the building's back door, planning to fade into the night like he did after shooting at Lyron and his buddies at the firebombing. Fuck, how they had run!

Bet they had to clean shit out of their panties.

The whole staged performance had gone off perfectly. The cops were blaming the Park residents for the car bombing, and the residents were screaming that the cops had opened fire on unarmed people running away from the car. And Tyrone, the poor little bastard, had picked the perfect day to succumb to his wounds, ramping up the strain between cops and civies before it even had a chance to ease off. Lyron had been more than willing to dish out some payback, and the line of volunteers had quadrupled in an hour.

Perfect. Absolutely perfect. The cops shoot Tyrone, Lyron torches a car. Tyrone dies, Lyron attacks the cop shop. And it would look like the cops had just killed Thriller, the one non-police witness to Tyrone's shooting. It was like a fucking Ping Pong match. With all this shit going on, the odd dead gangbanger would be lucky to make it on to a newspaper's back page.

"Pardon me, friend. Did you jus' hear sumthin'?"

Much like Thriller did moments ago on the landing, Ghost came up short, caught unawares. Reprimanding himself for his lack of attention, Ghost realized the night's work wasn't over.

Phil was out later than he had intended. But he had gotten to drinking with some buddies and the evening had slipped into night. It was amazing, in a sad way, how long it took to drink three beers when you were close to the big nine-oh. It was just shy of midnight and the cold damp air was playing hell with his joints as he and Bear trudged slowly along the Oak Walkway. It was a path he and Bear had navigated many times before, and he had no worries about making it home; he was old but he wasn't that old. Although, he would admit to himself—and maybe Bear if Bear asked, but that was the good thing about dogs: they asked very few questions—it might be a bit of a foot race with his bladder going up George Street to his home. That part of him was definitely old.

Bear waddled happily alongside Phil without a care in his doggy world. And why should he have a care? He could relieve himself whenever he found a likely tree or hydrant. Bear was a small dog—now chubby—of dubious heritage and had been Phil's closest friend for well over twelve years. Or it could be fifteen. Phil was a little cloudy on his friend's exact age; his memory, like his joints, didn't work all that well anymore.

"C'mon, Bear, time for—"

Phil stopped, his head cocked quizzically to the side. He thought he had heard something, a loud bang, like a firecracker. Not like the sissy little things they sold today—most of them didn't amount to much more than a loud fart—but one of the big cannon blasters he had loved as a child. He slowly turned in a circle, searching the dark for lurking troublemakers. He didn't want any young punks tossing bombs at Bear. If they did, they'd get themselves a whupping. Phil was old but he wasn't too old to tan any backsides that needed tanning.

He finished his circle and found himself facing a man who had just come out of the apartment building closest to the walkway.

"Pardon me, friend. Did you jus' hear sumthin'?"

The man jumped a bit, as if Phil had startled him, so Phil was about to offer his apologies when he heard another bang, but much, much louder this time. And with the bang came a sudden pain in his chest.

Bastard just punched me.

Phil staggered back a step and that's when he saw the gun. There was a second gunshot—*not a firecracker, you old fool*—coupled with another punch to his chest. Phil's bladder let go, and he felt the hot urine soaking his pants as his knees buckled under him. He fell over, shattering his pelvis as he hit the cold cement, but the pain down there was a hushed backdrop to the torture in his chest.

He could hear Bear barking furiously but couldn't see him; everything around him was getting awfully dark. He held out a hand, begging the man he could no longer see, "Please don't hurt Bear. Please don't hurt m' dog."

A final gunshot chased Phil down into a darkness that had no end.

51's Youth Bureau was tucked away in a second-floor corner of the old station, down the hall from the beehive of activity that was the detective office. Double homicides tended to have that effect. Jack sat in the dark, hiding from the cops, hiding from the questions, hiding from everyone and everything. But he couldn't hide from the pain.

Phil, a gentle old soul, a friend, was dead.

At first, it had been a simple sound of gunshots call. Nothing new or unusual for 51 or Regent Park. If a week went by without gunfire, then you weren't in 51. Jack and Aaron had been sitting at the Moss Park Armouries, the same place they had been last time gunplay happened in the Park. This time there was no frantic Jenny calling for an ambulance and backup. Just another idiot capping off some rounds. It only became serious if someone ended up catching one of the bullets.

Aaron was finishing off his latest assessment. Joey Horner, aka the Queen Street tackling dummy, had been threatening to kill himself with an overdose of Tylenol. When he'd seen who was working the CIT, he quickly changed his story, no longer wanting any attention.

"Did you want to go to that?" Aaron asked, not looking up from his checklist.

Jack shook his head, then realized Aaron was still looking at his paperwork. "Nah, just the sound of some idiot and his gun. We'll go if they end up finding a victim, but as Manny used to say, no victim, no crime."

"5103 to radio," the cop—Sue Dennis again, she and Paul were certainly lucking out on the gun calls tonight—sounded nervous. That wasn't good. "We need more cars at the Oak Walkway and Sumach. We've found a gunshot victim."

"Fuck, here we go again." Jack keyed the car to life.

"10-4, 5103, I have units heading to you." The dispatcher didn't bother voicing out for backup; she assigned every car in the division to the call, and to keep the air clear, if coppers were going, they simply accepted the call via the car's computer. *"5103, I have DAS on the line. Can you give the victim's status?"*

"Uh…" Sue hesitated, and that definitely wasn't good. Jack pressed down harder on the gas.

The dispatcher understood the hesitation as well. *"I've put a rush on the ambulance,"* she advised, but Jack, like the dispatcher, knew it was just a formality. Cops could only declare death because of three Ds: decapitation, dismemberment and decomposition. Jack was betting on a headshot. Not exactly decapitation, but close enough if the brains were scattered outside of the skull. Sue may have been on edge but she still had the sense not to broadcast that information over an open frequency.

And then things went completely to shit.

"We need backup here now!" Sue no longer sounded nervous. She sounded downright scared. "There's a large crowd gathering," she added, and Jack could hear Paul roaring in the background, "Get back! Get the fuck back!"

Not a minute later, Jack screeched to a halt on the walkway, less than a block from where Jenny's shooting had occurred, and the scene was virtually identical: two apartment buildings north and south of the walkway, each separated by parking lots that were technically part of Sumach Street. Scout cars littered the parking lots, and two were straddling the walkway, blocking the scene from each end.

But the cars, and the cops, were a fragile dam against the growing crowd.

There had to be a hundred people, most of them bunched on the south side of the walkway, and more kept coming. Crime scenes, especially violent, bloody ones, always drew onlookers: the simply curious and the morbidly fascinated. Those groups were generally placid and fluctuated in size as people came and went, but this wasn't a typical group of gawkers. It was a mob, and Jack was afraid it could turn into a lynch mob. Even in the car with the windows up, he could hear the angry shouts, could feel the vehemence radiating out from the mob like storm-wrought surf pounding against the shore.

Red emergency lights pulsated through the night, flickering scarlet over the multitude, and Jack was disturbingly reminded of the murderous, torch-bearing mob in the old Frankenstein movie.

Jack snagged the mike. "CIT to radio. There's a large crowd here, at least a hundred people and getting bigger and they're not happy. You better get some more cars from other divisions." Before getting out of the car he handed his collapsible baton to Aaron. The nurses didn't carry weapons, only radios. "Here, in case things get out of control. Stay close."

They ducked around the scout car on the walkway, keeping to the north side as the majority of the crowd was still gathering to the south. Jack eyed Paul and Sue standing near a body on the walkway, protecting the inner scene, Paul's hulking size dwarfing his redheaded partner. A line of coppers, a pathetically thin line, was trying to hold the mob back. The horde was angry, perhaps frightened as well, and they were venting their emotions at the targetable police. The shouts had no unity; there was no focus. For now.

And however scared or angry the crowd was, Jack doubted it was anything compared to his fellow officers. Their station had been brazenly attacked, and they were plunged into a potentially deadly situation. Jack was amazed—and impressed by the restraint—that no guns were in hand yet.

Sergeant Rose was striding the length of the blue line, shouting with her officers, "Move back, move back and let us do our job!"

Jack snagged her sleeve. "Where do you want us?" He had to shout to be heard over the unintelligible roar of the mob.

"Thank Christ," she said. The big sergeant was looking frazzled and more than a touch worried. But mostly pissed off. "Watch our backs," she ordered. "I don't want anyone realizing they could swing around and get in behind us."

Jack nodded. "I told the dispatcher to get more cars from other divisions."

"Good man. That's the first bit of good news I've had since this clusterfuck started. Who knows how much evidence's been trampled." She called after Jack. "And see if you can shut that damn dog up."

Only then did Jack become aware of a frantic barking, a continuous barrage behind the crowd's unruly din. A small dog faced off against Paul, who was unsuccessfully trying to shoo the little beast away from the body lying on the walkway. Jack looked for an owner, someone trying to call the dog. This scene was fucked up sufficiently without a dog tracking who knew what across the evidence.

Jack froze. His stomach fell as his balls crawled up inside him. "Bear? Oh, God, no. No!"

Jack pushed past Paul, shouldering the much larger

man aside effortlessly. He fell to his knees next to the body, praying it wasn't Phil. "Not Phil, please God, no."

But it was. Gone was Jack's friend. Gone was the kindly old man who shared a love for dogs with Jack. All that was left was a corpse. Blood stained the front of Phil's coat, the new Blue Jays jacket he wore with such pride. His right eye was a ruined mess, destroyed by the bullet that had exploded the back of his head. Blood, still steaming slightly in the cold air, pooled around his shattered skull.

Why? Why would anyone kill this gentle man?

A small nose nudged Jack's arm. Bear stood nestled between Jack's arm and thigh, shivering in fear.

"It's okay, Bear," Jack whispered. He pulled Bear close. "It's okay."

But it wasn't. How could it be?

Suddenly, all the grief, all the guilt and hatred, all the emotional agony that had eaten away at Jack's soul for months, for years, boiled up. He screamed. It was either spew out all the ugliness in him or choke on it.

His tortured wail did what all the ordering, all the shouting, couldn't. The crowd fell silent as they watched a cop cry over a dead man. In the shocked hush, Bear threw back his head and howled.

Jack sat in the darkened Youth Bureau, Bear curled up on his lap, his nose tucked under a paw. The old dog's leg twitched sporadically, and Bear whimpered in his sleep. Jack stroked the soft brindle fur, comforting himself as much as the dog. Bear had taken a nip at Jack when Jack had tried to pull him away from his master's body. Jack understood the bite, empathized with the pain and fear behind it. Bear had circled the YB continuously, whining, and had peed on the floor out of confusion, fear or frustration. Jack had cleaned it up, all the while assuring Bear it was okay, that Jack understood. In time, exhaustion had caught up to the old beast and he allowed himself to be lifted and held.

The office lights flickered to life. Jack turned his head, squinting against the sudden luminance. A migraine, thick, queasy, lay coiled deep in his skull. The bone around his eye throbbed with the brute's pulsing. Jack had an agonizing night to look forward to.

Staff Sergeant Greene stood in the doorway, clad and polished to regulation perfection as always. Jack and the platoon's boss had never gotten along; Jack had never agreed with Greene's archaic methods of supervising. His approach to policing was as outdated as the foolish handlebar moustache he kept tightly waxed and curled. A platoon revolt, spearheaded by Jack, which had involved officers parading for duty in their underwear, had shaken what Jack seriously considered an unstable individual. Later, in spiteful revenge, Greene had transferred Jack's partner, Manny, to Forensics, no doubt thinking the slow-paced, meticulous work would drive the hyper officer insane. Greene's plan had backfired when Manny had fallen in love with the work and requested that the six-month lateral be made permanent. The unexpected turnaround had further deflated the inflexible prick, and since then Greene had been nothing but a restless spirit wandering the station's halls.

Greene remained in the doorway, keeping as much distance from Jack as he usually did, as if Jack's unorthodox manner of policing was infectious.

The two police officers stared across the width of the office, neither speaking. Jack knew he had fucked up at the homicide scene, potentially contaminating the body—*Phil, his name is Phil!*—and then neglecting his duty by walking away. Add in that a second body had been found close by, and he assumed Greene was here to gloat over the impending documentation and possible Police Act charges.

Like I fucking care.

Greene broke the silence. "I don't like you, Warren," he stated, eying the sleeping Bear on Jack's lap with distaste. The prick most likely thought comforting an animal unprofessional and demeaning to an officer's authority. Again, Jack didn't give a fuck.

"You lack discipline and you've squandered your position of leadership on this platoon bestowed to you by your seniority. I know you hold me in contempt, consider my morals and principles old-fashioned and obsolete. You have no honour. You disregard and violate the laws you have sworn to uphold, and justify your actions as necessary to apprehend criminals. In my view, this makes you worse than those you arrest. You're a criminal with a badge and it sickens me to see you wear the same uniform as I."

Jack remained silent, still. Only his hand moved, stroking Bear's fur. The silence stretched across the office, and Jack realized Greene was waiting for an answer. Perhaps he expected Jack to defend himself, to offer some bogus explanation to avoid punishment, but Jack was tired, beaten to the depths of his soul, and just didn't—couldn't—care about Greene, any charges, or the fucking job.

Sighing, Jack said, "If you're going to charge me, then just fucking do it and get it over with."

Greene paused, as if he was considering doing just that, but then he surprised Jack. "The victim, he was a friend of yours?"

Jack nodded. "He was. He was a good man." Tears welled in his eyes, choking his words. "Some animal—no, some human piece of garbage—gunned him down as if he didn't matter."

"No one deserves to die like that." The staff sergeant dipped his head in condolence. "I don't know why, but someone appears intent on creating a war on our streets, and I fear many more will die unless he is stopped." Greene stepped away from the door, turned back. "Find him, Warren. And when you do, do what you do best."

Blood Rage

**Wednesday, 12 December
0247 hours**

The hot water swirled around Jack, throwing up a fine mist that dampened his face and hair like a gentle summer rain. Lillian's touch on his scar was nearly as light as the water droplets as she traced its length through his eyebrow.

"How did it happen?" she asked, her voice husky. Straddling his lap, she squirmed pleasurably.

Jack took a sip of cider then set the bottle back on the lip of the hot tub before answering. It was his third or fourth bottle. He wasn't sure. All that he knew, or cared about, was that the alcohol, combined with migraine meds, was blunting the pain in his head and soul. Blunting, but not obliterating. He doubted there was enough alcohol and drugs for that.

"Broken bottle neck," he said as he settled his hands back on Lillian's hips. "Guy wanted to provoke us into shooting him."

"And did you?" Lillian's throaty whisper was barely audible over the churning water.

He rested his head back on the foam pillow and watched her through lazy, slitted eyes. "Did I what?"

She leaned into him, her breasts brushing his chest. Neither of them had bothered with bathing suits. "Shoot him. Kill him," she sighed, her breath hot and moist in his ear.

He slowly shook his head. "Thought I was going to have to. Almost did, but just pepper sprayed him instead."

Pouting with disappointment, Lillian sat up, reached for Jack's cider. She had her hair up to keep it dry, and he watched, enthralled, as her lips kissed the bottle and her slender throat worked the liquid down. She smiled, pleased by his enjoyment of her show. As she shifted to set the bottle on the lip, she made sure she rubbed against his hardness.

Her hand touched the puckered scar on his right shoulder, her fingers probing where it dimpled the thick trapezius muscle. "This is where he shot you, isn't it?" She slid her hand over his shoulder and gasped when her fingers found the rougher, larger exit wound on his back. "You killed him, didn't you?"

"Yeah," Jack said, his voice coarse. "I shot him three times. Here, here—" he poked her twice between the breasts, trailed his finger to her quivering belly "—and here."

Part of him was disgusted by her reaction. She was a violence junky, she got off on it, but didn't that make her a better match for him than Karen? Karen, who abhorred violence in real life, who sat through all those Schwarzenegger and Stallone movies only because she knew Jack liked them? Not that there could be a future with Lillian; she was, after all, a married woman. And Jack definitely wasn't looking for a relationship. Hell, the corpse of his marriage was barely cold.

So why was he sitting here in the hot tub with a very naked Lillian on his lap? When, down in the secret caves of his heart, he still hoped for reconciliation with Karen? A foolish, doomed hope, but a hope nonetheless.

Maybe he was looking for a way to numb the pain, to get through one more night, to feel loved again, even if he was just being used by Lillian to fulfill some twisted sexual urge. Or maybe he was just tired of living in an empty house.

Well, not exactly empty.

Justice was lying in his favourite spot at the top of the deck stairs leading down to the grass. And huddled between the shepherd's front legs was Bear. The little dog had trembled and whined the whole ride home, but when Jack had opened the car door for him, Bear had been too scared to move.

Jack carried Bear to the front door, not sure how Justice was going to react to another dog on his turf. But Jack's trepidations proved unnecessary. He knelt with Bear in his arms, and Justice curiously sniffed the much smaller dog, then whined as if he sensed Bear's loss. Anyone who said dogs do not grieve was a fool; Bear, when not gripped by a fitful sleep, whined and moved with a lethargy that was far more than physical. And it seemed Justice understood this. He gently licked Bear's face, as if to comfort him and to welcome Bear to his new home.

Now Justice watched protectively over the sleeping Bear. Perhaps Jack was like the small dog: hurt, alone, and needing someone to tell him it was okay. Not that he expected Lillian to comfort him any time soon. Or ever. No, she was using him as much as he was using her. And maybe that was the best he could hope for.

So here he was with a woman he barely knew, who he had fucked once already and would no doubt fuck again before the night was over. At least when he was with her, he could take all the guilt, all the hate and soul-eating pain, and shove it down deep inside himself, be normal for a little while.

If foreplay consisting of scars and bloody, brutal stories could be called normal.

"Do you have any more scars?" Lillian asked as her hands explored Jack's chest and arms.

"Only on the inside."

She pouted again, and Jack decided she looked quite sexy when she pouted, which of course, she already knew; that's why she did it.

"Will you kill him if you find him?"

"Who?" Jack wasn't exactly listening. His hands glided down from her hips to cup her buttocks, then up her back. She was about the same height as Karen, but where his ex-wife had the firm legs of a runner and a toned upper body from weight training with Jack, Lillian was slender and supple. Her breasts were smaller than Karen's, but fit his hands perfectly. Her nipples hardened beneath his palms.

Moaning, she gripped his hands, encouraging him to squeeze harder. "The man your sergeant told you to find and kill."

Jack's hands suddenly clenched, startling a yip of pain from her. She only moaned louder and began gyrating her hips against him.

Why had he told her about Greene's comment? She had called him shortly after he had gotten home. She was in the area and wanted to come over. Jack didn't say no. The night's horrendous events had all come out as he explained Bear's presence: Phil's murder, rescuing Bear, Greene's suggestion.

She had ordered him into the tub, then slowly stripped out of her jacket, blouse and jeans. She hadn't been wearing underwear. Now she was thrusting against him as she arched her back beneath his rough hands.

Jack didn't want to answer her question; he'd had enough of talking. He grabbed her ass and lifted her onto the edge of the tub. Their bodies steamed in the cold night air as she guided him into her, then wrapped her legs around him and hungrily pulled him in deep. She bit him as she raked his back with her nails.

"I knew you cheated on me."

An icicle of fear stabbed Jack through the stomach as he turned to see Karen standing on the porch, her face a furious thunderhead.

He held out a hopeless hand to her. "Karen, I never—"

"That's it, don't stop." Lillian continued to grind against him, oblivious to, or uncaring of Karen's presence, and unbelievingly, Jack was still fucking her at a feverish pace. But it wasn't Lillian he was fucking, it was Jenny, and she was crying, "I thought he had a gun."

Jack turned to Karen and it was she who had a gun. His gun, his Glock, aimed at his head. "It's your fault, Jack," she was saying, the gun rock steady in her grip. "It's your fault I left."

"It's your fault," Jenny echoed, her legs refusing to release him. "It's your fault I shot him. You should have been with me. It should have been you."

"It's *all* your fault!" Jenny and Karen screamed in unison. Then Karen shot him.

Jack bolted upright in bed, his heart thundering in his

chest. As the last of the dream fled before the reality of his bedroom, he fell back, the mattress bouncing slightly beneath his weight. He stared at the ceiling, waiting for the booming of his heart to slow. He remembered what Connor had told him months ago about taking steroids, how he had hated lying in bed, listening to his heart pounding.

Yeah, well, I doubt he had to deal with dreams like that one.

A soft whine sounded in the dark beside his bed. Justice and Bear, curled up together on a single doggy bed—Jack had brought up Justice's downstairs bed for Bear, but the two insisted on sharing the one pillow—were staring up at him.

"Sorry, guys. Didn't mean to wake you." Jack reached down to pet them and found Bear, the poor little guy, trembling fiercely. "You miss him, don't you?" Bear simply whined.

"Come here, little guy." Jack scooped up Bear and set him on the bed. "Just for tonight, okay?"

Bear sniffed the covers, the pillows, then settled in next to Jack. Bear raised his head and looked at Jack with what could only be doggy gratitude. Jack gave him a scratch behind the ears. With a contented sigh, Bear nestled his nose under his paws and shut his eyes.

A cold, wet nose nudged Jack and when he rolled over, he found Justice staring at him, as if to say, *What gives?*

"I guess it's only fair. C'mon up."

Justice leapt onto the bed, stepped carefully over Jack and curled up next to Bear so the little dog was protected from both sides.

"Sweet dreams, guys," Jack whispered, and hoped it went for himself as well, but had his doubts. He shifted, trying to find a comfortable position for the deep scratches Lillian had gifted him with. That part of the dream was real at least. The rest, Jenny, Karen, the gun—what was that about?—was obviously his subconscious just fucking with him. Although it wasn't that hard to figure out. It was no secret he felt responsible for the marriage collapsing, and the thought had crossed his mind that if he hadn't taken the CIT spot, had been working with Jenny that night, then the whole thing might have turned out different. Not that he questioned his partner's abilities—he wouldn't be paired up with her if he did—but as partners, familiar with each other's abilities and policing style, they may have handled the situation another way. Or Jack would have been the shooter. Or they may have gone for coffee and missed the whole damn thing.

So, the guilt theme in the dream he understood. But the gun? That didn't make sense.

"Does it really matter?" Jack asked his bed mates, but neither of them answered. "Didn't think so."

But if it was of no consequence, then why had Jack, just as Karen pulled the trigger, felt so relieved?

Desmond Drummond was a fucked-up product of a fucked-up society. His mother had been a parent in the biological sense only. A crack whore quickly nearing the end of a downward tumble—twenty bucks got you access to any orifice in her wasted, skanky body—she squirted Desmond out in the bathroom of one of the more squalid bars in 51 Division, leaving him like another piece of shit lying in the puddles of urine and cigarette butts.

But even at a few minutes of age, little Desmond was a fighter. His outraged cries finally caught the attention of a bar patron who still had enough brain cells not yet drowned in alcohol to call 911. Desmond was rushed to the hospital where, despite being weeks premature and fed in utero a steady diet of crack and alcohol, he survived. He was never reunited with his mother, although she was located. Police found her in a crack house a short stumble from the bar where she had so unceremoniously dumped her son. Whether she had died from blood loss, an overdose or a combination of the two, no one really cared about another dead crack whore. Except maybe for the cops stuck doing overtime for the report.

Once Desmond was healthy enough—he grew like a proverbial weed; food that wasn't cocaine or alcohol really agreed with him—he entered the adoption circuit, but the demand for black crack babies just wasn't there. So he grew up in the system, floating from foster home to foster home. His surname, Drummond, was the only thing his mother left him, and he never learned who named him Desmond. Tracking down his father was just not possible; he could have been any guy with a twenty and a hard-on.

Desmond's childhood, like the pregnancy that had birthed him, was short-lived. When other children his age were learning their ABCs and taking naps in kindergarten, Desmond was having an important life lesson beaten into him: no one cared for him, no one would help him, he was alone. Whether at the fists of foster parents, foster siblings or complete strangers, it was a lesson driven into him so frequently that when a person or family did show him kindness he shunned it. He'd fallen for that trick before.

Despite his runty size when he slapped down onto that cold tile floor, Desmond grew fast, and he grew big, and he learned that a lot of what life offered—most, actually—was available for the taking if you were willing to go over or through anyone in your way. And Desmond was willing. By the time he dropped out of the eighth grade, he already was well known to the coppers of 51 Division for his penchant for violence and was regarded as a potential candidate for a future police shooting. If one of his fellow criminals didn't snuff him first, that was.

But here he was, eight years after relieving the public school system of the onus of his education, still alive and prospering. He made a very comfortable living and was well respected, or simply feared, amongst the criminal element in 51 Division, and more specifically, in the St. Jamestown area, his preferred stomping grounds. Desmond was a true 51 thug; born on the division's crack-infested streets, he rarely strayed beyond its borders. He occasionally went west of Jarvis Street, sometimes to catch a movie, mostly for his court appearances. Like many predators, he was very territorial.

And like a lifelong hunter, he had his favourite prey: other criminals. He was associated with various gangs in the area, and was frequently hired on to settle disputes with independents—crack dealers who thought they could undercut the organizations that controlled the drug trade in the division's north end—or other gangs. Usually the Philippino and Sri Lankan groups. Basically, Desmond was a mercenary, and would have most likely agreed with, even approved of, the description if he had known what a mercenary was.

If the contract work was a little slow, or if a particularly plump victim crossed his path, Desmond was not above taking what he wanted from regular people. They were usually easier, much easier, to handle than some gangbanger who might be carrying a blade or gun, but they also had a tendency to call the police. And if at all possible, Desmond liked to keep distant from the cops and their annoying habit of putting people in jail.

Which was why he was sitting at home on a Tuesday night—now early Wednesday morning. Two weeks ago, Desmond had helped himself to a tasty car stereo with the intent of making a few bucks with a quick sale, when the owner had come out of his house to confront him. Stupid bitch. Desmond had laid the boots to the man, but had also left his prints all over the car. Desmond knew that the cops didn't dust cars for fingerprints over a quick smash and grab, but they certainly did when the owner of the grabbed merchandise ended up in ICU.

So here he was, being the good boy, obeying his bail conditions while his lawyer went about "finding" witnesses who saw the car's owner attack Desmond with a baseball bat. He was sitting on his couch—the cushions and springs so worn his ass was nearly on the floor—watching some porn, well on his way to finishing off a twelve pack of Coors, when someone knocked on his door. On the big screen TV, a blonde bitch with big titties and a fucking hot Chink were getting nasty with each other, so whoever was out there could fucking freeze for all he cared.

"Mother*fucker*," he swore as the unseen caller rapped on the door again. Keeping one eye on the ladies—his remote's pause button was all fucked up—he snaked his hand down behind the cushions to grab his Taurus. A good little handgun, kind of like the cops' Glock, and Desmond's prize possession. His lawyer had begged him to ditch the firearm, at least until the charges were dealt with, but no way was Desmond going to give up the gun. He'd paid way too much for it to dump it, and being in the line of work he was, having a gun was just good business sense.

He flattened himself against the wall between the door and the front window. "What the fuck do you want?" he barked.

"Gerald sent me," a timid voice said through the door. "Your lawyer. He said we need to get our stories right."

Desmond grinned. That lawyer was one fucking sneaky son of a bitch. Send a "witness" around at a time when the cops aren't likely to be watching Desmond's place. Keeping the Taurus in hand—his lawyer may be sneaky, but Desmond was careful—he opened the door.

Some poor sucker was standing on the front step looking like a fucking drowned rat. The man's eyes flickered to the gun, then back to Desmond, and he had to look up; he was a fucking runt.

"Gerald said we should talk," the runt nervously said as Desmond loomed over him.

"Get the fuck inside before someone sees you, fuck wad," Desmond snarled. He shut the door behind the runt and went to turn off the TV. He'd pick up with the ladies later. "And don't get any fucking water on my couch, or I'll—"

Something smashed into Desmond's head, and his world exploded in darkness.

Desmond Drummond lived in the basement apartment of a rundown townhouse, his front door facing the street. The window was heavily draped, only a hint of light at the edges letting Ghost know someone was home. The units surrounding Drummond's were dark, lost in wet shadow.

Ghost plodded past the townhouses, his pace slow, defeated. Just a poor sap caught in the slushy rain on his way home with too far to go to bother running. He had his dark toque tugged low and the collar of his army jacket—a khaki green so old and dirty it was almost black—wrapped around the lower half of his face. Just another faceless, unimportant shadow in the rain.

He scanned the street, not expecting to find anyone; hours before dawn was the deepest fragment of night, a time Ghost had put to good use in the war.

He doubled back and walked openly to the front door. Keeping hunched against the rain, he knocked on the scarred wood. He could hear a TV and see the flickering light at the edge of the covered window. He knocked again. A muffled "Mother*fucker*," told him he had finally gotten Drummond's attention.

He tracked Drummond as he moved across the room—his source had told him the enforcer was a big bastard, and he certainly sounded heavy—then positioned himself next to the door. Like a bit of brick and wood would have saved him if Ghost had brought sufficient firepower. Unfortunately for Drummond, Ghost's plans for him were much more intimate.

The muscle for hire opened the door after Ghost gave him his spiel about being sent by his lawyer. The right keys—or words—could open any lock. Ghost acted suitably cowed and intimidated by Drummond's size and gun, and the fool invited him into his apartment. Drummond may have been a wolf, but he was one monumentally stupid wolf. Ghost's hands slipped free of his pockets, twin brass knuckles wrapped comfortably over black latex gloves.

"And don't get any fucking water on my couch," Drummond was warning him, "or I'll—"

Drummond may have been a fool, and his instincts dull, but something warned him as Ghost stepped up behind him, and Drummond twisted at the last instant. The punch that should have caught him on the ear and dropped him cracked off the back of his skull. Instead of falling to the floor, the big man stumbled forward, one hand instinctively covering his head, the other reaching for the gun tucked into his pants.

Ghost never gave him the chance to draw the gun. He struck Drummond a savage blow to the liver, the metal in Ghost's hand focusing the devastating impact, and the enforcer went to his knees, his hands wrapped protectively around his side, his gun momentarily forgotten. Ghost wasn't about to give him time to remember. He looped a punch into the side of Drummond's face, the shock of steel on bone jarring Ghost's arm, as the cheek shattered. Drummond fell back onto his coffee table, the rickety wood collapsing beneath him.

Ghost straddled the big man and snapped one, two, three fast punches into his face. Skin split, bone broke, blood flew. Drummond was barely conscious, and Ghost casually plucked the big man's gun free, slipping it into his own pocket. It was always useful to have a gun with someone else's prints on it; you never knew when it could come in handy.

Ghost gently slapped Drummond's face, staying clear of the deformed sagging jaw—X-rays would later reveal the jawbone was broken in five separate places—until his eyes came as close to focusing as Ghost figured they could.

"Don't worry, big man, I'm not here to kill you," Ghost assured him. "Just to teach you a lesson. You want to tune up assholes, go right ahead. You hurt another civvie, I'll come back and kill you. Do you understand, ass-wipe?"

"Who the fuck are you?" Drummond mumbled with a mouthful of blood and a broken jaw.

"I said, do you understand?" Ghost punctuated the question by driving his steel-shod knuckles straight into Drummond's collarbone. The enforcer's scream drowned out the snap of the bone.

Ghost slapped a hand across Drummond's mouth, the metal grip of the knuckles knocking out a tooth. He squeezed, smiling as he felt the broken pieces of the jawbone grinding beneath his hand. Drummond thrashed weakly under him, but Ghost kept baring down until the man's pain-filled eyes found his again.

"Do you understand?" Ghost repeated once he was sure he had Drummond's attention. The man nodded, a mere shifting of his head that brought tears to his eyes. "Good. Then we're done here."

Ghost straightened up, then hit Drummond one more time, levering all of his weight into the punch and shattering what was left of Drummond's jaw and cheek.

Ghost left the townhouse and faded into the rain-swept darkness. Drummond's neighbours, awakened by his scream, waited hesitantly in their rooms. Ten minutes passed before they felt safe to assume that whoever had caused the terrible noise in the downstairs unit had left. Only then did they call 911.

"…following up several leads at this time."

Can the bullshit. Let's get on with the good stuff. Millie shifted impatiently in her seat. The news conference was dull and dry, as was the woman giving it. Detective Sergeant Gregory, as she had introduced herself, wore a somber business suit that matched her personality perfectly, and for the last fifteen minutes she had reiterated information everyone already knew.

51 station had been burned and shot up in a brazen attack last night, but that wasn't the big news. Two homicides had occurred in Regent Park shortly after the assault on the cop shop. One tragic, the other extremely interesting. First, Frederick Franklin was shot to death, execution style, in a building stairwell. Moments later, Philip Robertson was also shot and killed, supposedly by Franklin's murderer to eliminate him as a witness. Enlarged photos of the two victims framed the detective. Franklin's was the typical static, face-on portrait of a police mug shot. The other, in contrast, was a candid picture of an elderly gentleman holding a small dog on his lap. The black face was heavily lined with age, but Robertson was smiling, and the dog was

looking up at him with the complete, loving devotion only dogs were capable of. The detective had mentioned that Robertson was walking the dog at the time of his death. Millie wondered what happened to the dog.

Millie also found it highly suspicious that the only non-police witness to Tyrone Johnson's murder—she could think of it no other way, especially now, with the fresh information she had—was killed before the investigation had barely begun.

"That is all I have for you now, ladies and gentlemen. We will keep you as updated on the case as possible." Detective Sergeant Gregory stepped away from the podium, obviously not taking any questions. Millie was going to have none of that.

"Detective!" she called, jumping to her feet. "Is it true that—"

"I'm not taking any questions at this time," Gregory responded over her shoulder, not bothering to slow her steps.

"Is it true," Millie bulled on, "that the shell casings found at both murder scenes are forty caliber, the same caliber and manufacture as the ammunition issued to Toronto police officers?"

It was a question the Homicide detective could not ignore in the expectant hush that fell over the room. She studied Millie for a moment, then asked, "And you are?"

Millie was very aware of how quiet the room had suddenly become, as if everyone present was holding their breath, and she knew she was the focus of that expectant hush. "Millie Templeton," she declared. "Of the *Citizen*."

There were a few muffled snickers and murmurs of derision at the mention of the once respected paper, and even Gregory seemed to relax a bit. Perhaps she considered information associated to such an ill-reputed paper not worthy of apprehension.

The detective smiled pleasantly, the first time since the conference began, and dismissed Millie's claim. "I cannot comment on that at this time, but I can assure you it is a common brand of ammunition and readily available."

"But doesn't it seem unusual for such high-quality ammunition to be used in a simple drug-related robbery?" That Franklin had been killed in a crack rip-off was the theory Gregory had presented to the press. Any supposed connection to any other shootings was pure coincidence. *Pure bullshit.*

"That's all I have today." Gregory gave Millie one final scrutinizing glance, leaving Millie feeling like she had just been examined down to her panties in that brief look, and left the room.

"Isn't it the same ammunition found at the sight of the car bombing?" Millie called after the detective's back, to no avail.

The members of the media packed up their cameras, recorders and notebooks and began filing out of the room. Some tried to pump Millie for more information, but if the Homicide Squad wouldn't let her confront them with it, then she was keeping it to herself. For now.

That's fine, bitch. No answer is just as good as any answer. Millie tossed her pad and recorder into her oversized purse as she began to mentally compose her next article. *Detective Gregory—no, Detective Sergeant Gregory, whatever the hell that means—refused to confirm or deny that the ammunition found at the double murder scene and the firebombing of the police car was standard—maybe issued?—police ammunition.*

"Miss Templeton, we need to speak for a few minutes." The Homicide detective cornered Millie before she could exit the room. The detective did not look happy.

Millie gave the other woman a friendly smile. "I thought you weren't taking any questions, Detective."

"I need to know how you came by the information about the shell casings. That wasn't released to the media."

"A good reporter is a lot like a detective, wouldn't you say? Now, if you'll excuse me, I have a story to write." Millie smiled pleasantly, stepping around the woman, but the detective blocked her way.

"You need to tell me who gave you that information."

"I don't *need* to tell you anything," Millie retorted, a little shaken by the woman's stony demeanor but refusing to show it. Once more, she tried to push past.

Gregory was not a big woman, but when her arm shot out, slapping her hand against the wall, Millie thought she could feel the impact vibrate through her feet. Uneasy, she quickly looked around. There were still a few media stragglers in the room, and they were all eying the unusual confrontation with great interest, but Millie also noted two large men in black suits—Gregory's henchmen, no doubt—casually standing guard about ten feet away, effectively isolating the two women in the corner.

Gregory smiled, a stretching of thin lips. The detective wore no lipstick. "I see you have a grasp of the situation now. Who gave you that information?" When Millie hesitated, Gregory leaned in close. "I can arrest you for obstruction. I'll get a warrant and seize your phone, your computer, your notes. Anything pertaining to this investigation, and you'll be left out in the cold, watching as others run with your story."

Millie suddenly was angry. How dare this bully bitch threaten to take away her story? She'd worked too hard, sacrificed too much to escape her former life and slogged through too much shit at the *Citizen* before catching a break. This story was her ticket to a bigger paper, a bigger paycheque and a better life. There was no way she was going to let this cop take that away from her. Millie's temper was up, and as everyone in Thunder Bay knew, when Millie got mad, her anger was ice cold.

Millie smiled, and this time there was nothing pleasant about it. "Drop the bitchy act, Gregory. If you could arrest me, you would have done it by now. The way I see it, I have something you want, and that puts me in the driver's seat. Now, do *you* grasp the situation?" Millie crossed her arms confidently. "You know what they say: you can catch more flies with honey than with vinegar."

"And the most with bullshit," Gregory countered. "One of us is bluffing, Templeton. Do you really want to find out if it's me?"

Millie paused, considering the detective's words. "What if we could come to a mutually beneficial agreement?"

"An exchange of information?"

Millie kept a poker face, but inward she was grinning triumphantly; Gregory's granite façade had just cracked. "Precisely."

It was the detective's turn to ponder her options. "Very well. Give me the name of your source and I'll tell you what I can."

"I may be new to town, detective, but I'm not new to the business." Millie dug out her notepad; she doubted Gregory would consent to going on tape. "Why don't I start? Let's call it a sign of good faith on your part."

Gregory crossed her arms, fixing Millie with a cold stare. "Don't press your luck, Templeton."

"Point taken," Millie conceded. "Were the bullets used at the murders and the car bombing police issue?"

Gregory sighed, then answered. "It was forty caliber, the same as we use, but—" the detective held up a cautionary finger "—that doesn't mean it was police-issued ammunition, or that the gun that fired the bullets belonged to a police officer. My turn. Who gave you that information?"

"I don't know," Millie said reluctantly, but quickly added when she saw Gregory's eyes tighten. "He didn't give his name. He called the paper last night, looking for me. I wasn't there, and they put him through to my cell."

"I need his phone number." Gregory held out her hand for Millie's phone.

"I have it," Millie admitted, unconsciously pulling her purse to herself. "But it's not your turn. Why is he so important to you?"

"He has knowledge of the crime scenes that was not released to the general public. That places him at the scene. Obviously." The look in the Homicide detective's eyes made it clear that she thought Millie should have figured that out on her own. "The number."

"That's a pretty big request, detective. I think I deserve something extra for that piece of information." Millie folded her arms over her purse. "I know, I know. You can arrest me and get a warrant."

"Actually," Gregory said, almost snarling, "I could arrest you and seize the phone without a warrant."

A flutter of uncertainty danced across Millie's new confidence. She knew she was fast approaching the detective's limit, if she wasn't already there. But Millie couldn't—wouldn't—stop now.

"It won't do you any good. My phone is locked. You wouldn't be able to get the number, and you wouldn't be able to hold me long enough for an IT guy to open it." *I hope.*

"True, you would be released on charges," Gregory acknowledged. "But your phone would stay here as evidence."

Crap. "Then I guess we're at an impasse."

"Not really." Gregory motioned to one of her henchmen. "I'll get what I want. It'll just take a bit of time."

"Okay, I'll give it to you," Millie hurriedly said. "I just want a promise in return."

Gregory held up a hand, stalling her hulking backup. "I'm listening."

"When you arrest this guy, I get first dibs on the story." When Gregory didn't immediately answer, Millie tried another angle. "I may be new, detective, but I plan on being around a long time. I can either be your friend, or be a major pain in your ass."

Gregory snorted, and Millie figured it was the detective's version of laughter. "The first thing rookie reporters learn about me is that I don't take kindly to being threatened. And one more ass pain won't amount to much." She waved her henchman away. "If this number leads to an arrest in the homicides, you get advance notice."

Beaming inside, Millie keyed her phone and looked for the number. As she scrolled though her recent calls, she mused aloud, "If he's involved, why would he want to give away that information?" She recited the number to Gregory, who jotted it down. "You think he's the murderer, don't you?" Millie gasped. "But that doesn't make any sense. Why would he give you a lead like that?"

Gregory tucked her memo book away. "When we find him, I'll ask him."

Shouldn't have had those beers before bed, Ghost chided himself as he padded to the bathroom after only a couple of hours of sleep. With his bladder contentedly emptied, he paused by the mirror to study his reflection, searching for any bruises or swelling. He didn't think Drummond had tagged him at all, but it was hard to tell in the midst of a fight; jacked on adrenalin, punches could land unnoticed.

His face was unblemished. He ran a hand over his hair, woven into tight rows. *Almost time to shave them off, maybe grow a goatee.* Yeah, once he was done here it would be time to change his appearance, disappear for a while.

Shouldn't be much longer.

The division was about to explode, ripe with anger on both sides. Crawling back into bed, he smiled. A good night's work. Drummond wouldn't be up to any shit for quite some time, if ever again. That ass-wipe had escaped punishment for far too long. And killing Thriller had added another log to the fire. If that wasn't damning enough, once that reporter wrote about the ammunition used... Well, people could draw whatever conclusions they wanted to.

It was too bad about the old man. But every war had its share of casualties. And it was about time those complacent cops learned what it was like to be in a war, and once the smoke cleared and the blood dried, only the strong ones would be left, the weaklings having fled to safer parts of the city. And with both sides of his homemade conflict—cops and the Park—busy at each other's throats, he was free to operate, safely hidden behind the chaos he had so carefully nurtured. After all, what were a few beatings or killings among the division's criminal element when the police were suspected of murder and the citizens were taking the law into their own hands?

Not only did he have Lyron and his crew ready to do anything he suggested, the rest of the Park was getting in on the action. Any cop in the Park was a moving target for rocks, garbage and the occasional gunshot. Ghost wondered if that had been Lyron acting on his own. No problem if it had been him, as long as he didn't get his ass arrested ahead of time. And it was only a matter of time before Lyron's prints on the shell casings were identified. Either at the station bombing or at the double homicide.

Once Lyron had admitted to being fingerprinted by the police it had been a simple task to make sure his prints were all over the ammunition. The eager fool was so careful to wear his balaclava and gloves, but had completely forgotten the bullets Ghost had let him handle back at the beginning of this little crusade.

With his fall guy in place, all Ghost had to do was walk away. And if Lyron talked? Or cried hysterically when he clued in he had been set up? What could he say? That he wasn't the brains behind the attacks. No, it wasn't him, it was some mystery man named Ghost.

"Yeah, good luck with that, kid," Ghost mumbled as he snuggled into his pillow.

Mason might realize the kid was telling the truth, might know who Ghost really was. If he did, it would only serve

Ghost's purpose, because there was no way Mason would let that story gain any credibility.

Fucking Mason. Turned out to be a coward like all the rest of them. Cut and ran when things got messy. Wouldn't even answer a phone call.

Well, things were going to get a lot messier and bloodier long before they got better. Ghost would see to it.

The dogs were barking. Jack was hauled out of a sluggish slumber by Justice's piercing yaps and a staccato coughing yip. The uproar at the front door, even with the distance of the stairs and hallway, sliced painfully into Jack's muddled brain.

"Justice! Enough!"

The raucous barking trailed off, and cursing a dog who saw anyone going past his house as a threat that needed to be warned off, Jack drew the covers over his head against the offending light that sneaked around the thick night blinds. His head throbbed with the echoes of the dogs' morning serenade, and he prayed he could recapture the sleep—as poor and meager as it had been—that Justice and Bear had set free. Just as Jack felt himself slipping mercifully away from consciousness, a ferocious pounding on the front door triggered yet another torrent from the hell hounds.

"Go away," Jack mumbled, but after only a moment's pause the hammering resumed. "Fuck me," he groaned, and literally rolled out of bed; he knew his skull would not take to standing very well. Kneeling with a steadying arm on the mattress, he raised his head to view the clock.

Through squinted eyes he made out 11:07.

"Oh, fuck me," he repeated weakly, and slowly pushed himself to his feet. Dragging on sweatpants and a T-shirt, he vowed never to mix migraine medication with cider again.

Awake, he was fully aware of, and susceptible to, the insistent knocking—it sounded like whoever was out there was trying to kick a hole through the door—and frenzied barking. Both of which were drilling holes into his skull.

"Whoever the fuck you are," he swore, "someone had better be dying, or you will be soon."

Justice was at the door, giving the unseen knocker canine hell. Bear was just as unwavering in the cause, but from the safety of the bottom of the stairs. The little dog hushed when Jack stooped—slowly and very, very carefully—to lay a calming hand on him. Justice's barks lulled to a low growl as Jack gently kneed him away from the door. Jack had no idea what the shepherd would do if someone was stupid enough to ignore the warning sounds and break in. He had known dogs who could sound as dangerous as Cujo run and hide at the first glimpse of a stranger. Remembering the sight of fangs mere inches from Joey Horner's face, Jack doubted Justice was the type to flee.

"All right, I'm here," he called as wood shuddered beneath someone's foot. "Stop kicking the fucking door."

"Where the hell have you been?" Jenny yelled at him as soon as she saw his face. Her eyes were red from crying, and she was on his front porch trembling, but not from the cold. She stormed into the house, and before he could ask her why she was here banging insanely on his door, she hauled off and slugged him in the jaw.

The punch hurt—his partner knew how to throw a fist—but it was a feeble slap to the explosion that tore through his head. Jack lost his vision in a blinding burst of silent whiteness, and staggered back. His feet tangled and he fell, landing hard on his ass which rocketed unbelievable agony straight up his spine to erupt behind his eyes. Crying out, his hands flew to his head as if he feared the bones of his cranium would blow apart.

Bear began a rapid-fire barking from somewhere behind Jack, each sharp utterance a red-hot icicle jabbing into Jack's brain, but it was Justice's deep growl that scared Jack. Not since the night he had rescued the shepherd from his demented owner had Jack heard such a dangerous and savage sound from Justice. The only reason the dog wasn't going after Jenny was probably because he was confused; he knew Jenny as a friend, or pack member in dog-speak, but Jack was suddenly afraid of what would happen if his partner moved.

He groped blindly for Justice as he warned Jenny not to move. His hand found fur, and Jack pulled the dog to him, reassuring him everything was good: "Jenny had a good reason to hit me. I just don't know what it is," he amended.

Jenny clarified it for him. "Why didn't you answer your phone? I've been calling all morning." Judging from her voice, she had calmed considerably, and thankfully she knew dogs well enough to keep her distance.

"My phone?" he asked, his ability to reason still jumbled by the fireworks going off inside his skull. "It died last night," he managed, the pain gradually receding. "I guess I forgot to charge it when I got home."

He settled Justice and got to his feet. The room swam alarmingly, and Jack almost fell again, but he found a wall and steadied himself. He opened his eyes and managed to focus on Jenny. She was crying, deepening Jack's confusion.

"Jenny, what—"

"I thought you were dead!" she keened, and threw herself into Jack's arms. Puzzled, he held her. Justice watched, his head cocked questioningly.

Me too, buddy. Me too.

"When I heard about the attack on the station I called you, but your phone kept going to voice mail. I called the station, but no one there knew where you were, if you were still working, or if you'd gone home, or…or…"

Jack reached across the corner of the kitchen table and took Jenny's hand. "It's okay, Jenny. Nothing happened to me."

"I thought you were dead," she sniffed, clutching his hand. "The news said an officer had been taken to the hospital, and when I couldn't get hold of you…It scared me. I had to know if you were okay." She took a shaky sip of tea and grimaced. "You put too much honey in it."

"There's no such thing," he joked, but offered to make her a fresh mug.

As Jack was filling the kettle, Jenny examined the tea mugs. "Where did you get these?" The mugs were made from lacquered, hollowed-out tree branches, and came complete with metal handles and bark, knots and all.

"They were a Christmas gift from Manny last year. He gave me a set of four. Karen thought they were disgusting, but I think they're kind of cool." He laughed dryly. "In fact, I'm surprised she didn't take them, just to piss me off. She took most of the kitchen's contents, but she left me the mugs and the table. Guess she didn't deem them worthy to take with her."

Jack set a steaming mug in front of her with the honey and a spoon. "Flavour to your liking." He sat and picked up her first cup. "Waste not, want not, and all that," he quipped. "The caffeine's making my head feel better."

"Sorry I woke you. If I'd known you had a migraine…"

"If you'd known I had a migraine, then you would have known I was alive and you wouldn't have tried to kick my door in."

"I guess," she said, returning his smile. "But still, I'm sorry."

"To partners who care for one another," he toasted, and they clunked mugs.

She watched Jack as he drank his tea, watched as the black T-shirt he was wearing pulled across his chest and shoulders.

He caught her looking and quickly checked his shirt. "Did I spill?"

"No," she said slowly. "I guess I'm just used to seeing you with your vest on. I never realized how big you are."

Puzzled, Jack said, "Thanks. I think."

"I mean I figured you looked that big because of the vest," she explained, giving him her patented look of condescending impatience. "Actually, when did you get all these?" Her fingers traced his forearm and the worm-like veins.

He shrugged. "I've been working out pretty hard since Karen left. Nothing else to do."

It was her turn to be puzzled. Jack seemed uncomfortable talking about his body, or maybe it was her touch. After all, the poor guy was in the middle of a nasty divorce that he hadn't initiated. She placed her hands on her mug, toying with the rough bark. It was a cool mug, in a weird way.

"It was really great of you to bring Bear home," she told him, gazing at the dogs curled up together on the kitchen floor. Jack had given her the heartbreaking news about Phil after she had calmed down.

"I couldn't let him go to the pound," he explained. "I wouldn't have been able to live with myself."

"I know the feeling," she said quietly, almost to herself.

He took her hand again—he seemed okay touching her—and gently scolded her. "Don't, Jenny. You had no choice. You thought he had a gun."

She nodded, not quite trusting herself to speak. "I know," she managed after a moment. "I keep telling myself that, but... Maybe I should have done something different. Maybe I should have waited, just another second or two."

"Enough!" Jack's hand slapped down on the table, startling Jenny and the dogs. "If you'd waited and he did have a gun, you'd be dead. You did nothing wrong."

"Then why does it feel like I did?"

"Because you're a decent person, that's why. If you were like the assholes we arrest, you wouldn't care. But you do care, and that's what makes you better than them."

She tried to smile and thought she succeeded. She freed her hand and folded both of them in her lap. She knew Jack wasn't going to like what she had to say, but if she couldn't tell him, who could she confide in?

"I've been thinking..." She took a deep breath and tried again. "I think I might not be cut out to be a cop." There, it was said, the hateful, upsetting concept that had been burrowing into her brain day and night, plaguing her waking moments and haunting her fretful dreams.

"That's your conscience, all the crap in the media, and you second-guessing yourself. Especially now that he died. You're a good cop and a good person. Don't damn yourself for—"

"For a mistake?" she finished for him. "Jack, I fucked up, and someone died. I shot him."

"And you tried to save his life," Jack reminded her. "You didn't stand there doing a victory dance or firing off rounds into the air. Once the danger was past you tried to help him."

"But there was no danger, Jack."

Jack sat back in his chair. "Then why did you shoot him?" he asked coldly.

Shocked by the sudden ice in his voice, she shot back, "Because I thought he had a gun."

"Exactly." Jack leaned in. "You thought he had a gun. No, you didn't *know*, but the only time we know they have a gun is when it's pointing at us. You didn't shoot right away. *He* forced you to. *He* didn't obey your commands. *He* gave you no option." Jack took her by the shoulders. "It…is…not…your…fault."

"I just feel so bad," she cried, and Jack held her as the stress, the self-imposed guilt, all the anxiety from the week burst through her defences. He held her, and she clutched at him, her arms wrapped around him, letting all the shit drain out of her and drawing on his strength, his solidness.

In time, the crying stopped. She felt drained, empty and utterly exhausted, yet better than she had in days. She pulled away—feeling a pang of loss as his arms slipped away—and wiped her cheeks with the heel of her hand.

"Sorry, Jack, I—"

"Sorry, nothing. You needed that."

"Yeah, I guess I did. Better here than in my SIU interview, right?"

He groaned theatrically. "Yeah, definitely better here."

She checked her watch. "Listen, Jack, I should go."

"No problem," he assured her, and walked her to the door. In the front hall, she hugged him once more.

"Thanks, partner." And she kissed him. She knew she shouldn't, knew it was wrong, but she kissed him anyway, and he kissed her back. His arms pulled her close, and she could feel him responding beneath the sweatpants, and suddenly she wanted nothing more than to have him carry her upstairs and love her.

In the bed he shared with his wife not so long ago.

She broke the kiss and pushed herself away, her hands on his chest. "I'm sorry. We shouldn't. There's Karen."

He nodded reluctantly. "And Brian."

"And Brian," she agreed. "And all of…" She waved a hand to encompass too much for words.

But he understood. "Yeah."

She touched his cheek, felt the stubble under her fingers as easily as the trembling in his hands resting on her hips. "Maybe some day?"

"Maybe some day," he acceded, and she heard her sadness and desire echoed in his words.

She left while she was still able to.

Jack stared at himself in the mirror. He knew he and Jenny had narrowly avoided something that could have torn apart their partnership, and worse, destroyed their friendship. She was a beautiful woman in every way, and she deserved better than him. That kiss had been an act of…

"Circumstances," he told the Jack in the mirror. Her grief and guilt, his familiarity with death, and the natural closeness between police partners had almost led to a mistake. One they both would have regretted come the new day.

"And besides," he told himself as he flexed his forearm, snaking the veins beneath the skin. "I don't think she'd like what I've become."

But it was something he needed, a way to cope with an ever growing sense of hopelessness and despair. It made him feel alive when nothing else did. It gave him the strength to make it through another day.

He cracked the top of another vial of steroids and readied the needle.

Paul Townsend pulled his leather jacket tighter. He had a thick fleece top on under the lined jacket, but the cold was still managing to seep inside. He should have worn his parka.

"Warm weather, my ass," he grumbled. People could talk about how it felt more like spring than winter, but just because the temperature wasn't below the freezing mark didn't mean it wasn't cold. Paul didn't do winter well. "Tell me again why I bloody well live here?" he asked himself.

He didn't have an answer.

Picturing his parka, all snug and warm, hanging in his locker, Paul cut across the parking lot. He was at the station early today after catching only a few hours of sleep. Everyone had done overtime last night, either at the homicide scenes or guarding the station. He glanced back at the station. The scorch marks and boarded-up windows gave the old building a haunted, broken look, but if anyone thought the appearance reflected the morale inside they would be seriously mistaken. The firebombing of the scout car was one thing, the attack on the station was personal, and the cops wanted someone to pay.

Which was why he was at work earlier than he had to be, and freezing his ass off. He had to talk to someone, and where he had to go a parka just wouldn't cut it. He didn't want to appear weak in any way. So he headed for Regent Park, a big man with a big burden on his conscience.

Paul had been a cop for six years, all of it spent at 51. It certainly wouldn't have been his first choice of divisions, or his last, but rookies had no say in where they were assigned, and after fighting all those years to escape the Park, he found himself right back home.

As one of the few black officers at 51, Paul knew he stood out, among both his colleagues and the black community. Standing six-four and looking like a competitive bodybuilder certainly didn't help him to blend in either. He knew there were some cops, stubborn in their racist views, who thought the only thing that should be black about the police service was the uniform, and there were those in the community who saw him as a traitor to his own people.

But his aunt had taught him there was no pleasing everyone, so he needn't bother trying. Cops were human, and by no means held a monopoly on racism. He would have run into that blind hatred regardless of the occupation he had chosen. And he had learned, just like every cop, that racism wasn't just about the colour of your skin. How many people hated him just because of the uniform he wore?

And just like every cop, every rookie, he had to prove himself. Which he had done. People, uniformed and not, learned that big muscles did not equal a small IQ, and he had quickly gained a reputation for a level head and fairness in his approach to police work. Unfortunately, he had also earned himself the nickname Black Hulk.

Tear one door off a car, and you get labeled for life.

Paul was the cop the criminals didn't want to see angry. He stood on Dundas Street, nervous to step into Regent Park, nervous to go home.

He entered the Park practically every day he was working, but that was different, that was work, where he was known as Officer Townsend. Paul Reynolds was a lifetime ago. A life he had left at fifteen, and never revealed to anyone on the job, not even his partner Sue.

Paul had grown up in Regent Park, the only child of a drunken, abusive father and a cowardly mother. When Paul was seven, his mother took off, fleeing her husband and his alcohol-fuelled rages. It was the only time she defied him, and she left Paul behind to suffer the consequences.

Paul's father blamed his son for his wife leaving, for abandoning him with a snot-nosed bastard. It was Paul's fault his father drank, it was because of Paul that his dad couldn't hold down a job, every shitty thing that happened to his miserable, crummy life he laid at Paul's feet. Paul could not remember a day without bruises. New ones always appeared before old ones faded. The child Paul had been went to the hospital several times for "trips" and "falls."

Only as Christmas approached did the beatings stop, and not out of any drunken notion or misconception of fatherly love. No. Paul had to look good, unblemished, for the family dinner. Every year, Paul's aunt—his mother's sister—and her husband had Paul and his dad over for dinner, even after his mother had run. Aunt Teresa and Uncle Bill Townsend were always generous with the gifts—which Paul's dad either exchanged or sold for cash—and were always good for a "loan." And Paul's dad was always good at asking. It was the repaying he was lousy at.

As charitable as his aunt and uncle were, Paul's dad kept them at a distance, limiting the contact to Christmas and perhaps birthdays, if Paul was presentable. Staying sober anymore than once or twice a year was just too formidable a task for him.

So Paul's childhood and early teen years passed beneath the fists of a bitter, defeated man. Paul was beaten for just about anything: coming home late, coming home early, interrupting his father with a bottle or a whore, mouthing off, not speaking up quickly enough when asked, poor grades or detention at school. Paul was ten when he realized the worst beatings he received were when he brought home good grades from school. It was then that Paul understood his father feared him, feared his son bettering him in any way.

Lying on a sprung mattress that passed for his bed, a threadbare blanket his only comfort—the sheets provided by Aunt Teresa sold unopened long ago—Paul silently suffered the results of a beating that would haunt his movements all summer long. He clutched the remains of his report card to his bloodied chest, the report card his father had torn apart, the report card and its column of A's that he had tried to hide from his father. That night, as three cracked ribs tortured his every breath, Paul vowed he would never be his father, would never allow himself to be dragged down.

As he shunned his father, Paul also rejected the temptation of the streets and the promise of easy money. In the gang members and the drug dealers, Paul saw future shadows of his father and a life he refused to live.

On his fifteenth birthday, as his father came at him with his heavy leather belt in hand—as Paul had grown, his father had resorted to using weapons—Paul finally said no. Tall for his age and muscled from the manual jobs he did after school to feed himself, Paul met his father in the middle of the living room. When the fight was done, the elder Reynolds lay truly broken and defeated, and Paul walked out of the apartment and never went back.

Paul walked all that night, a bloodied but proud man, and as a new dawn crested, he knocked on his aunt's door. When she opened the door, he fell unconscious into her arms.

His father never came for him, never called the police crying kidnapping, never sought out a lawyer. On his eighteenth birthday, Paul legally changed his name to Townsend, the name of his true parents, and kicked the dirt of the past off his shoes.

So, here he stood, almost ten years later, out front of 248 Sackville, and he bloody well didn't want to go in.

You got no choice, bud. This whole shit is partly your fault, remember?

How could he forget? God, it wasn't even a week ago. It seemed so much longer than that, and if it felt that way for him, what was Jenny going through?

She shot Tyrone, but I pointed her in his direction.

Friday, early in the shift—the sun hadn't quite set—he and Sue had responded to a call in the Park. Nothing major, just to chase some dealers off. But while they were cruising the Park, one of Paul's informants had surreptitiously flagged him down and had provided a little tidbit of information. Most informants waited until they were in trouble before they gave up any news or they waited for their handler to contact them. This snitch always liked to pay in advance. That way he was sure the information he gave was still fresh. You couldn't very well bargain your way out of an arrest with old info.

The snitch's news had been worthwhile. Or so Paul had thought at the time. There was a guy in the Park who went by the name of Thriller. He had this shit on his face and hands like he was turning white.

"What of him?" Paul had asked.

His snitch bobbed his head like a bird pecking at bread crumbs. "He's strapped, man."

"Strapped?" Paul knew what it meant, but wanted to make sure he was reading this right.

"He's got himself a gun, man. Letting everyone know it, too."

"What's this Thriller wearing?"

"How the fuck should I know, man? I'm just telling you what I heard. 'Sides, you can't miss him with that shit all over his face."

The rest had been easy. A quick computer search of nicknames brought up a name and picture. Paul passed the information and picture to the rest of the shift—he wasn't one to hog the arrests—and the rest, as they say, was fucking history.

I'm sorry, Jenny.

Things were out of hand and that was putting it bloody mildly. The shooting was tragic. Even the graffiti shit could be expected and tolerated until tempers cooled, but then his scout car got torched. Paul didn't think he was targeted purposefully; just the wrong cop responding to a fake domestic call. The attack on the station. And two homicides, one of them a witness who could sink or save Jenny, depending on what he said. The Park was like a guitar string wound too tight. One hard pluck could snap it, and Paul didn't want to think what would happen when that cord broke.

But there was one person who could ease off some of that tension and possibly save some lives. Paul knew she wouldn't talk to Officer Townsend, but maybe, just maybe, she'd listen to Paul Reynolds. He knocked on Devisha Lawrence's door and prayed to God Auntie Dee would speak with him.

The door opened, but the reception was anything but hospitable. "What the fuck do you want?"

Paul eyed the young man standing in the doorway, barring Paul's way into the apartment. Beneath his baby dreads, the man's face was a thundercloud of anger.

"Relax, friend. I'm just here to see Auntie Dee."

"Auntie Dee don't see nobody she don't know," the man—boy, really—sneered. "And I don't know you."

"And you don't look like Auntie Dee." Paul placed a hand on the door and shoved it open. "Auntie Dee? Are you here? It's Paul Reynolds."

A voice came out of the shadows of the apartment. "Little Paul? Is that you? Stand aside, Lyron, and let my Paulie in."

Lyron didn't move. "You sure, Auntie Dee? He looks like a cop to me."

"You behave, Lyron. Now, let my little Paulie in." The voice from the depths of the apartment was tired but still commanding.

Paul gave Lyron a satisfied grin as the smaller man reluctantly moved aside. The apartment was a typical Park one-bedroom, but where so many were filthy and unkempt, Devisha Lawrence's home was immaculate in its cleanliness, cheerful in its colours. But Auntie Dee was neither. Huddled on a large blue couch, she was lost in the folds of a heavy blanket despite the apartment being warm enough for Lyron to be wearing a sleeveless T-shirt. Her grey hair was disheveled, her face creased by deep lines of grief.

Paul, like everyone else growing up in the Park, had considered Tyrone's grandmother as aunt to the community. She was always there with a smile for hurt feelings and a kiss for skinned knees and elbows. She settled fights among children and adults alike, and more than one bully or gangbanger had hung his head before her in shame. She was the soul and spirit of the neighborhood, a constant in a troubled boy's life.

This woman wasn't her.

Paul hadn't seen Auntie Dee in person for years, but had seen her on TV the day after her grandson's shooting. That day her grief had been fresh, a painful mask over her strength, but in the days since, the sorrow had sunk in, become a part of her and stolen her life. The skin of her face hung loose, as if she had a lost a great deal of weight, as if the grief was consuming her from the inside like an insidious cancer. The dancing, merry eyes Paul remembered were listless and unfocused, deep within the sockets.

The TV was on, its artificial light casting an ashen hue over Auntie Dee's skin. A trembling hand lifted the remote and silenced Jerry Springer in mid rant. Auntie Dee's face lit up when Paul entered the room.

"It is you, Paul," she said, holding out her hands.

"Hello, Auntie Dee." Paul gently took her hands and kissed her cheek as he sat beside her. "I'm sorry about Tyrone. He was a good boy."

"Thank you, Paul. He's with God now, rest his soul." She dabbed at her eyes. "Now, how are Teresa and Bill?"

Paul smiled. As frail as she appeared, Auntie Dee's memory was still sharp. "They're good. Dad's retired now and they spend most of their time travelling."

"Good for them." She nodded in approval and patted his hand. "It's nice that you call them your parents. And what about you? Surely, such a fine-looking man as yourself is married."

"I am. We have two beautiful daughters. Twins. Not a year old yet."

"How wonderful. God can be very giving at times. I'm so happy for you, Paul. You deserve happiness after what that man put you through." She paused, her face growing serious. "I heard you became a police officer. Is that true?"

"Son of a bitch!"

"I'll have no such language in my home, young man," Auntie Dee warned Lyron, who was hovering nearby as if he expected Paul to attack the elderly woman.

"Yes, Auntie Dee." Lyron bobbed his head, docile before her admonishment, but when he raised his head, his eyes were hard on Paul.

"It is, Auntie Dee," Paul admitted. "I work here, in 51 Division."

Tyrone's grandmother was quiet as she mulled over

this revelation. "That's good," she decided. "It's good there's someone from here to represent us."

Paul cringed inside, ashamed to confess he'd kept his origins hidden.

"Did you come visiting as my Paulie or a police officer?"

"Both, I guess." Paul stilled the urge to squirm, feeling twelve years old under Auntie Dee's eyes. "I'm sorry to ask this of you—"

"I bet," Lyron scoffed.

"—but with all the tension between the Park and the police, someone could end up getting killed."

"Someone else, you mean." Auntie Dee's words were soft, but they cut like razored steel.

"Yes, sorry."

Lyron stepped up. "Why don't you get out and leave Auntie Dee alone? She don't need you upsetting her." Judging from his stance, Lyron was eager to help Paul out the door.

"Hush," Auntie Dee bid Lyron, then turned back to Paul. "You want me to ask people to calm down and let justice take its course, don't you?"

"Yes, ma'am." Paul laid his hands on hers. "I figure if you ask, people might listen."

Slowly, with care, Auntie Dee eased her hands free of Paul's. "And what about my Tyrone? Will there be justice for him?"

"Not from the cops, there won't be," Lyron declared. "Cops investigating cops. To them it's just another dead nigger. Ain't that right, Mr. Policeman?"

Paul returned the challenging stare. "No, it isn't. And it's not us doing the investigation. It's the Special Investigations Unit. A civilian body, not cops."

Lyron snorted. "No difference."

Paul focused on Auntie Dee; this Lyron wouldn't see sense if he was buried in it. "I know the officer who shot Tyrone. She's a good person, a good cop. She wouldn't have shot unless she felt she had to."

"But she didn't have to," Auntie Dee maintained. "He didn't have a gun. He was a good boy."

"The man he was with was telling people he had a gun." Paul reached for Auntie Dee, needing her to understand. "Maybe—"

"I think you should leave, Paul." Auntie Dee's hands slipped under the blanket. "I can't help you. Not when I have to bury my grandson. Say hello to Teresa and Bill for me."

"I will." Paul stopped by the door. "Goodbye, Auntie Dee."

She didn't answer.

Lyron followed Paul into the hall and shut the door softly behind him, but there was nothing soft about his face once Auntie Dee was safely hidden away.

"You got a lot of balls coming here, putting Auntie Dee through that." Lyron eyed him up and down. "She thinks you being a cop is a good thing. *Representing us.*" His words were mocking, and he sucked his teeth in derision. "You ain't nothing but another asshole with a gun, hiding behind his badge."

"You don't get it, do you? People—more people—could *die* over this."

Lyron laughed. "You seen the signs people been putting up. Ain't gonna be us bleeding. Ain't gonna be us dying." He smiled. "Cops die just like everyone else."

The Major Crime office felt like a tomb with all the shot-out windows boarded up. Mason had just one row of fluorescents on. With all the lights blaring, the room felt like a well-lit tomb.

Mason's phone rang. He stifled an acidic burp before snapping, "Mason." He listened, and suddenly his scowling visage cracked into a joyous smile. "You're certain? Yeah, yeah, sorry. Of course you are." He grabbed a pen. "Go ahead. Yup, got it. Beautiful. I love you guys."

Tank and Kris, Mason's twin second-in-commands, were staring expectantly at him. "We just got lucky, kids," he crowed, waving the sheet of paper triumphantly.

Tank, a huge slab of humanity, smiled back. It wasn't often his boss was visibly happy. "What have you got?"

"That was Ident. They got a hit off a print from one of the shell casings."

"From last night?" Kris wanted to know.

"From last night," Mason confirmed. "We grab him and squeeze him for the rest."

Kris looked doubtful. "A print on a casing says he handled some ammo, but it doesn't mean he was the one to pull the trigger." She eased back in her chair, crossing muscular arms over her equally massive chest.

"Ah, ignore her, boss," Tank encouraged. "She's dieting for a contest and you know how cranky she gets when she's low-carbing."

Kris was a competitive bodybuilder with a physique most men would kill for, and she pointed a shredded arm at her fellow detective constable. "Don't push me, Tanky," she warned. "I'm just stating what a defence lawyer will, come trial."

"Ooh, I love it when you get all nasty. Makes me all warm inside." Tank rubbed his considerable belly. He shared a love of heavy iron with Kris, but unlike her, he was a power lifter who thought the word "diet" should be deleted from the English language.

"Are you two lovebirds finished?" Mason growled.

"You bet, boss." Tank rubbed his hands gleefully. "Does this poor bastard have a name?"

Mason nodded, grinning wickedly. "Dove. Lyron Dove."

"Take a picture and pass them along. I want this guy's face imprinted on your memory." Mason waited until everyone on parade had a copy of Dove's picture before giving them the details. "We got lucky. He was pinched for assault a couple of years ago at a demonstration and his prints were found on a casing out front of the station."

A hostile murmur rippled through the ranks of coppers. The basement parade room was full, not quite standing room only, but more bodies than B platoon had seen in several years. All time off had been cancelled in response to the station firebombing, and the superintendent had tossed the budget out of the window, offering callbacks to anyone who wanted the extra time. Like Lyron had found in the wake of Tyrone's death, there was no shortage of volunteers.

Mason stood at the front of the room, an imposing, inspiring hulk of hostility. "I want him found. Tonight.

If he isn't the brains behind this, he'll lead us to whoever is. We don't have a current address on him, but he's in the Park, I can feel it. He's nearby, and he's laughing at us. And I mean to shut him up."

A hushed "I don't fucking believe it" breathed up from the back of the room.

Mason's stony stare skewered Paul. "What don't you believe, Townsend?"

"I…" Paul hesitated as all eyes turned to him. "I saw him at Auntie Dee's apartment this afternoon."

"You mean Johnson's grandmother? And just what the fucking hell were you doing there?" Mason's stare had gone from stony to curious. Intensely curious.

"I…ah, fuck me." Paul heaved a deep sigh. "I grew up in Regent Park," he admitted to the astonishment of everyone else in the room. "I know her from when I was a kid, and I went to see her hoping she could use her influence to calm everyone down. She's kind of a community leader," he added.

"That's all very touching," Mason snarled, "but what about Dove? What was he doing there? Does he live there?" The rough detective was all but frothing at the mouth.

Paul shrugged. "I don't know. I don't think so. I didn't know he was involved in anything when I was there."

"Okay, we've got a place to start. Tank, find Kris." Mason jabbed a thick finger at Paul. "You're with me. You've just become my newest best friend."

Ghost flipped open his phone. "What?"

The voice at the other end of the connection spoke quickly in hushed tones. Ghost killed the link without another word. He punched a number into the phone's keypad. He never used a phone's memory, memories could be broken into, stolen. And he never used the same phone for long even if it wasn't in his name. Mason had taught him that.

"Where are you?" he asked when the other end picked up. "Get the fuck out of there, right now. Why? If you don't want to end up in jail, you'll do what I fucking tell you and get your ass out of there. Now!"

Ghost shut his phone. If Lyron was smart, he'd be pounding the stairs right now. If he thought he knew better than Ghost, then fuck him. There were plenty more where he came from.

"I don't know where Lyron is. And even if I did, I wouldn't be telling the likes of you." Auntie Dee pulled the blanket tighter about herself and pointedly ignored the police officers in her home.

Paul looked beseechingly at Mason, but the burly detective jerked his head impatiently towards the elderly woman. Resigned to a path he didn't want to walk, Paul knelt in front of Auntie Dee and placed his hands gently on her knees.

"Auntie Dee… Devisha, please listen to me," he implored, hating himself for bringing Mason here, for tormenting this wonderful woman. "We need to find Lyron.

His fingerprints were found on some of the bullets shot at the station last night." Paul could feel Mason tighten up as he revealed that key piece of information, but if he was going to ask Auntie Dee to betray one of her own community, people she had loved and cared for all her long life, then it was going to be for a damn good reason and not just because Paul said please.

Auntie Dee's eyes flickered uncertainly then refocused on the wall behind Paul. "I know Lyron loved Tyrone a great deal, but what he's doing won't bring your grandson back. It will only get more people, most likely himself, hurt. Or worse."

"Like Philip Robertson?" Auntie Dee asked coldly, staring defiantly at the cop kneeling before her.

"Who?" Paul looked from Auntie Dee to Mason.

"The old gentleman on the Oak walkway last night," Mason supplied. Paul could hear the tension, the frustration in the detective's voice. They had apparently missed Lyron Dove by mere minutes.

"I'm not deaf yet, *officer*," Auntie Dee stated, and the *officer* hurt Paul more than he thought it could have. "I hear what people have been saying. It was police bullets that killed poor old Philip and the other young man in the stairwell, the man who was with my Tyrone the night he was shot. The only one who could tell what really happened. And now he's dead. How convenient for you all." Her scathing gaze took in Paul, Mason and the two officers from the MCU.

Paul had no answer for that and knew even trying to argue it would be pointless. "But that's what we're trying to avoid."

"What happened to Philip's little dog? Do any of you know? Do any of you care?" Auntie Dee's words were laced with venom that burned Paul to his soul. "That dog was Philip's best friend, at times his only friend, and you don't know what happened to him. All you care about is protecting your own. Well, that's just what I'm doing. Protecting my own." Her eyes returned to the wall, but her next words were for all of them. "I want you to leave my home now. And never come back."

Paul knew the last was meant for him. He was no longer welcomed in Auntie Dee's home. The door that was open for anyone, regardless of who they were or what they had done, was closed to him forever. The last bit of him that was Paul Reynolds was gone. Officer Townsend rose to his feet.

Mason stopped at the door, turned to Auntie Dee, who was still staring fixedly away from them. "You may have just signed that boy's death warrant, lady." His words were coldly truthful. "We would have taken him to jail, nice and easy. But now I don't have control over who finds him. And some officers are looking for payback."

The detective paused, waiting to see if his words had gotten through to the old woman, but she remained stubbornly mute. He shook his head and let the door swing shut behind him.

Auntie Dee was furious. The police, in her home, demanding she tell them where Lyron was. As if she knew. As if she'd tell them if she did. She told them all she knew—that Lyron had gotten a phone call then run like the proverbial bat out of hell—just because she knew it would vex them something sorely. And it had, especially that big, mean-looking one.

But coiled with the anger was a deep hurt, a hurt from seeing her little Paulie bending his knee before that big boss man and asking her what the boss wanted to know. When Paulie had visited earlier, she'd felt pride picturing him wearing the uniform. Pride and hope. Pride that he had escaped his hellish life and made something of himself. Hope that her community had one of their own wearing that uniform.

But he came back and spat on her pride, shat on her hope.

Well, all that's done now. You be careful Lyron. I'll be saying a prayer for you.

The apartment door swung open; she hadn't bothered to lock it after all that unpleasantness had left. A young black fella—*African Canadian, they call themselves now*—was standing in her doorway, studying her with a cool look. He was wearing a big, old baggy jacket and had those rows on his head with the silly corn name. He tipped his head to someone out in the hall, someone Auntie Dee couldn't see, but she'd be willing to bet all her savings it was that big, mean boss man. The young fella came in and shut the door behind him.

And locked it.

That's when Auntie Dee knew she was in trouble, knew a fear that all those big policemen and that one manly-looking woman couldn't inflict. Her bladder threatened to let go, and she fought not to wet herself.

"I don't know who you are, young man," she said, trying to keep the fear from trembling her words. "But I'm not having guests right now. I'll have to ask you to leave."

He smiled and it was a devil's smile, all slick and full of ungodly promises. And pain. The boss policeman had had a mean fix to his face, a look that said he'd hurt you to get what he wanted. This one's smile said he'd hurt just because he'd enjoy it. He knelt in front of her and put his hands on her knees much like Paulie had only minutes ago.

"Auntie Dee, it's a pleasure to finally meet you. Shush," he scolded her, touching a finger to her lips. "Unfortunately, this isn't a social visit. You know something we need to know. Don't you?"

Auntie Dee drew breath to scream for help, but the devil-man clamped his hand over her mouth. He bore down with a crushing strength, and she felt her jaw creaking, in jeopardy of breaking. He was still smiling when Auntie Dee's bladder let go.

"I'm surprised we're working together tonight. I thought you'd be back in uniform."

"So did I," Jack said, agreeing with Aaron. "I guess the sergeant figured it would spare the cars some unnecessary calls if the CIT was still out here."

"Nice to feel useful. Although, I can't see there being a shortage of cars tonight. Man, I've never seen so many cops in the station."

That was no exaggeration. All the cars were full, with

enough bodies left over to flood Regent Park with foot patrols. A mouse wasn't going to be able to fart without a cop hearing it.

"Just hope it's enough," Jack muttered.

"Say what?"

"Nothing. Just wondering how long this is going to take."

They were waiting in the cramped lobby of a rooming house on Winchester Street, twiddling their thumbs until the ETF finished up the call. Jack and Aaron had responded to a call where a man was threatening to kill himself; they had found him standing in his tiny room with one fucking huge butcher knife held to his throat.

"Don't you come near me!" the man cried, jabbing himself hard enough to dimple his skin. "I'll do it, I swear I will!"

Jack's head hurt. His back itched where the sweat ran into the souvenir scratches Lillian had given him. It may have been cool outside, but it was fucking boiling in the rooming house. Jack imagined a tenant had gotten control of the thermostat and that the owner was in for a nasty surprise next hydro bill. All in all, he didn't want to be here, in this hot, smelly shithole, waiting to see if this loser had the balls to slice himself or not. Jack hoped he didn't; he didn't need another SIU investigation.

Talking hadn't worked. Aaron tried first, then Jack. Commiserating had failed, as had joking, sweet-talking and ordering. Now they were waiting as the Emergency Task Force introduced Mr. Butcher Knife to their style of persuasion. Jack had been keeping half an ear tuned to the ETF ordering the suicidal male with as much luck as the CIT had. A loud crackling noise, uncannily similar to an electrical sound effect from a cartoon, sizzled through the ground floor.

"Time to go," Jack announced, perking up. "Taser," he clarified for Aaron's blank look.

A few minutes later, out came Mr. Butcher Knife, half walking, half carried between two grey-and-black-clad tactical officers. They hustled him outside and deposited him in the back of the CIT car. Jack extended his thanks for the speedy response time.

"We were in the area," the tac guy explained. "With what's going on at your station, everyone's in the area."

"What's going on at the station? We've been off the radio with numbnuts here."

"Something short of a riot, by the sounds of it." The Extra Tough Guy—as the bouncers down at the Guvernment nightclub called the ETF—took off his helmet and wiped sweat from his brow. "Nothing out of control yet, but we've been asked to stay close in case things get out of hand."

"Now what's happened? There was just the usual handful of demonstrators out front when we started work." Jack looked to Aaron, who nodded in confirmation.

"Not exactly sure. Something about an old lady getting tuned up."

"Any idea what he was talking about?" Aaron asked Jack as they headed to St. Mike's with their body.

"No, but I don't like the sounds of it. I'll call the station when we're at the hospital."

In the end, Jack didn't have to make that call; the afternoon's events were all over the news. Mr. Butcher Knife—considerably less lively after being zapped—was promptly and smoothly deposited into a private room that came with complimentary restraints should the need arise. Jack doubted it would; he'd never been tasered himself—some guys, masochists, the unbelieving, or plain idiots volunteered—but understood it hurt like a motherfucking bitch. The electrical charge locked up all the skeletal muscles, and the more muscle mass you had, the greater the pain. Jack was content to take the manufacturer's word on the effectiveness.

There was a small TV at the nurses' station and it was tuned to the news. Jack waved Aaron over, wordlessly nodding at the screen. A female reporter calmly spoke to the camera while bedlam cavorted behind her.

"What was once a peaceful, orderly demonstration out front of Toronto Police's 51 Division has turned hostile and unpredictable," the reporter conveyed as the camera shifted from her to pan the mob laying siege to the station. The numbers had swelled from about a dozen—the dedicated ones Jack and Aaron had seen at the start of shift—to an easy hundred, spilling off the sidewalk onto the street. Gone were the passive placards demanding justice. In their place fists punched into the air and a chant, too garbled to make out but clearly vehement, pounded the night air. A line of officers stood guard behind a row of metal barriers, protecting the station, which still bore its scars and bandages from the earlier assault.

The reporter was back on screen. "The demonstrators are protesting the supposed police involvement in the brutal beating of Davisha Lawrence, the grandmother of Tyrone Johnson, who was shot by police only days ago and who later died from his wounds. The demonstrators are demanding a full, impartial investigation into the grievous attack that has left Mrs. Lawrence in hospital in critical condition. Back to you, Gary."

"Sounds like they want to lynch someone," Aaron observed, and Jack agreed. No wonder the ETF were in the area.

The news cut back to Gary and his fellow anchorwoman, safely distant and detached from the ugliness in the street. "Thanks, Natasha," the trustworthy-looking, forty-something Gary said in his no-nonsense voice. "We'll keep you updated on events at 51 station house."

Station house? Next, he'll be saying precinct.

It was the anchorwoman's turn to gaze solemnly out from the TV. "Earlier this afternoon, a woman in her sixties was brutally beaten in her Regent Park home. The extent of her injuries is not known, but she was rushed by ambulance to St. Michael's Hospital for emergency surgery. We have been told she is in critical but stable condition."

Back to Gary. "Police are not commenting on the assault except to say an investigation is under way, but many residents of Mrs. Lawrence's building have their own notion of what occurred inside the one-bedroom apartment."

Cut to an outside shot, 274 Sackville Street in the background, a distressed woman crying to the camera. "It was the police that done this," she declared, no doubt or hesitation in her voice. "They came to see Auntie Dee—Davisha, I mean—but I don't know what for. Next, there's an ambulance taking her away."

"They wanted her to tell them where Lyron is," an infuriated black man stated positively. "And when she wouldn't, those pigs tried to beat it out of her. They say we're the criminals, but they're the ones beating up old women. It ain't right, and something's got to be done about it."

"What the fuck?" Aaron asked, but Jack could only shake his head in bewilderment.

"We remind our viewers that no police involvement in the beating of Mrs. Lawrence has been proven—" *a little late for that, Gary* "—but police did confirm officers had attended her apartment prior to the attack. They wanted to question her concerning the whereabouts of Lyron Dove, who is wanted in connection with the firebombing of the Regent Park police station Tuesday evening. Now, a check on tomorrow's weather."

"Fuck me," Jack breathed. "What the hell is going on?"

"I don't know," Aaron commiserated as he flipped through channels. "But it's on every station."

"Stop!" Jack barked, and Aaron's hand froze. "I don't fucking believe it. No, wait, I do."

Gary's news show must have missed this little tidbit, or thought it wasn't juicy enough to bother cutting into the forecast. But it was interesting to Jack. Interesting and fucking infuriating.

"Isn't that—"

"My father. Let me hear what the fucker is saying."

Mitchell Warren, looking simultaneously powerful and dashing, was standing outside St. Mike's emergency entrance. Like the interviews of Auntie Dee's neighbours, this segment had been taped earlier in the day, the sky just fading through twilight.

"I cannot comment on Mrs. Lawrence's condition right now except to say she is out of surgery, but not yet out of the woods." Jack's father always liked to toss in everyday euphemisms to maintain a connection with the everyday people. *That's my dad, a real people person.* "I am well aware of the allegations incriminating the police, but will withhold comment until the matter has been thoroughly investigated by the appropriate non-police agencies and my office."

Jack couldn't help being impressed in a sickening way. "Fuck, he's milking this for all it's worth."

"I am also aware of and am waiting to hear back from the police regarding the allegations against Lyron Dove, a childhood friend and companion of Tyrone Johnson, the poor boy who was shot to death by police last Friday."

"Waiting to hear back from police? What the hell does that mean?"

"It means," Jack groaned, "that good old Dad has already been in contact with the kid and is hiding him away somewhere until he can arrange a press conference before bravely escorting him to the station. Head quarters, most likely. Flashier that way."

Jack turned off the television, nauseatingly full of the news. He scrubbed his face with his hands, hoping childishly that the whole mess would disappear and he'd wake up in bed. No such luck.

"What do we do?" Aaron posed.

"Get back on the road," Jack suggested with a shrug. "Nothing else we can do."

"Do you think we can find a place willing to sell cops a coffee?"

Jack laughed. "Do you think Niagara Falls would be far away enough?"

Ghost had no such problem getting his coffee. He sat in the Tim Hortons near Yonge and Dundas, his old stomping grounds from his Ryerson University days. Except those days had been rather short-lived. Apparently, the school system at any level, frowned on violence, and Ghost was nothing if not exceptional at violence. He'd been birthed and raised amongst violence, waded through lakes of blood in his teens. But he was never a bully, never one to pursue and torture those weaker than him. In fact, many of those who had fallen to him were bullies, cowards at heart. He had donned the mantle of protector, but it made no difference to his mother who Ghost fought, or why. She had warned him that God intended the meek to inherit the earth, and she had tried her saintly best to beat the meekness into him.

Dear old Mom. The Good Book in one hand and a leather strap in the other. You never did learn, did you, Mom? If God meant for the meek to inherit, then He also meant for the sheep to have a shepherd to lead them, and sheepdogs to protect them from the wolves. Because the meek can't inherit shit if they're dead.

The coffee shop was full of mindless, obedient sheep, diligently pursuing their academic dreams so they could take their faceless, submissive places among the masses.

Sheep. Nothing but docile sheep. Lost and vulnerable without the shepherds, easy food for the wolves without the sheepdogs. Ghost had tried his hand at being the shepherd's weapon, both here and in distant lands, but in the end, there was too much wolf in him. So now he was a wolfdog, hunting outside the flock. And the hunting was good.

The coffee shop had a television bolted up in a corner and Ghost watched the news with a satisfied smile. He regretted hurting the old woman, but sometimes a sheep needed to be offered up as bait to lure the wolves into the open. He hadn't even needed to spread the police rumour. Whether the old woman had been able to say something to the neighbour who found her, or some of the sheep had managed to connect the dots he had lain out for them, didn't matter. Another barrel of gunpowder had been added to the powder keg that was Regent Park. If it didn't explode now… Well, there were always more sheep to use as bait.

But while he waited for the explosion he had people to visit.

**Thursday, 13 December
0917 hours**

"Shit, boss. Did you get any sleep last night?" Tank paused with his hand outstretched for the light switch; Mason was sitting at his desk, illuminated by the glow of his computer screen. The Major Crime detective's pallor was hellish, pale and sickly, and Tank was pretty sure it wasn't all because of the sterile electric light.

"I grabbed a few hours in the quiet room," Mason admitted. Every station had a room tucked away where cops too tired to drive or stranded between court and work could crash. 51's was hidden away in the basement somewhere. Tank didn't know exactly where; he'd never used it because he'd never heard of anyone changing or cleaning the blankets.

Mason yawned and scrubbed his face. "Go ahead, hit the lights."

Tank flicked on the overheads and decided the boss man definitely looked worse in the full light. He couldn't say for sure, but Tank thought Mason's hair was a bit greyer, the lines around his eyes a touch deeper. The sumo-shaped officer figured Mason could use a couple of days, or weeks, of bed rest, and not for the first time he worried what damage all the stress was wreaking on his boss's body. But the boss was just that, so when Mason asked what Tank had brought him, the plainclothes cop dropped the reports in front of him.

"Another bad night in the Park," Tank assessed. "Two times coppers were shot at. Luckily no one was hit. A couple of uniforms were swarmed when they tried to make an arrest. Fights, shit being thrown at cops and cars. It ain't settling down."

Mason nodded wearily. "I heard. And these?"

"These," Tank said, tapping the reports lying innocently on the desk, "took place while all the shit in the Park was happening. Two gang members in separate incidents were visited by someone armed with a small sledge hammer. It was left behind at the second scene."

Mason's eyes perked up. "Active members?"

Tank nodded. "Trafficking, robberies, serious assaults. One of them was a female. Whoever put them in the hospital certainly isn't sexist."

"Shit. And the other?"

"Happened over in 52. Hensio Carmichael."

Mason's brow furrowed. "Carmichael? Isn't he…"

"Yeah," Tank confirmed, filling in the blanks for his boss. "Rapist, pedophile. Suspected, never convicted. Someone took a pair of vise grips to his nuts." Tank dragged over a chair and dropped into it. "Real bad assaults. Real fucking bad, but not homicides, and assholes for victims. Nothing that would be considered important with all the other shit going on." Tank sighed. "He's back, boss. We gotta face it."

"Shit." Mason sagged in his chair, rubbing his eyes. "We have to know for sure. If it isn't him—by some fucking miracle—and we go after him, we'll be asking for a shit storm we don't fucking need. Would any of the victim's be able to ID him?"

Tank shook his head. "Hell, none of them will be in condition to talk to us for days, if we're lucky."

"God damn it," Mason growled. "God fucking damn it."

"I went through some recent reports and found one who might be able to help us," Tank said, offering a bit of hope.

"Don't fuck with me, Tank," Mason warned. "Who is it?"

Jesse Polan wasn't horny.

He was in far too much pain to be thinking about getting laid and way too fucking pissed at hurting all the time. He was pissed at the asshole doctors who ignored him when he told them they had to up his medication because he was in fucking agony. He was pissed at the bitch nurses who just smiled or frowned at him when he begged them—fucking begged!—to slip him a little extra.

No, there was no way Jesse was horny.

He stared at the clock on the wall with his one good eye, willing the second hand to move faster. Over an hour till his next dose of painkillers. No TV—he couldn't afford it, and the fucking doctors wouldn't tell anyone to hook it up—so all he could do was watch the clock and sleep, but he couldn't sleep unless he was doped up; the pain in his hand and head was just too fucking great. His right arm was in a cast from his fingertips up to his elbow. When he complained about how much the fucking thing itched, the asshole doctors or bitch nurses always liked to remind him that the fucker who had stabbed him in the hand had snipped a bone clean in half. And they always said it with a fucking smile.

"Fucking assholes," Jesse muttered. "I hope they all eat shit and die." He rolled his head to look out the window, and the room swam drunkenly. As fucked up as his hand was, it was nothing compared to his head. That motherfucking asshole had fucked up Jesse's head something fierce. Here it was a week later—he couldn't remember, just a week or two?—and his head was still wrapped up like a fucking Christmas present. His right eye, too. Some asshole doctor had said he might be blind in that eye. They could only wait and see.

Jesse's roommate, some old geezer hooked up to a breathing machine, had moved out that morning, giving Jesse a private room for the time being. He didn't know if the old fuck had died or not, and really didn't give a shit; the old guy made a fucking disgusting sucking sound as he breathed that had nearly driven Jesse ape shit. So now the curtain separating the beds—Jesse wished it had been a fucking soundproof wall—was drawn back, giving him access to the room's single window. Only to see out of it he had to roll his head to the right to use his good eye and any time he moved his head he felt like he was going to puke.

He carefully eased his head back to facing the ceiling. "Fuck me."

"Looks like someone already did."

Jesse almost turned his head to see who had come into the room but caught himself at the last moment. "Who's there?" He couldn't see shit out of the corner of his eye. "I need some meds, man. I'm in fucking agony here."

"You're breaking my fucking heart, Jesse." A man stood over him, filling the empty ceiling above the bed. It wasn't a doctor.

Short hair, a long grey goatee and hard eyes. Fucking stone-hard eyes. "Who the fuck are you?" Jesse whispered, very aware of how vulnerable he was. And how alone.

"You don't remember me? I'm hurt." But he didn't look hurt. He looked pissed off. Seriously pissed off and tired. A combination Jesse was sure wouldn't lead to a friendly conversation. No, not a conversation. More like an interrogation, like the ones the police—

Recognition hit Jesse and he forgot all about his pain. "You're a cop," he breathed. "You're that cop."

"That's right. I'm *that* cop." The big cop smiled, and Jesse felt his balls try to crawl up into his belly.

Back in the summer Jesse had made the mistake of sticking a gun in a bitch cop's stomach. They'd taken him to the cop shop, and in a small, windowless room this cop had talked at length with Jesse. He had tried to explain to the cop that he had just gotten out of the hospital—he'd still been all taped up for Christ's sake!—and had been all fucked up from the drugs they'd given him, but the cop hadn't cared. He wanted to know who had sold Jesse the gun and had dug strong fingers into Jesse's wounds until he had given up the seller.

Now the fucker was back, and once more Jesse was alone in a room with him. Or so he thought.

"C'mon, man," Jesse pleaded, close to crying. "I already gave you the guy who sold me the fucking gun. I ain't got no more."

"I'm not interested in the gun," the cop said. He leaned close to Jesse, pinning him to the bed with those fucking eyes. "I'm going to show you a picture—"

"Please, man, no. I can't rat again, they'll fucking kill me."

"—and you're going to tell me yes or no," the cop went on as if Jesse hadn't said a word. "But you're not going to know if I want to hear yes or no, so you might as well just tell me the truth. Trying to guess what answer I want will be rather painful for you."

A sharp stab of pain shot through Jesse's hand. This time he didn't remember to move only his eye, and when the room stopped spinning, he saw another cop standing on the other side of his bed. This one—a fucking huge bald bastard—was holding Jesse's hand, a motherfucking grin on his face.

"My friend there," the first cop said, regaining Jesse's attention, "can crush your hand quite easily. And if that isn't enough to ensure your truthfulness…"

"Yes! Fuck, yes!" Jesse cried as another agonizing jolt rocketed up his arm. "Whatever you want, man. Whatever the fuck you want."

"So maybe my friend won't have to lean on your skull," the cop mused.

"No, man. I'll tell you the truth. I fucking swear I will," Jesse gasped. He so desperately wanted to hug his tortured hand to his chest, to hold it until the pain went away, but the bald cop wouldn't let go. Jesse knew that if he wanted to survive this without getting hurt—fuck that, killed—he was going to have to tell the cop the truth. Whatever the fuck it was.

"I'm going to show you a picture," the first cop said.

"And you're going to simply say yes or no. Got it?"

Jesse nodded as best he could. "Yeah, man. I got it."

The cop held up a picture. "Is this the man who attacked you?"

The face in the photo was younger and the hair was cut short, not in cornrows, but Jesse recognized him. No doubt it was the fucker who had put him in the hospital, but Jesse was scared to death of saying so. And equally terrified of saying no. Because the collar peaking up from the picture's bottom edge wasn't part of an old army jacket. Not even close.

It was a colour he hadn't seen in years because they had all switched over to black shirts. To Jesse, it looked like the blue collar of a cop's uniform.

"Where you headed, boss?"

"Nowhere exciting, Tank," Mason replied, pausing in the MCU's doorway. "Just to the lunchroom. You want anything? Kris?"

"Nah, I'm good," Tank said.

Kris just shook her head, looking queasy.

Hope she's not coming down with something. We can't afford to lose anyone right now.

Mason trudged down the stairs, his thoughts occupied with what they had learned at the hospital. Silva was back. God damn fucking Marco Silva. Mason had thought—hoped—they had seen the last of that crazy fucker. At least now everything made sense. The car bombing, the shootings, the attack on the station. For a while now, Mason had felt as if someone was manipulating the Park residents and the police, moving them around like pieces on some bizarre chess board. And now they knew, all of it orchestrated by Silva to give him cover, a smoke screen, so he could carry out his demented plan.

Not that I think he somehow co-ordinated the Johnson shooting, but he sure as shit has taken full advantage of the situation.

"How do we stop him, boss?" Tank had asked on the way back from St. Mike's. "We can't just let him run around until he stops on his own. Hell, we don't even know if he will stop."

He'll stop. He's already planned his exit strategy: Dove. He's set the poor bastard up to take the fall. We were meant to find Dove's prints on those casings. When he's done, when he's put enough people in the hospital and morgue, he'll shove that kid in front of the nearest scout car. And if the kid talks, says it's all some nameless guy's doing—Mason would bet his mortgage Silva hadn't given a real name—*what proof would he have?*

But Dove wasn't the problem. Even Silva walking away wasn't the problem, not really. What scared Mason, what downright terrified him, was the thought of Silva not escaping, of him falling into police hands. Alive. A live and talking Silva was the worst-case scenario. It would destroy... Well, everything. There was too much, too many people, at risk. It was a gamble Mason wasn't willing to—couldn't—accept.

We missed him in the summer. We can't let him slip away again. But how do we find him? How? We can't stake out every asshole in the division.

With a Coke in hand, the detective headed back up the stairs and ran into Jack. "Doing a callback, Jack?"

"Couldn't turn down the extra cash," Jack said. "Not with the way my wife's lawyer is gunning for me."

"Love is a bitch," Mason replied, taking a swig from his can. "Aren't you a couple of hours early? I thought the next bonus round started at three."

"Yeah. I'm meeting Jenny for lunch."

Mason chugged more Coke. "How's she doing? What about Pest? Have you talked with him?"

"Jenny's hanging in there, but the kid dying certainly hasn't helped with her stress level." Jack frowned. "I feel like a shit, but I haven't talked at all with Connor. He's been labeled a witness officer so the situation isn't as bad for him, and I've been concentrating on Jenny…"

Mason waved away Jack's explanation. "Understandable. She's your partner."

"Paul said he talked with Connor the other night and said he's doing okay." Jack barked a cynical laugh. "Sounds like he's playing up the stress to wangle some pity sex."

"That's our Pest."

Changing topics, Jack asked, "Do you know how many assists there were last night?"

"Five. Must be some kind of record outside of Carribana or a major protest. Fuck, can you imagine if Toronto ever has to host something like a G20 summit? Fuck me."

"A what?"

"Don't you watch the news?" Mason kicked open the MCU door. "It's when a bunch of presidents and world leaders get together to act like they're actually doing something, and the city they're in gets shit on by protesters."

"Well, if one of those ever comes to Toronto, I hope it's long after I'm done on the job." Jack nodded hello to Tank and Kris, dim shapes in the office's gloom. The windows had yet to be replaced. "Kind of cheery in here, Rick."

Mason scowled. "Why give the assholes something new to shoot out?"

"Personally, I think the boss is just getting in touch with his nocturnal side. The whole Batman thing." Tank bumped fists with Jack as Jack perched on the big man's desk.

Mason glared at Tank. "You can go back to uniform anytime, kiddo. I'm sure Jack would gladly take your place."

"I don't know about that, Rick." Jack gestured at the windows and the shot-up ceiling tiles. "Doesn't exactly look to be the safest place."

"Is anywhere safe right now?"

The five assist calls last night were just the ugly tip of the shit happening in the division. Not only had assholes jumped cops in five separate occasions, but there had also been dozens of incidents where scout cars and officers were pelted with rocks, garbage and in one case a bag of shit. There had been foot pursuits galore, two of them drawing the chasing officers into deliberate traps, resulting in calls for help.

Mason had lived through combative times of strife with the Park before: the most recent not quite a year and a half ago when they were hunting for Anthony Charles, wanted for the murder of Jack's partner and Mason's friend. Before that had been…when? Ten, twelve years ago? A copper was stabbed on his way to work, and 51 had kicked the shit out of the Park until the asshole responsible was given up. This current shitstorm threatened to dwarf both of those little wars. But then, neither of those times had a madman playing puppet master.

Mason's cell phone started squawking, and he tugged it free of his belt. He checked the call display and smiled. "Well, if it isn't my favourite Homicide detective. How's life, Lizzy?"

"That's detective sergeant to you," Elizabeth Gregory told him. "And don't call me Lizzy. I'm not one of your impressionable rookies anymore."

"That you aren't," Mason agreed, still smiling. "But I bet you've still got the perfect ass that rookie had."

"That's sexual harassment, detective," she informed him icily. "Or it would be if I ever imagined a fat old man like yourself being able to back it up."

Mason laughed. "For you, Lizzy, I'd be willing to try."

She laughed with him. "How you keeping over there, Rick? Staying out of the line of fire, I hope."

Glancing at the boarded-up windows, he said, "Trying to. This a social call or business?"

Her mirth disappeared beneath professionalism. "Business, I'm afraid, old man. What do you know about Lyron Dove?"

Normally, Mason wouldn't be so willing to share information, even with Homicide, but Lizzy was ex-51 Major Crime. He had tutored and moulded the young PW into a tough, seasoned plainclothes officer, and at his urging, she had gone for promotion. Once she got her stripes she did stints in Hold Up and Intelligence, finally landing a spot at Homicide as a D/S. Lizzy was family.

"We found his prints on some shell casings from the station bombing, and we just missed him at the grandmother's place. Someone must have seen us coming and tipped him off."

"That sucks. You got an address on him?"

"Nothing current," Mason said, shaking his head, even though she couldn't see him. "He's gone to ground and all the leads are coming up shit."

"Well, well, well. Seems like I know something the great Rick Mason doesn't." She paused, and Mason could almost hear her smiling. "I've got an address on him."

"How did you get it?"

"Someone has been feeding a reporter at the *Citizen*—"

"That Templeton bitch?" Mason wanted to know.

"The very one. Well, this someone told her the casings found at your car bombing and the double homicide are Glock forty cal."

"And you think it's Dove?"

"Could be." The Homicide detective paused, obviously sensing Mason's hesitation. "What?"

"Hang on, Lizzy." It was Mason's turn to pause as he studied the three faces watching him. Tank, acutely intrigued and aware. Kris, also interested but less so and still green in the gills. And Jack. How much should—could—Jack be told? Too many people involved already, but if the situation ended up where Mason thought it was headed, then they'd need all the bodies they could get. But if Jack learned the truth, the *whole* truth…

Mason looked questioningly at Tank, and the big man lifted his hands as if to say *Your call*. Kris, when Mason turned to her, merely nodded weakly. When Mason looked at Jack, the scarred officer met his gaze frankly. It was obvious Jack knew something was going on around him, and he wasn't shying away from it.

If he learned the whole truth…

"Jack," Mason said, finally deciding. *And there'll be hell to pay if I'm wrong.* "Shut the door and grab a seat." With the office closed to accidental eavesdroppers, Mason let Lizzy know he was back.

"What is it, Rick?" she asked. "I just wanted to know if you'd checked out this address for Dove. What aren't you telling me?"

"It isn't Dove," Mason told her, his voice hushed. "It's Silva. He's back."

Jack sat in the dim office, not sure what he was hearing. Dove wasn't the one behind all the shit in the Park? There was someone else, someone staying in the shadows, someone Mason seemed to have a history with. And from Mason's side of the conversation with a detective from Homicide—Tank had let him know who Lizzy was—it was possible this someone had killed Phil.

"Sounds good, Liz. We'll touch base later." Mason tucked his phone back on his belt and heaved a tremendous sigh. It sounded like the detective was on his last legs. Jack didn't care.

"Who is this Silva? And what's he got to do with all the shit happening around here?"

Mason stared at Jack and growled, "I don't think I like your tone of voice, officer."

But Jack wasn't about to be bullied. "I really don't give a fuck, Rick. You and Tank look like somebody just kicked you in the balls, and Kris looks like she's ready to puke. What the fuck is going on?"

Mason's face stoned up. "I don't have—"

"Enough!" Jack snapped. He knew he was risking a spot in the MCU and a friendship with his attitude, but he could care fucking less. "If this guy is involved, he may have caused—shit, he may have *killed* my friend, and I want to know what the fuck is going on!"

A heavy silence muffled the office. At length, Mason blew out a breath and leaned back in his chair. "All right, I guess you do have a right to know. At least fucking sit down. You look like you're going to jump my desk and choke me."

It was only then that Jack realized he was leaning over the detective's desk, his fists planted firmly on the scarred metal top. "Sorry," he muttered, and took a chair.

"Marco Silva is a mad dog," Mason explained. "He was a cop here, briefly. You've been on the job, what? Seven, eight years? Silva was gone around the same time you got hired. He was given a choice: quit or face charges."

"For what?"

Mason sighed again. This was obviously some history he wasn't comfortable telling. "Silva had a tendency to be heavy-handed."

Kris snorted, the first input she'd had since Jack stepped in the office. "Tendency? The guy's a fucking bloodthirsty animal."

"Okay, so maybe 'tendency' doesn't quite cover it. More often than not, his arrests came in with injuries. Some pretty serious. I know, getting into scraps down here isn't uncommon, but with Silva, two out of every three bodies needed medical attention. Like Kris said, he's a bit of an animal."

"And?" So far, none of Jack's questions were getting answered.

"But it wasn't just that he liked to tune up the assholes. He had this…warped code of conduct, of honour. He went after the true assholes, the dealers, the kiddy diddlers, anyone who laid a hand on someone he considered weak or small." Mason squawked a laugh. "He used to say he was the wolf protecting the sheep, or some shit like that. You have to understand, Silva was a little messed up in the head. He did time over in the Gulf War, and I truly believe it fucked him up. Post traumatic stress, or something like it. His heart was in the right place—he hated the way assholes got off in court—but his way of solving things was just too messy. He would have been right at home in the Inquisition. Well, only so many complaints can be swept away, and eventually he was given the choice: walk or get done. He walked."

"That's it?" Jack asked when Mason added nothing else. "What has that got to do with the shit that's happening now?"

Mason heaved his shoulders. "Fucked if I know. I haven't heard from Silva in years. We kept in touch after he quit, but… You know how things like that go. What he's doing back here, I'm afraid to guess. He might be involved in all of this, or he could be harbouring a grudge for being forced to quit, and he sees this as us getting our just rewards. He may be here just to watch. Like I said, he's fucked up in the head."

"But you don't think he's here as a sightseer," Jack guessed.

Mason shrugged. "It's a hell of a coincidence, him coming back after all this time."

"Wait," Jack said, holding up a hand. "You told that Homicide D Silva is back, then you spend the next five minutes discussing how and when you're going to pinch Dove. I don't get it."

Mason picked up his Coke can, found it empty and tossed it in the recycle bin. "Ever since Jenny's shooting, someone has been riling up the Park, doing his best to create a war between us and them."

"Yeah," Jack agreed, cutting in. "That's what Greene said to me the other night."

Mason nodded. "Then give the old guy credit; he caught it before I did."

"But why?" Jack wanted to know. "Why attack the station? Why—" His voice hitched as he fought to say the words. "Why kill Phil? What's he get out of all this?"

"I honestly think your old friend was a mistake, a potential witness removed from the equation." The detective ducked his head. "Sorry, that was cold, but it's how Silva would see it."

"But what does it all achieve?" Jack persisted.

"Cover," Tank said simply, taking over from Mason. "Since all the shit started up, there's been a string of assaults in and around the division. I'm talking serious bodily harm and aggravated assaults."

Jack pondered what he was being told, and the MCU officers let him come to the conclusion on his own. "You're saying he's using this—" Jack swept his arm at the boarded-up windows "—as a smokescreen while he's out playing *Death Wish*?"

Mason nodded. "Exactly."

"Fuck me," Jack breathed, not able to completely wrap his head around the idea. This Silva was willing to risk lives and commit murder so he could be some righteous vigilante? "How does Dove fit in?"

"I think Silva's setting him up as his fall guy." Mason held up his hand and ticked off the points. "We find Dove's prints on shell casings from the station attack. He has a known relationship with Tyrone Johnson and his grandmother, giving him a plausible motive. The person who called Templeton at the *Citizen* used a phone listed to Dove. I'm willing to bet that when we find Dove, he'll be in possession of the handgun that was used at the car bombing or the two homicides. Or both. And as Dove takes all the blame, Silva will simply walk away."

"You seem pretty sure of this," Jack accused. "How can you be? I thought you hadn't seen Silva in years."

"I haven't." Mason opened a file on his desk. "But he has." He tossed Jack a stapled report.

Jack scanned the papers and scoffed in disbelief. "Jesse Polan? You trust him?"

"I don't *trust* him," Mason replied. "But I believed him when he ID'ed Silva. And he's got every reason in the world to hate him." He passed Jack a photo.

The face looking out at Jack was intense, angry. Silva's black hair was cropped to the scalp, almost shaved, and he was wearing one of the old powder-blue uniform shirts that the Service had dumped a couple of years ago.

"And you think," Jack said, handing the picture back, "that if we find Dove, we find Silva."

"If we're lucky, which I doubt." Mason stifled a belch. "'Scuse me. If Silva was using a phone number to lead us to Dove, I doubt very much that he'll be sitting there watching TV when we show up. But if we get Dove, we take away Silva's scapegoat and force him to cut short his actions. He disappears, the driving force in this fucking war disappears. Everything calms down and we go after Silva another day."

Kris laughed sorely, her first input to the conversation. "That is, *if* Silva lets us take Dove alive. I wouldn't put it past him to cap Dove and make it look like we did it. You know, a final *fuck you* for interfering with his plans."

Jack could tell from the look on Mason's face that her suggestion wasn't at all far-fetched.

Tank raised his hand. "We going to hook up with Lizzy?"

Mason nodded. "She's rounding up some guys from Mobile Support and getting the warrant for Dove's apartment. We're all meeting here this evening."

"There might be another way to get hold of Dove," Jack said quietly. "His lawyer is…my father." Ignoring the raised eyebrows, he added, "If I talk to my father, make him realize Dove is in danger, he might tell me where Dove is."

Mason pointed a finger at Jack. "All right. As of now, you're working for me. I'll let the parade sergeant know you'll be doing old clothes for the foreseeable future. Will your dad tell you this over the phone or do you have to go see him? I get the feeling things aren't quite all hunky-dory between the two of you."

"You could say that," Jack admitted. "And it's doubtful he'll talk to me at all, let alone over the phone. His office is downtown. I should go see him."

"Then go," Mason ordered. "The sooner we get our hands on Dove, the better our chance of cleaning things up."

Jack stood. "Let me grab my gun, and I'm good to go."

"Your gun?" Tank asked. "You need your gun to talk to your dad?"

Jack gave him a grim look. "With my father? Absolutely."

Jenny pulled her leather coat tighter about herself as she cut through the parking lot to the station's back door. It may have been unseasonably mild, but there was still a damp chill in the air. Hopefully, wherever she and Jack had lunch, there'd be a fireplace or something hot she could wrap herself around.

Jack could keep me warm. The thought popped up in her head unbidden. She banished the image, telling herself for the umpteenth time that she was with Brian and Jack was going through a traumatic, messy divorce. Not to mention all the stress and shit happening right here at work.

The back door banged open, and her partner hustled out, his head down as he dug through the pockets of his jacket.

"You look like you're in a rush," Jenny told him. "Trying to avoid our lunch date?"

"Oh, Jenny," Jack said, his head snapping up. "I was just about to call you."

"Is something wrong? You look like you're ready to kill someone."

Jack quickly brought her up to speed, then regretfully backed out of lunch. "I'm sorry, but I have to go see my dad, and try to convince him to do the right thing."

"Sounds like fun. Let's go."

"I'd love the company, but you're still off work."

"So what? It's not like you're going to get into a shootout at your dad's office, is it? I mean, judging from when you saw him at court, I realize it's not going to be a nice family get-together, but I can't see you dragging your dad back to the station in cuffs." Jenny brushed some hair away from her face. "Besides, I could use the company."

Jack smiled and relented. "Come on, then. I've got one of the MCU cars."

"A rogue ex-cop creating havoc and chaos for his own personal vendetta," Jenny mused as they waited for the cops guarding the lot's entrance to wave them through. "It sounds like the plot to a Dirty Harry movie."

"It does, doesn't it?" Jack tapped his fingers to his head in salute to the officers watching over the personal vehicle lot. The protesters were back in full force today, marching out front of the station like a medieval army laying siege to a castle. The hostility thrummed off the crowd in palpable waves.

"Greene said it looked like someone was trying to start a war in the division." Jack turned south on Regent, away from the demonstration.

"When did he say that?"

"Oh," Jack said, sounding as if he had just realized he had spoken aloud. "The night Phil was killed. He found me in the YB with Bear. I thought he was going to do me for leaving the crime scene, but he said no one deserved to die like that, and that he thought someone was intentionally starting a war."

"Wow," Jenny declared. "Who would've thought the old bastard had that much compassion in him?"

"Yeah, well, don't get all teary-eyed on his account. Before he left, he told me that when I find the guy who's doing this, I should do what I do best."

"Meaning what?"

Jack looked at her, amused yet grim. "I guess the staff thinks I'm good at killing people."

What could she say to that? The expression on Jack's face when he had burst out of the station had made her think he looked ready to kill someone. She was saved from speaking when Jack's phone rang.

He dug the phone out of his jacket pocket and flipped it open. "Yeah?"

Jenny couldn't hear the other person, but Jack's face immediately darkened. "Well, I can't.... I'm working, that's why." As Jack listened, his face grew even darker, and his fingers paled to white where he was gripping the phone. "I guess you haven't been watching the news lately," he snapped. "In case you don't know, there's a fucking war going on down here, and no one's on days off right now. Just mail it to me." He slammed the phone shut. "Bitch."

"Karen?" Jenny guessed.

"Yeah." Jack blew out a stressed breath. "She and her mom are with the lawyer right now, and thought it would be a good time for me to come down and sign away my life."

"I'm sorry."

"No big deal," Jack said, forcing a smile. "As long as I have Justice at home—wherever home ends up being—and you at work, I'm good."

She smiled and gave his hand a squeeze. Now was not the time to tell him she and Brian had spent the morning discussing her future, a future that did not include the Toronto Police. Or any police, for that matter. She wasn't set on any decision yet, but Brian had suggested she move in with him—dogs and all—while she went back to school or looked for a new career. Tempting, very tempting.

She surreptitiously studied Jack as he navigated the downtown traffic. Her partner, a good man, a man she could see herself falling in love with under different circumstances. Leaving the job meant leaving him. Oh sure, they'd remain friends, but would it be the same? Was it like staying friends with an ex? Was it possible to move backwards in a relationship, from an intimate relationship to mere friendship? Although she and Jack had never been physically intimate, never dated, the connection between permanent partners was just as strong, if not stronger.

But was staying with Jack reason enough to keep on with the job? Their partnership couldn't last forever. Eventually, one of them would move on, transfer. Maybe even go for promotion. She knew Taftmore was transferring out of the division, and rumour had it Jack was a shoe-in for his MCU spot, so who knew how much longer their partnership had to live?

Do I want to quit? A question she had posed too many times and never really answered. All she knew was that every night she relived Tyrone Johnson's death, and during the days suffered nauseating anxiety at the mere thought of putting that damn uniform back on.

"We're here," Jack announced, thankfully breaking in on her thoughts. "You sure you want to come up with me? You don't look so good, right now."

It was her turn to force a smile. "Just hungry, but I'm good to go."

Mitchell Warren's legal firm, Warren and Associates—no title sharing for Jack's father—was the entire thirty-seventh floor.

"Does the hourly rate go up with the floors?"

"Probably," Jack said absently as he studied the rising numbers above the elevator door. To Jenny he looked like a man watching the timer on a bomb tick down to zero.

A polite musical chime announced their arrival at his father's realm. To the left of the elevator stood a pair of glass doors with "Warren and Associates" emblazed in gold on their frosted panes.

"Abandon all hope, ye who entre here," Jack quoted as they headed for the doors.

"Is that from a movie?"

"*Dante's Inferno*," Jack informed her. "It's the inscription over the doors to hell."

"Oh, come on. It can't be that bad."

Jack opened a door and ushered her in, a sour smile his only answer.

"Wonderful," she muttered.

The firm's lobby was stunning. The leather furniture was so soft, Jenny could feel its sumptuousness just by looking at it. Paintings and sculptures proclaimed their outrageous value simply by being. But the winner was the floor-to-ceiling window that provided a spectacular view of downtown Toronto and the lake beyond. It was all a seamless merge of comfort and domineering control, a room designed to subtly remind you that you were here only at someone else's pleasure.

"May I help you?" The receptionist's greeting turned Jenny away from the windows. She was slightly surprised that the receptionist didn't comment on her response to the view; it had stopped Jenny dead in her tracks. But then, maybe the woman behind the desk had seen the exact same reaction so many times it no longer entertained her; the way cops quickly grew bored with people who held up their hands and joked, "I didn't do it." Yeah, that was only funny the first thousand times you heard it.

Or, it could have been the fact that Jack was pointedly ignoring the vista beyond the windows, a scowl etched deeply on his face.

If he doesn't smile once in a while, his face will break the next time he laughs.

"We're here to see Mitchell Warren," Jack told the receptionist, and Jenny could hear the tension in his voice.

The receptionist quickly consulted her computer, although Jenny was certain it was just for show. "Mr. Warren isn't seeing anyone today. Perhaps I could schedule something with one of the associates for after the holidays." If she detected Jack's tautness—Jenny didn't see how she couldn't; it sounded like Jack was using steel guitar strings for vocal cords—she didn't let it affect her professional smile. "And is this regarding a matter already being handled by us, Mister…?"

"Warren," Jack rasped. "Jack Warren, his son."

That elicited a reaction. Not a huge one, but some. "Oh. Well, let me see if Mr. Warren is available." She picked up the phone.

"Don't bother." Jack gently pressed the phone back into its cradle. "I just needed to know he's here."

"Sir! Mr. Warren is not to be disturbed," the receptionist called after them as Jack led Jenny past the desk and down a hall. "You can't go back there."

Faintly, Jenny heard a number being tapped into a phone. Giving the boss a heads-up, or calling security? *Guess we'll find out.*

Curious faces, alerted by the receptionist's alarmed cry, poked out of office doors as Jenny followed her partner deeper into his father's lair. She couldn't see Jack's face, but judging from the way most of the inquisitive people ducked back into their rooms, his scowl must have been in full bloom. What did it say about the boss when no one attempted to stop, or even question, a man who no doubt had a murderous expression carved onto his face? But then again, if it was anything like the look he had had on his face when Jenny met him in the parking lot, she really couldn't blame them.

The hall opened up into another reception area, this one panelled in heavy wood and still more leather. No relieving city view this time. Just sheer dominance. Jenny didn't need to be told they had just entered the senior Warren's lair.

Another receptionist, this one younger and male—a surprise to Jenny, who figured Warren for the trophy secretary type—greeted them as if he had been expecting them, which he no doubt had been, for the last thirty seconds or so.

"Go right on in," he said, gesturing to an imposing set of doors. "Mr. Warren is waiting for you."

Jack snorted. "Figures."

"What?" She followed Jack across the room, keeping half an eye on the receptionist. *If this was a movie, I'd expect him to pull a gun.*

"Dear old dad gets a call, telling him we're coming down the hall. He knows he can't stop me from barging in, so instead he acts like he's doing me a favour by welcoming us in."

"Jeez, we're you two always like this?"

Jack paused with his hand on the doorknob. "No, not really. Not until I told him I wanted to be a cop. Go figure, huh?"

Jack swept open the door, and the grand cityscape view that had been lacking in Warren's reception area slapped

Jenny in the face. The entire back wall was floor-to-ceiling windows, opening up on the lake. Even on a grey and dreary day, the view was magnificent. On a sunny day, after the deliberate dimness of the inner reception area, anyone walking into Warren's office would be momentarily blinded and mentally knocked off balance.

And Warren was positioned centre-stage, ensconced behind a massive wood desk, lord of all he saw, which would include any peons stumbling through the door and into the light. His immaculately styled white hair—no grey; Jenny doubted grey hairs would be allowed to blemish the snowy pelt—gleamed faintly in the weak sunlight. On a bright day, his hair would blaze like a white halo.

Petty, buddy. Real petty.

The monarch of Warren and Associates rose as Jack and Jenny approached the desk. "Jack. Miss Alton. To what do I owe this unexpected visit?" Although his tone was warm, inviting, Jenny noted that Warren didn't bother to come around his desk to greet his son, or offer them seats.

Jenny winced as Jack spoke without preamble or explanation. "I need to know where Lyron Dove is." She doubted a direct assault was the best tactic for Jack—son or not—to use against his father.

"And what makes you think I know the whereabouts of that young man?" Warren settled back into his chair, managing a subtle air of wounded dignity, as if Jack had been the one to neglect a courteous welcome. "And if I did, why in the world would I provide you with that information?"

Jenny watched as Jack visibly restrained himself. It was a mere hesitation in his breathing, the slightest physical pause. Jenny, like any good cop, had learned and grown accustomed to her partner's body language, could tell just by his stance and posture when he was on guard, relaxed or wanted to pound some asshole into the ground. And right now, Jack's father was close, extremely close, to a serious tuning.

What history do they have?

"His life is in danger. The safest place for him right now is with us." Jack all but ground his teeth as he relinquished that bit of information.

"With you?" Warren smiled. "You mean in custody, in a cell."

"Of course," Jack snapped. "You think we're going to put him up in a hotel? He was involved in the attack on the station, for fuck's sake."

"We believe he was coerced into participating," Jenny added, smoothly sliding in before Jack and his father resorted to shouting. Thankfully, Jack still had hold enough on his temper to see what she had done and backed off. "And we fear the person ultimately responsible is meaning to kill Lyron to keep his involvement secret."

"Please, have a seat." Warren, acting the gracious host or establishing himself in control by allowing them to sit, waved at the chairs before his desk. Jenny accepted, seating herself on a leather chair—how many cows went into the furnishing of these offices?—that was financially intimidating, but nowhere near as regal as Warren's throne. Instead of sitting, Jack remained standing behind his chair.

Warren studied his son for a moment, then smiled at Jenny. "And who would this mysterious person be?"

"Come on, Mr. Warren. You know we can't give you that."

Warren smiled at her again, and there was nothing friendly or warm in that predatory grin. "Then I believe we have nothing further to discuss. I trust you can see your way out; you had no trouble coming in."

"Oh, for fuck's sake," Jack grumbled. "We know you're in contact with Lyron. Hell, you've had your fingers all over this from the beginning, milking it for as much publicity as possible." He leaned over his chair, fixing his father with an unyielding stare. "Well, how's it going to look when one of your clients ends up dead? Again? Especially after I let it slip that *you*, not your firm, but *you*, had a chance to save his life."

"How would it look?" Warren pondered, seemingly amused. "Not nearly as pathetic as you coming in here, hoping to salvage a modicum of dignity out of the mess that your trigger-happy partner started."

Jack started around the chair, but his father stopped him with a derisive laugh. "Enough with the theatrics. I didn't put up with them from your mother, and I certainly won't entertain them in you. Besides, we both know that if you even attempt to touch me, you'll be lucky to write parking tickets for the rest of your miserable little career."

The pretense of civility in Warren senior was gone; he had stripped off his lawyer façade, exposing the ugly loathing beneath. A naked hatred mirrored in his son's face.

"Don't for a minute think I don't know why you're really here," Warren went on. "Did you hope to win me over with a pretty face and a nice set of tits?"

"What are you talking about?" Jenny blurted.

"Oh, come on," Warren scoffed across the desk at her. "Don't play the innocent with me; you don't do it very well." He targeted his venom back at his son. "What? You didn't think I'd know she's not working, that she's on suspension until those dim-witted asses in the Special Investigations Unit make up their minds and charge her with murder?"

"I haven't been suspended," Jenny protested.

Warren shooed her words away like bothersome gnats.

"The police can talk about you being off on stress leave after gunning down an innocent man, but we all know the truth, don't we?" He leaned back contentedly. "So you come here, hoping to steal Lyron Dove from me, and what? Use him as some sort of bargaining chip? A weight to tip the scales in your favour?"

Jenny followed Warren's eyes to Jack. Her partner stood rigid behind the chair, clasping its back so hard she feared it might snap apart in his hands. And Warren was smiling, a big shit-eating, self-satisfied, smug grin. Suddenly Jenny understood, realized this had nothing to do with her, or Lyron, or Tyrone Johnson for that matter.

"Why do you hate him so?" she asked Warren. "Your own son. What did he do to you?" Her soft words got through to both men, and they turned in unison to stare at her.

"What did he do to me?" Warren all but hissed. "I gave that boy everything. *Everything!* The best education, opportunities and contacts anyone with half a brain would kill for. And what did he do? He pissed it all away. And for what? So he could wear a worthless piece of tin and shovel human shit for the rest of his life. *That's* what he did."

Jenny didn't know what to say. How do you conceive such a sense of betrayal? But Warren wasn't quite finished.

"And if throwing away an education and career wasn't enough, he lets the best thing to happen to him since he put on that damned uniform slip through his fingers. How he ever convinced Karen Hawthorn to marry him, I'll never know." Warren sadly shook his head. "I certainly hope," he said, staring at Jenny as if she was the cause of all his sorrow, "you fuck as good as you look. I'd hate to think Jack ruined his marriage on a second-rate fuck."

Jenny was speechless at Warren's vehemence. In all her years as a cop, dealing with the dregs of humanity, she had never experienced such utter abhorrence. If some asshole on the street had given her even a fraction of this attitude, he'd be on the receiving end of a serious ass-kicking.

Before she could retaliate, Jack laid a calming hand on her shoulder. "Don't bother, Jenny," he said, his anger temporarily subdued. "He's not worth it. We'll find another way to help Dove."

"Save me the heroic speech," Warren called after them as they headed for the door. "And don't bother coming here again. As far as I'm concerned, I have no son."

Jack stopped in the doorway, turned to his father. "Fine by me. You stopped being a father a long time ago."

Jack was quiet as they waited for the elevator, but Jenny could see the muscles of his jaw quivering, his hands shaking ever so slightly. His face was a thunderhead ready to explode. She looked past his shoulder and saw the receptionist watching them intently. She gave the woman a scowl of her own, smiling when the receptionist ducked down to the safety of her desk.

The elevator doors slid smoothly open and they stepped inside. As the doors shut behind them, Jenny could almost see whatever tenuous bonds Jack still had with his father falling to the floor, severed permanently.

"Jack," she asked softly. "What did you mean by 'again'? When you said—"

"It was back before he had his own firm," Jack said sadly, not waiting for her to finish her question. "I was in grade nine, I think. He was defending some rich wife beater. I remember my father bragging to his golfing buddies that the police had this guy dead to rights, there was no way he should have been able to walk. But my father did it, got the prick off without so much as a suspended sentence. I snuck into his office one night and looked at the photos of the guy's wife." Jack turned haunted eyes to Jenny. "To this day, even with all the shit I've seen down here, I've never seen someone so badly beaten." He laughed softly, painfully. "But he walked. Thanks to my father."

Jenny waited, knowing Jack wasn't finished his tale.

"He killed her a couple of years later. Beat her to death with a hammer in the backyard, in full view of the neighbours. When the cops got there, they found him sitting in his office. He'd blown his brains out."

"My God, Jack," Jenny breathed.

"Yeah. Naturally, my father's previous involvement ended up all over the news, but he managed to distance himself from the first trial, saying he had only done his job, blamed the cops and Crown attorney for fucking up the case."

The elevator glided to a stop and the doors sighed open. Jack glanced at Jenny. "That was when I began to hate what my father was," he told her, and stepped out into the lobby. Wordlessly, she followed.

In the end, Lyron Dove was taken into custody with little fanfare. Silva watched what he could of the arrest from his apartment across the street. He watched as the police cars—all of them unmarked—pulled to the curb out front of 375 Bleecker Street and plain clothes officers rushed for the lobby. No doubt there were others stationed by the building's exits. Mason was easy to spot, his lumbering bulk proclaiming his identity even from across the street and twelve floors up.

Didn't bring the tac guys, Rick? Just the people you know and trust. Your people.

As the last of the cops—his former brethren, but no more—vanished into the gloom of the apartment building, Silva busied himself making a mug of tea. As he stirred in a generous amount of sugar he wondered if his protégé would be coming out under his own power or on a stretcher.

Or a body bag, if I know Mason.

That Lyron would end up arrested, Silva had no doubt. After all, he'd told the kid himself to stay put until directed otherwise. After alerting Lyron to the closing trap at the old woman's place, Silva stashed the kid in the St. Jamestown apartment, assuring him it was a safe location. And it had been, up to the point where the police tracked the phone number used to tip off the reporter.

That Templeton skank had turned out to be quite the disappointment. True, she'd gotten out the word that police-style ammunition had been used at the murders and the car bombing, but he'd hoped she wouldn't cough up the phone number so bloody quick. He wanted another day or two to play before shutting down the operation.

Here comes the parade. He blew on his tea as Lyron was ushered out of the building, sandwiched between Mason and Tank. *A lean wolf squashed between two obese shepherds. Alive, Rick? You must be slipping.*

Lyron was bundled into a car and whisked away. Show over. Silva sat on his couch, the only piece of furniture in the one-room unit. He sipped his tea, pondering what would happen next. Mason had enough to pin the station bombing on Lyron. The angry young man had more than enough motive and had not been shy about voicing his vengeful hatred of the police. Silva had seen to the rest, ensuring there were enough shells with Lyron's prints left at the scene. It was unfortunate his arrest had come so soon; Silva hadn't had the opportunity or time to make certain that Dove be found in possession of the murder weapon.

Oh well, I'm sure Mason will find a way to put the kid at the murder scenes, if not behind the gun. He's good at that sort of thing.

And if the kid talked? Told everyone about Ghost? Mason and a few others would know it for the truth, but they certainly wouldn't be corroborating the kid's story.

Sorry, kid. Even if you talk—which Silva doubted he would do; the kid had a stubborn, stupid sense of loyalty—*you're going to find out you're all alone. I told you I was a ghost in the machine.*

Another late night at the university. Dr. George Hawthorn drove home along streets nearly devoid of traffic. A gentle fall of wet snowflakes, melting the instant they touched ground, washed the downtown buildings with a façade of peacefulness and benevolence.

Well, t'is the season. Good will to men, and all of that.

The wipers, set on a slow, intermittent pulse, sang a fitting background score to Hawthorn's thoughts. Despite the festive season, his days at the university were growing longer, almost in direct proportion to the approach of Christmas. It may have been the time for good will and peace on earth, but there was very little of either in the Hawthorn household.

Karen's divorce had been a not-so-secret desire of his long before Evelyn had joined her voice with his, but once she had determined it was the best, the only option, his wife had taken the ball and run with it, to coin an old euphemism from his distant sporting days. But it had become an obsession with her, nearly the only driving force in her life. If she wasn't at the lawyer's office with Karen, she was scheduling the next meeting.

Meeting? More like war council.

Hawthorn could almost pity his soon-to-be-ex son-in-law. Yes, the man was a savage, and yes, his marriage to Karen was the equivalent of a medieval serf wedding his liege lord's daughter, but when Evelyn focused her vengeful nature on someone, it was nothing short of a bloodbath. He had seen her ruin several social and academic rivals, had been witness to the carnage and ultimate destruction. When his beautiful wife's ire was raised, it was a terribly wonderful thing to behold.

Hawthorn sighed. There had been a time when her passion for him, for their life together, had burned with similar intensity. Now, the fervor that had drawn him to her, that had led to so many nights of wild abandonment, ecstatic lovemaking, was nothing but a dim memory. He couldn't remember the last time she had touched him or allowed herself to be touched.

And it didn't help the situation, the frustration he struggled with daily, that Scott's office was just down the hall from Hawthorn's. Scott's wife—a sultry, exotic beauty—had taken to visiting her husband's workplace over the last few days. Hawthorn had seen her prowling the halls in a hungry, overtly sexual saunter as she found her husband absent from his office.

Ah, to have a woman like that in his life once again.

Tonight had been the piece de resistance, the crowning insult to Hawthorn's non-existent sex life. As he had passed Scott's office on his way to his car, he had heard noises emanating from behind the closed door. Telling himself he was simply ensuring the sounds were not of a distressed nature—but nowhere close to fooling himself—he stopped to listen. Above the heavy creak of furniture—Scott's desk, he was certain—he could hear a man's laboured, rhythmic grunts and a woman's throaty moans of pleasure.

Checking the hall and finding it empty, Hawthorn had leaned closer, the sexual cries fuelling his fertile imagination. He pictured Lillian leaning over the desk, its top swept haphazardly clear, her blood-red nails scoring the polished wooden surface. Her skirt—Hawthorn had never seen her wear bothersome pants—was hiked up over her hips, her animalistic desire too strong for the time it would have taken to undress, and Scott was behind her, thrusting madly.

"Harder, baby," he could hear her crying, too perfect to be his imagination. "Fuck me. Hurt me!"

"Keep your voice down," Scott warned, but the desk's wooden groans intensified.

Hawthorn smiled. Back in their youth, Evelyn would have screamed and not cared who had heard. He fell back into his voyeuristic fantasy once more. He watched as Lillian raised herself up to rip open her blouse and guide Scott's hands to her naked breasts—small, firm, perfect. She opened her eyes and smiled at Hawthorn.

So exact, so real was his fantasy that Hawthorn jumped back, his guilty eyes quickly scanning the hallway, then darting back to the door, convinced he had somehow nudged it open in his entranced state. The door was still shut, and safely locked he was sure, but the sounds from within had slowed, softened. Scott and Lillian's tryst was over, for now at least, and it was far past time Hawthorn should be gone.

Hawthorn shook himself back to reality, an embarrassed and longing smile on his face. *Evelyn*, he bemoaned, *where have you gone?*

Heading for the parkway, he passed Filmore's, the old strip club on Dundas. Hadn't he read something about it in the paper back in the summer? Something involving Jack? He let the thought go, but seeing the club's neon lights and unashamed sign guaranteeing the hottest girls in Toronto brought another memory bobbing to the surface of his sex-wrought mind.

This had definitely been in the summer; he remembered her flat, enticing stomach below her knotted T-shirt. He had been aimlessly cruising the streets of Jack's division when he had seen her standing boldly on the quiet side street's sidewalk. How many times had he driven past her? Each time believing it would be the last, and he would turn his car homeward?

And he had stopped, actually pulled over and waited for her to approach the car. Only a well-timed call from

Evelyn had prevented him from succumbing to his baser instincts. He had never sought her out again, but had never completely forgotten her either.

There. Pembroke. That was the road she had been on. He cast a furtive glance up the street as he passed it, hoping to see her, fearing he would. But the street was shadowed and draped with the soggy snowfall, and he was beyond it all too quickly.

Stopped at the red light at Sherbourne, he drummed his fingers on the wheel anxiously. A few quick turns would bring him back to her street. And if she was there?

Men like that cannot be trusted. His words to his daughter, spoken to her as they left her former home, came back to him.

The light turned green and, sighing heavily, he drove through the intersection.

"51 CIB, Constable Warren."

"Hey, Jack. Let Mason know Dove's lawyer is at the front desk."

"His lawyer?" Jack's hand clenched the phone.

"Yeah," the officer at the front desk confirmed. Then, dropping his voice, he added, "And he's one insufferable prick."

"Don't I know it," Jack grumbled. He hung up and searched the crowded office for Mason. The staff sergeant from Homicide—Gregory?—was here, plus the crew she brought from Mobile Support and a couple of hulking behemoths who looked too Neanderthalic to be carrying Homicide shields. Tank and Kris were lurking about but keeping their distance from Gregory's bunch, like wolves from different packs.

"Anybody know where Mason is?" Jack called out over the din of multiple conversations and the rattling of computer keys.

"Right here, Jack," Mason answered, rolling into the office with a Coke in hand.

Jack spun his chair, about to tell Mason about the visitor downstairs, but instead asked, "You okay? You don't look so good."

"I'm fine. Just some indigestion." To emphasize his words, he rubbed a hand over his large belly. A belly, Jack realized, that had gotten considerably bigger since he had first met the detective some eighteen months ago.

"And the Coke helps how?" Gregory asked from a nearby desk.

"It makes me belch," he justified and downed a defiant mouthful. A moment later he ripped out a massive, liquidy burp to prove his point. "See? Better already."

"You're disgusting, Mason," the Homicide D announced, but Jack glimpsed concern in her eyes an instant before her cop mask slid into place, effectively severing the softness from view. Gregory was in jeans and a sweatshirt, but as delectable—Mason's word, not Jack's—as she looked, there was a toughness to the diminutive detective that Jack wouldn't like to get on the wrong side of.

"Did you want me for something, Jack?" Mason lowered himself into a chair, looking out of place in the brightly lit detective office. Even with the boarded-up window, the CIB was still like outdoors at noon compared to the dingy

Major Crime office. Jack knew Mason hated that the MCU didn't have its own holding rooms for prisoners.

"Dove's lawyer's at the front desk," Jack informed him.

"His lawyer? You mean your…" Mason left the rest of the question unspoken, for which Jack was grateful; being known as the son of a prominent defence lawyer was akin to having the most hated teacher in school as a parent. It was a prejudice Jack could do without.

"You want me to go tell him Dove's being held and he can go fuck himself?" Jack was already half way out of his chair.

Mason raised a hand. "Hang on, Jack. Let me think." The detective gulped some more Coke and belched. "Ugh, felt that one in my nose," he complained, wrinkling up his snout.

"Are you seriously thinking about releasing Dove?" Gregory was looming over Mason, and for someone of her stature, she loomed surprisingly well.

"You bet your sweet ass, Lizzy." Mason was suddenly grinning. He quickly checked the office and, finding only his or Gregory's people, added, "What better way to bait a trap?"

The fat old white cop was droning on. "…not to be in possession of any restricted or prohibited weapon, ammunition or explosives. Finally, you are not to be outside of your residence from seven p.m. till seven a.m. Do you understand these conditions as I've read them to you?"

The old pig was staring at Lyron with his pig eyes as if he expected Lyron to say, "Yassay, massay." Like some old-time slave nigger.

Fuck you, pig.

"Do you understand the conditions?" the old cop repeated, wheezing between his words. Lyron hoped he had a fucking heart attack and died.

Lyron waited, silently amused as he watched a crimson flush creep up the fat cop's neck and across his flabby jowls. A vein was visibly pulsing in the old fuck's forehead. Just as the self-important cop—*you think those stripes your buddies gave you make you better than me?*—opened his mouth, possibly to tell the pigs flanking Lyron to take him back upstairs, he said, "Yeah, I do."

The pig's face screwed up something ugly as he bit back his words. Lyron matched the old fuck's stare until his bloodshot eyes dropped back to the documents he was holding. The papers quivered loudly in the quiet concrete room.

Lyron had been shocked when the cops had burst into Ghost's safe apartment, but he had played it cool, offering no resistance, giving the pigs no excuse to execute him right where he stood. And he had no doubt they would have gladly, joyfully gunned him down just like that bitch cop had done to Tyrone; Lyron saw the hate in their eyes and it made him feel good. People hated what they feared.

They took him to the cop shop and paraded him through the building, crowing with pride over how they had arrested him. All six of them for one unarmed nigger. Then they hustled him upstairs to the second floor, dumped him in a tiny, windowless room where two tough-acting pussies—he thought one of them was the bitch cop's partner or something—came in and had Lyron strip. They searched his clothes, made him spread his toes and open his mouth, even bend over and part his ass cheeks, but whatever they did, however they tried to humiliate him, it only gave Lyron strength. They could take everything from him, but they could never—never!—take away his pride. He had seen the busted windows, the burns left by the firebombs. No, they could never take away his pride.

Now the same pussies who had strip searched him—the bald fat fuck and the bitch's fuck buddy—stood silently alongside him back in the concrete room in which they had first flaunted his capture.

"Do you…" The old cop's voice faltered, his face still a fiery red. "Do you agree to abide by these conditions if released from custody?"

Lyron remained silent, enjoying the cop's frustrated anger. "Don't fuck around," his lawyer had cautioned. "Just yes sir, no sir. Sign the damn papers and get out. I can't be as much help to you if you're locked up." Lyron had no intention of staying behind bars, but he'd die before bowing and scraping to these white pigs.

"Perhaps you need more time to consider your options," the red-faced cop suggested, a satisfied smile twisting his ugly lips. "Officers, I think our guest will be staying with us a bit longer."

The cops gripped his arms, but Lyron held his ground. "Yeah, I agree."

Reluctantly, the sergeant held up a forestalling hand. "What was that?"

"I said, I agree."

"You agree, what?" the old fuck rasped.

Again, Lyron and the sergeant locked eyes in a silent struggle. *I ain't gonna say 'sir,' pig. I don't care what my lawyer says. Go fuck yourself.*

The tense moment stretched out, as palpable as the concrete beneath Lyron's shoes. Then, startling loud in the silence, the sergeant slapped the papers on the counter. He tossed a pen onto the documents. "Here, sign."

When Lyron stepped forward the old cop added, too quietly for the camera, "If you know how."

Lyron quickly attached his signature to the five copies, then skittered the pen back along the chipped and scarred counter to the pig.

"Bet you'd like to take a swing at me, eh Mr. Policeman?" Lyron taunted. "But only if your two buddies here held me down. Ain't that right? Wouldn't look too heroic, me kicking your fat ass all over this room."

The sergeant's face darkened from an enraged crimson to a furious purple. "Get this piece of shit out of my station," he managed to say, his voice quivering with what Lyron fervently hoped was the onset of a lethal heart attack.

The two pussies hustled him into the hall, past a gauntlet of hostile faces in black uniforms, and all but threw him into the station's tiny lobby. The fat, bald cop snarled, "Get lost," then disappeared back behind the door. Only the bitch's bitch remained, staring intently at him.

Lyron drew himself up. "What you looking at, bitch?"

The cop didn't speak, just stared at him, and Lyron felt an unsettling tremble in his stomach. The fat sergeant's eyes had been filled with impotent anger, a threat to no one other than his own overtaxed heart. But this cop's gaze, while burning with hateful rage, was at the same time empty, as if he would readily beat Lyron to death without care for witnesses or consequences. It was an expression Lyron found both unnerving and somehow familiar, like he had faced this cop before. Or seen a picture.

It suddenly hit Lyron, where he had seen the cop. It

was in an article that newspaper bitch had written, a story about what she had called a near-riot, a story about…

The Reaper.

Lyron glanced out the front doors and a shameful wave of relief quelled his unease; Auntie Dee's lawyer was walking towards the station, haloed by a TV camera's bright light. With the lawyer came a renewed bravado.

He sucked his teeth scornfully. "Think you're a tough guy? You ain't nothing but a pussy hiding behind a badge and a gun."

Even as the lawyer opened the door, the Reaper moved towards Lyron, and he found himself involuntarily falling back a step. Cursing himself for a fool—the pig wouldn't do anything with his lawyer here, would he?—he held his ground.

"I'll be watching," the Reaper told him in a hushed tone, and Lyron had to fight not to back away.

"Officer, step away from my client. Jack!"

The Reaper turned his head, and if Lyron thought he had seen rage in the cop's eyes before, it was nothing compared to the icy fury aimed at the lawyer.

"How dare you try to intimidate—" the lawyer began, but the Reaper had already shown him his back and was walking away, like the shadowed spectre that was his namesake.

Mitchell Warren walked Lyron Dove out of the police station and into the waiting hungry glare of camera lights, all the while a fatherly arm draped protectively across the younger man's shoulders. They paused in the spotlights, Warren's free hand gesturing expansively.

Jack observed his father's performance from the one intact CIB window. Next to him the shattered, scorched remains of the window where the poor copper had been turned into a human torch were still boarded over. He watched as the man responsible for such horrific injuries' was paraded as a heroic victim before the vapid media. Jack fisted his hands on the sill to keep them from trembling. Seeing his father coming to Dove's defence had ripped open a host of wounds, old and new. It had taken all of Jack's self-control not to—

Knock it off, Jack. Going down there won't accomplish anything.

Below, the circus was over. Warren was hustling Dove into a waiting car, the exhaust from its idling engine rising ghostly in the night air. The door shut behind Dove and Jack's father, and the car pulled smoothly away from the curb.

Elvis has left the building, Jack thought morosely. *I pray you're right about this, Rick.*

Down the street headlights flicked on, and a nondescript car slipped after Dove's ride.

I pray to God you're right.

"That cop has a real hate-on for you."

"Yes, so it would seem," Mitchell Warren replied offhandedly, not wanting to encourage conversation. The city outside the Town Car's window was damp and dreary from a lackluster snowfall.

"How come? You fuck him over in court or something?"

Warren turned away from his contemplation of the streets his son patrolled to face the man currently sharing the expensive automobile's back seat. Warren doubted Lyron Dove had ever been in a Town Car, except possibly to steal it.

Does he have any idea how much tonight's work would cost a real client? A paying client?

"All cops hate lawyers," he explained. "Especially defence lawyers; they know we're on the right side."

"Yeah, I see that." Dove shifted restlessly in his seat, clearly uncomfortable owing his freedom to Warren. Or had Jack unnerved him that much? Warren wouldn't blame Dove if Jack was the source of his discomfort; only Warren's pride and the presence of the TV cameras had prevented him from retreating before the look of utter contempt and naked hostility that his son had directed at him.

Damn it, Jack. If you had only focused that passion in the right areas. What a man you could have become.

Shaking his head ever so slightly at what could have been, Warren returned to business. "Forget the cop. He's nothing. You—" he pointed a finger at Dove "—need to lay low. That list of release conditions is your new bible, your ten commandments."

Dove smiled. "I ain't much of a churchgoer."

"You are now," Warren snapped, his patience at an end. "If you put a single toe out of place, if the cops even suspect you've breached a condition, your ass will be back behind bars instantly. And there'll be fuck all I can do to get you out next time. You understand?"

Dove made a rather disrespectful sucking sound through his teeth before saying, "Yeah, I hear ya."

Warren didn't know what the teeth sucking meant—he was not current with street slang and had no desire to be—but he doubted it was courteous. All he wanted was to get rid of this foul-smelling…person, then have the driver take him home.

And burn the back seat.

**Friday, 14 December
1212 hours**

Silva stood in the apartment gazing down at Bleecker Street where only yesterday he had watched as Mason and his flunkies had hauled Lyron away in cuffs. Part of him was surprised that Lyron had survived the arrest. Much easier to explain and justify killing someone who was armed and resisting than a death in custody.

"And why didn't you kill him, Mason? Because you know I'm out here. The question is, what are you going to do about it?"

The question, indeed. The sensible, the logical course of action was a strategic retreat, disappear as he had planned. Mason had his scapegoat; this could all end right now. But the scapegoat had been released.

"Was his lawyer—" Silva had witnessed Lyron's heroic rescue on television "—that good, or is Lyron bait?"

Every battlefield-honed instinct was telling Silva to

withdraw, live to fight another day. He had done enough here, hadn't he? The guilty had been punished, the weak protected. Like the hand of God, as his mother would have moralized, he had swept the land of the wicked. But not all of them. There would always be more.

"But one man can only do so much."

And with that, he knew what had to be done.

The blank screen of Millie's computer stared back at her, mocking her with its uninterrupted whiteness. Half a dozen times she had started writing and half a dozen times she had erased it all.

"Shit, shit, shit," she muttered, pounding her fists quietly on the keyboard. A line of nonsensical letters jumped across the screen. "About as good as anything I've written today," she bitched as she pressed down on the backspace key.

A story was out there, her story, but she had nothing new, no new angle. True, Lyron Dove had been arrested and released last night for the firebombing on the police station, but she had missed the whole escapade. She'd been forced to watch on the TV—just like every slob in this city—as Lyron's lawyer had walked him triumphantly out of the cop shop.

"Ungrateful bastard gets use of a phone and calls his lawyer, for shit's sake. I could have called his lawyer for him *and* he would have been front-page material. Bastard."

She could feel her story, her ticket to the *New York Times*, petering out. What had once been a roaring, uncontrolled firestorm was now nothing more than a backyard bonfire and getting smaller every hour. Lyron's arrest had put a face to the atrocities and had seemingly placated the cops for the time being. His release—unharmed and healthy—had soothed the community's fears that he would end up dead while in police custody. It appeared that everyone was willing to let the legal system move on in its tireless, plodding manner.

True, there were still some out there carrying on the fight. Most likely Lyron's crew from the bombing acting out from some shit-assed ideal of loyalty, or cracked-out idiots too caught up in the euphoria of shitting on the cops to realize that no one really gave a shit any longer.

She pushed away from the computer, sulking. "It would have been better if the cops had killed him."

"Little Miss Sensationalism at a loss for a story?" Ted Huntington asked as he strolled past her cubicle, a condescending smirk on his fat face.

"Go fuck yourself, Ted."

"Always a pleasure talking with you, Millie."

She glared at his back and shot him the finger. "Sanctimonious asshole."

Her desk phone buzzed and she glared at, it as well. *What now? The cops and the Park having a love-in at the community centre?* She hooked the phone and snapped, "Templeton."

"I have a job for you."

No hello, no greeting, but Millie knew who it was. Him. The mysterious player behind Lyron, the one who had tipped her to the ammunition, the one the Homicide bitch wanted to get her hands on. The day was suddenly looking a whole lot brighter.

Keeping the excitement out of her voice, she asked,

"And why would I do anything for you?"

He laughed, sounding amused at her attempted indifference. "Because without me, you have nothing. Without me, Lyron sits at home and you get to watch everything you've worked for fade away."

Bastard! "Meaning?"

Again that annoying, knowing chuckle. "Right now, Lyron has been effectively leashed, and I'm the only one who can set him free."

"Then why are you calling me, not him?"

"Use your brains, bitch. I've read your writing, I know you have some."

Millie bit back her anger. *I am so going to crucify you when the time comes, you asshole.* "You think the police have his phone tapped."

"Clever girl. You call him, tell him you want to come over for an interview."

"Why can't he come to me?"

"Now you're being a stupid girl. He's under house arrest, he won't risk going to jail just to talk to you. Fuck you, maybe, but not talk to you."

Millie's nails dug into the chair's armrest. "How do you know his release conditions?"

"I have my sources, just like you."

"Okay, so say I go see him. I suppose you want me to deliver a message?"

"Of course. You're going to tell him our work isn't finished, not by a long shot. You're going to tell him where and when to meet me."

"I thought you said he wouldn't break his conditions."

"Fuck, woman. Are you deaf? I said he wouldn't risk it for you. Now shut up and listen."

Millie shut up and listened, but as she jotted down what she was told she was busy determining her next step. Arrange the meeting then call Gregory at Homicide? No, too soon. Go with Lyron—tell him it's part of the plan if he balks—meet up with this cocky asshole, then call Gregory.

That way I get the story and credit for the arrest.

She was smiling as she hung up.

Jack powered up out of the squat, his muscles screaming in pain, screaming for more. He paused, sucked in a deep breath, then dropped down again, the barbell across his shoulders quivering beneath its load of iron plates.

"Up, Jack!" Tank bellowed. "Get your ass up!"

"Fuck!" Jack yelled as he pushed against the bar. Tank, spotting from behind, squatted with him, his hands poised over Jack's waist in case the weight proved too much. It didn't. Feeling strong, feeling fucking invincible, he drove up again, thrilling in the strength in his legs. He dropped the bar onto the rack with a satisfying crash that for a second obliterated Metallica on the stereo.

"Fucking good set, Jack." Tank clapped him on the back as Jack hung from the barbell, giving his legs a much deserved rest. "You doing another?"

"I'm done," he managed, straightening up. He loosened off his weight belt and let it drop to the gym floor, sighing in relief.

"I take it your workouts are going well," Tank asked with a knowing grin.

Jack nodded. "Yeah, real good." *That's a bit of an understatement. I just squatted four-oh-five for eight fucking reps.* Six months ago, a barbell thirty pounds lighter than that had folded Jack up on the fourth rep, cracking a rib. Now he felt like he could slap some more plates on and go again.

"You're up to what? Three injections a week?" Tank asked after making sure he and Jack had the station's small gym to themselves. Not that most coppers would care about steroid use, but it always paid to be careful. "I can see that you've put on some size. Feeling good?"

"It's like you said," Jack replied as he began stripping plates off the bar. "I feel like I could work out all day and fuck all night."

Tank laughed, a surprisingly tiny chortle from such a large body. "Well, I'll do what I can for the workouts, but for the rest you're on your own. Maybe Jenny can help you out."

Jack glared at him. "Like Kris helps you out?"

Tank looked startled by the edge in Jack's words, then held up his hands. "Sorry, man, just a bad joke."

"No, I'm sorry, Tank," Jack apologized, feeling deflated as suddenly as his anger had risen. "Everyone assumes we're sleeping together, but we're not. She's seeing someone, and I'm still kind of married. It's just a bit of a sore spot for me," he finished lamely.

"No problem, man. I understand. Divorces can really fuck you up. And with all the shit going on here, adding to your stress…" Tank paused, thinking. "Do you think right now is the best time to be trying the 'roids? I mean, with all the stress in your life."

Jack laughed. An honest, sincere bark of humour. "I think they're the only reason I'm doing so well. I don't think I'd have the physical strength to handle all of this, otherwise."

"That's good," Tank said, looking relieved. "Catch you upstairs."

Alone in the gym, Jack sat on a bench and dropped his head into his hands. He hadn't lied to Tank; the steroids made him feel physically strong and capable. In the gym he could push all the shit to the side, lose himself in the exertion of the workout, but unfortunately, the 'roids didn't do a damn thing for the rest of him.

I guess there aren't any steroids for the soul.

More and more frequently, the only reason Jack got out of bed was because Justice, and now Bear as well, needed to be let out and fed. If not for that responsibility he doubted he'd ever get to the gym, juiced up or not. His days were just a black mass of useless existence, a waste of time. The only bright spots in his life were the dogs and the brief periods he got to spend with Jenny.

Then talk to her, you idiot.

But he knew he wouldn't. She had more than enough trouble of her own right now, and besides, what would he say? That every day there seemed to be less reason to get out of bed? To keep trying? She didn't need that, and he'd be a selfish asshole to dump it on her.

So he'd just keep pushing forward. This crap couldn't last forever. Once the divorce was done, the house sold and all the shit at work died down, life could get back to normal. As normal as possible without Karen. But like Jenny, Karen didn't need or deserve to be subjected to him and all his problems.

"Hey, Jack. You okay?"

Jack quickly raised his head, feeling like he'd been caught with something ugly exposed. Paul was sticking his head inside the gym door. "You don't look so good, my man," the big cop stated.

Jack forced a weary smile onto his face. "Just tired, Paul. Tank whipped my ass in a leg workout."

"Yeah, he can do that." Paul grinned and disappeared back into the change room.

The smile vanished from Jack's face as if it had never been. "Just tired, is all."

"Hey, Manny, what's up?"

"You busy, Jack? Can you swing by Pembroke and Gerrard?"

"Yeah, sure." Jack frowned. Manny sounded guarded, hesitant. "You okay?"

"I'm good, dude. I just got something here I need to talk to you about."

"Okay. Be there in a couple of minutes." Puzzled, Jack flipped his phone shut and tucked it away. Not long after, he swung onto Pembroke and pulled in behind the Ident van. Manny, with a winter coat over his FIS golf shirt, met Jack on the sidewalk.

"I called the station and they said you were on the road."

Jack nodded. "Mason's got a play tonight, hopefully. I was just going to grab some dinner first."

"Sorry, dude, but this couldn't wait." Jack's friend and former partner had a silly grin on his face, yet still managed to look uneasy.

"What couldn't wait?" Jack rubbed his eyes. It had been

a hell of a day, a hell of a week, and to top it off he had a migraine building deep in his skull.

"With all the shit that's been going on, I was in the area," Manny quickly explained; working with Jack, he had learned to recognize migraine signals. "I spotted this guy talking to a hooker so I figured I'd give him a lecture before sending him home."

"And?" Jack looked past Manny, for the first time noticing the car directly ahead of the police van. It was an expensive-looking car, and a man—the would-be john, Jack assumed—was sitting in the open passenger door, his head in his hands.

There was something familiar about the john. *No, it couldn't be.* Jack stepped past Manny and slowly approached the slumped-over figure. At the sound of Jack's running shoes crunching on the salted sidewalk, the man looked up. Ashamed and horrified.

George Hawthorn.

Jack's guts twisted at the sight of Karen's father. All the pain of the last year came back, flooding Jack in a mess of guilt, shame and anger.

"You okay, Jack?" Manny placed a cautionary hand of Jack's arm.

Nodding, Jack turned his back on Hawthorn.

"Normally, I'd just give the guy a lecture, threaten to call his wife—" Jack could feel Hawthorn flinching at the thought "—and cut him loose. But I thought this was a set of special circumstances. A quick statement from the hooker and he's done." Manny gestured at the woman standing a short distance away, and Jack glanced her way, noting absently that with the long dark hair and slim build she slightly resembled Jenny.

Jack laughed quietly to himself. Special circumstances. An understatement at best. This was a gift from heaven, a chance at payback, to throw back some of the shit Hawthorn had been dumping on him since Jack and Karen had first started dating. If there was a face to be put to the failure Jack's life had become it was Hawthorn's. Who had never stopped telling Karen that Jack wasn't good enough for her? When Jack's job had become a wedge between him and Karen, who had done all he could to drive that wedge deeper? Who had welcomed Karen home with open arms, encouraging her to stay, to escape the savage? Who had hired Karen's fucking lawyer?

Hawthorn.

Jack faced Hawthorn, and the man wilted beneath that icy stare. Jack knew a charge of communicating for the purpose of prostitution wouldn't survive. Hawthorn's lawyer could probably crush it at the first court appearance, but the damage would be done. The tale of how Hawthorn had been arrested with a hooker—and a cheap streetwalker, not a high-class escort—would spread like wildfire through the university and Hawthorn's snob-filled society. He would be humiliated, ostracized. Perhaps he would even learn the pain of a wife walking away.

But he was Karen's father. Any pain Jack inflicted on him would be felt by her. She would see this as an attack, as Jack striking back the only way he could. He would prove he was the monster she believed him to be.

"Cut him loose, Manny. It isn't worth it."

"Okay, boys, heads up. Our boy is on the move and looks like that reporter chick is playing chauffer." The Mobile Support officer, formerly of 51 MCU and Homicide, gratefully relayed the info; sitting on the rooftop across from Dove's Regent Park townhouse was getting to be a pain in the ass. Literally.

"Roger that. Over."

"Cut the crap, Stevens, and quit fucking around. Send Timmins to pick me up. If we lose Dove, the boss lady will have our asses."

The second-floor patio of 259 Sherbourne Street was the ideal site for a clandestine meeting. Open on three sides, the field of view was excellent. Anyone approaching would have to come across Bleecker, Sherbourne or a playground. The apartment building itself blocked the patio's south end except for a narrow walkway on the Bleecker side, but Silva had taken care of that. It would require too many bodies to establish an effective perimeter, too much area to cover and too many gaps—and Silva was good at slipping through the cracks. Good views and good escape routes in virtually any direction. A quick drop to the ground and he could vanish.

Manned by volunteers drawn from Lyron's crew, Silva had three cars waiting for him if the need arose. And he would be surprised if a need—a very urgent need—didn't arise. Hotshot lawyer or not, there was no way Lyron should have been released, not on those charges. Unless Mason was casting the kid out as bait. Bait for whom?

Why, for me, of course.

He grinned in the dim light. Conveniently, all the lights for the area were broken, and only the street lamps on Sherbourne threw any illumination this far. Crouched behind a concrete planter, Silva was one with the shadows.

Meeting with Lyron was a risk, a huge risk. Silva knew—he absolutely *knew*—that Lyron was being followed, that he himself was the ultimate goal for Mason's pawns. So why chance arrest? He could tell himself his work wasn't done yet, that he could not leave the scourging of the guilty incomplete—did the angel of death strike down only some of Egypt's firstborn?—but it would be a lie.

I'll leave this game when I'm damn good and ready, on my own terms. Not forced out by the likes of you, Mason. If that was pride talking, then Silva considered it an acceptable price for the punishment of many.

Already the fire in the Park was dying down. Like the bonfires at the shift parties on Cherry Beach he had attended back in his uniformed days, when the flames were allowed to die with the approach of the sun, so was the passion, the craze, flickering out in those waging the war against the police. No, this could not be allowed to happen. Not yet. Silva knew what was needed to reignite the conflagration, and for that he needed Lyron.

One more task, Mason, then he's yours for the taking.

Footsteps in the damp, cold air. Silva shifted to peer around the planter and stifled a curse.

Fucking bitch! What's she doing here?

No matter. Silva would grab Lyron and get the fuck out of here before the cops following him and the reporter got close. If that bitch imagined she was getting an interview, then she was a bigger fool than Silva thought. Checking the twin handguns tucked into his belt, Silva stood up, motioning for Lyron to join him. The bitch let out a tiny squeak when Silva rose out of the shadows, but quickly recovered, hurrying to catch up with Lyron.

"Why the fuck did you bring her?" Silva snarled, scanning the night around them.

Lyron opened his mouth, puzzled. "You said she was to come. Right?"

"You fucking idiot. I didn't—" Broken glass—the shattered light bulbs Silva had strewn in the darkened walkway—crunched under foot.

"She brought the cops!" Silva grabbed Lyron and threw him to the ground as he drew his Glock. He capped off three quick shots at the shadows, the muzzle flashes tearing at the darkness. Not pausing, he kicked Lyron to his feet and shoved him towards the railing.

"Jump!" he yelled, and fired off another two rounds. He couldn't see the cops that he knew where there, just wanted to keep them down.

The bitch was screaming, a shrill piercing that cut through the gunshots' bouncing echoes. Silva waited until Lyron leapt from the railing, then thrust his gun at the yowling woman.

"Fuck you, bitch," he said, and fired twice—a perfect double tap—just as gunfire erupted from the walkway. Bullets tugged at Silva's flesh as the bitch went down. He dropped to a knee and emptied his clip, not bothering to aim. As his gun locked open, empty, he vaulted over the railing. He landed next to Lyron. Mason's scapegoat was crouched low, frozen, but time was a luxury they didn't have. The situation was rapidly falling to shit. Dark shapes were converging, and Silva knew the trap would soon be too tight to escape. Grabbing Lyron by the scruff of his neck, Silva hauled him to his feet.

"Run!" Silva commanded, pointing across Bleecker, into St. Jamestown. Lyron ran.

Silva could hear frantic shouting up on the patio and in the playground. Gunshots barked behind them, and Lyron actually slowed down, looking over his shoulder.

Who the fuck do you think they're shooting at? "Move!"

They cut through the basketball court between 325 and 375 Bleecker, forcing any pursuit to be on foot. Lyron was beginning to lag, but Silva kept pushing. As they ran, he ejected his spent clip, letting it drop. He didn't care if the cops found it; the only prints on it were Lyron's. He slapped in a fresh magazine and racked a round. Good to go.

"Here," Silva gasped, and shoved Lyron towards an idling car. Lyron stumbled the last few feet, pinwheeling his arms to keep his balance.

Silva ripped open the back door and pushed Lyron in, telling him to get low. To the driver, Silva ordered, "Nice and easy. Down Parliament. You blow a red light, roll through a stop sign, catch the cops' attention, and I swear to God I'll put a bullet through your fucking brains." The driver nodded his understanding and pulled calmly into traffic.

Silva huddled down beside Lyron. "Fucking stupid, bringing that bitch with you."

"She said it was part of the deal," Lyron protested, still winded. "She said you wanted to talk with her. How was I to know?" he whined.

Useless fuck. Aloud, he asked, "First time in a firefight?" Not that Lyron had been actually involved in the shooting, but it was time to see what this scapegoat was capable of.

Lyron nodded, his eyes wide. "And when we hit the station."

"Right." *Buildings don't shoot back, bitch.* "You did good. Didn't freeze." Silva heaved a deep breath. He hadn't sprinted like that in some time. "They shot at us, no warning. Didn't try to arrest us. You see what they're willing to do?"

"Yeah," Lyron breathed. "Fucking pigs."

Silva fixed Lyron with a steely stare. "The question is, what are *you* willing to do?"

Lyron didn't shy away. "Blood for blood, man."

"Good man," Silva praised, gripping Lyron's shoulder. "It's time to kill the cop who started it all."

"The bitch who shot Ty?" Lyron's words were a strained hush, excitement and disbelief.

"The very one," Silva confirmed and handed Lyron his Glock.

Mason trudged across the parking lot, a beaten, disheartened man.

God, what a fucking mess. A gunfight right in the open, that bloody reporter—what the fuck was she doing there?—shot, may not live. Fuck, what a mess.

Everything had been going well, according to plan. The guys from Mobile were following Dove and the reporter, doubtless on the way to meet up with Silva. Mobile had the three of them cornered, but before everyone could get in place, draw the net nice and tight, all fucking hell had broken loose.

And what did they have to show for it? A civilian—a fucking reporter, no less!—wounded, possibly fatally. A cop with an ankle broken from jumping after Silva. Thank God he'd been able to limp away before any uniforms responded to the gunshots. Worst of all, no Dove, no Silva.

And his guts were killing him. It felt like a bucketful of acid was burning its way up his throat.

Should maybe see a doctor, he mused, then laughed scornfully. *Exactly when would I find the time?*

His Chev, a boat from earlier days, was tucked away in the lot's far corner. The hood was sadly decorated with the last of the autumn's leaves. Small leaf drifts had built up against the wipers.

When was the last time I went home?

There was no reason to stay any longer. After tonight's debacle Silva would disappear into the woodwork, and they'd have to wait for him to surface again, six months, a year from now. Who fucking knew when?

The shooting was being treated as any crime scene. After all, there was nothing to link the gunfight to the police, although initial reports from the scene confirmed that some of the spent ammunition was forty caliber. Police ammo. Silva's, no doubt, and just as guaranteed, Mason knew any prints found would belong to Dove.

You really nailed him to the cross, didn't you?

He reached out to brush the leaves away, but a burning pain in his guts doubled him over. With one hand on the car's cold metal to keep from falling, he pressed the other to his chest as the pain seared its way up from his stomach. Gasping for air, he twisted to lean against the car door, his hands searching frantically for his antacids. He was fumbling with the bottle when a voice came out of the dark, out of the past.

"Not doing too well, Rick?"

Mason turned his head—he couldn't have moved his body to save his life; the pain was sucking the strength out of him—to face a ghost, his own version of the Ghost of Christmas Past.

"You don't look so good, Rick," Silva assessed, stepping close to peer at Mason's pale face. "You're sweating like a turkey basting in its own fat."

"Why..." Mason tried to talk, but there was a vise clamped on his chest, crushing his ribs.

"Why? I could ask you the same fucking question, Rick." Silva jabbed a finger at Mason's chest, but the detective barely felt it beneath the sledge hammer pounding him. "You tried to kill me," Silva hissed.

Mason weakly shook his head. "I didn't..."

"You look like a fish." Silva laughed, pinching Mason's cheeks, puckering his lips grotesquely. "Don't lie to me, Rick. I'm tired of all your lies, you ass-wipe." He pulled Mason close until his hate-twisted face filled Mason's vision. "I came here to return the favour, but it looks like God got here before me. I think I'll leave it up to Him. Besides," Silva chuckled, "I can always kill you later."

Silva stepped back, surveying Mason. "Don't feel too bad, Rick. You ain't the only one dying tonight. The bitch that started it all is getting her ticket punched, too. My little buddy Lyron is seeing to her personally. Who knows? Maybe you'll be lucky and live long enough to hear about it."

Mason's eyesight was shrinking as a terrible blackness ate at the edges of his vision. The vise over his heart squeezed once more, an uncaring iron hand crushing his chest, and a cold numbness flooded his left arm. The antacid bottle fell from fingers he could no longer feel, hitting the pavement with an echoing plastic *pop*.

Silva squatted, examined the bottle. "I don't think these are going to do any good, Rick." He stood up. "But—"

Mason had his Glock in hand, his elbow braced on his hip.

Snickering, Silva pointed at the gun. "As if you could—"

A single shot ripped through the night, but Mason barely heard it over the roaring of his own blood in his ears. He saw Silva stagger back, hands clutching his side.

I hit him, Mason thought grimly. *I shot the fucking bastard.*

The gun sagged in Mason's grip. He tried to raise his arm, screamed at himself to lift the damn gun, to get off another shot, drop Silva while he had the chance. But the gun didn't rise. It slipped from his fingers, and he heard it clatter on the ground as the clamour in his ears ebbed away.

Silva stepped forward, a dark hazy figure.

I guess he's going to kill me after all.

But Silva didn't pick up the gun, didn't kill Mason. He stopped, then suddenly ran off, almost instantly vanishing into the shadows of Mason's eyesight.

Well, fuck me.

What little strength Mason had left quickly drained from his body. His legs buckled, dumping him on his ass. Sitting against his car, he waited to see if he was going to die.

Jack was heading up the outside stairs from the basement change room when he heard the gunshot. He instinctively ducked even though he was still below ground level, but didn't stay down. The shot had been close, close enough to have come from inside the parking lot, and he wasn't about to hide, not when a cop could be bleeding a short distance away.

Unarmed, unprotected, he ran into the lot. Others were streaming out of the station, guns in hand. Jack was painfully reminded of the attack on the station and how a bloodbath had been averted when cops hadn't charged outside.

Fuck, we could be running into an ambush.

"There!"

A shadowy figure was sprinting from the lot, making for the Park. Officers took off in pursuit. Jack wanted to join the chase, but without a gun or radio he could easily end up being a hindrance or worse. As well, the lot needed to be searched. Who knew what the person had been up to and what the gunshot meant.

Jack prowled among the personal cars, not knowing what he was looking for but fearing he'd find the worst. If a copper had fired the shot, he or she would have let everyone know. If some asshole was responsible, why come right into the lot? He could have shot at the cars from beyond the chain-link fence, if cars were the target. No, it didn't make sense that the cars were the objective, and that left only one other possibility.

Jack found Mason a couple of minutes later.

He was slumped against the side of his car, and Jack feared he was dead. Even under the poor light he could see how pale, how drained of life Mason's complexion was. But as Jack knelt by him, the detective's eyes flickered open.

"Jack?" Mason's voice was deathly weak, less than a whisper.

"It's me, Rick. Hang on." Uniformed figures were milling about the parking lot. "Over here! Get an ambulance and put a rush on it!"

Jack returned to Mason. "Help's coming, Rick. Don't you dare fucking die on me." Cursing himself for not having a flashlight, he ran his hands over Mason's torso, searching for blood.

Mason raised his hand, tried to knock Jack's hand away. His arm fell limply to his side. "Not…shot…heart…my heart."

An officer Jack didn't recognize skidded to a halt, banged his knee off the car's bumper.

"He's not shot," Jack explained before time could be wasted on stupid questions. "He's having a heart attack."

"Then who got shot?" the cops asked, puzzled.

"No one got shot, you idiot. I think he shot *at* someone." Jack gestured to the Glock on the pavement. "Now get me a fucking ambulance."

"Right, right." The cop yanked out his radio, stepped away to make the call.

"Hang tight, Rick. Help's on the way."

"No time," Mason wheezed. "Silva…"

"Silva was here? Okay, don't worry about him, we'll get him later. I need you to—"

"Shut the fuck up," Mason growled, some of his old iron will strengthening his words. "Silva told me…said Dove's…"

"Dove?" Jack leaned closer. "Dove's what?"

Mason grimaced. "Fuck…it hurts. Dove's…going after…"

"Who's he going after, Rick?" A cold, sick foreboding twisted Jack's guts. "Who's he going after?"

Mason drew a ragged breath. Jack could see he was fighting to stay conscious. His breath escaped him, and on its tenuous wind, Jack heard what he feared most.

"…Jenny."

A fine rain was falling, starring the cheerful lights decorating the homes along Jenny's street. She was anything but cheered by the lights. Another horrific day, another abysmal date with Brian. The late dinner at a local pub—she wasn't up to fine dining these days—had been going well, or as well as could be expected, when the television over the bar had delivered the shocking news that a reporter for the *Citizen* had been found shot in St. Jamestown. Police were searching for the suspect, Lyron Dove, who had been seen with the victim shortly before the shooting.

Dear God, how many more people are going to be hurt or killed because of me?

Brian had tried to convince her it wasn't her fault, but he just didn't understand. If she hadn't shot Tyrone Johnson then none of the rest—the poor officer burned at the attack on the station, that sweet old woman beaten half to death, dear Phil, Jack's friend, shot to death—would have happened.

The date had ended miserably with Brian heading off to work when he had originally planned to take the night off. Now she was walking home in the rain, alone. Her heels tapped out a lonely pace on the sidewalk. She considered calling Jack but decided against it; he had enough troubles of his own, and besides, he was working tonight. No, she'd just go home and curl up with the dogs. If she was lucky she might even manage to sleep for a while.

Inside her purse her cell phone, muted, flashed unseen.

"Damn it! God fucking damn it!"

Jack thumbed his phone off and clamped both hands on the steering wheel. *She didn't hear it, that's all. That's all.*

He tromped on the gas and the old Taurus laboured beneath his demands. The engine chugged, lurching the car along the rain-slick road.

"Don't you die! Don't you fucking dare!"

As if it had heard him, the motor gave a massive belch then revved to new life. Jack pressed even harder on the accelerator as he dialed 911.

Jenny lived on a little side street that overlooked the Don Valley. It was a street of older couples, and at this time of night very few of the windows weren't dark. Even most of the Christmas lights were off. The cold drizzle falling through the winter-bare trees gave the street a stark and dismal feel.

Snow would be nice, Jenny thought as she pulled the collar of her leather coat tighter.

"Jennifer Alton?" a voice asked from behind her.

Crap, not another reporter. How do they keep getting my address? "Listen," she began, turning, and found herself staring at a gun.

"Thought it was you, bitch. Just wanted to be sure."

A young black man held the gun, his face radiating hate. Raindrops clung to his baby dreadlocks and glistened in the streetlight. Jenny had the bizarre thought it looked like he was wearing Christmas lights in his hair.

"Nothing to say, bitch?"

The handgun was centered on her face. It didn't waver. Whether by plan or fluke, the man stayed just out of reach. Not that it mattered. A heaviness had sunk into her limbs, as if her body had already accepted the outcome and given itself to a fitting, if not just, punishment.

She shook her head sadly, felt a raindrop trace down her cheek like an icy tear. "What do you want me to say? What can I say?"

"That you're sorry, bitch!" he yelled, stabbing the gun at her for emphasis. "How about that, huh? Sorry that Tyrone's dead, that you killed him."

"Of course, I'm sorry," she whispered miserably into the echo of Dove's tirade, recognizing him from Jack's description. "Do you think I actually wanted to kill him?"

"It sure as shit looked that way, bitch. *You—*" he jabbed with the gun "—shot *him* and *he's—*" another jab "—dead. He didn't even have a gun."

"I didn't know that!" she screamed, all of the guilt, agony and regret exploding out of her. "I didn't fucking know that!"

Dove stepped back, shocked by her vehemence, but his uncertainty was short-lived. "Bullshit. You just saw another nigger you could shoot."

"Shut up!" she shrieked. "Just shut up! I thought he had a gun. He—"

"That's a lie!" Dove threw back at her. "Tyrone would never have a gun. Not even a toy one." The gun, which had been dropping, came up on target.

"Not him," Jenny whispered, her rage spent. "Not

Tyrone. It was the other one." Oblivious, uncaring to the gun trained on her, she sagged against a car parked on the street and buried her face in her hands. "We weren't looking for Tyrone," she said, her words muffled by her hands. She raised her face, turned agonized, tearful eyes on her would-be executioner. "Freddy Franklin was telling everyone he had a gun. We were looking for him, not Tyrone."

Dove paused, and Jenny could see confused anger on his face. "So you killed Tyrone instead? That it?"

She shook her head as she palmed away her tears. "No. We told them to stop, both of them." Her eyes stared past Dove, back to a cold night on a dimly lit walkway. "Franklin put his hands up right away, but Tyrone…Tyrone didn't. He wouldn't listen to us, to me. I kept telling him to stand still but he wouldn't. I thought Franklin had passed him the gun when he saw us coming."

"That's all bull—"

But Jenny wasn't talking to Dove, not really. "At one point Tyrone ducked behind Franklin, and I thought he was going to use him as protection, a human shield." Her eyes were unfocused, her voice heavy with memories. "Then he started going through Franklin's pockets, like he wanted to find the gun. I don't know."

"He probably meant to grab it and run away so his friend wouldn't get in trouble. That's what Tyrone would have done." Dove sounded unsure of himself. His gun hung somewhere between the ground and Jenny.

"Could be." Jenny shrugged. "But we'll never know. Tyrone's hand came out of Franklin's pocket and he was holding something. Something metal. He pointed it at me, and I…" Her voice broke, and for several heartbeats she was silent. At length she looked at Dove. "And I shot him," she admitted.

Dove's face contorted, as if he was fighting to control, or perhaps force, his anger. "What was it? What did Tyrone die for, bitch?"

"A crack pipe. Franklin's fucking crack pipe." Jenny pushed off from the car, and Dove moved away, keeping a distance between them. She faced him, resigned. "I shot him because he pointed a copper crack pipe at me, and it's something I'll have to live with for the rest of my life."

Dove raised the gun. "Who says you ain't going to die right now?"

"Dove!"

Jenny and Dove both turned. Jack was there, his hands held out beseechingly. "Don't do it, Lyron. It won't solve anything."

"She killed Tyrone," Dove snarled, positioning himself so he could see both of them.

"And you think murdering her will fix that? Is that what Tyrone would want?"

"Shut up!" Dove snapped the gun around at Jack. Keeping his eyes on Jack, he pointed a finger at Jenny. "She killed him. She deserves to die."

"What will that accomplish?" Jack asked. "It won't end here. More people will be hurt, killed. Tyrone and your Auntie Dee wouldn't want that."

"Shut the fuck up! You don't know them. You don't know what they want." Tears were shining on Dove's cheeks, mixing with the faint rain. He swung the gun from Jack to Jenny and back.

"You're right, I don't know them." Jack's voice was soft but sure. "But I know what Silva wants, and if you kill either of us you'll be playing right into his hands."

"What the fuck are you talking about?" Dove's doubt sounded greater than ever, but the gun was still up.

Jenny saw what Jack was doing, drawing Dove's attention to himself. She knew that if she could ask him, Jack would say he would want to be the one shot, the one to die. She wasn't about to let him make that sacrifice. Not when the blood was on her hands. She slid a step closer to Dove.

"Silva. Marco Silva," Jack was saying. "He didn't tell you his name, did he? What did he say? That he was on some police most-wanted list, that it would be safer for you not to know his name?"

"I don't know what you're talking about." Dove licked his lips as his eyes darted repeatedly from Jack to Jenny.

But he did know. Jenny could see it in his face, hear it in his words. She took another step.

"He's using you, Lyron," Jack said bluntly. "He's lied to you from the start. He isn't some criminal mastermind. He's a cop."

Dove staggered back a step, as if Jack had physically hit him. "No. That doesn't make any sense. He ain't no cop."

Jack had obviously seen that he had rocked Dove and wasn't about to let up. "He used to be, used to work at 51, but had to quit because he was too violent. Now he's back, and he's using you and all the shit in the Park—everything he'll make sure you get blamed for—as cover, a smoke-screen. He's killing people, Lyron. Criminals, gang members, anyone he thinks should die. And when he's done he'll disappear, and you'll be left holding the bag."

"I don't believe you," Lyron whispered. "I don't fucking believe it."

"How do you think we got your fingerprints?" Jack slowly, carefully, pointed at the gun in Dove's hand. "He gave you that gun, didn't he? I'll bet he used it to kill Freddy

Franklin and the old man with the dog. Were you with him tonight when he shot the reporter? With that gun? The gun that now has your prints all over it."

Dove's eyes widened, focused on the gun he was holding. "He shot her?" Jenny could see pieces of a puzzle falling into place in Dove's mind. She moved closer and saw Jack mimicking her action. She tried to warn Jack away with her eyes, but he refused to see her.

Jack nodded. "Yeah, he shot the reporter, left her to die, and gave you the murder weapon. He's the one who attacked Auntie Dee."

"Bullshit!" Dove raged. "That was the cops."

"He did," Jack assured him. "She gave us a description: black, with his hair in cornrows. That's him, right? He's been playing all of us for fools. The cops, everyone in the Park. And he's set you up to take the fall."

In the distance but growing louder were the screams of sirens.

"Drop the gun, Lyron," Jack pleaded. "Drop the gun and we can make him pay for everyone he's hurt, for everyone he's killed. Don't let him use you anymore, Lyron."

Dove was staring at Jack, Jenny forgotten. "I...I didn't..." Jenny watched Dove's face, and for a moment she thought he'd do as Jack was asking, but then his features hardened.

Lyron raised the gun, sighted on the bitch. It didn't matter what that cop, the Reaper, said, she was the one who killed Tyrone. She deserved to die.

And yet he couldn't pull the trigger. The trigger of the gun handed to him by a man who called himself Ghost, a man Lyron suddenly realized he knew nothing about. Doubts flooded his mind.

Ghost, a cop? It couldn't be, it couldn't be.

He shook himself. It didn't matter. Even if everything the cop said about Ghost was true, Tyrone was still dead, and she was the one who killed him.

And yet still, he stayed his hand.

He had come here eagerly, with vengeance in his heart. Confronting the cop before he killed her, he had expected fear or defiance from her, possibly tears and begging, but not the raw remorse she had shown him.

She's just acting, trying to save her own skin.

But as he looked at her anguished eyes, he discovered that shooting someone in cold blood was a far cry from tossing firebombs at a car or shooting at the windows of a police station.

"It's over, Lyron," the Reaper was saying. "Drop the gun."

Lyron turned his eyes from the bitch and found himself surrounded by police, their guns all aimed at him.

"It's over. Drop the gun, Lyron. Please."

The Reaper was right, it was over. Regardless of what Lyron did, he would not walk away from this. He lowered the gun to his side. He had a choice: open his hand and let the gun fall, or fight. Did he want to spend the rest of his life in a cell, a trophy for the police? Or did he want to see how many he could take with him? Surely, shooting a faceless cop behind a gun would be easier than killing her while he looked into her eyes.

He used me.

Ghost had planned this all along. All of Lyron's decisions had been made for him. Was Ghost laughing at him? Most likely, but maybe, just maybe, Lyron could earn his respect.

He raised the gun.

**Saturday, 15 December
1230 hours**

The sun shone high in a cloudless sky, yet the air held a chill, sharp but not unpleasant. Jack and Jenny stood outside of the small group of mourners, not wanting to intrude on a private affair. Most of the group were elderly and huddled within thick winter coats despite the sunshine. One woman, though, had her face turned up to the sun, a small smile belaying the gleam of tears in her eyes. She brought her eyes down from the sun to the casket where it lay within the cold ground, and in passing briefly paused on Jack, a flicker of recognition crossing her face.

The interment over, the mourners began to head for the cars, a long walk for those who felt the bite of cold on aged bones.

"Did you want to say goodbye?" Jenny asked.

"No." Jack wiped away a tear. "I already have."

They turned away from Phil's final place of rest, and

Jenny took Jack's gloved hand in hers. "It was a beautiful service," she commented. "There were a lot more people here than I expected."

"Yeah, more than I thought, too." Jack had secretly feared he and Jenny would be the only ones on scene to say goodbye to Phil. "It was awfully nice of her to have his friends driven here. I doubt any of them would have been able to attend otherwise."

"Excuse me," a woman called, hurrying to catch up to them. While others had their heads bowed in prayer or grief, hers had been smiling at the sun. "I'm Phil's great-granddaughter, Lisa. I don't mean to be rude, but are you Jack? The police officer?"

"I am, and there's no need to apologize." Jack extended his hand. "This is Jennifer, my partner."

"It's a pleasure to meet you," Jenny said, shaking hands with the woman. "I'm sorry we had to meet this way."

"Thank you. Daddy Phil was quite taken with you," she told Jenny, then laughed. "He joked that if Officer Jack hadn't been so big, he would have courted you."

"I wish I had the chance to know him better."

"So do I," Lisa said sadly, looking back at the grave. "I hadn't seen him in over ten years, and now he's gone." He hands slipped over her stomach. "He won't get to meet his great-great-grandchild."

"It may be a small conciliation," Jack ventured, "but the last time I saw Phil, he was ecstatic over your visit. Said it was the best damn day he'd had in a long time."

Lisa laughed. "That sounds like Daddy Phil. That's what he wanted me to call him: Daddy Phil. He said great-grandfather took too long to say and made him feel old." A single tear rolled down her cheek. "He called me that day, right after you visited him. He wanted to tell me all about the special beers you gave him. He was so happy. You know, he shared them with his friends the night he…the night he…"

"I didn't know that," Jack said, saving her. "It certainly sounds like something Phil would do."

The young woman nodded sadly. "Yes, it does. I'm glad his friends were able to come today."

"That was awfully nice of you to arrange for them to be here," Jenny said.

"I just hope the outdoor service wasn't too hard for them." Phil's great-granddaughter smiled. "When I was a child, I remember Daddy Phil saying that God could see you better if you were under His sky, so anything important should be done outside. I'm glad I could find him a place in the sun."

Jack smiled, remembering. "He liked to sit in the sun in Allan Gardens. Him and Bear."

"That's what I wanted to ask you about, Jack. Do you know what happened to Bear? No one knows where he is. I've checked the pounds and with his friends, but I can't find him," she said, her voice growing tight. "I have to find him. He was Daddy Phil's best—"

"It's okay. I have him," Jack was saying, but in her desperation and despair, Lisa wasn't hearing him. Jack had his hand on her arm, and finally had to give her a little shake to grab her attention. "Bear's safe, he's with me."

"You have him?" she asked quietly, as if she doubted she had heard correctly.

Jack nodded. "I have him. I took him home that night. I hope you don't mind, but I couldn't stand the thought of him going to the Humane Society."

"Oh, thank you!" Lisa cried, and threw her arms around

Jack. "I'm sorry about that," she said after stepping back. "It's just that I was so worried."

It was Jack's turn to apologize. "I'm the one who's sorry. I should have contacted you, but I just didn't think of it. If you…" He cleared his throat of sudden fears. "If you want Bear…"

"Is he happy with you?" she wanted to know. "Do you have children?"

"No. I mean, yes. Yes, he's happy, but no, I don't have children," he finally managed. "I have a German shepherd and the two of them never leave each other's side."

Lisa smiled, relieved. "That's nice. If it isn't an imposition for you…"

"None whatsoever," Jack assured her, feeling quite relieved himself.

Phil's great-granddaughter was silent for a moment, then quietly said, "I heard in the news that the police killed the man who murdered Daddy Phil. Is that true?"

"It looks that way," Jack admitted after a heartbeat's pause. "We won't know for certain until the tests come back on his gun, but they're pretty sure it's him."

"Thank you," Lisa said. She hugged them both then walked away.

"That was nice of you to give her that," Jenny said, watching as Phil's great-granddaughter paused at his grave before moving on to join his friends waiting for her at the cars.

Jack snorted. "What could I say? That we didn't get the right guy, but we killed the poor sap who had been set up to take the blame for your Daddy Phil's murder?"

"I guess."

They walked in silence for a while, weaving through

the headstones; they had parked away from the other cars. "Coffee?" she asked once they reached the car.

"I have tea at home if you've got time." The funeral had been east of Jack's house, and Jenny had picked him up. "I don't have much in the way of furniture, but I have tea. And cookies."

"Chocolate chunk?" she asked.

"Perfect for dipping."

"Done."

A short while later they were settling on the carpet in front of the fireplace. The fire popped and sparked as Jack jabbed at it with the poker. "I'm going to miss having a fireplace," he said, hanging up the iron.

"Are you still thinking about selling the house?" Jenny asked.

"I might be able to carry the house on my own after buying Karen out—I haven't done the figures yet—but I don't think I'll bother." Jack looked around the empty living room. "Too many memories."

Jenny nodded in understanding. "I can't believe all she wants now is half the house."

"Well," Jack said with a humourless chuckle, "I don't know if it's what she wants or what her father told her she'd get. All I know is that her lawyer has been reined in."

"I can't believe Hawthorn did that." She sipped her tea and stretched out on her side facing him. "Why do you think he did it? The lawyer, not the hooker. I don't want to know why someone like him would be trolling for a 51 hooker."

"Don't know," he admitted, taking his own drink. "It could be a not so subtle bribe to keep my mouth shut, or a thank-you for letting him go. All I know is that the lawyer sounded royally pissed on the phone. I think he was enjoying squashing a bug like me."

Jenny made a face. "Don't say things like that. You're not a bug."

Jack hid his grimace behind a drink. "To that guy I was."

"You're too hard on yourself, Jack."

He shrugged. *Someone has to be.*

"The kids are getting along," Jenny said, changing the subject.

"They are," Jack agreed. Justice was curled up by the fire, soaking up the heat, with Bear in his customary spot between the shepherd's front legs. Justice liked lying close to the fire but would always have to move once he got too warm. Jack imagined he would stay put longer than normal as Bear really enjoyed the heat.

It must feel good on his old bones. And whatever the little guy wants, he gets. I'll look after him, Phil. I promise.

"How's Mason? It was a mild heart attack, wasn't it?"

Jack nodded. "I'd hate to see what they call major." He remembered how the detective had looked slumped against his car. "He should be out of the hospital soon and staying home."

"But knowing Mason, he'll go straight back to work," Jenny surmised with a smile.

"I'm surprised he hasn't checked himself out already."

"I heard the same news that Phil's great-granddaughter did. They talked about Dove but didn't mention Silva." Jenny dunked a cookie in her tea then plopped the half-soggy mess in her mouth. "Mmmm."

Jack's face grew dark. "I don't know what's going on there. I talked to Tank about it, and he gave me some bullshit about wanting to keep Silva's name out of all of it. Said that's how Mason wanted to run it."

"That doesn't make sense," Jenny argued.

"It doesn't. But Tank pointed out that we really don't have any evidence that Silva was involved."

"What about Polan? He ID'ed Silva, gave Mason a description."

"But that doesn't tie Silva to the murders, or the attack on the station, or even Dove. If Dove had lived, maybe he would have co-operated, testified against Silva, but the fool decided to go out in a blaze of glory."

"Any idea why he didn't give up?"

Jack shrugged. "I've given up trying to figure out how people think. I'm just surprised he lived as long as he did." Shot numerous times, Lyron Dove had died in the ambulance on the way to the hospital.

"What about the reporter? Didn't she see Dove and Silva together?"

"I'm not sure. It's the impression I got listening to Mason and Gregory talking, but I can't say for sure. Anyway, she still hasn't woken up after her surgery, and no one seems to know if she will."

"I still don't see why Mason wants it all hushed up. Sounds kind of fishy."

"Tank said something about it having to do with Silva being an ex-cop. If it gets out he's gone rogue every case he was ever involved in could be reopened and a shitload of assholes would be back on the streets."

"So Silva just walks, free and clear?" Jenny sounded pissed, and Jack could sympathize.

"That's how I took it, too, but Tank says Homicide is looking for him."

"But when they catch him they'll be facing the same problem."

"Maybe they don't plan on taking him alive," Jack offered as he snagged a cookie from the bag.

"My God, Jack," Jenny gasped, shocked. "Do you really think so?"

"Dunno," Jack admitted, dunking and eating. "It's their problem, not mine, and I really don't care what they do. What about you? How are you doing? You seem different today, not as down." *And I'm an expert on that.*

It was Jenny's turn to shrug. She flipped her hair over her shoulder, and Jack watched longingly as it flowed back into place, a midnight wave tinged scarlet by the firelight.

"I feel better. I don't know… It's like telling Dove what happened somehow made it all more…" She tossed up her hands, lost for the right word.

"More acceptable?" Jack offered. "Maybe by telling the story, the truth, to Dove—to someone who definitely wasn't on your side—you convinced yourself you didn't do anything wrong. Remember, he came there to kill you, certain you were guilty."

"Maybe," she said softly. She looked him in the eye. "Does it get any better, Jack?"

He nodded. "In time. And I think you just took a big step in the right direction."

Comfortable with each other, they fell silent. Jack's eyes wandered about the living room, its once warm embrace now devoid of furniture, familiarity. Like the rest of the house, it was a naked corpse, cold and empty of life, waiting to be discarded.

"That's a sad smile."

It's either smile or cry. "Just thinking it isn't going to be the merriest Christmas this year."

"Hey, what am I? I'm right here, you know."

Jack's smile grew a touch brighter. "You know what I mean. I've lost a lot, nearly lost you last night." *And whose fault is that, Jack? This is the second time Jenny's almost been killed because I wasn't there. I should have been there.*

Jenny took his hands in hers. "But you didn't lose me, did you?"

"Yeah, but am I going to lose my partner?" he asked, forcing out the dreaded question.

Jenny looked surprised. "How did you know I was thinking of quitting?"

"Just got the feel from some things you said, some you didn't." *But that's not an answer, Jenny.*

"Brian wants me to," she said, stabbing Jack's guts with an icicle.

"And you? What do you want?" His hands were clammy in hers. He tried to pull free but she gripped his fingers.

"I'm not going anywhere," she said with a smile, melting the ice in Jack's stomach.

"Really?"

"Yup. Face it, you're stuck with me."

She smiled, and Jack thought it might not be such a terrible Christmas after all.

Monday, 11 March

Appearing on page twelve of the *Citizen*:

> SIU CLEARS OFFICER IN REGENT PARK SHOOTING
>
> The province's Special Investigations Unit says a Toronto police office was justified in using lethal force last December against an unarmed suspect.
>
> Ontario's civilian police watchdog says that on the night of Friday, the 7th of December last year, police were searching for a male whom they had reasonable grounds to believe was in possession of a handgun.
>
> Officers located the male in company of the suspect. The suspect refused to obey the officers' commands and reached into the male's pocket. The suspect produced a metal object and pointed it at the officers. One officer fired a single shot, striking the suspect in the chest. He was taken to hospital for emergency treatment, but later died of his injuries.
>
> "In my view, the subject officer was justified in discharging her firearm at the suspect—she reasonably believed that she was in imminent danger of death or grievous bodily harm when the suspect began raising, what appeared to be a handgun in her direction," said the director of the SIU.

Made in the USA
Middletown, DE
07 January 2016